Love Immortal

Felicity Heaton

Copyright © 2011 Felicity Heaton

All rights reserved. No part of this publication may be reproduced, stored in a retrieval system, or transmitted, in any form or by any means mechanical, electronic, photocopying, recording or otherwise without the prior written consent of the publisher, nor be otherwise circulated in any form of binding or cover other than that in which it is published and without a similar condition being imposed on the subsequent purchaser.

The right of Felicity Heaton to be identified as the Author of the Work has been asserted by her in accordance with the Copyright, Designs and Patents Act 1988.

First printed January 2011

First Edition

Layout and design by Felicity Heaton

All characters in this publication are purely fictitious and any resemblance to real persons, living or dead, is purely coincidental.

CHAPTER 1

Monsters existed.

Lauren had always suspected it to be true, and now she had all the evidence she needed.

One was standing twenty feet in front of her.

It towered over her, yellow eyes glowing in the dim alley between the old redbrick houses of her neighbourhood. Tufted black wiry fur covered it from tail to pointed ears, from the long claws on its colossal paw-like hands to the thick trunks of its hind legs. Her fevered mind said that it was only an escaped wolf from London Zoo, but Lauren couldn't bring herself to believe it. She'd seen the wolves once. This creature was nothing like them. This was something else.

Its mouth opened to reveal jagged teeth, each the size of her thumb.

Why Grandma, what big teeth you have.

All the better to eat you with.

Icy fingers clutched her heart and Lauren trembled, cold sweat trickling down her back beneath the skinny-fit brown t-shirt. The mad rush of her pulse made her dizzy and unexpended adrenaline stole her strength. Whoever had said that adrenaline made you invincible was a liar. Her legs were shaking so much that they were close to buckling, the gym bag on her shoulder was too heavy, and her thick black winter jacket felt impossibly tight, as though it was squeezing the air from her lungs.

Instinct told her to run.

If only her feet would cooperate.

Her shoulders slumped when the monster took a step towards her and her kit bag dropped to the ground. The shinai case slid down her other arm but she caught it at the last second. The feel of the bamboo sword through the black canvas bag was reassuring and instilled a strange sense of calm in her. Lauren tried to remember her kendo training and everything she had just practiced in class but nothing came to her. She stared at the monster, still trying to comprehend what was happening.

Instinct changed its mind.

Her other hand automatically reached across and undid the ties on the shinai bag. Lauren swallowed and kept her movements slow, not wanting to startle the beast into reacting. The end of the bag flapped open and she reached inside, locking her right hand tightly around the white leather hilt of the bamboo sword. She drew it and let the carry-case fall to the ground.

This was insane.

Her shinai would last five seconds against such a huge creature.

It didn't matter. Her only chance of escape was to stun it with a direct hit and run for her life. Her knees wobbled. That was, if she could run.

Taking deep breaths, Lauren shuffled backwards as the beast advanced and moved into a fighting stance. She brought her shinai around in front of her, clutching it so tightly with both hands that her knuckles turned white.

One breath. Two. Three.

With a loud cry, she launched herself at the creature. It reacted slowly, glowing yellow eyes widening. Lauren struck it between its ears and it yelped. The sound brought a smile to her face.

It was a short-lived smile.

The monster lashed out, flinging a heavy paw into her stomach and sending her flying into the wall of the alley. Her breath left her on impact and pain blasted through every inch of her. She grunted and fell onto the hard tarmac. Another huge paw flew at her and she rolled forwards to avoid being pulverised. She turned at the last moment and grabbed her shinai, desperate to protect herself. She was too damn young to die.

A low snarl sent a shudder down her spine and fear stole her breath away. Lauren scrambled to her feet and backed off, her bamboo sword trembling in front of her. The moon peeked out from behind a cloud and lit the world. Her heart stopped.

Holy God, the monster was more frightening in the light than it had ever been in the darkness. Long strings of saliva rolled down its fangs and dark fur tufted down its spine, raised like hackles. It wasn't a wolf, but it wasn't a man either. It was somewhere in between. An abomination. Something straight out of her dreams.

She'd dreamt of wolves and monsters before, and each time she had ended up fighting for her life.

It lowered its head and snarled again, hunkering down. It was going to attack.

This wasn't a dream. It was a living nightmare.

Lauren's fight left her and she moved backwards, faster now. Her heart started at a pace, thumping erratically in her throat. She clutched her shinai and glanced around. It was only just gone ten at night. Someone would pass by. Her neighbourhood wasn't normally this quiet. Any moment now, someone would come and help her. She'd only left her kendo class fifteen minutes ago and she'd been first out of the door. A couple of the men in her class lived near her. One of them would come. Someone would. Anyone? Thirty-four was definitely too young to die. She didn't want to be killed in the night as her parents had been.

She opened her mouth to call out for help but no sound left her lips. Her voice had died the moment her eyes had locked with the monster's ones. She saw her death reflected in them, saw how easily it would tear her to shreds and how she wasn't going to make it out of this alive. Emptiness settled in her mind, ringing in her ears.

Cold stillness shrouded the world.

The beast leapt.

Her heart leapt too.

Shrieking, Lauren raised the bamboo sword to defend herself and flinched away, screwing her eyes shut. Only sound came to her.

The sing of metal cutting through air, an ear-splitting howl of pain, and then a wet slapping noise.

Silence followed.

Lauren breathed hard, hunched up with her bamboo sword still held in front of her face. Her rough gulps of air filled the night. When everything had been quiet for a minute, she realised that something had happened to the monster and that she wasn't dead. She cracked an eye open.

The first thing she saw made her retch.

Spread across the alley were guts, blood and the two halves of a naked man. Her stomach rolled in response to the gruesome sight and she took a step backwards. It hadn't been a man a moment ago. Her eyes hadn't been lying to her even though her mind had. It had been a monster—a wolf that could stand on its hind legs, over six feet tall, and had tried to kill her. She looked at her bamboo sword. Splatters of blood covered the length of it, soaking into the white leather cap at the end. She couldn't have killed him with it. It wasn't possible.

The sound of steel sliding against something made her look up.

Her eyes widened and she dropped her weapon.

A tall man stood opposite her on the other side of the dead person. His long black coat fitted snugly to his slim frame and the stand up collar rose so high that it created a funnel that masked the lower half of his face, held closed by two thick bands of bright gleaming metal across the front. The wind tousled the finger-length spiked strands of his dark hair, shifting them across his pale forehead.

Shimmering silver eyes stared at her, pupils wide in the low light.

Her heart thudded in response to the jolt she felt when her eyes met his.

How many times had she looked at someone and not felt anything? Every day she met the eye of people on the Tube or at work, or even her opponent in kendo, but she'd never experienced a jolt that shook her to her core.

Never had she been so aware of making eye contact.

The longer she looked into his eyes, the calmer and warmer she felt, until she wanted to stare into them for forever. Something about those eyes, about this man, was so familiar. She was sure that she didn't know him, but at the same time, she was certain she did.

He stood unmoving, a sense of resolve about him. Everything suddenly felt like nothing but a nightmare, a vivid dream that this man had roused her from. His eyes narrowed. Invisible arms wrapped around her, holding her as soothing whispered words filled her mind. She was safe now.

Instinctively, she took a step towards him.

He lowered his head, giving Lauren the impression that he was bowing to her, awaiting a command or perhaps something else.

The man raised his head a fraction, so his eyes met hers again.

She snapped out of her trance when, without any sign of emotion, and with precise and practiced grace, he slid the long curved katana he held into the sheath hanging at his waist. The blade was clean but blood splattered his hands.

Lauren swallowed her heart and the fear that rushed through her again. Lost in his eyes, she'd forgotten what had happened. Everything had seemed so normal and the monster hadn't existed. Now she was back in reality, standing in an alley with a dead man at her feet and the man who had killed him opposite her.

His silver eyes flashed in the moonlight.

Another monster?

She made no move to run, or to look away, not when he approached her and not even when he stopped two feet away, towering over her. She couldn't move. His eyes had mesmerised her again. They melted from brightest silver to ice blue and she didn't even try to convince herself that she'd imagined it. They had changed. Ribbons of black hair caressed his forehead and her fingers itched to brush them away, to stroke his skin in their place and sweep them from his eyes so she could see them more clearly. A strange wave of calm washed over her again, only this time the feeling went deeper. She felt at peace with the world.

Because no matter what happened, this man would protect her.

He extended his hand to her. Before she could consider what she was doing, she was reaching for him.

"We must leave." His voice was smooth and sensual, deep and accented in a way she couldn't place but she knew that she liked it because the sound of it added to her boneless feeling.

Without hesitation or fear, Lauren placed her hand into his. His fingers closed over hers.

A sense of connection filled her.

"It is not safe here," he said and, without thinking, she nodded.

His hand left hers and claimed her upper arm. He strode at a pace so quick that she was almost jogging. Lauren gazed at the back of his head, catching glimpses of his profile.

It seemed right to go with him. Something inside her said that she knew him and she knew he would never hurt her. He had saved her from the monster.

She didn't care where they were going. She ran with him, empty and unable to think clearly. Her mind raced over everything that had happened, darting back and forth through her encounter with the monster. The man was right. It wasn't safe. A monster had attacked her and she had a feeling that more were coming, some sense of imminent danger that she couldn't ignore.

She had to run and she had to stay with the swordsman. Only he could keep her safe.

"What was that thing?" she said between breaths and tried to look over her shoulder towards the dead man. The world wobbled so much she couldn't focus.

"They are after us."

Her stomach fluttered and she looked at the swordsman. It was worth asking, even if it would only confirm that she'd gone insane.

"Who are they?" Her voice trembled enough that she was certain he would know that she was frightened of asking that question.

He stopped and looked at her, his pale blue eyes narrowing with his frown. Lauren wished she could see the rest of his face, could open the collar that obscured the lower half of it. She hadn't realised until now just how much of what a person was thinking showed in their expression. His eyes betrayed nothing.

"The monsters?" he said and her heart skipped a beat. "I almost lost you in the alley. I was foolish but I will not allow it to happen again. We must hurry."

When he looked past her, she glanced over her shoulder. Two men were coming down the street. She stepped towards them, convinced that they were from her kendo class, but the man held on to her arm, stopping her. She looked at him and then back at the two men. The streetlights highlighted their faces and she realised that she didn't know them. The sense of danger inside her worsened and the voice at the back of her mind told her to keep running. They were coming for her.

Before she could speak, the swordsman was running with her again. His grip on her arm was unrelenting, his pace so fast that she struggled not to trip.

Lauren looked over her shoulder. The men were following them. She rushed on, her thoughts running at a million miles per hour now. Was she really safe with the swordsman? She wasn't so sure, but he did seem to be the lesser of two evils. If the two men that were following them were actually monsters then she'd probably chosen the right side.

A flash of silver eyes crossed her turbulent mind.

Perhaps she hadn't. The swordsman was possibly as much a monster as the wolf-man had been. She glanced at the man's hand and then at his face. He had his eyes fixed on the distance, his jetty eyebrows knitted tight. She had to get away before something happened. The man had said they were after them, but she couldn't believe that. What reason would they have to be after her? She hadn't done anything in her life to enrage monsters or make a single enemy. It had been quiet and safe. Now she felt as though she'd fallen into someone else's life and she wanted her own boring one back. She had to get away.

It wasn't far to her house now.

The man turned down a side road between two houses, heading towards her street. He knew where she lived? Sodium lights flickered on the walls high above. The heavy stomp of boots echoed in her stomach and she turned as the swordsman stopped. The men had caught up with them. They came to a halt a short distance away and the swordsman moved to stand in front of her. Lauren had the terrible feeling she was about to witness a showdown.

"Stay close," the swordsman said.

He threw his arm out, sending his long coat swirling from the waist down and revealing his katana. In one swift, graceful move, he drew it and was in a fighting stance. Lauren backed into the wall, fascinated but frightened.

A low growl caught her attention. Her knees threatened to give out when the men tore their t-shirts off and dark fur erupted in waves across their skin. Their bodies twisted and distorted, limbs elongating as their noses and chins pushed outwards and became muzzles. Ears sprouted from the top of their heads and their eyes changed to yellow. They snarled in unison and she pressed hard into the wall.

It was real.

The swordsman changed position, raising his katana. He looked over his shoulder at her. His silver eyes gleamed as brightly as his blade in the streetlight.

Oh God, it was real.

The swordsman disappeared. A loud cry split the silence a moment later. No, he hadn't disappeared. The monsters and the man were both moving so fast that it was hard for her to keep track of them. They were a blur in her eyes, shifting violent shapes as they passed her. Turning, she clung to the wall and watched the fight. She had never seen a man move with such agility or fight with such astounding grace. Each attack was beautiful and polished. Each counter by the monsters just as fluid. A deadly ballet.

A perfect chance.

He couldn't stop her and the monsters at the same time. They wanted him, not her. She hadn't done anything to upset them. If she just left quietly, perhaps they would leave her alone. She could go the long way round to her house, get some things and then leave before the swordsman could find her. She could go to her friends' house and hide until everything was sane again.

Backing away into the shadows, Lauren breathed slow and shallow, afraid that even that sound could alert either the man or the monsters to the fact that she was leaving. Her hands trailed along the brick wall, rough under her fingertips, a feeling that grounded her and kept her going. The darkness engulfed her but she didn't take her eyes away from the blur of the fight, not until the very last second when her hand finally ran out of wall.

With a sigh, she turned away and then froze.

Black tufted fur filled her vision. Her gaze rose to take in the massive bulk of the wolf-like monster and stopped when it reached its jaw. Sharp teeth greeted her as its jowls peeled back in a snarl.

She began to shake her head.

The monster backhanded her, sending her crashing into the wall. Pain erupted across her skull as her head hit the pavement and a trembling sickness passed over her. She pushed herself up on unsteady arms and looked towards the man where he fought the other monster, keeping it at the other end of the alley, and then behind her at the one that had hit her.

It was coming.

Vivid yellow eyes filled the darkness. She couldn't look away. The sound of fighting swam in her ears and then drifted into the distance, replaced by the noise of heavy feet pounding the tarmac. She threw a glance back towards the man to see the other monster coming for her. Her stomach heaved. She had been wrong. The monsters weren't after the man at all.

Lauren froze right down to the marrow of her bones.

They were after her.

Turning back to face the one nearest her, she screamed when she saw that it was almost on her. Its sharp jaws opened.

Blood exploded up the wall and the monster tumbled to the ground. Lauren shuffled backwards, away from it, not even thinking about the other monster that had been coming at her from behind.

Her hand hit a puddle.

Only it hadn't been raining.

And puddles weren't warm.

Sick to her stomach, she snatched her hand back and retched when she saw the blood covering it. She frantically wiped it on her jeans, her heart fluttering against her ribcage. Both men were dead, cleaved cleanly in two. Her stomach heaved but nothing came up. Bending over, she grasped the pavement with both hands and tried to be sick again. Nothing.

The swordsman grabbed her arm and hauled her to her feet. The motion jarred her vision and made her headache worsen.

"Are you hurt?" he said, voice soothing. Lauren looked up at him, instantly lost in his silver eyes.

He frowned when she didn't respond and then touched her forehead above her right eyebrow. It stung and Lauren flinched away. His touch lightened, becoming so tender that it felt like a lover's caress rather than a simple concerned touch. She stared into his eyes as he inspected what she presumed was a cut. The pain seemed so distant. Everything did. His eyes gradually changed from stunning silver to icy blue again and she found herself wondering why he worried so much about her safety.

And why she felt as though she knew him.

His hand caught her wrist and they were moving again. She almost tripped when they passed one of the bodies and it began to disintegrate before her eyes.

"Stay close," the swordsman said.

Lauren glanced at him and then down at his hand on her wrist. She didn't think that she had much choice. The strength in his grip was incredible.

Why was he protecting her? What did he want from her? Why were monsters after her?

She had to be insane to be running around London with a man she didn't know and fighting monsters that were after her for some reason.

The man turned down another street. Lauren yanked her hand free and started back in the opposite direction. This had gone on long enough. She wasn't sure where she intended to go but she had to get away before it all got crazier. She didn't think it could, but something deep inside said that it was going to if she kept letting the madman drag her around.

He grabbed her wrist again.

Lauren tried to tug it free but his grip tightened. When she hit his hand, he let go and backed away a step. Was he trying to calm her down?

Finding her courage, she avoided looking him in the eye and put her hands on her hips.

"I'm leaving and you'd better not try to stop me," she said and it sounded quite convincing to her own ears.

The man stepped back again. His coat fell open to reveal the hilt of his sword.

"There is no going back," he said. "They will find you again."

Her head was splitting now that she'd stopped moving and threatening a man with a sword suddenly didn't seem so clever.

She edged backwards.

"There is no going back," he repeated, his tone as calm as a millpond, instilling a sense of peace in her. He was right. She told herself that he wasn't. He was wrong and he could do strange things to her with his voice and his eyes. She had to escape. "If you do, you will die."

Lauren's head snapped up, her eyes locking with his. She wasn't sure whether he was threatening her or insinuating that the monsters would kill her.

"But my bag," she whispered, desperate for a reason to get away.

"Is there anything in it that could link you to tonight?" he said and she thought for a moment. She touched her jeans pockets and then her jacket pockets. Her purse, keys and mobile phone were all with her. The only thing in her bag was her kendo armour.

She shook her head.

"Forget it then." With a move so fast that she didn't even see it happen, he snatched her wrist and began walking. She stumbled along behind him, trying to prise his fingers off her. As a last resort, she slapped his hand again but this time he didn't let go. "My duty is to protect you. We must leave before others come."

Great, now she had her own Terminator and she wasn't even sure how she'd come to have him. Was she someone important?

Important enough to protect?

The swordsman had fought to defend her. He'd killed three monsters for her sake and she got the feeling that he would kill more if he had to. Her gaze roamed over the strong line of his shoulders and up the funnel neck of his coat to his face. His eyes remained fixed on the distance. She had an overwhelming urge to pull down the collar of his coat so she could see what he looked like. His eyes were incredible but something told her that collar hid a face that was more than that.

"Where are we going?" she said, her voice weak.

No answer.

Lauren was about to ask again when the redbrick Victorian houses of her street came into view. She'd never been so glad to see her home with its bay sash-windows and red door. Memories of her childhood and her parents came flooding back, filling her with a strange mixture of warmth and cold, and reminding her that no comforting arms waited for her in the house, not anymore. Her parents were gone and the pain of losing them hadn't faded in the months since their deaths. At the door, Lauren fumbled with her keys and then breathed a sigh of relief when she finally managed to slot the key in and turn it.

The slam of her house door behind her was comforting and she leaned back against it. The house was quiet and cold, but it still made her feel safe. She glanced at the man where he stood to her right, looking around her messy living room. When his gaze came back to meet hers, her heart began to slow and her breathing came normally. He'd saved her and for some reason she didn't feel threatened by him. She felt safe. A dry laugh pushed past her lips. She was definitely going crazy.

Or was she?

Everything that had happened seemed so incredible and impossible, yet she knew that it was real. She closed her eyes and tilted her head back into the door, sighing on an exhale.

The alley flashed across her closed eyes, the scene playing out again in the darkness of her mind. She'd never seen anything so horrible.

Her eyes shot open when she remembered all the blood. She raised her hands and stared at the crimson stains, her breathing laboured and throat dry. Her fingers shook, wavering so much that she couldn't focus on them. If the blood was on her hands. She looked down at her chest. Black lines criss-crossed her brown t-shirt. Where else had it hit her? With trembling fingers, she touched her face and felt sick when she found wet patches.

Lauren raced up the stairs in front of her, following them around the corner, and ran into the small peach coloured bathroom at the top. She slammed into the sink and grasped it with both hands.

Her dark brown eyes widened when she saw her reflection in the cabinet mirror.

Red streaks marked her face, matching the colour of her hair.

The monsters flashed before her eyes, followed by the swordsman.

Her gaze fell to her hands and she raised them palm upwards. The blood had seeped into the cracks of her skin, leaving dark jagged lines. Her fingers trembled and her stomach twisted. She turned on the tap and tried scrub the marks away with a nailbrush, rubbing her skin raw. A tight swirling feeling mounted inside her. The blood wouldn't go away. Each glance at her hands revealed it was still there, coating them as it had in the street. It wasn't going away. She wanted it to go away.

She didn't want monsters to be real. They weren't real. She clawed at the blood. It wouldn't come off. A noise from downstairs made her tense and she stared wide-eyed into the mirror. The man was coming. He was a murderer. Any feeling of safety he'd given her was just an illusion. It was her mind playing tricks, just as the monsters had been.

Monsters.

She saw them again, bisected and dead.

Why wouldn't the blood come off?

Lauren locked the bathroom door, yanked the shower curtain aside, turned the shower on, and stepped under the warm jet. It soaked her clothes through but the blood on her hands still wouldn't go away. She sank to the floor and hugged her knees to her chest, burying her face in them as she sobbed, weak and tired. The water bounced off her back and trickled over her scalp. It dripped from the ends of her near-shoulder length red hair and masked her tears as she rocked back and forth.

Was it real or was she going insane?

Why was the swordsman so familiar and why did she want him to come to her, need him close by?

Her eyes widened and she stared at the water running down the plughole.

She had a horrible feeling that he was right.

The monsters were after her.

And only he could protect her.

CHAPTER 2

Julian looked around the small messy living room. His gaze scanned over the haphazard piles of women's magazines on the coffee table, the open face-down book on the beige couch to his left, and the bookshelves filled with DVDs that stood either side of an old television and its stand in front of him. He moved to the window on his right and checked the street in both directions. The area was silent save the sound of distant traffic but it didn't soothe him in the slightest. Three werewolves. It couldn't be coincidence. The one by itself or the two together he could dismiss, but two separate attacks left him worried. He needed to get Lauren to safety as soon as possible. For that to happen, he needed to tell her why monsters were after her.

And then he needed to get her to believe him.

He stared up at the ceiling, sensing Lauren in the bathroom above. She had been there a while, her feelings in disarray and her fear running through his blood. She was still fragile but he couldn't allow her to be alone as she needed to be. He couldn't risk her attempting an escape, not now that he'd found her.

He'd never resorted to kidnapping her before, but he was beginning to consider it if he couldn't convince her to come with him of her own free will.

There was a first time for everything, or so they said, but countless centuries had passed since he'd experienced such an event. At his age, it was almost impossible to find something he hadn't done before.

He walked up the stairs, his footsteps dulled by the thick carpet and his focus fixed on Lauren, monitoring her feelings in case they grew worse. His duty now was to ensure her survival and to protect her. Being in her home would reassure her and make it easier for him to explain things, but now that she was somewhere safe, she wouldn't want to leave, and they had to get away from this place before other werewolves came. He considered knocking on the white bathroom door and then continued down the hall, giving her some privacy. She would come out soon enough and if she didn't, he would go in and get her. He paused on the threshold of her bedroom.

Her soft scent lingered in the air, warm and comforting, filling him with a sensation of need he had long forgotten. He shook it away. He needed to get some clothes and things together for her. Having some of her personal belongings might ease the transition and make things less confusing and painful for her.

It was always difficult for her to believe what he was going to tell her, and this time he didn't have the luxury of years in which to break it to her. He wasn't sure how long it was until her awakening but it was close.

In a small wicker basket on her chest of drawers, he found something that would answer that question. Her passport. The date of birth in it revealed that it was one month to her birthday. He was cutting it close.

Julian pocketed her passport and then looked down at her bedside table. The books stacked there were all about swords, fighting, and history. The movies near the small television opposite the end of her bed were mostly tales of hit men, martial arts and horror films. Her instincts were there. He wondered if she knew why she liked these things. There were another two shinai propped up beside the wardrobe next to the television. She had been courageous to attack the werewolf with such a flimsy weapon. It had surprised him enough that he'd kept back and watched her rather than intervening as he should have. He had never seen her so brave before the awakening.

He found an empty backpack in her wardrobe and crossed the room to a pile of ironed clothes on the wooden trunk under the window. They were recently washed so had to be clothes that she favoured. He packed some of them. She would feel better for having a new pair of jeans to wear and a clean top. He lifted a top off the pile and held it up. The sight of the small black camisole made his heart beat hard and he couldn't stop himself from imagining her in it. It had been a long time since he'd seen her in such revealing clothing and even longer since it had affected him. He reined in his feelings and shut them down, reminding himself of his position and his duty.

Julian went to leave but stopped when he saw a picture beside her bed. He rounded the bed again and picked it up, frowning beyond the image of Lauren and an older couple to the man crossing the park behind, seeing him for what he truly was. A werewolf. He opened the frame and removed the back. The date printed on the rear of the photograph was six months ago. His stomach dropped. The attacks hadn't been random. Lycaon knew where she was.

He dropped the picture onto the bed.

Illia.

Julian spun to face the bedroom door. Lycaon was hunting her. He raced down the hall to the bathroom.

He had to protect her.

He couldn't lose her again.

They had to leave.

He banged on the bathroom door, his heart thundering and his chest tight. Fear stole his strength and left him weak. He clenched his teeth and fought against the feeling. He wasn't weak.

"Illia!" He banged again but she didn't answer.

She wasn't there. He told himself to calm down. She was there. He could sense her and feel her heart beating. There was no reason to panic, so why couldn't he stop his heart from racing and his limbs from shaking?

"Illia!" Julian stepped back, his mouth turning dry, and assessed the door.

He was about to break it down when it opened and she peered around it.

"Who's Illia?" She looked so small clinging to the white door, her rich brown eyes red with tears and wide with fear.

All of Julian's strength left him and he sank back against the wooden banister, relieved that she was still safe. He leaned there a moment, gathering himself and regaining control. It wasn't like him to react like this when she was in danger. Was it because she was still fragile?

She twisted the wet strands of her near shoulder-length dark red hair around her pale fingers and stared at him, an expectant look surfacing in the depths of her warm eyes. Her teeth teased her lower lip, reddening it and drawing his attention there. A surge of hunger pushed through him, a desire to do the impossible. He balled his hands into fists and swallowed.

Or was his reaction because of something else?

Julian dropped his gaze and realised with some dismay that she was still wearing her black jacket, brown t-shirt and jeans, and that they were soaked. He looked down and frowned at her damp shoes. She hadn't even removed them. The clothes stuck to her slight frame, emphasising her slender figure, and the fact she was trembling. He looked into her eyes, studying the pale beauty staring back at him. A fierce need to protect her gripped his heart, seizing control of him, and he stepped towards her, raising his hand to brush the tangled threads of hair from her face. He wanted to tell her that he would protect her, and would never allow anything to happen to her. No monster would ever lay a hand on her so long as he breathed. She had no reason to fear now. He was here.

His hand fell to his side when he realised what he was doing and thinking. It was impossible. Such things went against his duty.

He reached behind him to grip the banister and felt the towel there. Pulling it off the banister, he walked towards her. She tensed and then watched his hands as he placed the cream towel around her shoulders and drew it closed over her chest. He held her shoulders, tempted to rub the towel against them to dry her. She was still fragile. She needed to take more care of herself. Releasing her, he stepped back to give her more room.

She pulled the towel around herself and walked past him. Her hand went to her jeans pocket and she tugged her mobile phone out. She started pressing numbers, muttering at the phone and cursing it. When he caught her arm, she frowned at his hand.

"What are you doing?" he said, studying the faint flicker of emotion he could feel surfacing in her.

"I'd like to call the police now." She removed his hand from her arm and tapped her phone, glaring at the blank display.

He knew enough about technology to know that electronic devices didn't respond well to large quantities of water dousing them. The phone had been in her pocket when she had been in the shower. He doubted it would work even if it dried out.

"Not necessary," he said and tried to remember if he had seen a phone in her house. He couldn't allow her to do such a thing.

Lauren backed off a step when he advanced one.

"Oh, I think it is." She moved again, working her way towards her bedroom door, still pressing buttons on her phone as though it would miraculously spring back into life. He followed her. "I'm going to call the police about those men and then I want you to leave."

"I cannot do that." He advanced another step, his pace slow so he didn't frighten her. The hard look that had entered her eyes said that she was serious. "And I cannot allow you to call the authorities."

"Why not?" She took another step towards her room, glanced over her shoulder at it and then back at him.

"What would you tell them?"

She paused and frowned. Her mouth opened and then closed. She glared at him. "I want you to leave now."

"I cannot. You are in danger."

"You're telling me," she muttered and backed away. "I don't know what you're after—"

"Nothing, Lauren." That name still felt foreign to him. Illia. She was Illia but, at the same time, she wasn't. None of them had ever been Illia. Not really.

Her pulse quickened, rushing in his ears. "How do you know my name?"

He hadn't meant to frighten her by revealing that he knew about her. It had come out before he could stop himself. He took another step towards her.

"I will explain everything, but right now I need you to answer something for me."

She stared at him for a full minute and then slowly nodded.

Julian went into her room and picked up the picture from her bed. He looked at the photograph of her and the couple. Her parents? Of course. She had parents. Or at least, she'd had parents.

He held the picture out to her. She snatched it and stared at it. When she blinked, tears tumbled down her cheeks.

"When did your parents die?" he said and her head jerked up, her eyes betraying her shock as much as her thundering heart did. "Was it shortly after this picture was taken?"

She looked confused and then nodded. Her eyes searched his. "They were attacked in the park. The police never caught their murderer."

"And they never will."

She gasped. "Those things? Oh God."

He dashed forwards when she collapsed, dropping her phone and the picture on the floor, and caught her under her arms. He lowered her so she didn't hurt herself. She was freezing in her wet clothes. He drew the towel around her and covered as much of her as possible. When she was kneeling, he knelt before her, waiting for her to take it all in.

"No," she whispered, shaking her head. Her eyes met his, swimming with tears that filled him with a strange ache to wipe them away. He couldn't. "How? What are they?"

"Werewolves."

She paled. Another tear dashed down her cheek.

"Werewolf?" A bark of nervous laughter. "A werewolf?"

He nodded and her smile faded.

Before Julian could say another word, she ran past him towards the bathroom. A moment later, she retched. He got to his feet and went to check on her. She'd knocked her head in the fight and there was a chance that she was dealing with a concussion on top of everything else.

He wished he could make it easier on her.

It was never easy.

Getting her to believe the existence of werewolves wasn't normally the hard part. It was all the rest. It was the awakening, her duty, and the strange tale of her history.

He walked into the bathroom to find Lauren at the basin. She splashed water over her face and then gripped the edge of the sink, staring blankly at the peach porcelain.

"I will not hurt you, Lauren," Julian said and she looked over her shoulder at him. "I am only here to protect you from those creatures."

"The werewolves?"

He nodded. "The werewolves." Amongst other things.

Lauren swallowed and closed her eyes, looking as though she was struggling to stop herself from being sick again.

"Why did they kill my parents?" Her voice was small.

Julian stepped into the hall, giving her some space, and thought about how to explain things to her. They didn't have much time. He needed to convince her to come with him as soon as possible. They needed to go somewhere they would be truly safe.

"Come and sit down," he said and she turned to look at him.

"I'm fine here." Her stubborn streak had remained with her then. It was something she always had. For once, he wished that she didn't.

"You need to be sitting." After her collapse at the mention of her parents' death, he wasn't taking any chances. In the cramped bathroom, he wouldn't have room to get to her if her knees gave out and he didn't want her to hit her head on the basin. "And we need to get you changed into something dry."

"I said that I'm fine. Just answer my question."

"To weaken you."

Her expression changed to one of confusion.

"Lauren, you are special, born to serve a purpose... a destiny that is three thousand years old, born thirty lifetimes ago."

She swallowed several times. "I think you were right. I need to sit down."

Julian stepped aside. She fumbled her way along the wall and into her small bedroom. When she reached the double bed, she collapsed onto the dark covers and leaned forwards so her head was between her knees. Her rough breathing and the fast beat of her heart filled his head.

She was taking it better than he'd expected. Kneeling in front of her on the floor, he waited for her to emerge before continuing.

"Why are they after me?" she whispered. "I felt as though they were. I thought they wanted you and then I... I realised... they wanted me... and you were protecting me. Why?"

What did he tell her, the long version or the short? He needed to convince her quickly to come with him. He couldn't take her searching for the safe house during daylight when he wasn't strong enough to protect her.

"Because of who you are," he said.

She laughed. Not the reaction he'd expected.

"Who I am? I don't know who I am! Christ, my friends have been teasing me something chronic about my whole 'find myself' gig recently and all of a sudden I have a strange masked monster telling me that I have some purpose and werewolves want to kill me because of who I am."

Julian frowned and touched the tall collar of his black coat. Masked monster? Is that how she saw him? He'd never considered himself a monster before. If he was, then she was a monster too, she just didn't realise it yet.

How was she going to take that?

There was only one way to find out.

"That is because you have not yet awoken," he said. She stared at him in silence. He took it as a cue to continue. "You were born almost four thousand years ago as Illia and are the daughter of the minor goddess Selene who looked favourably upon a man named Lycaon. This favour angered Zeus as he had banished all form of contact with Lycaon. As punishment to Selene, he placed you on Earth. Zeus promised you that your task would redeem your mother, so you willingly accepted it and Zeus bound your fate to Lycaon's. Zeus ordered his brother Hades to refuse your soul entry to the underworld on death until Lycaon has been defeated, so each time you are reborn."

She just stared at him, her rosy lips parted and her eyebrows raised high.

Her heartbeat was steady though. Either she didn't believe him, or she did and it was beginning to make a little sense.

He hoped it was the latter.

She laughed.

The former.

"I'm having a hard time with this," she said. "You're telling me that I was born to some goddess in God-knows-what-BC and I'm supposed to defeat some man named Lycaon?"

"In essence, yes." He paused and tried to think of a way to put it that would make her believe it. Back when he had been human, people had believed in the gods. He'd understood that Illia was the daughter of the goddess that he and his men worshipped. He'd accepted his duty without hesitation. "Lauren... Illia's soul resides within you. Each death at Lycaon's hands sees you reborn, but it is only her soul and her purpose that carries over to her new incarnation."

"So I'm not really her?" Lauren said and her heartbeat picked up a little. Thirty times of telling her and he still hadn't found a good way. "So how do you know I'm her... reincarnation... or whatever it is you think I am?"

She was beginning to believe him. He just had to keep her calm and explain things clearly, and she would eventually understand.

"Yes, you are her reincarnation, and when you reach thirty-five you will awaken and be ready to continue the fight against Lycaon. My fate is tied to yours and has been for three thousand years. When Illia was sent to Earth, she was given two hundred Arcadian soldiers to carry out her orders. I was their commander."

"And now you've been reincarnated, like me?"

Julian hesitated. This never went down well but he had to tell her the truth.

"Lauren, I have not been reincarnated."

Her jaw dropped.

She blinked.

"I died three thousand years ago, the last of your Arcadians, and you bestowed this gift upon me so I could continue to help you." Those words grew harder to say each time. They brought back every ounce of pain he'd felt that day and more. It hurt to remember the things that Illia had said to him then but had never said again.

Lauren stood and stormed past him, heading for the stairs. He hadn't locked the front door.

"This is insane. I'm out of here." She ran down the stairs, grabbed the door handle and yanked it hard in her attempt to escape.

Julian was next to her in an instant, his fingers closed tightly around her wrist. She turned and hit his hand, scratching it and trying to prise it off her. Losing patience, he spun her around and pinned her to the door by her wrist, holding her hard and tight. She struggled and he tensed his jaw, steeling himself against his desire to grab her other hand.

"I will not let you leave," he said and she stilled, her eyes round and shining with fear again. He sighed to release his anger and reminded himself that it was his duty to protect her, not frighten her.

She punched him hard across the face and then hissed in pain, shaking her hand and scowling at him. He wasn't sure what she had expected to gain from turning violent. She hadn't hurt him, if that was her intention. She had only hurt herself by hitting the metal bands that held his collar closed. She shoved his shoulder hard enough that he had to step back to steady himself. He held her wrist tighter and thought about what to say.

"I cannot let you leave. I must protect you."

She stared up at him. Fear still widened her eyes and her heart was beating fast.

"Lauren, you know that they are after you. I know you must have felt something tonight, a sense that you were in danger even when there was no imminent threat."

A distant look filled her eyes and she nodded a fraction.

"I assure you that you are safest with me. I must keep you with me in order to protect you. I have no choice," he said and she slowly leaned back into the door, relaxing enough that he could loosen his grip without fearing she would attempt to escape. "You are not my prisoner, but I cannot let you leave, and I cannot leave you. Come, sit back down and I will answer your questions."

He released her arm, hoping she would see that he trusted her and that she would begin to trust him.

"And what do you want in return?" Lauren said with a sceptical look and rubbed her wrist. It was red where he had been holding it too tightly. He hadn't meant to hurt her but the thought of her leaving, of losing her again after all the mistakes he had made with her, had made him react. "What is it you want with me?"

"I ask only that you come with me to meet some people and that you grant me time to explain things to you and make you see that all of this is real and that there is no escaping your destiny. I will protect you from the monsters, Lauren."

She frowned.

"You're a monster."

"We are not monsters."

"We?" Her voice was tiny. In her eyes, he could see that she knew the answer to that question.

"When you awaken, you will become like me again. That is why in three thousand years you have only lived thirty lifetimes. Sometimes you live for longer, sometimes for only short periods. All of you awaken on your thirty-fifth birthday because it is the mortal age at which Illia was cast to Earth to fulfil her task."

She paled again and surprised him by stepping away from the door. His gaze tracked her as she walked to the stairs and sat down. He was tempted to lock the door but knew that she would think he didn't trust her if he did and that she would feel threatened. He needed to gain her trust and trusting her was the first step.

He knelt in front of her again. She was quiet for a while, the myriad of feelings flickering across her face telling him that she was struggling to take it all in.

"And what is this... awakening... thing? Who's Lycaon? What does this all really have to do with me? And why the hell am I beginning to believe you?" she said.

"Because in your soul, you know me. When you died the first time, Zeus heard your plea and gave me the task of finding and awakening you so you could continue your duty. He brought me over, just as you wished. You know me, Lauren, only your mind and heart is reborn clean so you have no memory of me."

Lauren buried her head in her hands and exhaled long and slow. "I'm going insane."

"You are not."

"I am, because when I first saw you and you killed that... werewolf... I felt I knew you and I felt you were protecting me."

Julian placed a hand on her shoulder and squeezed it, hoping to reassure her. "Because you do know me and I am here to protect you. I will do all in my power to protect you from Lycaon so you can complete your destiny."

"Who is Lycaon? Why does Zeus hate him? Why do I have to kill him?"

"Lycaon once tricked Zeus into eating human flesh. As punishment, Zeus cursed him into the form of a werewolf. He was told that he would become human again if he abstained from his cannibalistic ways for ten years. Lycaon did not. He refused to and embraced his new life as a werewolf, quickly learning that he could spread his curse to others." Julian wished that he had more time, could break everything to her slowly, but that wasn't an option. Lauren was in danger. Lycaon could be tracking her. He needed to tell her as much as she could take right now. "Lycaon hunts you so that he may be rid of you for another period. He wishes revenge on Zeus and for whatever reason he is willing to go to great lengths to achieve it."

He wasn't sure why but the thought of Lycaon killing Lauren made heat coil in his stomach and his fingers itch to grasp his sword. He hadn't felt like this since Illia. He wouldn't let Lycaon kill her. Not Lauren. He would protect her.

She raised her head and looked into his eyes. Their beautiful dark depths soothed the anger inside him. She was looking at him so strangely, with warmth that made him want to ask her what she was thinking and why she looked at him that way. She'd done it several times now. None of her predecessors had ever shown him such feeling.

"And I have to kill him... because Illia's mother favoured him," she said with a slight tremble in her voice.

She seemed to be getting to grips with her role now but Julian still wasn't sure if she fully understood what was happening to her or her duty.

"We must stop him from achieving his revenge," Julian said.

"He had my parents killed. I want him to pay for that. I want revenge too." She leaned forwards causing the towel to slip off her right shoulder.

Julian leaned back, sitting on his heels. The steely determination in Lauren's eyes backed up her brave words. She did want to avenge her parents and kill Lycaon. None of the others had ever had a personal reason for fulfilling their duty before. Perhaps where they had failed, Lauren would succeed.

Perhaps.

First, she had to make her decision. Her desire for revenge wasn't her answer. When she'd come to terms with what was happening to her, he would ask her whether she was willing to go through with the awakening and take on her duty once again. Until then, he could only wait and tell her all that she needed to know. He could only protect her.

Julian covered her shoulder with the towel again. "I will explain more soon when we leave this place. If you have any more questions—"

"I do," she said, looking straight into his eyes. "What is this awakening thing you keep mentioning?"

He wasn't sure if she was ready for the truth about it. None of Illia's incarnations had ever taken this part well. All of them had feared death. Only Illia herself had embraced it.

"Your blood flows in my veins. When the time is right, I will offer it to you." He peeled back the left cuff of his coat to reveal the many pale scars on his wrist and watched her closely.

A familiar look entered her eyes. Hunger. A desire to feed and grow stronger. Her teeth sank into her lip. She reached out towards him and then took her hand back a fraction before continuing and using her index finger and thumb to measure the distance between the marks on his wrist. Her touch was light and warm, and sent a spark chasing up his arm. He didn't understand. She had never affected him like this before.

Lauren measured another set of marks with her fingers, and then brought them to her teeth. The gap between them fitted her canines perfectly. Fear and confusion laced her scent. She recoiled, drawing back into herself and frowning at him. It was too soon for her to understand her desires.

"My blood will awaken you and you will regain your powers and become like me again." He covered his wrist.

"An immortal?"

Julian nodded. It was better than calling him a monster, although not a true definition of his existence. He could die. As could she. He was painfully aware of that.

"Come, you need to change into something dry." He stood and offered his hand to her. "Then we shall go somewhere that we will be safe."

"I still don't understand what's happening." She surprised him by catching hold of his hand, clutching it tightly in her own, but not standing. Her feelings were in disarray, her heart beating hard and fast. He couldn't push her any more today. She'd already reached her limit.

He hesitated a moment and then covered her hand with his, completing the tangle. She needed reassurance and that was all he was offering. This touch didn't break the rules.

"Rest for now. Give yourself time to take everything in but know that I am here to protect you, Lauren, as I have always been. That is my duty. I am not a threat to you."

A small smile graced her lips and she nodded. He released her hand but she didn't move. She remained sitting, staring at the door. He leaned against the wall and waited for her to come out of her thoughts.

"Er... I'm so rude... I don't know your name," she said and Julian smiled behind his collar.

It had taken her more time than usual to ask that question, and less time to ask about the awakening.

"Julian." He leaned the back of his head against the wall. The tip of his nose brushed the funnel neck of his coat.

"Julian?" The note of trepidation in her voice matched the one in her heartbeat.

"Yes, Lauren?"

"I should thank you for saving me... I mean... you did save me from those werewolves."

"I did."

"So, erm, thanks." She stood on the bottom step of the stairs and smiled at him, her heart steady now. He liked the gentle patter of it in his mind. It was soothing. He liked her smile. "And Julian... I knew... I knew that you wouldn't hurt me."

Those words sent a jolt through him. Julian closed his eyes, relishing them and the soft way she'd said them.

He listened to her breathing, slow and calm. She'd never taken things this well before. It was a good sign. It might mean that when he told her everything else that she would be able to cope with it too.

"So where are we going?"

"A group that I met and have worked with to find you. People with special abilities like you and me." Julian looked at her. The questions were another good sign. Sometimes she went into a catatonic state when he told her. Normally when she questioned him, she turned out to be a fighter, one who lived for years before succumbing to defeat.

That word sent a chill through him. For Lauren's sake and his own, he hoped that she was a fighter. He'd seen her books and movie collection, and seen her fight a werewolf with nothing more than a bamboo sword. She could fight. She could survive this time.

He thought about where he was taking her and the implications. They had never worked with others before but it could only be a good thing. The greater their numbers, the greater their chance of defeating Lycaon.

There were other advantages too.

Duke and his team would be able to protect them during Lauren's awakening, but whether she survived the process of regaining her powers was up to the Fates. Julian could only do so much to ensure that she lived. The

Fates were fickle and didn't always heed Zeus's order to allow Illia's soul to return so she could continue her fight. Julian had lost her before during the awakening. He looked at Lauren. The thought of losing her turned his insides. He wouldn't let it happen. For her, he would face the Fates and demand Illia's soul crossed over. He wouldn't let Lauren die. His fists clenched. He hadn't felt this way in so long. Since finding her, he'd watched her closely. She fascinated him, and he felt intensely protective of her, far more so than he'd ever done with the others.

She started up the stairs and then stopped.

"Do they have a name?" Her wide brown eyes shone with curiosity.

He would protect her. They would protect her.

"Ghost."

CHAPTER 3

Protection and answers.

They were the most prominent reasons why Lauren was going with this man and the ones that she was going to stick with until everything started making sense. There were other reasons floating around her mind but she ignored those. So what if she felt attracted to Julian? She was only going with him because he could protect her from the monsters that were out to kill her.

Lauren adjusted the straps of her backpack and walked in silence beside Julian through the centre of London. He hadn't said much since they had left her house other than telling the taxi driver to drop them off at Piccadilly Circus.

They passed through several side streets, heading deeper into the heart of the city, and entered a square with tall Georgian townhouses on all sides. Their pale stone, uniform black iron fences and black doors made them mirror images of each other. A fine layer of frost covered the fancy cars parked on the road outside them. A tall iron fence enclosed a wooded park in the middle of the square, the gates closed. The trees were bare, silhouetted against the sky. Where was Julian taking her, and why couldn't they have continued in the taxi?

He'd said something back at her house about them going to see some people who were special like her. An organisation called Ghost.

The mention of that name had piqued her interest but Julian had told her to get ready. He'd said it with such insistence that she'd fallen silent and done what he'd asked. She'd changed out of her wet things, mulling over everything he'd told her about her past lives, her apparent mission, their opponent, and himself. She hadn't said a word since then.

She didn't have a problem with reincarnation. Belief in that was common enough and it was comforting to think that there was something beyond death.

The thing she found hard to swallow was the fact that ancient Greek gods were involved, and Julian and the werewolf named Lycaon were thousands of years old. Immortal. That was the stuff of movies and fairytales.

But so were monsters, and they were real.

Julian hadn't told her what would happen if she chose not to 'awaken' on her birthday, which left her wondering if she really had a choice at all. Would something bad happen to her or the world if she didn't? What if one of Illia's reincarnations said no? Did it all just end?

No. Lauren knew the answer to that. Lycaon was after revenge, something she could empathize with since learning who had ordered her parents' deaths. If she chose not to carry out Illia's, her, duty then Lycaon might just get his wish. She wasn't sure how it worked but Julian had made it sound as though her role was a necessary one and she was important.

She'd never been important before.

It was a nice, if daunting, feeling.

She wrapped her arms around herself in an effort to keep warm. The night sky was clear, leaving the world frosty and far colder than her clothing could protect against. Her warmest jacket had been wet so she'd had to dress in her thinner brown combat jacket. Even when combined with the black jumper and camisole it wasn't warm enough to keep the chill off her skin. She looked up at the heavens. It would be dawn in only a couple of hours. Darkness had already started to give way to a strange kind of twilight that made it easier to see her surroundings but more difficult to make out any detail.

Lauren looked at Julian. He stared straight ahead, eyes intent on the distance and the tall collar of his coat masking the lower half of his face. He didn't even blink when the wintry wind blew the black strands of his hair across his brow. She kept her gaze fixed on him as much as possible, taking him all in. He moved the black carry case he had borrowed from her to conceal his sword to his right shoulder and straightened. He was much taller than her, enough that she barely reached his shoulders, but she liked it and the fact that he radiated strength and confidence. She wished he would speak more to her though. The sound of his voice soothed her. It was warm and calming, adding to the way she felt when she was around him. She didn't feel as though she was in danger. She was safe with him. Even though she knew that she shouldn't feel that way, she did. She couldn't help it.

He blinked slowly, shuttering his beautiful blue eyes. She had never imagined that such pale eyes could have such intensity. They sent a tremor through her whenever he looked into hers, a spark that gave her a warm feeling in the pit of her stomach. When he looked at her with silver eyes, she felt mesmerised.

She moved ahead of him a little and looked back. He glanced away from her, towards the park in the middle of the square.

His behaviour was starting to give her the impression that he was avoiding looking at her. What reason did he have to do that though?

Julian stopped, scrutinised the pavement, and then walked a few steps and crouched down. Lauren leaned forwards to see what he was doing. When he held his hand above the paving slab, something flared into existence. The flash of green light faded to reveal an intricate glowing symbol just beneath Julian's palm on the pavement. He stood and the symbol disappeared.

"What was that?" Lauren said. Shiny glyphs didn't just appear out of nowhere and they certainly didn't disappear without a trace.

"A marker," he said and the sound of his deep accented voice made her want to close her eyes.

"And it does what?" Lauren crouched and waved her hand over the pavement. Nothing happened.

"It responds only to me." Julian knelt on one knee beside her. He held his hand out and the marker appeared again, glowing brilliant green and lighting his hand and the pavement. The swirling pattern shifted beneath his fingers. Twin circular bands edged the central symbol. The smaller glyphs inside them moved in opposite directions. The ones in the outside ring turned clockwise and those in the inside one anti-clockwise. "It tells us which way to go."

"How does it know where we want to go?" She reached out and touched the marker. It was freezing cold. An unsettled feeling grew in her. Julian took hold of her hand and moved it away.

"They do not just appear of their own accord. Duke placed it here to guide us. I came ahead of the others and do not know the location of the Ghost office here in London." Julian stood and brushed off his knee before offering his hand to her. She took it and pulled herself back up.

"And who is Duke?" Everything Julian said left her with more questions and she wanted answers.

"You will meet him soon enough." Julian held his arm out to one side, indicating the way forward.

She could sense he wanted her to be silent again so he could concentrate. One more question first.

"How do you find the markers?"

Julian paused mid-stride and looked over his shoulder at her. The funnel neck of his coat shifted and she caught a glimpse of the rest of his nose. It was perfectly straight. She wished that she could see all of his face. Perhaps when they reached Duke and the Ghosts he would remove his coat. She wanted to know what Julian looked like.

"I can sense them."

"Can you sense me too?"

He nodded. "Come, we must not keep them waiting."

Lauren followed him again, feeling somewhat like a small child just told off by their father. Julian was old enough to be her great-times-one-hundred-grandfather. Lauren couldn't imagine living for that long. He would have seen the world change, for better and for worse. More questions came to her but she kept them to herself this time.

Julian led her down a side street and then an empty pedestrian street. He stopped and placed his hand against the redbrick and cream sandstone wall of an old factory building to her left. Another symbol appeared between two large white-framed arched windows. Pale blue this time. It matched Julian's eyes.

Lauren frowned at the comparison.

When had she become so interested in him? He'd been on her mind since she'd met him. He'd told her so much about herself and Lycaon, but he'd barely mentioned himself. The fact that he kept half of his face hidden only increased his aura of mystery and when she combined that mystery with his incredible sword skills and need to protect her, she found herself desiring him.

He took the black carry case from his shoulder, pulled out his katana and slid it back into place under his coat. He handed her the case and she put it into her backpack. Had they arrived?

Julian stepped back, looked up at the building and then at the similar one opposite.

Before Lauren could ask what the symbol had said this time, one of his arms was around her waist and the other went behind her knees. He lifted her effortlessly. Her eyebrows almost touched her hairline and she looped her arms around his neck. Her feet crossed. No man had ever picked her up before. She stared at his face, right into his eyes, able to see every tiny fleck of darker blue against ice. This close to him, she couldn't deny her attraction to Julian. Her heart jigged in her chest and heat scorched her where his hands pressed into her body.

"Hold on tight," Julian whispered and Lauren nodded, captivated by the dark ring that encircled his irises and the wide black abyss of his pupils. His eyes were so beautiful. "Do not look down."

Lauren frowned. She wasn't that high off the ground. Come to think of it, why was he holding her anyway? Did he intend to carry her across the threshold like newlyweds? That thought brought an odd warmth with it but it quickly dissipated. Immortals probably didn't marry and she barely knew him. If her friends were here they would think she had either gone crazy or was finally seizing the day just as she'd said she would.

She blinked and then frowned again, remembering that she'd left her bag in the alley. The body of the man had disappeared but her things were still there, covered in blood. What if the police could link them to her somehow? They could contact her friends and then they would think that she had been murdered or kidnapped.

Well, they would be right about one of those things.

Julian had practically abducted her and he'd told her things that she still didn't fully believe. The people at Ghost were like her. How much like her? Were they like Julian, or were they different?

He turned with her and jumped, pushing all thought from her head. Her arms tightened around his neck. She expected him to go a few feet and then hit the pavement. He didn't. He soared upwards towards the building opposite at incredible speed.

He was going to jump to the roof. That was impossible. No one could jump that far. Could Julian?

The second storey windows of the building came at them fast.

They were going to hit it.

Lauren leaned into Julian's neck and braced for impact. His arms tightened around her in a delicious way and just as they were going to hit the wall, his foot came out. He pushed off from the second redbrick warehouse, pivoted, and they were sailing upwards again.

Her heart pounded as they sped towards the roof of the building that bore the symbol.

Julian landed silently on a low wall that edged the flat roof and then stepped down, still holding her. She stared up at him, mouth working silently as she tried to speak. He gently lowered her until her feet hit the gravel. Her legs wobbled beneath her and her arms refused to come unlocked. Strong hands firmly gripped her waist, steadying her, warming her until she burned inside. She stared into silver eyes. Her reflection shimmered in them.

"Are you well?" Julian said, his low voice making her quiver with delight.

She swallowed and then nodded. "That was incredible."

His eyes narrowed as though he was smiling behind the funnel neck of his coat and he reached around behind his head, took hold of her hands, and removed them. Lauren looked down at their joined hands when he kept hold of one of them. It felt nice. What made it feel even better was the fact that the hand holding hers was his left, the opposite of the one he used to draw his sword. He was still protecting her. If something happened, he would be able to defend her in a heartbeat.

Did his heart beat?

"Stay close." He started walking.

Lauren followed in a daze. If Julian had wanted to make her believe that all this was real, he'd found the perfect way by leaping up to the roof. Now she couldn't deny that he was different and she couldn't help wondering if she would be able to do that too when she awakened. Jump building to building. Soar over the gaps between them. Fight like him.

She frowned and tracked back through her thoughts. When she awakened? Shouldn't that have been 'if'? She was on the verge of agreeing to something before she had all the facts. There were definitely things that Julian had skirted around during their conversation, or had omitted completely. There was more to this than he was telling her, just as there was more to him.

They stopped in front of a small square structure with a dark metal door and Julian held his free hand out to it. A red symbol appeared this time. The markings matched the green one that had been on the pavement. The door clicked. Julian opened it and walked in, his grip on her hand increasing.

Lights flickered into life above them, dull and tinted green. They barely lit the steep concrete steps that led down into the building. Lauren clung to Julian's hand and looked back at the door. No one was there and her footsteps on the stairs were so loud that she would have heard someone walking down them if they had opened the door and then left. Who had unlocked the door and turned on the lights?

A red dot on the sloped ceiling caught her attention. A small black security camera pointed at her and the door. She stared into the dark lens, wondering who was looking back at her.

They turned right down the corridor at the end of the steps. The industrial lighting stole all warmth from the cream walls. She hunched up, feeling cold as she walked through the eerily silent building.

They passed several dark doors. Some of them were open, revealing modern and spacious offices. No one was in them. She wasn't surprised considering that it was nearing dawn now. Everyone had probably gone home for the evening. That was, if Ghost operatives went home.

Julian's boots were loud on the beech wood floor, echoing along the hall ahead of them. She looked down as they passed a staircase on her left. A brown carpet stair-runner led her eye downward and she frowned when she heard noises coming from the floor below. There were still people in the building, and they were awake.

Julian's grip on her hand tightened and his pace slowed. They were nearing the end of the corridor now. Only two doors lay ahead of them, both closed. Was his contact behind one of them? She looked at Julian. His increasing grip on her hand and his hesitation gave her the impression that whomever they were meeting, he didn't fully trust them.

At least not with her.

That thought made her heart thump hard against her chest. Julian stopped and looked back at her.

"Is something the matter?" He frowned.

Lauren could only draw one conclusion.

He could hear her heart beating.

She hadn't tensed, gasped, or made any move or sound that might have alerted him to the sudden spike in her emotions caused by the thought that he wanted to protect her. Had he sensed it? Was this another of his abilities? Super hearing.

"Nothing," she whispered and then stepped towards him. "What… what gave you the impression something was wrong?"

He looked down at her chest. His blue eyes showed a flicker of hunger. She liked the way he looked at her. Fire, passion, desire. No man had looked at her like that before.

"Your heart." He turned away. "It sounds frightened."

It was galloping in her chest, racing over the way he'd looked at her rather than the revelation that he could hear it or anything like fear. After witnessing firsthand that he could leap up buildings, she was sure that nothing about Julian could shock her.

"I'm not frightened." When she said that, he glanced at her out of the corner of his eye.

He walked to a dark wooden door and knocked.

Without waiting for an invitation from within, Julian opened the door and held it for her. She hesitated, uncertain about going in first, and then took a deep breath and laughed internally at how ridiculous she was being. Fear had lived too long in her heart, making her play it safe when everyone else was taking chances. It was time that she changed that. If she could accept everything that Julian had told her, then she could face whatever was in this room.

Head held high, Lauren walked into the large office. There was nothing more than a man sitting at a grand mahogany desk working on a laptop. Papers were scattered across it. A mug sat in one corner under a green glass and brass lamp. Three tall arched windows behind the man revealed a panorama of London rooftops. The sky was starting to grow brighter.

The man looked up at her. Short dark tangled waves touched with silver framed his tanned handsome face. He looked no more than ten years her senior. Deep intense brown eyes met hers with confidence and a sparkle of amusement. He smiled, adopting an almost seductive expression, and then with quintessential Italian charm, he stood, walked around the desk to her and took hold of her hand, bringing it to his lips and pressing a kiss to the back of it.

"Lauren, I presume?" he said in a husky voice and glanced up into her eyes.

She nodded, stunned by his greeting. His thumb brushed the back of her hand. Was he flirting with her?

The sleeve of his silver-grey suit fell back, revealing a tattoo on his forearm and his palm. Black outlined roses and stems wound their way up his arm, spread out as they disappeared under his shirt but grouped closer together on his palm. The flowers close to his shirt cuff were empty but some of the ones on his wrist were coloured in, as were all of the ones that she could see on his palm. They varied from crimson through to a red so deep that it was almost black.

He waved a hand towards two dark red leather armchairs in front of his desk. She shook her head. She didn't want to sit down. She would only start fidgeting and showing her nerves.

"I thought Julian said not to frighten her?" The female voice caught her off guard and Lauren turned on a pinhead to face the owner of it. The woman was stunning, wearing a tight long black dress that revealed an hourglass figure, abundance of cleavage and legs that Lauren would kill for. Red heart-shaped lips, near-black eyes, and glossy straight black hair that reached mid-way down her back topped off the vision of perfection.

This woman was sin personified.

The man let go of her hand, smiling all the while, and leaned against the large mahogany desk. He placed his right foot up onto the seat of one of the leather armchairs. Shiny expensive leather shoes. He seemed accustomed to luxury. His office was a lot different to the others she had seen down the hall. It was larger and more grandly furnished, superior, and it showed signs of life, albeit ones that unnerved her. She hadn't failed to notice that the wall to her left was painted dark red when all the others were cream, and that a huge wooden glass-fronted cabinet full of guns took up most of it. One of the doors was open behind the other. None of the guns it contained were automatic or modern weapons. They all looked antique, and there were a couple missing.

"I would think that sort of greeting would be more frightening than mine. You made the poor girl jump." The man folded his arms across his chest.

Lauren looked from him, to the woman where she stood framed against the strip of cream wall between two massive mahogany bookcases, to Julian. His pale blue eyes were narrowed, his eyebrows drawn tight together. If she had to guess at his feelings, she would say that he wasn't happy. Had it been the man's flirtatious greeting or the fact the woman had scared her?

Lauren stepped back towards him, distancing herself from the two new people. The closer she moved to Julian, the calmer and safer she felt. He moved forwards until he stood beside her, so near to her that their hands were almost touching.

"Perhaps we should introduce ourselves more formally?" the man said.

Julian nodded and his expression lightened.

"My name is Duke." With a flourish, the man motioned towards the woman. "And this is Astra."

Duke and Astra. Only two of them? When Julian had told her they were going to meet some people, she'd imagined more than two. But they had powers. Maybe they only needed two of them to help.

"Ghost," Lauren said and Duke nodded, a smile winding its way across his face again. She glanced at Julian, wondering what his smile would look like. He still showed no sign of removing his coat.

"The organisation that we work for is called Ghost. It formed around a century ago to deal with maintaining a balance between the human and the demon worlds. Ghost is made up of small teams of five, each with their own mission. Normally that mission is to eradicate any species thought to threaten human existence or thought to be in danger of revealing the existence of demons."

"Like some sort of paranormal investigation company," Lauren said and the man laughed.

"Not quite, but close enough. I have led several missions with Ghost. Demons, portals, magic, we deal with anything and almost everything. My team's current mission is to assist Julian in finding you."

"But that mission seems to have concluded." Astra leaned back against the patch of cream wall between the two crammed bookcases, distant from all of them.

Astra crossed her arms, pushing her breasts up even higher. Lauren snuck a glance down at her own meagre offering. Her gaze shifted to Julian and she was relieved when she found him looking at her, not at Astra. She wondered why either man was paying attention to her when a goddess was in the same room. Most men she knew would have been fawning over Astra by now.

"So are we included on the second part or not?" Duke's smile held.

"It is up to Lauren." Julian moved away and a cold feeling stole through her.

She moved closer to him again. Astra smiled across the room at her. There was a hint of malice to it.

Lauren realised that everyone was looking at her. She stared at the intricate Chinese rug that covered most of the floor in the office, her gaze following the flowing forms of dragons and arched bridges and pretty buildings. The room was silent and filled with an air of expectation. If they thought she was going to announce her decision right now, they had another thing coming. She wasn't going to decide either way until she had all the facts. She knew nothing about her so-called 'awakening' or these people. At least she could remedy that. She looked up at Duke.

"Julian says you're both special, like me. You have powers."

Duke grinned and leaned back, raking his gaze over her. "You are definitely special."

"We have different abilities to yours." Astra came away from the wall to stand near to Julian. She turned her dark eyes on him, her smile becoming seductive. "Yours are like Julian's."

Julian looked at Astra. Jealousy hissed in Lauren's mind. In a competition of looks, Astra would win hands down, but Lauren wasn't about to just throw in the towel.

When Julian's gaze moved back to her, Lauren turned her attention to Duke. Determined to ignore Astra's attempts to make her jealous, she gave Duke her best smile.

"Show me what you've got," she said and couldn't quite believe those words had left her lips. For a brief moment, she'd considered adding 'big boy' to the end of her sentence and was glad that she hadn't. Things were crazy enough without her falling into a flirt-off with a woman that had twice her talents and then some, for a man who she wasn't even sure of her feelings for.

In the blink of an eye, Duke had disappeared and then reappeared right by her elbow. He hadn't moved like the werewolves and Julian, quicker than her eyes could keep up with. He had literally disappeared. Teleported. He raised his hand, showing her that it was empty save the tattoos that marked it, and then produced a red translucent ball of something that morphed into the shape of a heart.

Not a cartoon heart.

A human one that was beating rapidly.

Lauren's eyes widened. It matched her heartbeat.

That wasn't some cheap parlour trick magic.

Her stomach turned and she backed away from Duke, bumping into something. Turning, she found herself staring up at Julian. His pale blue eyes were fixed on Duke in a scowl but dropped to her in a heartbeat. When had he moved so close to her? Astra laughed but there was only anger in her eyes.

Lauren looked back at Duke. The heart was gone and he was toying with something. A gun. It looked like an old six-shooter, like the large collection in the glass cabinet on the wall to her left, but there were more rounds in the chamber than that. She'd never seen such an elaborate gun before. The metal was golden and intricately carved with roses, and the grip was mahogany.

"A wizard?" Lauren said, unsure whether it was the right word to use.

"Of sorts." Duke spun the chamber of the gun. "Although I rarely use magic to fight with nowadays. I rely more on man-made weaponry, albeit with an edge."

He opened the chamber, removed a bullet and tossed it over to her. Lauren caught and stared at it. Strange symbols similar to those on the markers covered the silver casing. She looked at Duke for an answer to her silent question.

"It is an incantation. It will kill any demon that it penetrates."

"Not all demons," Astra said and Lauren's attention was immediately with her. "Some of us are immune, aren't we, Julian?"

Lauren frowned at her and then Julian. "A demon?"

He shook his head. "Astra is the only demon in this room."

Astra laughed, high and tinkling, her hand delicately covering her mouth. When she opened her eyes again, they were glowing bright blue, flickering as though they had turned to flame.

"I am the only demon, vampire?"

Vampire? Lauren's gaze shot back to Julian.

Julian's eyes flashed silver. "I am no vampire!"

"You drink blood to live… a vampire drinks blood to live. Tell me the difference. We are not so different." Astra's eyes narrowed.

"Astra!" Duke stepped between them. Lauren moved behind Julian. His hand was on his sword. "Stand down. Julian is not a vampire or a demon, and neither are you, not for a long time."

Astra turned away and walked to the last of the three tall arched windows. When she reached it, she looked back at Lauren, her eyes still vivid blue, as bright as a summer's sky at noon.

"I apologise, Julian… but do not expect me to pander to your little girl's desire to know of my 'power'."

Lauren stood her ground, unflinching under Astra's eerie stare. Whatever power the woman had, it was strong and Lauren got the feeling that it was dangerous.

"She's been grouchy all day. If she was mortal, I would say it was her special time." Duke shrugged and Astra turned her back on them. Lauren watched her for a few seconds more and then shook off her bad feeling and faced the two men.

Her eyes sought Julian's. They were pale blue again, unreadable. Any emotion he was feeling was well-masked, hidden beneath layers of ice that made her feel cold. He'd shut her out. Until now, she hadn't even realised that he'd let her in but she felt the loss keenly. Whatever barrier he'd brought up, she wanted to break it down. She wanted back in.

"Is she right about you?" Lauren's voice quivered the tiniest amount. She clenched her fists to steel her nerves and settle them. So what if he drank blood? She was growing accustomed to people being different to her.

Or not so different. If she chose to awaken, she would become like Julian. When Julian had shown her the scars on his forearm, she had reacted to the sight of them. The thought of taking his blood had frightened her, but she'd felt a compulsion to bite him, to taste the strength in his veins. The desire had been almost irresistible, and completely confusing. Now, it made a hideous kind of sense. In the same way that she instinctively remembered Julian, she'd remembered her need to feed.

"Normal sustenance is no longer possible for me, just as it was never possible for you. It was your blood which brought me over and I have inherited my abilities from you—my immortality, my speed and strength, and my need for blood," he said.

A very eloquent if unnerving reply. She didn't like the way he spoke about her and Illia as though they were the same, and she didn't like the fact that she was beginning to think that way too.

"I am not like a normal vampire."

Her eyebrows rose. "But you drink blood."

And she would too when she awakened.

Julian nodded. Duke glanced towards Astra. Lauren looked there too.

"What does she drink?" Lauren uncurled her fingers and then clenched her fists again. Her insides trembled. She was glad that Astra remained facing away from them. If Astra had been looking her way, Lauren would have lost her nerve. "She said that you weren't so different, Julian... if you drink blood... is she a vamp—"

"Dare call me that filthy word and I will—" Astra stopped mid-stride as Julian drew his sword and stepped into her path.

Lauren's heart jumped. She hadn't realised that calling someone a vampire would cause so much trouble.

"What are you then?" Lauren found her bravery now that Julian was between them and showed no sign of backing down.

"We have no name." Astra settled back onto her heels. "But I am not a vampire. I do not feed on blood." Her eyes fixed on Lauren's, sending a chill through her. "I need souls to survive."

Lauren stepped back, her hand coming up to her chest.

Duke laughed. It did nothing to ease the tension in the room.

"It has been a long time since Astra has devoured a human soul. She has acquired a taste for demon souls," he said but the knowledge that Astra had changed her tastes didn't comfort Lauren in the slightest. Astra had implied that she wasn't the only one of her kind out there.

Lauren added soul-eating demons to her list of things to avoid.

"Julian?" She ventured a step towards him.

He turned, sheathing his sword at the same time. His eyes were still cold. Even when provoked into defending her, he'd been emotionless.

Seeing that he wasn't going to ask her what was wrong this time, she gave a brief small smile and then said, "How do I regain my powers? You never really told me what happens during my awakening."

A flicker of hesitation crossed his eyes and then disappeared as though he'd erased it.

"Lycaon was already spreading his curse to others by the time I fell. You were confident that you could do something similar by passing your blood to me. As I lay dying, you fed me your blood and asked Zeus to save me. He did because I carried your blood and promised to protect you. He charged me with finding you and reawakening your power each time you are reincarnated."

He'd told her as much already, although he'd been vaguer about it. She nodded, wanting him to continue so she could finally learn more about what was happening to her.

"During the awakening, I will give your blood back to you, and bring you over," he said.

"Bring me over?" Several pieces fell into place in her head and she didn't like the connotations one bit. Julian had mentioned something about Zeus bringing him over. He'd also mentioned that he'd died in order to meet Zeus. "As in, die?"

"You will die either way, so what's the difference? One way you'll come back." Duke's bright air tailed off when she turned and stared at him.

Her mind raced.

"Wait… I'm going to die?" She didn't know who to look to for an answer. Julian danced around his answers and Duke said things straight—both of them knew what was going on when she didn't.

Duke winced and looked at Julian. "I thought you would have told her."

Julian's eyes were still cold and empty, even when he took hold of her hand.

The sound of raucous laughter filled the silence and a moment later the door burst open.

A young dark haired woman stood on the other side, grinning over her shoulder at something behind her. She almost tripped over her feet as she walked in and two young men followed. The two men were identical in every way, right down to their alternative clothes, broad builds and dark spiked hair that was tinted red at the tips. Their smiles fell off their faces when they noticed her. The girl smiled again in her direction and then at Duke.

"You called?" she said, her voice light in the heavy atmosphere of the room.

Duke nodded. "I wanted to introduce you all to Lauren. Julian found her."

There was a babble of incoherent noise as they all spoke at once and Lauren just smiled. She was sure they must have introduced themselves at some point in the mess of voices but she hadn't caught any of their names.

"Lauren is tired. We should retire. It has been a long day." Julian's hand tightened against hers.

She looked up at him, thought about it and realised that she was tired.

Had Julian sensed it in her?

Uncomfortable with the feeling that he was controlling her, she said, "I'm fine, really."

Julian gave her a knowing look.

"We were about to retire ourselves," Duke said and there was a murmur of agreement from the others. Lauren looked at them all in turn and then at the windows. The sky was lightening fast now.

"It's almost dawn." It seemed strange that they had all been awake during the night. Horror movie clichés came to her in droves. She glanced at Julian, wanting to ask whether he was going to be dead to the world when the sun rose, just like a vampire.

Pale skin, blood drinking, immortality, and superior abilities. They were all the hallmarks of a vampire. Only why would he react so violently to that word if he were one?

"We work at night," Duke said with a broad disarming smile. Another murmur from the group.

"We have arranged rooms close together for you." Astra's smile was as wide and charming as Duke's. It reminded Lauren of a snake, giving her the feeling that any moment now Astra would strike and suck the soul from her body. "I can take you to them."

"Not necessary. I will take care of Lauren." Julian's hand was firm against Lauren's lower back, pressed just below her backpack. Close enough to her bottom that she blushed.

"Fine. Next floor down. Your room is the second door on the right. Hers is two doors further down on the left, at the end of the corridor." Astra turned to face her. "Sweet dreams, princess."

Julian led Lauren towards the door. Lauren looked back at the five Ghosts. They all stared at her so closely that she wondered what they found interesting and whether they were going to talk about her when she was gone from the room.

"'Night," she said with a feeble wave and then Julian had escorted her out of the room and they were walking down the pale corridor.

Her gaze shifted to him. Was he going to explain about the awakening and the fact that she was going to die? It was definitely the catch that she'd felt. No wonder he hadn't wanted to tell her. If the younger Ghosts hadn't come bursting in and distracted her, she would have given him a piece of her mind. Better late than never. She wasn't about to leave anything up to chance now. If she didn't mention it, he might not either.

"So I'm going to die?" Her tone was as breezy as she could make it, as though she was talking about the weather or something inconsequential. "On my birthday I'll die if I don't go through with the awakening."

Julian led her down the stairs they had passed on their way to Duke's office. When they reached the bottom, his hand left her back. He adjusted his coat. He was thinking of what to say.

"Just say yes if I'll die."

"Yes," he said. Never had that word sounded so menacing and cold.

"Will I die if I go through with it?"

She was too damn young to die. It wasn't possible that she'd found her purpose in life, her reason for being on Earth, and now she was going to die. It wasn't going to happen.

"Duke is correct. It is part of Illia's curse. You will die either way, but one way you will come back."

"And be like you... a vampire?"

He turned on her, his eyes dark and full of deadly intent. Lauren backed away and bumped into the cream wall. She raised her hands and cringed.

"What are you then? You drink blood... live forever... clearly eternal youth is on your side... and then there's those amazing abilities of yours."

"I am not a vampire." That same black tone of voice he'd used on Astra. Lauren made a mental note not to call him a vampire again. "Vampires are filth."

She noted that too. Vampires, werewolves and soul-eating demons—three species she was definitely going to avoid as much as possible.

"Then what are you?" Lauren risked a step towards him, relieved when his expression altered and all sign of his anger melted away. "Tell me so I can understand. There's so much I still can't get straight in my head. Please?"

When his look softened, concern touching his pale eyes, her heart warmed and she took another step forwards, wanting to be closer to him. Her fingers itched with the temptation to reach up and pull the funnel neck of his coat down so she could see his face. She wanted to see if he was as handsome as she was picturing. She needed to see him.

"Yours," he whispered and her heart leapt. A wave of warm tingles spread through her. He looked away from her and then back again. All affection was gone from his eyes. His tone was empty. "Your Arcadian. Your protector."

He moved past her, leaving her rooted to the spot and staring at his back. He still hadn't answered her question. In fact, he'd only left her more confused. He flitted between cold and warm so rapidly that she couldn't keep up.

"And the awakening? Do I really have a choice?"

"Yes," he said, still walking away from her.

He stopped in front of a dark door just past a junction in the corridor and turned to face her.

"Have I ever said no?"

A shake of his head. He opened the door.

None of Illia's previous reincarnations had said no. She could understand that. When faced with death or the chance to live, she would have to choose living. If she went through with the awakening, she would change, become different like Julian. She wasn't sure if it would be such a bad thing. Her eyes met his and she walked towards him. Would it be wrong to do it purely to remain alive and with him?

She shook her head to clear it of such ridiculous thoughts. Living was reason enough. Death didn't bear thinking about.

Lauren walked into the room and looked around. It was large and the pale blue walls made it appear cold but the furniture looked comfortable. A dark wood double bed stood to her right against the same wall as the door, flanked by two small cupboards. Three tall rectangular windows lined the wall opposite her. Drawn white muslin curtains blocked out the world, framed by open long Wedgewood blue ones. She walked to the window nearest her and pulled the muslin curtains open a crack. The office building opposite was dark. She looked up. The sky was pale blue now, the scattered clouds touched with pink and gold. Turning back into the room, she let the curtain fall closed and looked to her left, past the bed. There was a white armchair and wooden side table in the corner against the same wall as the windows, and another door on the adjoining wall to her left. It was open, revealing a white tiled bathroom.

Lauren sat down on the bed and removed her backpack, dumping it down on the blue bedspread.

"Is something the matter?" Julian frowned.

"I'm not sure," she whispered and dropped her gaze to her feet. One moment she wanted to go along with it all and the next she thought she was crazy and wanted to go home. Her mind was going in so many directions that she feared it was going to fall apart completely. The only thing that felt solid and real right now, that felt safe, was Julian.

"Would you like me to stay?" he said and her eyes widened at the thought. "I can stay if it will make you feel better."

Lauren stared at Julian. He stood by the door, tall and straight, his eyes fixed on her. There was such fire in them, a promise of passion that she knew she had to be imagining. He hadn't really given her a reason to believe that he found her attractive, but right now, she could easily fool herself into thinking that he did.

With that hunger shining in his eyes, she didn't doubt that he could make her feel better, better than any of her lousy ex-boyfriends ever did. And while some part of her said to reach out and take what she wanted, to live life to the full just as her friends did and lose herself in the moment, the greater part said that it wasn't going to happen. She'd learnt from experience that men like Julian, strong, undoubtedly handsome and sexy, were so far out of her league that they were in another galaxy.

She lowered her eyes again, tracing the grain of the wooden floor, and shook her head, letting the moment slip through her fingers as she had done a million times in her life. She might have told her friends she was going to seize the day from now on but she wasn't quite ready to after all. "I need some time alone."

It wasn't a lie. She needed a little space in order to gain perspective. With Julian around, it was so easy to go along with things.

"My room is just down the hall should you need me," he said in a low voice that made her want to look at him again. "Goodnight, Lauren."

"'Night," she whispered. The door closed and she continued to stare at the floor, taking it all in.

Unzipping her backpack, she removed the picture of her parents with her in the park. Werewolves had killed them. Because of her. Whoever Lycaon was, he had a sadistic streak. Her fists clenched. She would make him pay for their deaths. But how?

She remembered the way Julian fought, his incredible abilities, and what he'd told her about her destiny and duty.

The thought of dying filled her with cold dread but the choice she had to make was easy when she thought about the alternative and what Julian had said.

She was born to die and rise again to fight the man who had killed her parents.

She just didn't think that she was strong enough to go through with it.

CHAPTER 4

Tremendous pain engulfed him. Julian's knees hit the dirt beside her. His vision blurred with hot tears and his heart tore in two, ripping him apart until he felt as though the sense of loss alone would kill him. Emptiness followed in its wake, sweeping up from below and turning him numb. He pulled her off the dusty ground and into his arms, cradling her broken body against the solid armour covering his chest. His hand found hers and he held it, desperately tried to close her bloodied limp fingers around his but they would no longer hold him.

He brought her hand to his face and pressed his lips to the back of it, until he tasted his tears on her skin. Illia was gone. He closed his eyes and buried his face in her long dark hair, holding her tight against him. She couldn't be gone. What was eternity without his love? She'd given him a cruel gift—a world without her.

"Illia," he whispered, rocking with her. The Fates had played a terrible trick on him. They had sent him back to Earth too late to save her.

He couldn't go on without her. He couldn't bear the pain. How could he live without his heart? It had shattered, scattered on the wind along with her last breath.

His Illia.

Julian looked up at the man who had taken her life. Lycaon. He stood a few metres away, bathed in moonlight and towering over them, his dark armour scarred and his body bloodied from the battle. The warm summer breeze carried the scent of blood and earth, and tousled the long wavy strands of Lycaon's black hair, blowing them across his face. They caught in the short stubble that covered his jaw. He stood motionless save the rise and fall of his chest with his heavy breathing. His dark brown eyes fixed on Illia where she lay in Julian's arms. A flicker of regret shone in them and then he turned away, his blood-soaked sword held limp at his side, and walked into the night.

A sickening swirling feeling grew inside Julian. He braced himself, clinging to Illia as he became aware of what was coming.

In the darkness of his closed eyes, he saw horror after horror. Death after death. In one bright blinding burst, he saw the last moments of every incarnation of Illia. He saw their final fight, each more violent and bloody than the last, and witnessed the change in Lycaon. All sign of regret at taking Illia's life faded until Lycaon showed nothing but glee as he drew out their death, toying with them. They didn't stand a chance. Nothing Julian did could save them. No amount of time to prepare helped them. Lycaon was too strong—his skill with the sword and his lust for death unparalleled.

Lycaon's laughter rang in Julian's ears as he held each incarnation of Illia while they breathed their last and looked at him with fear in their eyes. Every shred of pain Julian had felt compounded into one burning feeling that made him ache to die, but he had to go on, for their sake. He had to continue the duty he had been charged with, regardless of the pain and suffering it caused him to live eternity alone even when he wasn't, to be denied love and physical contact, to be isolated from humanity. He grieved thirty deaths in one heart-breaking moment until silence shrouded him and he swore he could take no more.

A scream shattered the night air.

He looked up and his eyes widened, horrified by the fight playing out before him. He tried to rise to his feet, to protect her as he had sworn but he couldn't move. Lauren fought desperately, his own sword in her hands as she struggled against Lycaon. Lycaon forced her backwards, her strength no match for him. Julian reached for her, tried to call her name but no sound issued from his lips. His eyebrows furrowed and he cursed the Fates for making him witness such a terrible act of murder. She wasn't strong enough. She never was.

Lauren shrieked and clumsily blocked Lycaon's heavy sword. Lycaon pressed on, using his weight to force her sword down, and cut into her shoulder. She screamed again and turned towards Julian. Julian stretched out his arm to her as she reached for him. Lycaon grinned, triumph shining in his dark malicious eyes.

Julian shouted her name but it was too late.

Lycaon's blade came down and Lauren arched forwards, the pain in her eyes unbearable, and cried out as the sword cut down her back.

She fell and Julian closed his eyes, not wanting to see Lauren die. He couldn't take it.

A soft breath caressed his face.

Julian opened his eyes and drew back. Lauren lay in his arms, her eyes swimming with fear. A spray of blood marred her pale cheeks, blending into her red hair at her right temple. Her hand twitched in his and her expression softened. His eyes closed briefly when she brushed the fingers of her other hand across his cheek and smiled up at him. The fear in her deep brown eyes turned to sorrow and, in his heart, he knew that it was for him. Tears rolled down her cheeks, cutting through the blood and dirt. He squeezed her hand, choked on the words that he wanted to say. Her palm cupped his cheek. Her hand turned cold against his skin.

She was so different to them. He needed her more than anything, anyone.

He shook his head, cursed the gods and then wrapped his arms around her and pulled her to him.

"I will not let you die," he whispered into her hair, raw pain stealing his breath.

Her hand slipped from his cheek and his arms were suddenly empty. He could still sense her. She was alive but distant. Cold stole through his veins, freezing the fragments of his heart. His eyes opened to reveal nothing but eternal darkness. He couldn't breathe. His heart thundered. The dust choked him. Panic broke over him in a nauseating wave and he scrambled forwards in the inky black.

His hands smacked against something solid and he groped around, finding nothing but icy stone.

No.

Not this again.

Not this.

A muffled scream reached his ears.

Not again.

He looked up in the darkness, knowing that she was above him somewhere, alone and fighting for him, afraid.

Julian's breathing came in sharp bursts. He dug through the rubble with his bare hands, desperate to escape the cloying darkness. It enveloped him, went down into his lungs and stole his strength away. Another scream. He scrambled up the rocky incline until his head hit the ceiling of his prison. He banged his fists against it, using all of his remaining strength in an attempt to break through and get to her before it was too late. Dust scattered down and filled his mouth and lungs, shortening his breaths. He clawed at the rocks until blood trickled down his fingers.

His heart tightened as everything went quiet.

It became empty as he felt her die.

Illia.

Not this.

Please.

Not again.

"Lauren!"

Julian sat up with a jolt, trembling and cold. He couldn't breathe. He needed to breathe. He needed to escape. He gulped down air so hard it burnt his lungs. His heart hammered against his ribcage, filling his head with a staccato beat. He needed to get to her.

He clawed at the air and then realised there was nothing there. No rubble blocked his path. No dust choked him. No sound of battle came to his ears.

Gradually, the darkness faded, revealing the unlit bedroom surrounding him. He quickly reached across the bed and fumbled with the lamp on the wooden side table there, almost knocking it over. The light was bright when it came on but it was a relief. He should have turned it on when he had come into the room. He shouldn't have slept in the dark.

Still trembling, he sat back in the middle of his bed on top of the pale green covers and looked down at himself. He must have fallen asleep before undressing. His jaw tensed and he ran shaking fingers through his hair. Images of his nightmare flashed across his mind and he clenched his fists. He wasn't there. It wasn't happening again. The pain in his heart reminded him that it had been once and part of his nightmare could come true.

He needed to see her. He had to make sure that Lauren was alive.

Julian swung his legs over the edge of the bed and tried to stand but his knees gave way. He hit the wooden floor hard. Every muscle in his body quivered—weak and tired, unresponsive. He knelt on all fours, breathing hard, and tried to convince himself to move. He had to move. He had to check that Lauren was safe.

He ripped open the twin clasps that held his coat collar closed and sucked in deep breaths. Slow. Steady.

It took every ounce of his will to crawl to the door across the room and pull himself up. He leaned into the cream wall beside it for support, his legs threatening to give out again. He didn't dare close his eyes. He didn't want to go back to the darkness, not until he was able to face it, to bear it for her. Several attempts to open the door failed but eventually it gave and he made it out into the hall, his limbs shaking so much that he felt as though he wasn't in control.

He wasn't. Panic and fear were. Two emotions that he was too familiar with for his liking. He grew frustrated at himself for being so weak but the sense of need spiralling through him crushed any strength that anger might have given him. Only his need to see her gave him the will to continue and he stumbled on unsteady legs towards her room, leaning heavily against the wall, and then tripped across the hall to her door. He grabbed the handle to stop himself from falling, determined to overcome the weakness infesting him.

The door opened and he fell into the room, hitting the floor hard. His eyes immediately sought out Lauren. He had to see that she was alright. If he could then this feeling of desperation would pass. Fear would no longer rule him. He would be strong again, for her.

She lay on the bed to his right, the blue bedclothes barely covering her breasts. Moonlight cascaded through the crack between one set of curtains and over her skin, highlighting her peaceful face as she slumbered, unaware of his fear and pain. Relief and comfort eased him and gave him the strength to stand. He pushed himself up and crossed the room to her.

Her heart was calm and her breathing was steady. They soothed him. A need surfaced with him, so intense that he couldn't deny it. He had to touch her. It didn't matter that it was forbidden. He needed to feel that she was safe and here with him at last. In this moment, he didn't just want to break the rules, he wanted to shatter them.

Julian hesitated and then reached out and swept the short strands of her red hair from her eyes. The touch became a caress before he could stop himself and he brushed the backs of his fingers across her forehead. Her skin was warm and soft, smooth against his. His hands trembled, his breathing shaky. He was so weak for her, but this time that weakness felt stronger than ever.

Stronger than his weakness for Illia had ever been. He didn't understand it. Didn't try to. He just accepted it. Lauren affected him deeper than her predecessors. He needed her.

His frail legs threatened to give out but he refused to leave. He needed to stay a while, to take in the sight of her until he was sure that she was real and it had only been a nightmare.

Lauren rolled her head into his hand. Her face became shadowed but he could still see her, continued to watch her sleep. His heart whispered that he wasn't strong enough to lose her this time. He absorbed the soft warmth of her against his hand and vowed that he would do anything to protect her. Anything. He wouldn't fail Lauren.

His breathing slowed and his heartbeat steadied, matching Lauren's.

He stroked her cheek, fascinated by the satin feel of her skin. Being with her like this made him realise that something had changed in him over the years and filled him with a sense that his feelings had altered in some way. He felt different.

Lauren's rosy lips parted in a sigh.

She felt different.

Julian ran his fingers over her brow.

She was beautiful in a way none of them had been.

She smiled in her sleep, as though she could hear his thoughts and was pleased.

At least her dreams were good. She needed her sleep. Soon her nightmare would begin.

He would do all in his power to ensure that she survived.

CHAPTER 5

Lauren woke to a feeling of peace. It soon changed to the sensation of being watched. She kept her eyes closed, afraid of what she might find. She'd been dreaming of her parents, only Julian had been there too. He'd been watching her.

She cracked an eye open.

It seemed that he was still watching her.

He sat in the white armchair in the corner of her room, his eyes on her. The lamp on the table beside him cast a warm glow over his skin. He still wore his coat, half of his face hidden so his expression was unreadable. She blinked sleep away and sat up, gathering the blue bedclothes to her. Dread replaced her sense of calm.

"What is it? Is something wrong?" Lauren said.

Julian blinked and then looked at her as though he'd only just noticed that she was awake. His eyes were lifeless. She reached across and turned the bedside lamp on. He flinched, glanced down at his hands and then back at her. A shadow of pain crossed his features and his eyes shone in the light.

Tears?

He stood, crossed the room and paused at the door to her left. Lauren turned on the bed and looked at him, waiting. His eyes met hers. She'd seen that melancholy and drained expression on someone's face before.

Hers.

When her parents had died.

"Is something wrong?" Her chest tightened. "Did something happen?"

Julian gave her one last pained look, and then left the room. The door closed with a soft click. Lauren leapt out of bed, dragged her jeans and black jumper on, and bolted out of her room. She raced barefoot down the corridor to his room and flung the door open. He wasn't there. She ran on, searching for him. When she came out into the brightly lit open foyer of the building, she leaned against the banister on the black balcony. There was no one in the foyer below. The moon shone in through the rows of tall Victorian factory-style windows that lined the wall opposite, stealing all warmth from the exposed brick walls. She leaned over the banister, trying to see the two floors below her in case Julian was there. No sign of him.

He had to be somewhere. He couldn't have disappeared so quickly.

She needed to find him, had to know why he'd looked so sad.

"You're up," an unfamiliar female voice said, its tone high and bubbly.

Lauren looked around to see the young woman from last night. She hadn't caught her name.

"Where's Julian?" Lauren said, not caring that she sounded rude. She had to find him.

The young woman pointed over the balcony. "He said he had business."

Lauren stared down at the black double doors. Why hadn't he answered her questions?

"Did something bad happen today?" Lauren's heart lodged in her throat.

The young woman's dark eyes widened and her eyebrows rose so high that her straight-across fringe hid them. She shook her head, sending her brown ponytail swishing side to side.

"Why?" she said.

Lauren's gaze went back to the doors. If nothing had happened, what had been wrong with Julian?

"Is it Julian?" the young woman said, her voice strained. "Did he say something? Should I get the others?"

There was an increasing note of panic in each question. Lauren managed a smile, feeling terrible for frightening her.

"He didn't say anything." Lauren moved back from the banisters, forcing her eyes to remain away from the doors and her focus to stay on the woman and not Julian.

"That's not like him." The young woman smiled at her, high beam and full of feeling.

Lauren laughed. It was a good joke. Julian was hardly the talkative type. Even when he'd been explaining things to her, he'd been economic with his use of words. The girl's look turned serious.

"It isn't?" Lauren said. Were there two Julians—hers and this talkative one?

Hers?

"I mean, he doesn't say much but if there's something wrong, he'll always tell us... even when he goes out alone to kill."

Lauren realised that the 'business' the woman had mentioned actually meant killing monsters.

"Do you know where he went?" Her heartbeat picked up again and she breathed slowly to control it. There was no need to panic. Julian had killed three werewolves in front of her and had come away without a scratch. He would be fine.

"I don't know, but I do know that you're not going out. My orders on that front are dreadfully clear. If you set foot out there, he'll kill us all."

Lauren got the feeling that the young woman wasn't joking that time either.

The woman took hold of her arm and smiled again. "Don't worry! He'll be back soon. How about some breakfast?"

"It's dark." Lauren glanced at the windows.

"You'll get used to it." The young woman's smile only grew wider and her deep brown eyes twinkled. "We're having bacon sarnies tonight."

Lauren's stomach grumbled in approval. Bacon sandwiches did sound good.

"Oh! I'm so rude." With a little hop and another smile, the young woman held out her hand. Lauren didn't know what else to do so she shook it. "I'm Piper. I think Kuga and Leo drowned me out last night. They're so bloody loud sometimes."

"Lauren." Saying her name felt so redundant. Piper already knew it.

Lauren's gaze drifted back to the door.

"He'll be back soon." Piper looped her arm around Lauren's. "Let me introduce you to the boys. I'm sure you're as curious about us as we are about you."

Lauren couldn't deny that. She'd wanted to meet the three younger Ghosts this morning. They were so different to Duke and Astra. Half their age or more for a start. Piper couldn't be older than eighteen, almost half Lauren's age, and the two men had looked as though they were in their early twenties. All three of them had been dressed in black jeans and dark t-shirts. Now the young woman was wearing a thick roll-neck jumper striped in various shades of pink and pale blue jeans. Piper gave her an impish smile as she led the way down the stairs to the next floor. Lauren's gaze wandered to the open doors they passed, catching glimpses of a modest sized gym and a tidy library. The smell of bacon grew stronger.

Laughter flowed down the hall.

It stopped when Lauren walked into the kitchen. The two broadly built men stood frozen to the spot, both looking over at her. They were as identical as she remembered them, right down to the tight black t-shirts stretched taut over their muscled torsos and the red spiked tips of their brown hair. One was leaning against the black counter near a tall white refrigerator, the coloured tips of his hair almost blending into the cherry-wood cabinets behind him and a slim glass of orange juice in his hand. The other was still smiling as he stood in front of a wide stainless steel and black stove holding a pair of tongs and a grill full of bacon.

"For a moment, Pip, I thought you were going to miss out," he said with a wide grin and went back to turning the bacon over.

"Yeah, and Hell is going to freeze over," the other man said with a laugh.

They sounded the same, but there was a stronger sense of kindness in the first one's words.

"You promised not to call me Pip anymore." Piper released Lauren's arm, walked around the kitchen island to the offending male and prodded him in the side. He turned to face her, his build and height making Piper look tiny and petite. With a smile and warmth in his brown eyes, he reached up and looked as though he was going to touch Piper's face in a tender caress. Were they an item? Just as his fingers were about to touch her cheek, a spark of electricity leapt from their tips and arced along the three metal hoops in Piper's right ear.

She swatted his hand away and covered her ear, scowling at him. "Shit, that wasn't funny the first time!"

"Aw, Piper... come on," the man said, leaving the grill on the stove and following Piper across the room. "Don't be mad."

Piper shot him a glare. He reached out to touch her again but ended up skidding backwards into the counter, as though someone had pushed him. The other man laughed.

"You reap what you sow, Brother." He pushed off from the counter and walked over to Lauren. He wiped his hand on his thick jean-clad thigh and offered it to her. Lauren eyed it with suspicion. She wasn't stupid. It seemed this man's brother could do something with electricity. It probably ran in the blood. The man grinned at her, as though he'd realised that she wasn't going to take his hand and was impressed. "I'm Leo. The idiot there is my younger brother Kuga."

"Younger?" she said.

"By a whopping twenty two minutes," Kuga said and gave Piper an odd look before returning to his duty at the grill. He slid it back under the flames.

"They're both morons," Piper said and then sighed when both men frowned at her. "Kind hearted morons."

"Don't forget who raised you, little girl." Leo's frown stuck.

Piper put her hands on her hips. "I'm not a little girl anymore."

Kuga gave Piper a look that said he might have noticed. If they had grown up together, it was no longer brotherly feelings that Kuga was having towards Piper. The hunger in his warm brown eyes was unmistakable.

"So you can both do that thing with electricity?" Lauren asked.

Leo cut open some white floury baps. Kuga took the grill out again and started filling the buns with bacon. They both nodded.

"They can conduct it, manipulate it, create it... it's really quite cool." Piper sat down at the kitchen island and patted the padded wooden stool next to her. She was still smiling wide, her brown eyes bright with it.

Lauren remembered what she'd been like as a teenager and how smiling had come so easily to her too. Now she didn't really have much to smile about. Life got complicated fast and it was hard to keep her spirits up sometimes, especially since her parents had died.

She sat down beside Piper. Leo slid a glass of orange juice her way. She reached for the other one to give it to Piper but it moved across the smooth black counter all by itself and stopped in Piper's hand. Lauren's eyebrows rose.

"Pip is the real talent." Kuga slid his broad muscled frame onto the stool the other side of Piper. He held his hand up and arcs of white lightning danced across his fingers. His look turned thoughtful. "Electricity is nothing when compared to what she could do."

Could do? Lauren looked at Piper.

For the first time, she wasn't smiling. She was staring at the glass, turning it back and forth in her hands.

"You'll get it one day." Leo sat down at the other end of the kitchen island.

Piper shrugged and then sat bolt upright, the smile back on her face. It was forced this time. What was Piper thinking? Lauren liked the breezy, happy and youthful vibe that the young woman gave out. It made her feel as though she might gain a friend while she was here. Perhaps someone that she could talk with about things. Piper seemed to know Julian well, and Lauren wanted to talk about him most of all.

She looked across at Kuga. He was watching Piper, concern in his light brown eyes. Piper toyed with her bacon sandwich. Leo devoured his as though nothing was wrong.

"You can move things... that's pretty cool," Lauren said in the hope it would lift the heavy atmosphere and get Piper smiling again.

"Yeah," Piper muttered and raised her hand. Kuga's food shot over to her. "Sometimes. The problem is, I can't control it."

"Yet." Kuga touched Piper's shoulder. "You'll get there. Duke said it would take time. Your gift is strong and those are the ones that can take years to master."

"It's been years," Piper whispered and then sighed. "I don't feel any closer to finding a way."

"But you moved that, and you pushed Kuga," Lauren said, impressed by Piper's ability and hoping to get her talking more about it so she could understand her better. If she was going to be working with Piper, Kuga and Leo, she wanted to know everything about them. She wanted to know them and hoped they would want to know her too.

"Little things." Piper pushed Kuga's plate back to him. "I can move small things and sometimes give a psychic push, and read people's minds, but I can't control my power when I have to fight or use it over great distances or tap into minds that are strong. I've been practicing since I joined Ghost when I was nine, and now I'm almost eighteen. I just don't feel as though I've made any progress at all."

Lauren wasn't sure what to say to that. Kuga's arm slid around Piper's shoulders and she leaned into his embrace, her forehead against his neck. Kuga closed his eyes and turned his face towards the top of Piper's head, taking a deep breath as though savouring the smell of her. When he opened his eyes and looked at Lauren, she smiled. He definitely felt something for Piper and it wasn't the brotherly type of love.

"Cheer up, Pip." Leo pushed his empty plate away. "You'll crack it one day and then you can come out on missions with us."

Piper didn't look so sure. Even though she was curious, Lauren knew better than to ask what happened when she lost control. After seeing Piper shove Kuga with her mind, Lauren could easily imagine the devastation Piper could cause. She could probably throw Kuga through the window, or maybe even take down the entire building. It was incredible to think there were people in the world with such powers.

Leo moved around the island and grabbed Piper, wrestling with her when she struggled and grinning ear to ear when he ruffled her hair.

"Come on, Pipsqueak, being all mopey won't change a thing. You've just got to practice."

Piper pushed him away. He laughed as she tried to straighten out her hair. Kuga laughed too. It was sticking up all over the place. Piper gave up and giggled. Lauren watched them with envy. They were like brothers and sister, all smiles and jokes, all grouping together to cheer each other up. She'd always wanted siblings.

"Have you all been with Ghost since you were young?" Lauren said, wanting to be a part of the group again.

The laughter died. Kuga exchanged a glance with Leo.

"We've been here seventeen years, since we were six. People's powers awaken at different times. When mine did, I caused a fire," Leo said.

"There are other people with powers out there, people like you... you are people, aren't you?" She felt a little ashamed of asking such a question.

Leo laughed. "I see Astra has made her usual impression. We're human, just like you."

"For now," Lauren mumbled.

"Ghost has hundreds of operatives around the world and all of them have a power of some sort, and quite a few of them don't register as human," Kuga said in a warm tone and with an understanding smile. "It's a good place to be though, and far better than being out there and having to act normal for fear of someone finding out that we're different. Personally, I don't want to be someone's science project."

Lauren smiled now. Kuga was probably right. People had a tendency to mistrust anything that was different, and you couldn't get more different than people who could use telepathy or control electricity.

"So how did you join Ghost?" She looked around at all three of them.

"The orphanage didn't know what to do with us when my powers awakened. They thought we had set fire to things on purpose. Then Ghost came and Duke took us in. Kuga's powers appeared a few months later. Duke made sure that Ghost trained us well. He raised us. Probably a better life than we might have had if we had been normal." Leo sat back down and gave her a smile.

Both Leo and Kuga had above average looks, warm and friendly, but while Kuga didn't seem to pay much attention to his looks, Leo did. He was well groomed and obviously aware that with a little effort he could make most women's pulses race. His was a well-practiced smile. Aimed straight for the heart.

"You're orphans... my parents died a few months back," Lauren said.

"Mine died when I was a child," Piper said in a strained voice and Lauren placed her hand over hers, holding it to comfort her. She couldn't imagine how hard it would have been if she'd lost her parents when she had been a child. "It's why I came here... to learn to control my power."

God. Lauren could only draw one terrible conclusion. Piper had lost control and killed her parents. Was this how dangerous her powers were? She stared at her with wide eyes and Piper nodded, as though she'd read her thoughts.

Lauren frowned. Piper had mentioned that she could read minds. Was she reading hers now?

Could she read Julian's?

"I'm sorry." Lauren wasn't sure what else she could say. "Julian thinks that Lycaon murdered my parents."

Stony silence filled the room. Perhaps it wasn't the best thing she could have said.

"That's terrible!" Piper's hand caught hers. "I didn't know. He must have guarded that thought."

"Guarded?"

Piper's expression turned thoughtful and then she looked at Kuga and Leo. "Duke wants you."

The two men nodded, stood and left the room.

"I can read most minds, but some people can guard their thoughts. Normally Julian isn't so guarded with them. I have an agreement with him. I've promised to keep them secret because his mind calms me. His thoughts are steady... constant. I like them."

Lauren wanted to ask if they were about Illia or her. Piper had made a promise though and she didn't want her to break it, not if Julian's thoughts were soothing to her. The young woman had been through a lot by the sounds of things.

"Can you turn it off? I mean, can you choose not to hear their thoughts?" Lauren said and then bit into her sandwich. The salty rich taste of bacon made her mouth water and she devoured another bite. She eyed the orange juice. Coffee would have been better. She could use a caffeine jolt to wake her up and help her take in everything.

"Yes," Piper said and then started on her own sandwich. "I leave my mind open to Duke so he can send us information or orders. He keeps a lot of thoughts protected, like Julian has started to."

"What about Astra, or Kuga and Leo, can you read them?" Could she read her?

"Astra is open with her mind. She doesn't care about the fact I can hear her thoughts because she knows I don't like to be in her mind. It feels too sharp and dark. Leo is guarded sometimes but a lot of the time, he's open. Kuga... I find him difficult to read to be honest." Piper toyed with her juice, frowning at it. "Do you want to know about you?"

There was a slight smile to those words. Lauren was dying to know.

Piper's eyes met hers.

"I can't read you at all."

"Why not?" Lauren said, feeling a little disappointed but pleased at the same time. She didn't want Piper probing around in her mind, not when she couldn't stop thinking about Julian. Her gaze went to the window above the steel sink. It was so dark out tonight. Grey clouds filled the sky now. Where was Julian? Was he fighting werewolves without her? She didn't know how to fight as he did, but she wanted to be there with him, wanted to see those monsters again and seize hold of her destiny with both hands.

"I don't know," Piper said, drawing Lauren's attention away from the window. Piper tore a chunk out of her bacon sandwich, and then spoke with her mouth full. "Maybe you're subconsciously blocking me. Or your mind's empty."

She grinned, her teeth full of bread.

Lauren frowned and then smiled at her. Something about Piper made her feel at home.

"So what do you think of us?" Piper stood and put the empty plates and glasses into the dishwasher.

"I think we're all crazy."

"I thought that too at first. You'll get used to us."

Lauren thought about them, about what she really felt. Except for Astra, they all seemed so nice, especially Piper and the twins. She really did feel at home.

"I like you... I even think I might one day grow to like Astra." When she said that, Piper gasped, her face a picture of mock shock. Lauren smiled again. It was nice being around someone so full of energy and laughter. She wished that Duke hadn't called Kuga and Leo away. They had been taking her mind off Julian. "I like the twins, and you. You're all so... I don't know."

"Stupid?" Piper grinned again. "Don't be fooled by Kuga and Leo. Those two aren't always laughing or joking. They have a serious side too, and a competitive streak. When they start getting that way, leave the room. Normally it ends in a fight and I've been shocked one time too many already. Of course, Kuga always wins."

"Which one is Kuga again? Is he..." Lauren trailed off. She had wanted to ask if Kuga was the one who clearly had feelings for Piper, but thought the better of it. Instead, she said, "Is he the one who sat near you?"

Piper nodded. "I can't wait for my birthday. I'll turn eighteen in a few weeks. Kuga has promised that he'll take me out of the city when I do."

"Have you never been out of the city?"

"Of course I have, silly." Piper laughed. Her dark eyes twinkled. "But not with Kuga. He's been practicing something. When he asked what I wanted for my birthday, I told him to surprise me. It's something to do with his power. I love it when he makes shapes with it. You'll have to get him to show you some time."

Lauren nodded, more fascinated by the light that shone in Piper's eyes when she spoke about Kuga than what he could do with his powers. Did Piper even know that she was in love? It was unmistakable, in both of them. The teasing, the little touches, and the quick concern. If they weren't already an item, they soon would be.

"And of course I'm hoping that Duke will let me go out on more missions. I've done a few since turning fifteen, all with him or Kuga or Leo, but I would like to do a solo mission. I'd like to try my powers again. I've been practicing but it's different when you're out there." Piper was speaking so quickly that Lauren struggled to keep up. "It's frightening of course. Kuga doesn't think they are… but the werewolves frighten me."

"Then why do it? Why go out on missions if they frighten you?"

"Because I owe a lot to Ghost. I want to be useful and gaining control of my power would help them a great deal. Duke says that when I can control it, I'll be one of the most powerful operatives. Maybe even more than him. I want to control my power. I want to pay Ghost back for the belief they have in me."

It had been a long time since Lauren had seen someone so excited about something. It had been even longer since she'd felt excited about anything.

Piper had a purpose. She wanted to repay Ghost for their belief in her. Lauren knew without asking that Julian believed in her, and hearing Piper talk made her want to live up to that belief.

She thought about the prospect of taking on the duty of defeating Lycaon, of embracing and regaining her powers, and realised that it wasn't so frightening after all.

In fact, it was quite exciting.

CHAPTER 6

Lauren paused when she heard the door close. Hot water bounced of her hands where they were frozen against her head, halfway through rinsing the shampoo out of her hair. She focused and was surprised when she could feel there was someone in her bedroom. It was similar to how she had felt the night that Julian had saved her—an indescribable sensation in the pit of her stomach. That time it had said she was in danger. This time it was the opposite. A strange aura of calm washed over her.

Julian.

The bathroom door was open. She hadn't been expecting company, but she wasn't about to leave the shower now that company had walked in uninvited. It seemed like forever since she'd had a shower and the hot water running over her body felt too good to give up. She was willing to risk something happening. She didn't have a perfect figure like Astra, or come anywhere close to her in the beauty stakes, but she wasn't ashamed of her figure either. Although some bits needed work in the toning department, she was still the average weight for her five feet seven inch frame. Would Julian think she had an attractive body if he caught a glimpse?

A butterfly didn't jig in her stomach, a whole army of them rushed around, sending it spinning like a hurricane. It wouldn't settle, not when her thoughts were fixed on their current favourite topic—Julian.

He'd been a perfect gentleman so far and didn't seem the type who would take advantage of a situation like this, even if she did want him to.

"How long have you known these Ghosts?" Lauren hollered over the noise of the shower.

Silence. She listened for a while and started to wonder if she had been wrong about him being in her room.

"Five years." His voice was so clear and loud that she jumped.

He was in the bathroom.

Her heart started at a canter and rapidly increased to a gallop. She breathed deep to slow it again, knowing that Julian could hear it. He didn't mention the change in it this time.

Lauren stared at the white shower curtain. Where in the room was he? She shook her head. Her heart was never going to settle if she thought about him. Leaning back, she tilted her head under the water. The hot beat of it against her hair quickly stole her attention away from Julian. It was exquisite, easing all of the tension from her body and re-invigorating her.

She let out a long low groaning sigh of satisfaction.

Her cheeks burned with the blush that covered every naked inch of her. Her attention shifted back to Julian. Suddenly, she was very aware of the fact that she was nude and alone with him. Her mind leapt forwards, imagining the possibilities. Passionate, hot images of him in the shower with her, their naked bodies entwined and his lips on her throat, sent fire sweeping through her body and her heart pounded out a rapid rhythm.

She really needed to get a life. Julian had barely looked at her, let alone shown much interest. The small more courageous part of her said that he might show a little interest if she accidentally on purpose tugged the shower curtain aside enough to flash him, or fell in the bath so he'd come to check on her.

Lauren ignored it.

"Can you hand me a towel?" She squeezed the water out of her hair with one hand and turned the shower off with the other.

A white fluffy towel greeted her when she turned around, Julian's arm sticking through the gap between the shower curtain and the tiles. Lauren went to take it from him and then froze when she saw the scars on his wrist.

An incredible urge to bite him rushed through her, sweeping up from below and engulfing her. It was exhilarating.

She snatched the towel and wrapped it around herself. It was wrong. She didn't want to think about the blood-drinking aspect of the awakening. She wasn't sure how she was going to take to it. The thought repulsed her. Her body said different. The sudden desire to bite Julian had left it warm in all the good places. She tucked the end of the towel in, making a fuss of it to distract her from such disturbing thoughts, and then pulled the curtain aside. Julian looked up, most of his face still hidden beneath his coat collar. He was so close to her.

Fire flickered in his blue eyes. A hunger that both confused and pleased her. When he looked at her like that, she felt beautiful. She just didn't know what he felt.

Lauren stepped out of the bath and walked over to the sink. She grabbed another towel and rubbed her near shoulder-length red hair. Julian stood behind her, reflected in the cabinet mirror. Not a vampire then. In all the stories she'd read, vampires didn't have reflections. She looked at him, meeting his gaze in the mirror and studying his face. She longed to see what he looked like. His eyes were stunning under the bright light of the white bathroom, so pale and icy but holding such incredible warmth. He looked away towards the bath. The long black strands of his hair obscured his eyes but she didn't miss the way they narrowed and his pupils widened. She swallowed. Had he sensed the way she'd reacted to the sight of his marks? He'd said that he could sense her. Could he detect such things? Did he know that she wanted to bite him, and that just the thought of it bordered on arousing?

He stepped to one side when she turned around and she walked past him into her bedroom. She picked up her backpack from the white armchair in the corner, determined to distract herself from thoughts of biting Julian and acting on her desires, and placed it down on the bed. Heat touched her cheeks as she pulled a fresh pair of knickers out of her bag and thought about the fact that Julian had packed them for her. He'd touched her underwear. She cleared her throat and quickly pulled some clothes out and set them down on the blue bedcover. They were all of her favourites. She was glad of that. They made everything feel a little more normal.

Lauren sat on the bed beside them. When she had gone through her bag this morning, she'd found her mobile phone. She'd checked it then and again this evening. It was dead. She glanced at Julian where he stood by the bathroom door and then looked at the three sets of drawn blue curtains to her left. She wanted to ask Julian if she could call her friends to let them know that she was safe, but already knew what his answer would be. He would tell her that it might place both herself and her friends in danger, and a part of her knew that he was right, but she needed to contact them. They would be worried about her by now. She worked with one of her friends, Vicky, pushing paper in an office, and was sure that when she hadn't shown up for work, Vicky would have tried to call her.

"Something is troubling you." The sound of his voice still sent a shiver of delight through her. Was it a Greek accent? It had probably changed throughout the ages but he still sounded foreign to her. Exotic.

"You said that you were a commander of some men." It seemed like a better topic of conversation than her friends. She would find a way to check on them and let them know that she was alright.

"Arcadians," he said and moved across the room. He stopped a few feet short of her, tall and towering, menacing in a way but not one that frightened her. She liked his presence, the way she could sense him when he was near to her, and the way that made her feel. His strength, his power, radiated through her. It wasn't just comforting or calming. It was more than that. It stirred desire in her. Everything about him was alluring. Everything about him said that he wouldn't hurt her.

He would protect her, just as he'd promised. Her knight in shining armour.

"My protectors." Her eyes met his. The fire in them grew stronger. He narrowed them on her and she swore they had fallen lower, towards her towel, for just a brief second. She stood and the action put her close to him, to within a foot. Heat spread through her along with a desire to lick her lips.

Her fingers twitched again, desperate to lower his collar. She was strong enough to do this. She stepped past him instead and when she turned back around, Julian was sitting on the edge of the bed, his sword lying beside his hip. She crossed the room to the three tall windows and opened the middle set of curtains a crack. It was still dark out but it was heading towards dawn. Where had Julian gone tonight? She glanced at him and then went to the armchair and dragged it across the room so it was facing him. She sat in it and stared at him.

"Illia was given two hundred men, her army. Arcadians have always worshipped Zeus, and my men and I have always worshipped Selene. It was an honour to be chosen by Zeus and Selene to protect Illia. I was honoured to serve my goddess, Selene." Julian paused and glanced at the window and then back at her. The fire in his eyes had faded but reignited again while he looked at her, his gaze boring into hers. "Know that they fought and died for you, just as I died for you, and continue to fight for you. We lived to serve you."

Lauren swallowed hard, trying to keep her emotions in check. It was strange to hear someone say that they had died for her. It made her heart flutter. She reminded herself that Julian had died for Illia. He hadn't died for anyone else since then. Would he go that far for anyone other than Illia herself? Would he die to protect her?

"And I was your commander?" she said with a quiver in her voice.

"You are my commander."

She swallowed again.

Julian frowned at her, his gaze dropping to her chest the same way it had done in the hall when they had first come to Ghost, and then rising to her face again. He was listening to her heartbeat. It was off the scale at the thought that he might die to protect her, and at the thought of having to be his commander.

Whoever she'd been back then, she wasn't that person now. Her entire body felt tight at the thought of having to make decisions that could get someone killed—that could get Julian killed.

"I don't want to be," she admitted and felt better for it but worse at the same time. There was a glimmer of something horribly like disappointment in Julian's eyes. It faded an instant later, erased like all his other emotions were when they began to show. "I'm not strong enough."

Meeting Julian and the others had made her painfully aware of that. She couldn't compare to any of them. Even Piper, who feared monsters, desired to go into battle because of her faith in her fellow Ghosts and her sense of duty.

She was braver than Lauren.

Julian leaned forwards, his elbows coming to rest on his knees. She could see down his collar. The light was dull but she could see enough to tell that he was good looking. Her gaze darted to the lamp beside her bed. If she could just turn that on, she would see him properly at last. She would see that her instinct about him had been right.

He was more handsome than anyone she'd ever met.

Her heart skipped.

A soft look entered his eyes, his expression earnest and open.

"I am your guardian, Lauren," Julian said in such a calm and gentle tone that the tight feeling inside her began to melt away. She liked how he said her name, pronouncing it slowly and carefully as though he was savouring it. "I would bleed myself dry if you willed it. I am yours to command. It is not a matter of strength, but if you believe it is, then use mine until you find your own."

Her heart thudded now, hard and heavy against her ribs. God, could this man be any more wonderful? All of her tension melted and her bones began to follow it. Warmth glowed inside her, happiness that this man believed in her even though he barely knew her. He believed that she was strong and she could feel the truth in his words. He would do everything he said. He would lend her his strength, and he would bleed himself dry for her.

"Would you really do that? Bleed yourself dry?" she said, captivated by the romantic notion of him doing anything for her, even risking his life. She wanted to hear him say it again.

His pale eyes narrowed slightly and she couldn't take hers away from them. There was something about his eyes. She could look into them for forever. The world could end and she wouldn't care if he were looking at her as he was now.

"If you desired it," Julian husked. Tingles chased down her back, spreading through her. "My blood is yours. If you needed it all, you would have it."

Even when he talked about blood, she felt intensely drawn to him, willing to do whatever he asked if he could promise her eternity with him. It was crazy. Insane. She didn't know enough about him to be dreaming that kind of future. Perhaps she'd been alone too long. But then, a man had never looked at her the way that Julian did.

With love.

With intense passion.

With need that said he might die without her.

If he kept looking at her like that, she would go through with the awakening just so he would continue.

"How much blood do I normally need... to awaken?"

"Enough that I am too weak to protect you. Should Lycaon attack, we will be vulnerable."

Those words sent an unpleasant shiver through her and made her realise that she didn't like the idea of Julian bleeding himself dry for her after all. She didn't want him to die. She wanted him to live. Even the thought of her awakening weakening him left her cold. Had he learned from experience that they were vulnerable during her awakening?

"Is that why we're here?" Lauren leaned forwards a little, her eyes still locked on his, searching them for answers.

He nodded. "It is. The Ghosts will protect us. They do not fully understand the situation, but they will not fail us should there be an attack."

"Would you fight?" That question made her stomach turn.

He nodded again, solemn and slow.

"Why?" She sat back in the armchair, horrified by the thought that he would risk his life for her by fighting when he was weak.

"Because my duty is to protect you."

Lauren didn't have a response to that. He really did believe in his duty, and he'd carried it out for millennia. He knew his purpose in life and he was sticking to it. She knew hers and couldn't decide whether to embrace it or bury her head in the sand.

It wouldn't get her anywhere if she did that though. Burying your head in the sand didn't stop death.

Julian was still looking at her with a soft tenderness in his eyes. How far would he go for his duty? She tried to think of a way to test him, to plumb the depths of his dedication to her.

"Would you do anything I asked?" Lauren said cautiously, looking deep into his eyes to check if he was telling the truth when he answered.

He nodded again. The look in his eyes hardened for a moment and a shadow of pain crossed them. Lauren leaned forwards again. What had he been thinking? She hated seeing hurt in his eyes. When he'd left her room this morning looking so sad, it had torn her apart inside with worry. Something terrible had happened to him in his past. It had to have to make him look at her as though he was dying inside.

"Even kill Lycaon?" she said.

"If I could." His voice was low and as cautious as hers had been.

"If?"

He took a deep breath and sighed. "It is forbidden. The death of Lycaon is your duty and yours alone to carry out. I cannot interfere in that battle, just as Lycaon cannot interfere with my existence. When Illia died, Zeus realised his mistake. Zeus did what he could to help you. He made me immortal as you wished, and he made me invulnerable to the threat of Lycaon, but he could not change your curse to make you invulnerable to Lycaon's blade. He could only ensure that you would be reborn and that I would be there to awaken you." Julian leaned closer, his eyes on hers, and then cast them downwards at the floor. "If I could spare you from the horrors of battle, I would."

There was an edge to his voice. Lauren could read between the lines. He wanted to protect her and it seemed duty didn't have anything to do with it.

Lauren stared out at the night through the crack in the curtains of the middle window. The sky was growing light in the distance above the building opposite. The air in the room was heavy, hard to breathe, thick like tar in her lungs. She didn't know what to say. Did Julian want to protect her for another reason? Was that reason anything to do with the way he looked at her sometimes?

Did it have anything to do with her, or was there more to her reincarnation than she knew?

"Am I always the same when you meet me?" she said slowly, unsure of whether she wanted to know the answer to that question.

"Your instincts sometimes carry on," he said in a distant tone. She continued to stare out of the window. "There is a reason you are drawn to swords and combat."

"A shinai is very different to a real sword… but when I'm facing my opponent in kendo, when I'm fighting, I feel a strange kind of peace, as though everything is right in the world. Is that my instincts too?" She glanced at his katana where it rested on the bed beside him. She'd never held one before.

How was she supposed to fight with a sword when she was used to nothing more than a glorified bamboo stick?

"Perhaps. The principle of combat is the same in real life as it is in kendo, and I will train you."

Her gaze darted to him long enough to see he was looking at the sword now, and then went back to the window and the beginning of dawn.

"I will see to it that you can fight, Lauren. Do not fear."

The niggling feeling of doubt and fear in her stomach disappeared. She was sure that he would keep his word and teach her how to fight. She just wasn't sure how good she would be at it. She was only at second grade level in kendo.

She pushed away her worries and watched the sky. The dawn was fast becoming beautiful, as peaceful as she felt inside. Pink traced the sky. Gold lined the scattered clouds.

"Do I always look the same?" It was the question she'd originally wanted to ask and the one that she feared the most.

"Yes." His eyes were on her now. She could feel them. A blush touched her cheeks and she was glad that the low light would hide it from him.

"Sound the same?"

"Yes, but the language is often different."

Lauren looked at him, her heart on the verge of falling into her stomach. It had risen so high, so far into her throat that the drop was dizzying, like plummeting down a rollercoaster.

Julian had mentioned that Illia had changed him. She had desired him to live. In her heart, Lauren knew what that meant. Illia had loved Julian.

Had Julian loved Illia?

Lauren was just a carbon copy, a replication of the original that he'd loved.

Her heart hit her feet. She frowned at the sky, trying to pretend that she found it interesting even though it had lost all its colour and warmth the moment she'd realised that all the looks Julian had given her were really about Illia.

She tried to say something but the words stuck in her throat. She coughed to clear it and then breathed deep in an attempt to steady herself so he wouldn't hear the hurt in her voice when she spoke.

"Will I remember my past lives when I awaken?" Her voice was still tight. She feared that he would notice her change in feeling—her hurt. If he did, he didn't mention it.

"I do not know." His gaze was still on her. She could feel it and she wished she couldn't. She wanted to make him leave. She ached for her old life—for the time when she'd been normal, not some reincarnated demi-goddess. "Sometimes you remember little things."

Lauren stared into the distance, hoping that she remembered nothing this time. The thought that she was continually reincarnated had begun to feel comforting but now it choked her. It made her feel small and insignificant. To

Julian, she was just another Illia. It was probably instinct making her fall for him, not her real feelings.

She was such a fool.

She'd been an idiot to think that someone like Julian would really look at her that way. When he looked at her, he was looking at Illia. Well, whatever he believed, she wasn't Illia. She didn't know who that woman was, but she was sure that Illia had been strong and brave and everything that Lauren wasn't.

Lauren wanted to laugh at herself but her gut twisted when she thought about Illia. She pressed her hand to it, surprised by the violent feeling. Jealousy had never hurt like this before.

Gentle fingertips against her jaw made her start. Heat danced around the spots they touched. Julian slowly brought her head around so she was facing him. Her gaze dropped to her bare feet. She couldn't look at him now. If he saw her feelings, she didn't know what she would do. Right now, she felt vulnerable and weaker than ever, and one wrong look from him could break her.

His fingers brushed through the strands of her wet hair, his caress tender and soft, very careful.

"You seem so different this time," he whispered and her heart started at a pace, lodging itself in her throat and trembling. "Your hair…"

"It's dyed," she said, eyes shooting to his.

"I know." There was a faint hint of a smile in his shadowed face. Her insides flipped. What he said next made them jig and her head spin. "It suits you. It brings out warmth in you that I have never seen before."

Her eyes widened. Warmth that he'd never seen before? Were all her predecessors cold? Even Illia?

"I understand that this is difficult for you, Lauren. Each time you are so different, you react so differently, but it is always hard for you to come to terms with what is happening." His fingers paused in her hair, resting gently against her scalp. His palm brushed her cheek and she was tempted to lean into it. "I should have reached you sooner. I am sorry that I took so long… and that because of me you have less time to make your decision."

There was such an earnest look in the depths of his pale blue eyes, tinted with regret, that Lauren found herself reaching up and covering his hand with hers, wanting to comfort him. Her fingers closed over his, pressing into his palm. His hand was so warm.

"How did you find me?"

"I told you. I can sense things. That sense is strongest when it comes to you. It guides me to you." He paused and drew a deep breath. This time, he didn't sigh. The hurt was back in his eyes. "I normally find you faster, but I was… delayed."

Lauren knew better than to probe into that answer. Whatever the delay had been, it had pained him. As much as she wanted to know, she couldn't ask. After the way he'd looked at her this evening, she never wanted to hurt him.

Because he already held a world of pain in his eyes.

His hand left hers and she sat back, again becoming aware that she was only wearing a towel, only now she didn't care.

Lauren stared deep into Julian's eyes, mesmerised by every dark fleck against palest blue. A sense of calm filled her, as though she'd found a haven in a storm and knew that she was safe at last. The things he'd told her lost their frightening edge. Everything seemed strangely normal.

Everything felt fine again.

Julian was immortal—a vampire of sorts. She'd lived thirty lifetimes and was on a mission to stop the king of werewolves before he managed to get revenge on the ancient Greek gods. Soon her latent abilities would awaken and she would become immortal again. Perfectly normal. Completely insane.

When she looked into Julian's eyes, the world was right again. When she looked into his eyes, strength surged through her and she was ready to take on Lycaon and defeat him at last.

It felt so warm and quiet here with him, drifting through her life one breath at a time, one heartbeat after another.

Lauren frowned.

"Is the hypnotism thing a power of yours too?" It had to be a power. He hadn't told her all of his abilities yet and she was sure that this was one of them.

"Hypnotism?" His left eyebrow rose and then they both knitted into a frown.

"Yeah. You did it the night we met and you're doing it now. When I look into your eyes—" She cut herself off when it struck her that he wasn't hypnotising her. There was another possibility. She really did like him. First, the instant attraction, then the jealousy and now she turned into a daydreaming little girl whenever he looked into her eyes. She might as well just melt into a puddle around him.

It was fortunate that she could speak or look at him at all without falling apart. Lauren chided herself. She was stronger than this. No man was about to reduce her to a quivering wreck. "Forget I said anything."

The ardent way he looked at her sent a blush blazing across her cheeks. Standing, she turned away and walked into the bathroom, taking her clothes with her.

She stopped in front of the mirror and looked in the reflection at Julian. Her stomach flipped. He was watching her, his gaze drifting down her back towards her legs.

Was she really different to Illia? Warmer? If anyone would know, it would be Julian.

When Julian looked at her, did he see her or did he see Illia?

She hoped that he saw her.

Because when she looked at Julian, she saw a man who was stealing her heart piece by piece.

CHAPTER 7

Lauren kicked the hem of her dark jeans so they covered the tongues of her black trainers and then tugged on the sleeves of her plum long sleeve kimono-style top. She smoothed the thin material over her breasts, allowing a modest amount of cleavage to show. It was cold in her top but she wanted to look good. She wanted Julian's attention.

She combed her fingers through her red hair, twisting the ends so they flicked up and out.

She only wished that she could straighten out her nerves as easily.

Julian had left when she'd been dressing. He'd told her to pass the day away with Kuga, Leo and Piper if she couldn't sleep, and to come to Duke's office the next night. Piper had kindly gone out and bought her some beauty products and other necessities. She'd used all of them to make herself look more presentable and as pretty as she could manage. It had taken a while, giving her time to see the night fall and to think about why Julian would want her to go to Duke's office. Now she stood outside it, trying to get her feelings into order and still wondering what awaited her on the other side.

Only one way to find out.

She opened the dark wooden door and stepped inside. The first thing she noticed was Astra talking to Julian. He stood to her right near the bookcases, with his hand resting on the hilt of his katana where it hung at his side, hidden beneath his coat. Astra glanced over at her and then smiled at Julian with bright red lips, touching his shoulder as she did so. She moved closer to him, a sway in her hips that Lauren didn't like. It caused the slit up the side of Astra's long black dress to open and reveal her thigh. Her smile widened and she ran her fingers through her glossy black hair, pushing it out of her face. A flicker of jealousy flared into life inside Lauren when Astra's fingers slid slowly and sensually over the black material of Julian's coat and she laughed, high and very feminine, about something.

"You're looking better." Duke came out from behind his large mahogany desk and crossed the room to Lauren. "Are you feeling better?"

Lauren threw a furtive glance Julian's way and saw that Astra was now smiling right into his eyes.

"I was," she muttered and turned her back on Astra.

Duke frowned. It didn't suit him. It made his face dark and vicious, and gave him a menacing look when combined with his backdrop of the huge gun collection mounted on the dark red wall behind him. Lauren smiled, hoping to alleviate whatever was bothering him. She touched his arm.

"I'm fine." Her hand slid down his arm. His gaze followed it intently. She was about to withdraw it when his hand came forwards so they touched. She went to take her hand back but he caught hold of it and turned it palm upwards. His fingertips grazed the lines on her hand, tickling her. "Are you going to tell me my future?"

He laughed—a rich deep sound that made her smile and made his intense brown eyes sparkle. While Astra's laugh had been forced, Duke's one had been real, like Kuga and Leo's. It seemed all the male Ghosts enjoyed a good laugh. Lauren didn't have the energy to laugh with her heart. She could only manage one as fake as Astra's.

"I don't tell fortunes." Duke's thumb brushed hers again, a caress that was both sensual and alarming. She stared wide-eyed at him, not knowing what to do. Julian wasn't watching, and so what if he was? He probably wouldn't do anything about Duke's over-attentiveness. She probably meant nothing to him. Her life was a mere blip in his and when she died, another would come along to take her place. "But I could try... for you."

"That's fine." Lauren extricated her hand from his. "I was just joking anyway."

Duke swept the pad of his thumb over his fingers. Lauren stared at the roses on his palm.

"They're beautiful tattoos." She tried to get a closer look but Duke curled his hand up and lowered it.

"They would be if they were tattoos." He smiled but this time it was as phoney as hers were recently and it didn't touch his eyes. They were cold and empty, fixed on his fist where it hung at his side.

Another peal of laughter from Astra made Lauren's fists clench. What on Earth was Julian saying to her that was so funny? Lauren glanced over at them. Julian said something she couldn't quite hear but his look was serious, no sign of humour in it. When Astra touched Julian's hair, brushing a rogue black strand from his eyes, Lauren's temperature shot up.

She couldn't believe that Astra was openly flirting with Julian, acting as though she wasn't even there. Not that Julian was hers.

"Are you feeling alright?" Duke said with a look of concern.

Lauren shook her head, cursing the hot tears that burned her eyes. She hated how confused her feelings were, especially when it came to Julian.

Unable to bear hearing Astra with Julian, Lauren looked around her. To the left of the three arched windows was a white door with a green fire escape sign on it. Escape sounded good.

"I need some air." Lauren went straight out of it and climbed the black metal spiral staircase to the flat roof.

The night was cold, a bitter wind blowing, but it was fresh and soothing, and it cleared her head. Astra's flirting had hurt her more than she'd thought possible and she didn't want to think why.

Lauren gripped the black metal railing that edged the roof around the fire escape and stared up at the sky. It was cloudless and inky, but it did nothing to make her smile as clear starry winter nights normally did. She felt as though she was drowning in it, pulled under by feelings that were out of control and that she didn't understand.

There was a laugh from the room below. Astra.

Lauren's grip on the icy railing tightened and she glared at the sky. Why wasn't Julian coming to her? Hadn't he seen her leave? Had he even noticed that she'd arrived or was he too busy with the beautiful Astra?

She almost laughed at herself. She'd come out into the cold for a reason other than the fresh air. She wanted Julian to come to her. She wanted him to choose between her and Astra. Where had it gotten her? Five minutes had passed and he wasn't coming. All she'd gained for her stupidity was heartache and misery, and probably the start of a cold.

The door below opened and that same heart jumped for joy until Duke appeared on the staircase. She turned away again. The old warehouse opposite was full of people working. She watched them, remembering that today was Friday and that it was only just gone five. Soon everyone would be going home for the weekend. She wished she could go home.

Her gaze tracked the people. Normal life was going on around her, unaware of the monsters that lurked in the darkness or even walked amongst the office workers. Werewolves appeared human at times. How many of them had jobs? Was one of them down there now, in that office working amongst innocent people?

How many had she met during her life?

"It's best that you're not alone right now." Duke leaned against the railing beside her.

Lauren didn't look at him. She stared into the office, trying to spot any unusual behaviour that might give someone away as a werewolf and trying to ignore the creeping jealousy and anger in her heart.

"I want to be alone," she whispered. A man walked past the window on the floor down from her in the office building. He seemed inconspicuous enough and he didn't pay the slightest bit of attention to her. In the darkness, he probably wouldn't be able to see her. The moon wasn't strong tonight. It was nothing but a sliver in the sky, surrounded by bright twinkling stars that not even the city lights could drown out.

"So you didn't come out here to get Julian's attention then?"

Lauren tensed. Was it that obvious? If it was, why hadn't Julian come? Didn't he want to be with her?

She laughed, more at herself than at what Duke had said. "Not at all."

Duke sighed and ran his fingers back and forth along the black railing, his short fingernails scraping at the paint.

"Astra can be incorrigible and Julian is too polite." He paused and turned around so his back was resting against the bar. Lauren looked over the edge and wondered how Duke could be so trusting of the balcony railing. It was a long drop to the quiet road below and the rail didn't feel that sturdy under her fingers. Wasn't he frightened of death? "Come back in."

"I'm fine out here." She wasn't. She was freezing and miserable, but it was better than being around Astra. In the office, people were coming and going, some were leaving for the night. Life was going on without her. This past day she'd lost touch with the world and had felt as though only her, the Ghosts, Julian and the werewolves had existed. She'd forgotten that people still had lives to lead.

Lauren expected Duke to go back inside but he didn't move. He hummed a tune for a while, a melody that she didn't recognise, and then sighed. Her eyes shifted to him. He was watching her. When he saw her looking, he smiled.

She wished that it was Julian with her.

"How are you holding up?" Duke's words were quiet and cautious, giving Lauren the impression that he felt as though he was handling fragile glass that was likely to smash at any given moment.

She was stronger than he thought then, but weaker than she needed to be.

"This wasn't exactly what I had imagined when I had wanted to know who I was and what I wanted out of life." Lauren smiled back at him, genuine and heartfelt, amused by how she'd longed to discover who she was and now that she had, part of her wanted to go back to her old life. "It isn't what I wanted."

Duke placed his hand on her shoulder. The weight of it against her was comforting, the warmth of his hand noticeable through her top. He frowned, removed his dark grey suit jacket and placed it around her shoulders. It warmed her through and she took hold of both sides of it, pulling it as closed as possible, and smiled her thanks at Duke.

"There isn't a person here who hasn't been through this moment of disbelief and fear." His voice was low, intimate. It unnerved her slightly but she didn't pull away from him. Instead, she looked up at the moon, feeling drawn to it tonight. "None of us felt more than a shadow of what you must feel though."

It was hard to drag her eyes away from the moon but she managed it. Duke's brown eyes were black in the low light, dark pools that were bottomless and empty but shining with feeling. Was he flirting with her again? She was never sure whether Duke was just being friendly or whether he was after something more than that. Just a few days ago, she would have said that he was too old for her because he was in his forties. Now she couldn't use that excuse, not when she wanted a man who was three thousand years her senior. Duke touched her chin, making her jump, and slowly tilted her head back.

"I never imagined that you would be so—"

The sound of sliding metal sent ice racing over her nerve endings. Duke's hand fell from her face and the corners of his lips lifted into a smile. His eyes slid to the side, towards the staircase.

"All yours, big man," he said with an easy, unaffected air. "I was just giving her a little needed company."

He walked away, taking his jacket with him. Lauren's gaze followed him but halted when she saw Julian. He blinked slowly. The tiny trace of moonlight made his eyes shimmer. He'd changed into whatever state it was that he normally fought in. His sword was slightly drawn, a sliver of blade reflecting the moon. He slid it back and looked at the staircase with a frown as the door below closed, and then back at her.

Did he perceive Duke as a threat?

Lauren dragged her courage up to her chest and turned to face Julian. He stared at her, his silver irises eerie but beautiful. She stepped towards him, until she could feel the heat coming from him. Her heart sped, driven by her rising fear, but she reached up towards his face. His gaze shifted to her hands but she didn't stop. Not this time.

This time she was going to seize the moment.

She was going to be strong.

With trembling fingers, she unclipped the two bands of metal that held the thick funnel collar of his coat closed. She sucked in a sharp breath of anticipation that he stole when the collar fell open to reveal the defined line of his jaw and his straight nose—all masculine and classical beauty. Her gaze fell to his sensual dusky lips. They tempted her, begging for a kiss that she would all too willingly give him. Her tongue swept over her dry lips and she swallowed. Her whole body warmed when she thought about what she wanted him to do right now, and the things she dreamed he would do in private.

"Show me." Her eyes locked with his.

A flicker of a frown creased his brow and his eyes searched hers, as though he was trying to read her mind.

Now that he was unmasked and she'd leapt the first hurdle with relative ease, she found the strength to continue. It was a shame that she couldn't find her voice. It failed her, but where it did, a touch could succeed, and it would be a far sweeter form of success.

Her thumb caressed the line of his jaw, as light as she could manage, running over scratchy dark stubble until she reached his chin. A momentary shiver danced through her along with a sense of concern. Her eyes widened as she stared into Julian's. Not her feelings but his. They were all there in his silver eyes. He was worried. He'd realised what she was asking of him.

Did he think that it would frighten her? She wanted to see what would happen to her. She'd seen the scars on his wrist. Bite marks. When his lips parted, she would see fangs instead of teeth. And she needed to see them. If he showed her, if she saw them with her own eyes, then maybe she would finally totally accept that this was real and that it would happen to her soon.

"Let me see," she whispered, low and coaxing, no longer nervous.

His lips parted to reveal the barest hint of pointed canines. Caught in a trance, transfixed by the sight of them, she rubbed the pad of her thumb across his lower lip. It was soft and warm. He breathed in sharply, his reaction empowering her, and his mouth opened to reveal his fangs. They glistened in the moonlight, white and sharp, but they didn't frighten her.

What did was the fact that his gaze shifted to her neck.

Her heart hammered against her chest, blood rushing through her head. She shifted her eyes upwards to his and froze, mesmerised by the way he was staring at her neck with such forceful hunger glowing in his eyes. The silence stretched between them, his eyes locked on her neck and her thumb against his lips. His breath was warm against it, coming out in short heavy bursts that matched her racing heartbeat. She licked her lips again, couldn't stop herself from imagining what it would feel like to have his mouth on her throat, his teeth in her flesh. The very thought made her tremble and prickly heat scorched her body.

"Do you… need to… need… blood?" Those words were harder to say than she'd thought they would be. Her fingers shook against his jaw.

Julian's gaze snapped to hers as though she'd startled him and he stepped backwards, leaving her standing with her hand held in the air. In an instant, his eyes were pale blue again.

"Go inside," he said, tone commanding and urgent at the same time. His fists shook at his sides.

Lauren edged towards the staircase and then stopped, looking back at him. "Are you coming too?"

He shook his head. The muscle in his jaw twitched as though he was grinding his teeth. Clamping them shut? His body language screamed of restraint. Had her touch triggered this internal war she was witnessing? He seemed to be fighting something.

"Where are you going?"

"To hunt."

Her heart missed a beat. He was hungry. She hesitated and then moved back towards him, her throat tight again. She didn't care how he would react. She had to know.

"Can you feed without killing?"

He nodded and then his gaze dropped to her neck again. She touched it. His eyes switched briefly to silver and he backed away another step.

"Go inside." This time his voice was strained, his eyes showing the struggle that she could now feel in him. They switched again, flashing between silver and blue, darting between her throat and her face. "I cannot be near you. Not when I am hungry. Go… stay with the others."

"Why?" Lauren ignored him and took a step towards him. He countered it with another step back, keeping the distance between them steady. Sheer agony filled his eyes and his expression changed to one of pleading, as though he was silently begging her to do as he'd asked. She trusted him. He wouldn't hurt her, not even when he was hungry. She believed that.

His eyes melted back to silver and, when he spoke, she saw his canines had extended again. "They will keep you safe."

"No," Lauren said with a frown, unwilling to go until he'd answered her real question. "Why can't you be near me?"

His eyes went to her neck. He frowned. When he met her eyes, he looked pained.

"It is forbidden."

Before she could ask why, he leapt over the edge of the building. She gasped and leaned over the railing, only to see him land on his feet in the street far below and then disappear. Her heart started beating again. He could have told her that he could fall that far and not be hurt.

Lauren stared in the direction he'd gone.

More importantly.

She touched her bare neck, his hungry look burned on her memory.

He could have told her why it was forbidden.

CHAPTER 8

Julian stopped on a rooftop a short distance from the Ghost safe house. He looked back towards it, a part of him hoping to catch a glimpse of Lauren still standing there watching for him. She was beautiful tonight. He had noticed her the moment she had walked in and looked at him, had felt her gaze burning into him and had felt her turn away to speak with Duke. When Duke had touched her, Julian had wanted to go to Lauren and take hold of her. Instinct had told him to stake his territory. A ridiculous idea. Lauren wasn't his. She was free to talk to whoever she wanted.

But it hurt to see her talking to Duke and ignoring him, until he had sensed the change in her feelings. It had been a hint of sadness or pain. He couldn't quite pinpoint the emotion but she had felt something, and then she had left the room. Why? He had considered it while trying to end his conversation with Astra and the only conclusion he could find was a ridiculous one. Lauren hadn't liked him speaking with Astra and she had left to get his attention. He couldn't bring himself to believe something so fantastical. He was reading into it. But if she was jealous, it would explain the way she acted around Astra, and the feelings he saw in her eyes sometimes. He wished that he had gone to her straight away, as he'd wanted to, but Astra had stopped him from following Lauren, hindering him long enough that Duke had gone instead.

Julian's fingers curled into tight fists, the darkness he'd felt in that moment reclaiming him with a vengeance. Lauren didn't realise just how beautiful she was, how the clothes she wore tonight emphasised her delicate figure and made him burn for her. It had been a struggle to keep his eyes off her, to resist the temptation she placed in his path. And it had made him think, so much so that he hadn't heard a word that Astra had said to him. His focus had been wholly on Lauren and his thoughts, on trying to figure out just what it was about her that felt different. In the end, he had found no satisfying conclusion, only a sense that there was something new about her, something that distinguished her from the rest.

When he had gone to her, found Duke with his hands on her, a rage blacker than any he'd felt before had consumed him.

He'd been ready to fight Duke for her.

But then Duke had left and Lauren had looked at him with such tenderness that he had found himself believing that she did want his attention and that she had been jealous. His heart had been pounding by the time she'd approached him, stepping so close that he could clearly smell her sweet scent and feel her warmth. He'd thought she would change her mind again and wouldn't go through with unmasking him but this time she hadn't backed down. There had been such determination in her eyes, not just about overcoming her fear of what she would become but also about seeing him. He'd caught her glancing his way, seen how she'd stared at the collar of his coat with her fists clenched in restraint. He'd watched her when she thought no one was.

He was always watching her.

She entranced him.

He stared back towards the Ghost building, replaying every moment. From the instant she had walked into the room, he had been aware of her. Her beauty and warmth captivated him. When he looked at her, he was looking at a different person. Not Illia or the incarnations that had followed. He was looking at Lauren, a woman nothing like her predecessors. A woman who stirred feelings in him, desires and needs long forgotten or ignored. His canines sharpened at the memory of her standing before him on the rooftop, her neck bared and the smell of arousal lacing her scent.

Without thinking, Julian touched his face, his fingers following the same course that hers had taken. His thumb brushed over his lower lip. Hers had trembled against it, hot and sweet, gentle but strong at the same time. Her touch had been so light and the feel of her hands on him divine. It had been beyond anything he'd imagined possible, stirring his hunger until he had bordered on losing control.

That touch had triggered a battle within him, a fight between surrendering to desire and breaking the rules she'd laid down over the years and continuing to obey those orders. If he hadn't left, he was sure that he would have given in to temptation and tasted her. His whole body ached and tightened at the thought of her warm throat and her blood. She had been offering it so willingly, had wanted him to bite her. It hadn't been mere curiosity but a true desire. Why?

Her behaviour, her touch, made him realise something about himself.

Three thousand years without a woman's touch, without so much as a concerned caress or tender look, had left him cold in his heart and soul.

Julian's gaze tracked upwards to the moon. The brilliant white crescent shone kindly down on him, a companion that sent calm washing through his body whenever he saw it. His protector.

Only tonight, she didn't hold his attention as she normally did. His eyes lowered again, seeking the distant rooftop where Lauren had touched him.

She'd touched more than his face. If only she knew what she'd done to him, how she'd opened his eyes and placed him on a dangerous precipice where all he could do was fall.

Her shy glances and the way she blushed when he caught her looking had paved his path up to the treacherous peak on which he now stood. No matter how many times he told himself to defend his heart against them, to save himself from what would only end in pain and misery, he'd still climbed the path one step at a time.

When he'd spoken to her in the shower, and afterwards when she'd only worn a towel and had held his hand, he'd reached the summit. She affected him so deeply, had rekindled lost feelings in him, but it was more than that this time. He knew it. It felt deeper, more than it had ever done, and it tore him apart.

He couldn't let himself believe the things that he thought he saw in her shy glances and blushes. They weren't real and it hurt too much to fool himself into thinking they were. He'd suffered too many long lonely years with and without her, always alone even when she was with him.

Yet he still found himself recalling Lauren's tender looks and the way that she'd held his hand, touched his face, and stared at him with something akin to adoration and need.

His knees hit the roof and he slumped forwards, staring into the distance.

His jaw tensed.

His fingertips pressed into his knees, clutching them.

Raising his head, he stared up at the moon, beseeching Selene to listen and answer his call. Why do this to him now? Why torture him when his heart had endured so many years of pain and loss, had grieved so long that he'd lost all sense of feeling and all hope?

A cloud stole the moon from view.

Julian continued to stare at it, at the bright spot behind the thin layer of cloud, and pleaded the gods to take pity on him. His shattered heart ached.

He pressed his hand to his chest, rubbing the spot over his heart as though he could stop the pain.

The moon returned to him, bright and mocking with her reply.

This feeling wasn't his love for Illia. It ran deeper, poison in his veins, filling his heart with a toxin that would surely be the death of him. He cursed Selene when he realised the truth of it.

His love for Illia had faded from the moment of her first reincarnation. His feelings had crumbled in time and with each withering glance and harsh word that she'd thrown at him, until they had finally died six centuries ago. He'd clung so fiercely to what had become normal to him that he'd been blind to the change in his heart. He'd been blind to the fact that his sense of purpose had dulled into routine, his desire to do his duty weakening with it and leaving him dead inside. He'd been blind to the fact that the incarnations had been changing in ways other than just their strength and abilities. Illia's traits had gradually disappeared from them, leaving them less and less like the original, and Lauren was the most different of them all.

When he looked at her, he saw no trace of Illia. Her heart was different, her personality more caring and her feelings ran deeper. She wore the same face but even that was different now. Lauren was more beautiful.

Julian stared at the moon, not seeing it as it dawned on him.

This feeling and attraction he had for Lauren was new.

She had reawakened his soul, making him feel as he had over three thousand years ago.

Julian dragged himself to his feet and stared hard into the distance. Filled with resolve, he scanned the night for a sign of werewolves. He would protect Lauren. She would live, even if he had to take her hand and strike Lycaon down himself.

He wouldn't lose her. Not this time.

Not when there was hope that she might grow to love him.

Not when he finally felt alive again.

CHAPTER 9

This was a bad idea and if Julian found out what she was doing, he was going to be angry.

Lauren stared up at the blue neon sign that promised 'Seventh Heaven' and stuffed her hands into the pockets of her dark brown combat jacket. Piper stood beside her in the street, hunched up in her shiny blue bomber jacket with the chill winter breeze tousling her ponytail. Leo stood to her other side, his hands jammed into his jeans pockets, pulling his open long black coat back and emphasising the breadth of his build. He frowned at the sign.

She'd told everyone the name of the club but had neglected to mention it was a strip joint. Leo wouldn't have come with them if she had and she needed him around in case werewolves somehow found her.

The wind chased over her skin, freezing her to the bone. The man on the door of the club called over to her, asking whether they were coming in or not. Lauren's gaze remained fixed on the sign.

This was a very bad idea.

When she'd gone back into the building after Julian had left her to hunt, she'd gone straight to her bedroom and found her phone vibrating on the bedside table. She'd been shocked to find it working and even more surprised to receive a voicemail message from her friend Vicky saying they were worried about her and asking whether she was still coming tonight. Lauren had tried to call her back but the phone had died again when it was ringing at the other end. She'd left the phone on her bed and had gone down to the kitchen. Piper had been there with Kuga and Leo, all laughing about something. Lauren had tried to join in, to get Julian off her mind and to stop herself thinking about her friends, but it had been impossible. In the end, she'd given in and asked the trio to help her.

She had to see if her friends and let them know that she was okay.

Piper had told her that Julian wanted Lauren to stay with her. Lauren had responded by asking her to come too. Kuga had been against the idea, but Leo had surprised her by offering to go with her. She only wanted to see them and make sure they were fine. She would leave as soon as she'd explained things.

Her heart beat fast in her throat and her skin crawled when she cast a glance around at the shadowy streets, afraid the werewolves would find her.

Leo looked back over at her and she nodded. They would go in, find her friends, and get back to the Ghost building. No messing around. Nothing bad was going to happen.

Lauren walked forwards, leading the way towards the club. She still couldn't believe that she had agreed to go to such a place with Vicky. It wasn't like her. She'd never been to a strip club before and she didn't want to go to one now. She stopped and turned around. This was insane. They had to get back before someone discovered they were gone. She couldn't remember Vicky's number to call her but she could put the card from her phone into another and see if it would work. A phone call would be enough.

Just then, a taxi pulled up and her three friends spilled out of it, all giggles and broad smiles.

Vicky laughed about something and adjusted the skimpy black boobtube and mini-skirt that she was wearing and then checked her hair, her fingers running over the twisted knot at the back of her head and the long brown spikes sticking out. The man at the door of the club wolf-whistled and she looked over, the smile dropping off her face when her brown eyes fell on Lauren.

"You're here!" she shrieked.

Lauren didn't have time to say anything before she Vicky pulled her into her arms and squeezed her tight. Vicky took hold of her shoulders and pushed her back, looking her over.

"I thought you were dead!" Vicky said, her brown eyes sparkling with relief and a laugh to her tone, as though she had really believed Lauren had died and felt foolish.

Lauren opened her mouth to explain but Sharon slung her arm around her shoulders.

"I said she'd be fine." Sharon's long blonde hair danced across her face and obscured her broad smile.

Lauren looked around her three friends, feeling more out of place than ever. All of them were leagues above her on the beauty scale but never more so than tonight. They were gorgeous and every man passing them by was staring, smiling, tossing lewd suggestions their way.

None of them had even noticed her. Who could blame them? She just about scraped by as above average, even with the make-up she was wearing tonight, and her clothes weren't anywhere near as provocative as her friends' were. She was still dressed in her jeans and kimono top that barely showed a little cleavage, and was freezing to death. Her friends were showing more flesh than the strippers probably would be and didn't seem to care about the cold.

"I should go," Lauren said, her nerves getting the better of her. She glanced around them at the people gathering outside the club. A voice at the back of her mind whispered words about werewolves and how upset Julian and the others were going to be with her.

Thinking about Julian turned her stomach and increased her desire to return to the Ghost building.

"No!" Vicky grabbed her hand. "You're not chickening out now. Where's all that 'live life to the full' and 'find out who I am' crap that you spouted the other night? How are you going to find yourself if you don't try a few things?"

Her friend had a point. She'd decided to find out who she was and her place in life. Recently, she'd had a feeling that her life was missing something and that she was destined for greater things than pushing paper in an office. She hadn't realised that those greater things included fighting werewolves, becoming immortal, and falling for her protector.

Lauren sighed. "I wasn't exactly imagining men gyrating to bad European techno music when I said that."

"Don't be such a prude." Jackie this time. She flipped her blonde wavy hair out of her face and winked at a passing group of men. They grinned at her, their eyes blatantly on her breasts and the tight little black dress she was wearing. "When was the last time you saw a naked man?"

In the flesh and still breathing? Too long ago for Lauren to remember the exact details but it hadn't been the most romantic encounter.

"But I really do have to get back." Lauren looked to Piper and Leo for support. Her three friends looked at them too.

"You brought friends?" The smallest of frowns marred Vicky's perfectly smooth brow, and then she smiled wide when she spotted Leo. "Hello, Handsome."

Leo smiled right back at her, flashing straight white teeth to devastating effect. All three women were instantly giggling.

"We should go, shouldn't we... Leo?" Lauren said with a meaningful jerk of her head to one side.

Leo ignored her and stepped towards her friends. "We could stay for one drink."

Lauren's fingers curled into fists and trembled. She was going to kill him. They had agreed that they would see her friends, let them see that she was alright, and then go back. He was changing the plan. She looked at Piper, who was still staring at the sign above the club, and then at Leo where he was walking towards it with Vicky and Jackie both on his arm.

"Come on." Sharon took hold of Lauren's hand, forcing her to follow the others.

Lauren grabbed Piper's hand and Piper tried to pull back. She shook her head and stared wide-eyed at the man on the door.

"I'm not old enough," she whispered.

Piper was right. She was only seventeen. But they had to go in. Leo was already through the doors and Lauren couldn't leave Piper outside by herself while she went to find him.

"We'll be in and out, gone in a second. Just long enough to get that idiot back."

"I wish Kuga had come with us." Piper's look turned desperate as they approached the club and then melted into an expression of pure horror when the doors opened and she could see inside. Lauren looked there at the barely dressed waiters walking around in nothing but tiny shorts and white angel wings. "Actually, I'm really glad he isn't here now. If he saw me in a place like this, he'd kill me... he's going to kill Leo."

Lauren smiled and started to tell Piper that she didn't doubt Kuga would kill Leo for letting her go into a strip club but the music drowned her out. As they moved farther in, low lights flashed in erratic patterns that gave her a headache and heat assaulted her along with the smell of too much perfume and alcohol. Perhaps this wasn't a good idea. She should have stayed where it was safe.

Lauren did laugh at herself this time. Where it was safe? Wasn't that the story of her life? She'd spent every minute playing it safe and look where it had got her. Thirty-four and only just realising that her life was missing something, and now life as she knew it was over.

Sharon dragged her further into the club and then let go, leaving her and joining Sharon and Jackie as they flitted between flirting with Leo and toying with the waiters.

Lauren looked one over. A spark of envy flickered inside her when Jackie ran her hand across his muscular bare back, shoulder to shoulder. She would never find the courage to go up to a man and do that, especially one who was wearing nothing but a pair of white trunks and a broad smile. He winked at her. Lauren expected her heart to jump into her throat but it didn't. He didn't affect her at all.

Jackie openly flirted with him, touching his bicep and then his face, her eyes full of sinful invites that Lauren knew she would go through with. Watching her, she couldn't help wondering if she could ever be like that—confident in her beauty, strong enough to just reach out and take.

It struck her that she could if it was Julian. If he was standing before her in nothing but his underwear, she could damn well reach out and take what she wanted. At least, she thought she could. In reality, she would probably clam up and turn shy.

She remembered touching him, unmasking him. Could she go any further when it had taken so much for her just to find the courage to do that? What would it be like to kiss him? Would he respond if she did and return the kiss? The very thought made her blush.

The waiter smiled at her. She hurriedly looked away, towards Piper. She wasn't blushing over him but she'd clearly given him that impression. Only Julian could make her cheeks blaze the way they were right now, so hot that every inch of her was burning.

"Are you okay?" Piper said, clinging to her arm and staring at the room with round frightened eyes. Every time a waiter came within four feet of Piper, she jumped. Lauren had to get her away. She had to get them all out and back to the safe house.

Her friends had found their table. When Lauren sat down, she realised that they were right at the front. Two men were on the stage near to her, both wearing identical black leather pouches and police hats. Heavens. She covered Piper's eyes and turned her chair so she had her back to the stage. She wasn't about to be responsible for corrupting her.

Lauren uncovered Piper's eyes and cast a glance around the other tables. They were either full of middle-aged women who probably had kids waiting at home for them or young nubile girls who were almost as naked as the men on stage were. Could she be more out of place? She held Piper's hand to comfort her and tried to get Leo's attention again. He was definitely ignoring her, flirting outrageously with her friends. All three of them were rapt with attention and he was drinking it up.

A charming trunks-clad waiter stopped at her table and flashed perfect white teeth. He fussed over Vicky, Jackie and Sharon, flirting so much that all three women were giggling messes when he took their drinks order and finally left, leaving Leo looking more than slightly annoyed.

"We really should go," Lauren said loud enough that he couldn't fail to hear her this time. He looked around the club and then reluctantly nodded.

Lauren went to stand but Vicky caught her wrist. There was disappointment shining in her brown eyes. "You're not leaving?"

"We really have to." She looked at Leo and Piper. They both nodded.

"Lauren..." Vicky's look turned gravely serious. Lauren sat back down, wondering what had gotten into her friend. In all the years she had known her, Vicky had never looked so intense. Not a trace of laughter touched her face. It was laden with worry. Vicky leaned towards her and hesitated a moment before saying, "The police came to speak to me. They said that someone had left some kit or something in an alley, and it was covered in blood. They'd contacted your class and it turned out the only person they couldn't get hold of was you, so they called me."

Lauren's blood chilled. She swallowed and then forced a smile, followed by a laugh.

"And you thought it was mine?" She laughed again and then nudged Piper under the table with her foot. Piper laughed too. "I really hope no one at my class was hurt but it wasn't mine. My stuff is at home."

"You disappeared, Lauren. I've been calling you and I couldn't get through. You haven't been at work..."

"That's our fault," Leo said and everyone looked at him. "We sort of crashed her life."

"And you are?" Sharon this time and Lauren got the impression that she was only interested in finding out more about Leo rather than what was happening.

"Her cousins!" Piper shouted so loud that everyone on the tables around them looked over. She shrank down into her coat. "From out of town."

"Cousins?" Vicky frowned.

"Yeah, cousins." Lauren wished she was better at thinking on her feet.

"But we couldn't get through to you."

"Uncle Duke and us came down and whisked her away," Piper blurted.

Lauren looked at her with raised eyebrows. She shrugged and then sank back into her jacket, so far that the funnel collar covered her nose and made her look like Julian's younger sister. Piper was as good at lying as Lauren, which wasn't saying much. Uncle? How old did Piper think Duke was?

"They suddenly came down and I've been so busy since then. My phone is in for repairs because I dropped it down the toilet and I had to come here tonight to let you all know that I was okay. So here I am, all okay, nothing wrong with me. And we really do have to be going," Lauren said, standing again. This time, Leo and Piper stood too.

Piper took hold of Lauren's hand and she could feel her shaking. She had to get them all out of here and back to the warehouse. It had been foolish of her to make Piper come out to this kind of club.

"I really want to go now." Piper nervously scanned the crowd, her eyes stopping on people at random. Lauren wondered if she could hear what they were thinking. She didn't want to know what sort of sordid thoughts went through people's minds in places like this. "Julian will be mad."

"Who's Julian?" all three of her friends said in unison and Lauren blushed again.

"Her boyfriend." Piper smiled at them and Lauren clenched her hand tight until Piper grimaced and frowned at her. Lauren widened her eyes to tell her to keep quiet, her cheeks blazing over what Piper had said. Julian was definitely not her boyfriend.

"You have a boyfriend now?" Vicky's round eyes almost matched Lauren's own. "Since when do you have a boyfriend?"

"It's a recent thing, and he's not my boyfriend."

"Yet," Piper muttered beside her and Lauren cast her another dark look.

"Well, it's about time you got some action," Jackie said with a wide smile.

Lauren pulled a face of discomfort and tried to smile back at her. She didn't think she would be getting much action, not with Julian, no matter how much she wished she would.

"We really have to get going," Lauren said and hugged Vicky when she stood. "I'll contact you again soon."

"What about work?"

Lauren paused, trying to think what to say. There was only one thing she could say.

"Tell them I quit." She smiled and waved at Jackie and Sharon, and then shrugged when Vicky looked shock. "I have a new job now."

She grabbed Piper's hand and was heading into the crowd before her friends could say another word, following Leo as he led the way towards the doors. When they reached them, cool air washed over her and Lauren had never felt so free. It felt good to be away from her dead end job, and she was happy that she'd managed to let her friends know that she was okay. She looked around at the dark streets and then at Leo and Piper. A niggling feeling replaced her sense of happiness, something inside her saying to get home as soon as possible. Piper wasn't the only one who didn't want to get into trouble.

They hurried down the shopping streets back towards the Underground station. Piper's grip on her hand was still tight and Lauren had an inkling of her feelings. She was frightened. Lauren looked at Leo. He walked ahead of them, his confident swagger not just for show. She could feel him too, knew that he would handle anything that came after them, just as he'd promised.

Her mind flashed back to the club and the moment when Piper had said that Julian was her boyfriend and then back further to the waiters. None of them had affected her as Julian did.

Her heart missed a beat.

Julian was gorgeous, and not just average good looks like Leo and Kuga. No, Julian was Greek god gorgeous, the kind of man that she'd fantasised about marrying when she was a teen and into her early twenties. After that, reality had set in and she'd begun to notice that she didn't have the looks, the money or the body to win that kind of man.

Still, the way Julian looked at her, the way he'd reacted to her touch tonight, made her feel as though the impossible might be possible after all.

Perhaps she could win the man of her dreams.

No. A man beyond her dreams. Julian was flesh and blood, and his looks weren't the only thing that made him gorgeous. It was everything—his concern, his desire to protect her, and the tenderness he showed her sometimes. He was beautiful through and through and she was sure that he cared about her.

And she had gone out. She had gone against his desire to protect her, to keep her safe, and risked everything because she had wanted to see her friends. What had she done? He wouldn't just be angry with her if he discovered that she was gone. He would be disappointed and it would shake his trust in her.

It was a relief to see that her friends were all fine but she had to make it back to the Ghost safe house before Duke and Astra, or worse, Julian, realised that they were missing. Kuga had promised to cover for them, but she didn't hold out much hope of him convincing Julian that she and Piper were in her locked room.

Piper had used her powers to shift the lock into place from the outside.

Julian would see through it in five seconds, the length of time it would take for him to sense that she wasn't in the room.

Lauren prayed that they made it back before he did. Her niggling fear of werewolves finding her was getting worse now that she'd seen her friends. It was a long way to the safe house and there were patches of fog in the air. They walked through one, Piper clinging to her arm and staring at the drowned out world with wide eyes. Leo was always a few steps ahead, playing with a globe of electricity as though it was a ball. The light helped Lauren keep an eye on where he was, but it lit up the fog and made it hard to see.

When they reached a crossroad, Leo stopped. He motioned towards a busier road. Red double-decker buses and black taxis drove along it, disappearing into the fog as though it was swallowing them.

"I'm going to buy some fags," he said with a guilty smile. "Don't tell Kuga 'cause he'll blow his nut. Just say I went to check something out. Take care."

With a wave in their direction, he was gone. Lauren stood there, her eyebrows high. So much for their chaperone and all his talk about protecting them. Piper's grip on Lauren's arm increased. Lauren took hold of her hand and squeezed. Out of everyone in Ghost, Piper had been the friendliest to her. Lauren liked her and she wasn't about to let anything happen to them.

"It's just a short walk," she said with a smile and zipped up her jacket to keep out some of the cold. "We'll be home before you know it."

"Home," Piper echoed, hope in her eyes. "Home sounds good... home and a cup of tea."

"That sounds even better. Come on, let's hurry. It's damn freezing." Lauren led the way towards the Underground station, refusing to let the menacing fog and her fears get the better of her. They would be home in less than half an hour and then she would feel stupid for believing that they were in danger outside. The chances of someone finding them were slim to none when it was misty and soon they would be lost in the Underground.

Her heart said that she was lying to herself. Lauren ignored it too. The werewolves wouldn't find her.

It said that they had found her twice before. They would find her again.

Lauren told it to shut up and kept walking, brisker now, tugging Piper along beside her. Piper's hand trembled in hers. She looked down at it, and when she looked up, they were at another crossroad.

A shape materialised in the yellow streetlight-lit fog ahead of them. A man.

CHAPTER 10

Lauren's heart started to pound, and she pulled Piper closer. The man looked like a thug in the shadows. When he came closer, she saw that it was the waiter who had smiled at her in the club. He was dressed now, wearing a black leather jacket and jeans. When he saw her, he ran his fingers through his short sandy hair and then smiled. He was just a man. Lauren's heart lifted and the tension melted away.

She glanced at the man.

He passed them and she exhaled the breath she'd been subconsciously holding and then shrieked into the heavy hand that closed over her mouth. It pulled her backwards against the solid bulk of his chest and she lost her grip on Piper's hand. An arm wrapped around her stomach like a steel band, squeezing the air from her. Lauren struggled, frantic to escape. Two thoughts pounded through her spinning mind.

They had found her. They were everywhere.

"Lauren!" Piper screamed and started towards her.

Lauren reached out to her. The waiter held her tighter, his body pressing against her back. The fear in Piper's eyes spurred her on. Lashing out, Lauren kicked the man hard in the shin. He dropped her and she stumbled forwards, hands skimming the pavement as she tried to regain her balance. She snatched Piper's hand and ran. Her legs shook but she kept going. Her breathing was loud in her ears, creating a cacophony when combined with her thundering heartbeat and the words screaming in her head.

Run. Run fast. Don't stop and don't look back. Just run, and don't let go of Piper.

Her legs started to tire. She couldn't see the Underground station anywhere. The area didn't look anything like the one where it was.

They were going the wrong way.

Piper tripped, almost dragging her down too, and Lauren made her first mistake. She looked back. The man was almost on them, his lumbering gait making him look like bull.

A bull that wasn't about to stop its charge.

Lauren swallowed.

Her heart screamed his name.

Julian.

In a desperate attempt to keep Piper safe, Lauren pushed her out of the way. The man slammed into Lauren, knocking her to the ground and landing hard with her. The impact pushed the air from her lungs but Lauren fought back, scrabbling and clawing at the man with all her strength. She pressed both feet into his stomach and shoved him backwards. Regaining her feet, she dashed over to Piper.

"I can use my power." Piper's voice quivered.

Lauren held her arm out to stop her, shielding her from the man as he approached. He grinned and she could only stare at him as his eyes lightened, turning yellow like a wolf's.

"I can do it," Piper said but Lauren didn't let her pass. Piper was nervous about using her abilities, and that meant that she couldn't control them. She couldn't let Piper face the werewolf when there was a danger that she would possibly hurt herself, or someone else. The man was after her. Lauren swallowed her fear. She would face him alone.

"Stay back," Lauren whispered and stepped forwards to meet the man.

An amused look entered his dark eyes.

"Where's your chaperone?" He grinned again.

Lauren stood silent, trying to think of a plan. There had to be a way out of this. She quickly scanned her surroundings, eyes running over the dark shop fronts and office buildings. The man stood between them and the way back towards the club and the Underground station. If she could dodge his attacks for long enough, she could turn things around so they were on that side. If.

Suddenly, she wished that Piper could read her thoughts so she could tell her what to do.

"Never mind." He shrugged. "I have a score to settle with him, but it can wait. Business first. If I'm lucky, he'll show up and I can take you both to see the boss."

Lauren realised that the werewolf wasn't talking about Leo. He was talking about Julian and he was talking about taking them to Lycaon. A wave of nausea passed over her but she held it together, facing him and not letting him see the fear that turned her stomach and made her insides shake. She wasn't frightened of him. She and Piper were faster and if they could get past him, then they could get home.

Julian was going to kill her.

He'd been right. She should have stayed where it was safe. She was an idiot for thinking she wasn't in any danger outside.

It wasn't time for regrets though. The man wanted to take her alive. He might go easy on her and they might get a chance to escape. Would he take both of them if they failed to get away?

She hoped Julian would show up. This man was a definite threat to her and Piper, but he would be no trouble at all to Julian. She was sure of it.

Lauren focused on Julian, silently calling his name in a desperate attempt for him to hear her. He'd said that he could sense her. Could she make him sense her now? Did the connection they shared run that deep?

"Lauren?"

She vaguely sensed Piper move forward and held her arm out.

"It's okay." She looked over her shoulder at Piper and smiled. "I'll deal with this."

The man laughed. Lauren glared at him, straightening to her full, if a little short, height. He cast his gaze over her, slow and assessing, with a hungry flicker in his eyes that made her skin crawl.

"How?" He laughed again. "You don't have a weapon."

"Neither do you," she shot back and then regretted it when he stretched his fingers out and his fingernails turned to claws.

Fur erupted along his fingers and over the back of his hands. She stood rooted to the spot, horrified as he began to change in front of her. He shed his clothes, twisting and writhing as his body transformed, bones popping out of place and changing shape to fit his new form.

Lauren had forgotten that he was a living weapon.

It didn't matter. She had to keep Piper safe. She had to literally face her demons and find the strength to fight. If she couldn't do it now, she would never be able to.

She couldn't rely on Julian's strength.

She wanted to stand on her own two feet and fight for herself.

She could do this. She could take hold of her destiny and face the awakening.

The werewolf rolled its shoulders and then howled at the sky. While it wasn't paying her any attention, Lauren gestured to Piper to move left and circle around. When Piper had made it a few metres, Lauren began to move too. The werewolf growled at her and pounced. Lauren reacted in an instant, throwing herself forwards and onto the ground. She hit it hard and rolled. The werewolf's foot slammed down. Lauren squeaked as she curled into a ball to avoid it and then scrambled to her feet.

Before she could move, a heavy paw smashed into her shoulder, knocking her over again. She fell to the side, hitting her ribs on impact and gasping as pain spread across her right side. Dodging a werewolf had sounded a lot easier than it was turning out to be.

It swiped again, its fist plummeting towards her. Lauren scooted backwards and managed a quick glance at Piper. She'd made it as far as a lamppost and had stopped, clinging to it. The fog was thinner here but Lauren couldn't make out much beyond fifty metres.

The werewolf growled again. Lauren hurried to her feet. It attacked and she ducked under its arm and ran at it, shoving it backwards and off balance.

She forced herself to keep going, to keep ducking and dodging whenever it attacked. It was just an overgrown puppy, nothing to be scared of. It wasn't going to kill her. It wanted to capture her and she was going to make that work against it. It tried to grab her, two arms flinging towards her, and she leapt to one side to avoid it.

Lauren made it back past the werewolf and was about to test whether she could run when the werewolf grabbed her wrist. It yanked her arm up, so she dangled in the air. Her shoulder threatened to pop out of the socket.

The werewolf bared its fangs and then launched its huge paw at her, aiming straight for her head.

She flinched away but the impact she'd expected never came.

Peeking through one eye, she was surprised when she saw that the werewolf had stopped dead, its paw mid-strike and its jowls still peeled back to reveal huge fangs.

In fact, it wasn't moving at all.

"Lauren." Piper's voice was small and strained.

Lauren looked over her shoulder to see Piper standing close by, her palms facing the werewolf and her eyes narrowed. Had she stopped the werewolf?

"Hurry." Piper gritted her teeth and sweat broke out across her brow.

Lauren reached up and pulled on the claws locked tight around her arm. She clenched her jaw and tried harder. It was no use. Pain shot through her shoulder and Lauren cringed. She couldn't get the werewolf's paw open.

"Lauren?" This time, Piper sounded scared.

Lauren looked at her again and her eyes went as wide as Piper's were when she saw the blood trickling down from her nose. Piper was hurting herself. The young woman gave her a confused and sorry look, and then collapsed. The werewolf dropped Lauren with a long low growl.

Lauren ran to Piper.

"Piper?" She shook her but Piper didn't respond.

The blood reached Piper's lip.

Sharp pain burst across the back of Lauren's skull.

Her vision swam out of focus as she slumped to the ground. The last thing she saw was Piper's face.

And it was the first thing she saw when she came around.

Only now, they weren't in a street. Wherever they were, it was freezing and smelt of mould. A single dull light shone down on them. Lauren frowned, wishing her head would clear. It ached and spun, a dull throb at the back marking the spot where the werewolf must have clobbered her. She pushed herself up onto her hands and knees, and crawled across the cold stone floor to Piper. Her stomach rolled with the urge to be sick. It ebbed and flowed, one moment so strong that she feared she would throw up and the next barely noticeable.

"Piper," Lauren whispered, afraid to raise her voice in case the werewolf heard. She didn't want him to know that she was awake. For all she knew, he could have taken them to Lycaon already. If she could wake Piper, they might be able to find a way to escape before someone came to check on them. She wouldn't let Lycaon win so easily. She was going to go through with the awakening and she was going to make him pay for the things that he'd done.

Piper didn't stir. She remained silent and prone on the floor, blood caking her nose and top lip. Lauren licked the cuff of her brown combat jacket and used it to clean the blood away. Whatever Piper had tried to do to help her, it must have taken tremendous effort to control it, enough that she'd hurt herself. Lauren stroked her cheek, willing her to wake. Her breathing was steady but shallow, not strong enough to comfort Lauren.

At least they were alive.

For now.

She looked around her, chafing her stiff cold fingers and trying to get a feel for where they were. It was freezing. The corners of the large room were dark. There were no windows. A basement? Just her luck to be tossed somewhere with only one means of escape.

A low groan made her head snap around. Piper's nose wrinkled and she frowned.

"Piper?" Lauren whispered again, more urgent this time. Even if there was only one means of escape, they were still going to have to try it. She rubbed her arms through her jacket and sighed. Her breath turned opaque in the chilly air.

"Lauren?" Piper sounded groggy. Her hand went to her head and then her eyes opened a slither.

"Are you alright?" Lauren leaned over so Piper could see her without straining herself.

"My head is killing me." There was a smile to those words. As much as Lauren loved Piper's way of making light of situations, she didn't think that this was a laughing matter.

"Promise me that whatever you did back there, you won't do it again. It hurt you."

Piper pushed herself up. Lauren took hold of her arm, helping her into a sitting position. The young woman rubbed her eyes and then frowned when she touched her nose and saw the blood on her fingers.

"Noted." Piper screwed her eyes shut. "I could use some painkillers."

"We need to get out of here for that to happen. Can you hear anything?"

Piper shook her head. "It hurts too much."

That wasn't a comfort. Lauren had been relying on Piper being able to hear the thoughts of any people in the building above them so they could know what they were up against and could avoid them if possible.

Piper opened her eyes and looked around. "Where are we?"

"I don't know."

Piper was as pale as marble in the dim light, her eyes enormous and dark. Lauren took hold of her hand, moving closer to her. They were both filthy and cold. The basement was grey and dusty, and looked as though no one had used it in decades.

"We'll be okay," she said and wondered if she actually believed they would.

Was Julian coming for her? Lauren focused all of her energy on him, convinced that he would sense her if she did. He had to come for them.

She needed him.

She needed to feel him close to her, because only then would she feel safe again.

"I'm sorry," Piper whispered.

"Don't be. This is all my fault. If I hadn't been so stubborn and had stayed in, none of this would have happened. I'm sorry."

A door creaked open above them to her left and light streamed in, silhouetting the man stood in the doorway. Was it Lycaon?

Lauren got to her feet, willing to face him if necessary. She stood in front of Piper, blocking the man's path to her.

The man walked slowly down the steps and then into the light. Not Lycaon. The man who had captured them. The light cast dark shadows on his handsome face, turning his features evil and menacing.

"Won't be long now." He smiled at her, setting her nerves on edge. He tossed a water bottle her way. It landed by her feet. "Clean up. Boss will want you presentable."

Lauren stood her ground. Lycaon couldn't have arrived yet. She glanced down at Piper to see that she was glaring at the man, her fingertips digging into the damp stone floor.

His smile became a grin. "Can't wait to watch you get what you deserve."

He headed up the stairs and slammed the door.

Lauren stood there a few seconds longer and then looked down at Piper. "Anything?"

Piper rubbed her temples and closed her eyes. "It's fuzzy but I think he's alone. I couldn't hear anyone else and he was thinking about preparing for Lycaon's arrival."

A sigh escaped Lauren. She tilted her head back and stared up at the ceiling. Was Julian coming for her?

"Don't worry," Piper said and got to her feet. She brushed her dark jeans down and then stretched. "I'm sure that Julian is on his way."

"I wish I was so sure."

"Then you don't know Julian." Piper looked up just as Lauren glanced at her, giving her the impression that she was avoiding her, but then she met her gaze and grinned. "I've never met a man like him. He found you once... tracked you down even though he didn't know where in the world to start looking. Now that he's found you, Lauren, he isn't going to lose you. Believe in him, trust him, because he's incredible. We'll be long gone before Lycaon arrives."

Lauren didn't have a response to that. She stood staring at Piper. She'd never thought about how amazing Julian must be in order to find her, one person in a world crammed with over six billion. He'd found her. He'd overcome that challenge so he could be here for her when she awakened. Her heart warmed. She pressed her hand to her chest and looked down at it. Piper was right. Julian was incredible.

She believed in him. He would come for her, and together they would defeat Lycaon.

Piper looked thoughtful and then grinned at her.

There was a loud crash up above.

"Julian?" Lauren said.

"I wouldn't want to be that werewolf. I've never heard Julian this pissed off before. Oh." Piper gasped. Her cheeks darkened. There was a sound like an explosion.

"What is it?" Lauren grabbed her hand, blinded by concern for Julian and fear that his anger was for her.

Piper bit her lip. "Kuga."

CHAPTER 11

Julian stormed through the dark boarded up house, his sword drawn and his silver eyes darting around, searching for Lauren. He had checked all of the rooms on the ground floor at the front of the house. They were bare, not even carpeted. The only sign of life had been a grey blanket on the living room floor. He reached out with his senses and a single werewolf signature came back to him, and then two other heartbeats. It was difficult to get their location.

Kuga and Leo were close behind. The concern he could feel in them distracted him, making him aware of his own fear. Lauren was alive, but he didn't know what state she was in. She could be hurt. On the way here, he'd repeatedly told himself that there was every possibility that he would find her unharmed, but his mind had kept conjuring images of her injured or dying, and he was finding them impossible to ignore. They played on his nerves, unsettling him and making it difficult to follow Lauren's scent that so clearly marked the lingering fog. For the first time in several millennia, he was acting rash, heading into a situation he knew nothing about with hands so unsteady that he could barely hold his sword.

The fact that it was daylight wasn't helping.

Kuga tried to pass him. Julian sped up, running up the flight of stairs to the first floor in an attempt to pinpoint Lauren and Piper's location, and that of the werewolf. Even if he was weak during the day, Julian wasn't about to be coddled by a mere child. It would've been bad enough to have Duke or Astra treat him as though he was delicate and feeble. Having Kuga and Leo trying to protect him was insulting.

He was still stronger than them. He wouldn't back down and let them take the lead. A single werewolf wasn't about to stop him from rescuing Lauren. He might not have his abilities and his normal strength, but he could still wield a sword with three thousand years of skill and experience.

A sickening sense of fear washed through him. Lauren. He stopped dead on the stairs, absorbing the feeling, savouring it almost. She was worried. She knew that he was here. Piper must have heard him and told her that he was coming.

He was coming. He tried to send that message to her, needing her to know that he was here for her. She wouldn't be able to sense him clearly before her awakening, but she might be able to catch a glimmer of his feelings. He wouldn't fail her. The werewolf that had taken her was going to pay and then he was going to get her out of here, and take her far away to somewhere safe.

"What is it?" Leo hissed up the stairs towards him.

"The basement. They know we are here," Julian said.

"Who knows?" Kuga this time. Julian turned on the stairs and looked down into his eyes.

"Lauren, and Piper."

The relief that filled Kuga was palpable. Julian wanted to tell him not to be so quick to feel that way when they hadn't saved them yet, but he felt a similar sense of relief deep in his heart. Lauren was alive. He moved down the stairs, following his senses. The closer he got to her, the clearer she became. She was hurt and she was frightened.

Julian wanted to take both of those feelings away for her and make her feel safe again, just as she'd felt these past few days with him.

His focus on Lauren, Julian didn't sense the werewolf until it was almost too late. He evaded the claws that slashed through the air at head height, coming out of the darkness. Bringing his sword around, he lunged forwards. The blade cut through something soft. The werewolf growled and rushed him. In the narrow hallway, it was impossible to avoid a collision. The werewolf barrelled into him, knocking his katana away and tackling him to the ground. Julian pushed back and buried his own claws into the werewolf's shoulders. Landing on top, he slammed his fist into the werewolf's jaw, knocking its head hard to one side, and then hit it with his other fist, flinging its head back again.

The werewolf lunged forwards, huge jaws flashing bright teeth that snapped close to his face. Julian struggled to hold it down. Fighting werewolves during the day wasn't something he relished, and this one was stronger than he'd anticipated. It pushed back, overpowering him. Julian could only bring his hand up to defend himself. Long fangs punctured his palm, smashing bone and coming out the other side. The werewolf shook its head and slammed Julian into the wall. His mind reeled and his vision swam. He cursed and ripped his hand free of the werewolf's teeth. White-hot pain rolled up his arm, burning so fiercely that the blood that streamed over his hand and forearm felt cold. Julian clutched his hand to his chest and kicked the werewolf in the face, his boot connecting solidly with its jaw, sending its head snapping backwards.

A blue-white blur shot past his head. Julian rolled away before it impacted, filling the air with the smell of singed fur and burnt flesh.

He held his broken hand and stared at the twitching corpse of the werewolf. The bolt had blown its head clean off. He looked up at Kuga, offering him silent thanks for his intervention. The twin extended a hand and Julian didn't hesitate. He grabbed it and hauled himself up onto his feet, keeping his injured hand close to his chest and upright so the bleeding slowed enough for him to heal. Kuga pulled a face of pure disgust, released his hand, and stared at his own.

Blood covered it.

Leo laughed. Kuga pulled his long heavy black cotton coat to one side and wiped his bloodied hand on his black jeans.

Julian did the same with his own uninjured hand. The boy should have known that he had blood on his hands from where the werewolf had bitten him. More than that, he should be unaffected by getting his hands dirty in battle. As a child, one of the first things Julian had learned about battles was that they meant bloodshed. War was never a clean affair.

He picked up his katana and slid it back into its sheath. His focus switched to Lauren. Her fear left a foul taste in his mouth and rekindled the anger in his heart. The death of the werewolf hadn't satisfied his desire for blood and violence. Part of him wanted to wait for Lycaon to arrive so he could slake his thirst for vengeance, but Lauren was mortal, vulnerable. It would be too easy for Lycaon to kill her. Julian couldn't allow that to happen.

Vengeance would have to wait. His priority was getting Lauren to safety.

With a sneer, Julian kicked the door to the basement open. Twin gasps made his jaw tense. He reined in his anger, regretting his actions, and stared down at the two women where they stood huddled together under the single light. He could smell blood. His gaze scanned over Lauren and then Piper. It was hers.

Lauren moved forwards, pushing Piper behind her.

Protecting her.

It seemed Lauren was stronger than she realised. She was protecting a girl that could easily crush every bone in his body if she willed it, and Lauren was still only mortal.

Julian descended the stairs. When he stepped into the light, Lauren's expression changed from one of sheer determination to utter relief. She moved forwards and he found himself doing the same. A long dark bruise darted across her cheek. He frowned and reached out to touch it.

"Christ!" Lauren took hold of his hand, her grip light and careful. "God, Julian."

The force with which she said those words warmed his heart. He'd never felt her so worried before, not about him at least. Lauren was treating his broken hand as though it was a mortal injury. The bones had already healed.

"It is nothing," he said and found the strength to cover her hand with his. It stilled against him and her eyes met his. "It will be gone by tomorrow."

Tears lined her eyes, trembling on the brink of falling. "I'm so sorry, Julian. I'll never do anything so stupid again. I'll listen to you."

The thought that those tears were for him sent his head spinning. Everything about Lauren was too good to be real. It felt as though he was in a dream, a world where the loneliness he'd borne over the millennia had never existed and all he'd ever known was this warm, joyous feeling.

Her eyes darted between his, full of fear that he could sense in her.

Any anger he might have felt about what she had done disappeared, leaving only disappointment at himself for having failed to protect her. She had been hurt. He should have been there for her, just as he had promised.

"There is nothing to apologise for." He wiped her tears away with the pad of his thumb. Her skin was cold beneath his touch. "You are safe and that is all that matters."

More tears came, dashing down her cheeks and cutting through the dirt that covered her. He'd never had much practice at saying the right thing to a woman. His attempts over the years had gained only criticism or rejection. Now he'd made Lauren cry rather than smile.

Kuga passed them, gathering Piper into his arms and berating her. Julian ignored his harmless tirade, knowing that it was only fear for Piper's safety speaking and that Piper would know it. How would Lauren react if he gathered her into his arms?

He looked at her and when she wiped away her tears and smiled, he almost found the strength to do it, but then the moment shattered.

"We gotta move," Leo said from the top of the stairs.

"Lycaon is coming," Lauren whispered.

Her increasing fear was enough to make Julian act. He took hold of her hand with his uninjured one and led her towards the stairs. Checking her over to make sure that she wasn't hurt was going to have to wait. She reached out behind her and Piper took hold of her hand. Kuga brought up the rear as they moved through the house and then out into the black van.

Leo was already in the driver's seat with the engine running. Julian helped Lauren and Piper into the back and then stepped in and slid the wide panel door closed. He turned to Lauren, removed his coat, and placed it around her shoulders. She pulled it closed over her chest and smiled at him, one full of gratitude and warmth. He returned the smile, hoping to alleviate some of the fear and guilt that still laced her scent, and pulled the collar up so it protected her neck. He didn't think offering her his coat was a great sacrifice. Her clothing was flimsy and she was freezing. He would bear the cold for her, would face the frozen winds of Antarctica if it meant she would be warm. He would do anything for her.

He noticed that she had closed her eyes and stood with her head inclined slightly towards his hand where it brushed her neck, still holding the collar of his coat. He hesitated a moment, telling himself that he would be breaking the rules again if he went through with it, and then found the courage to move his hand to her cheek and hold it.

"I am sorry," she said and opened her eyes, looking up at him.

"It is done now. I am glad you are safe."

She smiled again and moved back to Piper.

They sat on the bench over the rear wheel arch. Lauren's arm went around Piper's shoulder, holding her close. When had Lauren taken responsibility for Piper's safety? None of the other incarnations of Illia had ever acted this way. Not even Illia herself had.

Lauren looked over at him, fatigue written in her expression. He wanted to comfort her. He wanted to ignore his duty and the rules and go to her, take her into his arms, and hold her. Piper curled up against Lauren with her head on her shoulder. Kuga sat next to him, staring at Piper. Was Kuga thinking the same as him? Did he wish that Piper was with him and that he was holding her? Julian wanted nothing more than to have Lauren close to him, and for once in his existence, it had nothing to do with protecting her.

He looked away from her, focusing on other things so he wouldn't be tempted to break the rules. He had bent them so far but couldn't overstep the mark and disobey his orders, no matter how much he wanted to.

Julian stared at his injured hand and thought about the journey that lay ahead. A tight feeling settled in his chest when he remembered the last time Duke had done this to him. It was only a short period this time and he could cope with it if it meant Lauren passed undetected out of the country. At least, he thought he could. He would only find out what his real reaction would be when it came time to go through with it.

The van stopped. Kuga opened the door and hopped down, helping Piper when she went to him. Julian followed, stopping on the road to help Lauren down. She thanked him with a smile and a blush that made his heart beat faster.

He hoped that she didn't react too badly to what was coming.

Lauren frowned at her surroundings.

Julian didn't bother to take them in. He knew the docks well enough, with their large warehouses and the smell of rotten fish. To a human, it would be undetectable. To him, it was overpowering.

A group of men gave them strange looks as they passed. It was going to be difficult to explain what they were doing here if someone saw what Duke was about to do.

"Where are we going?" Lauren stared straight ahead at Duke.

He and Astra were standing in the shadow of a massive rusty red and dull black tanker next to an open shipping container, a pile of luggage beside them. Julian still wasn't sure how he was going to explain to Lauren what they were going to do. Duke had said it was best not to try at all. Julian hated the thought of doing that to Lauren, and he wouldn't.

They stopped in front of Duke. He held out Lauren's black jumper to her. Julian took his coat from her and put it on. Lauren removed her own jacket and put the jumper on, and then her jacket again. She would need what little warmth it would give her in the journey ahead. A sigh caught his attention and he looked at Astra. She stood behind Duke, her arms folded and a mild look of disgust on her face. She hated the daylight as much as he did but they had to leave straight away. By nightfall, Lycaon could be after them. They had to lose him now and buy Lauren some time.

Kuga and Leo walked over to the luggage and grabbed two cases each. Piper picked up Lauren's backpack and followed them onto the large tanker.

Julian looked out towards the sea. The weather was clear and crisp, and the water in the distance was calm, but he knew from experience that it wasn't a sign that it would be just as smooth out to sea. The English Channel in winter was rough and violent.

He turned to face Lauren and placed his uninjured hand on her shoulder. A flicker of concern surfaced in her eyes again.

"Everything will be fine. We need to leave the country and this is the best method. I need you to trust me." He held her gaze.

Lauren nodded but didn't look sure.

"It's time to go," Duke said and before Julian could continue his explanation about what was going to happen, he'd jabbed a needle into Lauren's neck.

She looked shocked for a moment and then her eyes slipped shut and she fell. Julian caught her, cradling her in his arms while ignoring the pain in his hand, and glared at Duke.

"There isn't time for niceties. We have to leave now."

Behind his collar, Julian bared his fangs. A desire to lay Lauren down, unsheathe his sword, and cut Duke in two filled him. Instead, he held Lauren close and stared at her peaceful face. He should have told her in the van. He'd asked her to trust him and then Duke had turned that trust against her. Would she still trust him when she woke up, or had Duke ruined everything?

"Ready?" Duke armed himself with a second needle. Kuga stopped next to Duke while Piper and Leo loaded the last of the luggage onto the ship.

"Give me a moment," Julian said and looked down at Lauren. He needed to look at her for a minute, to take in that she was back in his arms where she belonged, safe with him. When he'd found her missing, it had shaken him worse than his nightmare had. He'd feared that it was coming true and that he would find her dying. His strength had failed him. Never before had she had power over him like this, an ability to make him feel so weak and defenceless.

But at the same time, a smile from her, or a single concerned look, was enough to make him feel invincible.

He looked at the dark, cramped metal shipping container. He took a deep breath and handed Lauren to Kuga.

Julian closed his eyes and nodded.

A sharp pain pierced his neck. Ice filled his veins. His mind numbed.

"We don't have enough to keep either of you under the entire way." Duke's voice was distant.

Julian frantically knocked Duke's hand away and yanked the needle from his neck. It was too late. His vision wavered. He tried to hold on, afraid of waking trapped in darkness, but it was no use. All strength slipped from his body and he fell forwards into the inky black, fearful of the nightmare that awaited him.

His last thought was of Lauren. She would be there with him.

He wouldn't be alone this time.

For her, he would endure the dark, because she was his light.

CHAPTER 12

Lauren woke to a throbbing head and cold endless darkness. She pushed herself up on the freezing floor and something slid off her. What little warmth she'd had from her cover disappeared. She felt around and found the blanket, and pulled it to her chest. The ground lurched. Wherever she was, she was moving.

She crawled forwards, taking deep breaths to control the rising panic inside her, and tried to remember what had happened. Julian had told her to trust him. They had been at the docks near a huge red and black ship. She'd looked at him and then everything had gone dark. She stopped and touched her neck. Duke had put something in her. She remembered the eerie way the drug had flowed through her, turning her blood to ice.

Lauren got to her feet and stumbled to her left as the ground pitched and rolled, losing her blanket in the process.

A ship. They were on the ship. Panic set in when she remembered the shipping container with its open corrugated rust-coloured metal doors and dark inside. Her hands hit something solid and her shoulder smashed into it shortly after. She felt around and gasped when her fingers found the same contours as those of a container.

She was in one.

She trembled and stumbled forwards along the wall, clutching the icy metal for support. It numbed her fingertips. The ship lurched again and she slammed into another wall. She followed it. A short distance away, she found another wall. It was a container. They had put her in a container. God.

Lauren leaned against the short wall and banged it with her fists.

"Help!" she yelled at the top of her lungs. "Someone help me... open the door!"

The freezing darkness chilled her and stole her breath. No matter where she looked, no matter how wide she made her eyes, she couldn't see anything. She banged again.

"Someone... help!" She leaned hard against the wall, her strength leaving her as she realised that no one was coming. Outside the wind was howling. It crept in through the cracks around the door, freezing her until she felt too tired to raise her fists to bang again.

She managed another strike with her hand and then pressed her forehead against the icy metal. She silently begged someone to come for her. She needed to get out, away. It felt as though the darkness was getting inside her, into her lungs and mind, swallowing her. They couldn't leave her here. She was sorry that she'd broken the rules and gone out. She was sorry that she hadn't listened. Didn't they know that?

The ship rolled again and she hit the side wall hard. She slid down it and curled up, sobbing into her knees. The wall was cold against her back, stealing all of her warmth until her body on the outside felt as numb as it did on the inside. She hadn't meant to upset anyone. She'd been stupid. She was sorry.

Burying her face into her knees, she struggled to breathe through her tears. Why wasn't anyone coming for her? Were they going to leave her here in this wretched place, alone?

"Julian," she whispered and then raised her head, looking into the nothingness above her. "Julian!"

She hiccupped on a sob and then broke down, clutching her knees.

"Please, Julian. Don't leave me here. I'm sorry… please forgive me. I don't want to be alone. Don't leave me here alone."

Her heart ached. She didn't want to be alone. Not anymore. She'd been alone too long. She needed him.

She jerked to the side when something touched her shoulder and then scrambled backwards, away from it. She hadn't imagined it. Her heart missed beats and she desperately tried to see in the dark. Footsteps. Panic stole her breath when she hit the corner of the container. Trapped.

Someone was close. She could sense them. Closing her eyes, she reacted on instinct and lashed out with her leg. It hit something. That something grabbed her ankle.

"Let me go!" she shrieked and tried to pull her leg free.

A moment later, Lauren was off the floor and in someone's arms, cradled against a warm body. A familiar feeling of calm broke over her and her fear subsided. She clutched his shoulders and buried her face in his neck.

"Hush," Julian whispered in the darkness and held her close. "I am here."

It felt so good to be in his arms that she wanted to cry harder but she didn't have the strength. Instead, she relaxed into him and his arms tightened around her. He carried her through the gloom and set her down on her backside. It was warmer here away from the door and with Julian close to her.

He placed a blanket around her shoulders, pulling it closed and almost tucking her in, and then sat down beside her. Surprise claimed her when he put his arm around her and gathered her close to him. She shifted, pressing her right side against his and turning so she could rest her head on his shoulder. He stroked her arm through the blanket, the slow motion soothing her raw nerves and settling her.

"It was a necessary precaution." Julian sounded tense, as though he liked their predicament as much as she did. "In here, I can enter France without a problem, and Lycaon will find it difficult to trace your movements."

Lauren moved closer to him and shut her eyes. If she didn't see the darkness and focused on the melodic sound of Julian's voice, then she could pretend that they were just sitting outside on a winter's day.

"So we're going to France?" Her voice seemed loud in the small space. "I've been to Paris once. I bet you've been there before."

"I have." The tension in his voice increased.

"With me?" She felt him nod. "I bet you've been to lots of places."

It seemed like a good way of distracting her from their current location. She could easily picture Paris in her mind. Were they going there? The thought of Paris in the snow was romantic. Paris, snow and Julian? That sounded even better.

"I have been many places on this Earth, either with you or searching for you."

"So many different time periods too. Did you see England in the Georgian period?" she said and he made a noise of confirmation. "France during the revolution?" Another noise. "Ancient China or Japan? Egypt when the pharaohs reigned?"

"Only the late pharaohs. The rest are far older than me." He sounded amused.

Lauren tried to think about a time and place she'd always wanted to be. Georgian England was at the forefront of her mind. Balls, beautiful dresses, and rich gentlemen in huge country houses. Julian would have looked amazing in the clothing of that period. Lauren had the feeling that Julian probably hadn't experienced too much of that side of things though. He'd probably been fighting werewolves.

"Lauren… I am sorry that Duke did not give me a chance to warn you." The regret was there in his voice, lining the edge that it had gained. Was he angry with Duke? Was that why he was so tense?

He was silent for a while and she listened to his heart beating steadily against her ear and savoured the way he was holding her. It drove all fear away, leaving her feeling safe again.

His hand shifted to her hair and he stroked it, playing with the tips.

"Are the others on the ship?" The feel of his hands in her hair warmed her until she no longer felt the chill of the container. She couldn't recall a man ever running his fingers through her hair, or holding her like this. Piper was right. Julian was incredible, in more ways than just abilities and his immortality. He was the most wonderful man she'd ever met. Not one in a million, or a billion, but more like one in a universe. Unique. Perfect. Hers? She wished.

"They have quarters. Duke knows the owner of the vessel." He paused and she felt the tension rise in him. "You know you could have travelled with them without rousing suspicion."

Lauren frowned. "Then why didn't I?"

She thought about being up with the others or trapped in a box with Julian. She would rather be here with him. She didn't want him to be alone, just as she'd feared that she'd been. Sometimes he seemed so lonely. She hated to see that in his eyes.

"Duke thought that you would not want to be away from me," Julian said and Lauren looked up.

She wished she could see him in the darkness. Could he see her? Did his abilities allow him that? Could he see how wide her eyes were and feel how shocked she was? If Duke believed what he'd told Julian, then he knew more about her feelings than she felt comfortable with and more than she'd wanted anyone to see. Until she was sure of her own feelings and Julian's, she wanted things to continue as normally as they could. She needed to see where things went and needed to get her head straight. Julian's fingers combed through her hair, his breath soft against her face.

How close was he? A sense of anticipation stirred and built in her stomach. Was he close enough to kiss her?

"Duke believes that you are attracted to me."

Lauren's cheeks blazed. If he was fishing for an answer, he wasn't going to get one. She looked down, desperately trying to think of something that she could say to divert his attention away from her and her feelings. Julian had switched from cold to hot on her so many times that she wasn't about to confess anything without being able to see him and read his expression. Her history with men was a bloody battlefield and she'd been defeated there too many times. She couldn't bear the thought of Julian hurting her too.

His hand caught her shoulder and she remembered how bad it had looked in the basement.

"Is your hand okay now?" she said, relieved to have something to talk about. The air between them instantly felt lighter.

"It has healed." He touched her face. "You have a bruise. I saw it back at the basement."

Lauren touched the spot where he had and it hurt. He was right. The werewolf must have hit her harder than she'd thought.

"Do we always heal so fast?" If she were like Julian, would her bruise be gone by tomorrow? Would shaving cuts on her legs no longer be a problem?

"Not always. Silver slows the healing process if any trace of it is left in our bodies."

"Does Lycaon heal like us? Is he as strong as you?"

"Lycaon has been growing stronger since Zeus first cursed him. By the time he met Selene, he was strong enough to promise her that he would help her in the fall of Artemis."

"Who's Artemis?"

"The goddess of the moon and Zeus's daughter."

"I thought Selene was the goddess of the moon?" She wished she could see Julian.

"Selene is a Titan, one of the old gods, and she envies Artemis and the gods who usurped them." The ship rocked. Lauren clung to Julian. In her mind, she imagined that it was the gods angry with Julian for saying that they had usurped the Titans. She couldn't remember the name of the Greek god of the sea, but she was sure that he was making the ship sway. "Selene wanted revenge, as do many of the Titans, and made a pact with Lycaon. When Zeus discovered it and decided to punish Selene, she promised to break the pact and not attempt to overthrow him and his kin."

"And I'm her daughter... does she drink blood too?"

Silence.

"No."

It was a very curt answer that made her want to ask more even though she had the impression that Julian wasn't going to expand on what he'd said.

"Did Illia's father drink blood?" she said with a tremble in her voice. Julian hadn't really said much about Illia's father. In fact, he hadn't mentioned him at all. She'd read books for history classes that talked about goddesses and gods, and they always seemed to have a lot of children and a lot of partners. She was sure that Selene hadn't been any different. Maybe they didn't know who her father was.

"Selene told me once that Illia's father needed blood to survive and that is why you need blood, and why I need blood."

"Tell me more about her... about Illia and Selene." She rubbed her arm to keep warm. She liked to hear about the gods and what things had been like in Julian's days as a mortal. She could picture him back then, his skin sun-kissed and his hair longer, dressed in chest armour, sandals and little more than a loincloth. She wasn't sure if that was how Arcadians had dressed, but in her mind it was, and he looked fantastic.

Julian sighed and adjusted her blanket so it reached up her neck. A shiver bolted through her when his fingers brushed her throat and his fingertips paused against it, as though he'd felt her reaction. He was still a moment and then swept his thumb across her neck as his hand left her. Another thrill chased through her and she knew his second touch hadn't been an accident. He had been testing her reaction. If he asked, she would confess that she liked it. Here in the dark, she felt bolder, courageous almost. Here in the dark, she could find the strength to kiss him if she tried.

"There is a lot to tell. Before she came to Earth, Illia lived on Olympus with the other gods. She never told me much about her time there, but she did mention that she had lived with Selene and had often watched over the people who worshipped her mother. They had been close and she had not hesitated when Zeus had charged her with the duty of defeating Lycaon, because she knew that it would save her mother." He drew her closer. The braver part of her said that he wasn't holding her close to keep her warm or protect her. He wanted her near him. He was attracted to her too. Her heart fluttered at that thought. It was the clearest sign she'd had so far but she still wasn't going to act on her own feelings, not until she was certain of his.

She told herself to focus on learning more about Selene, Illia and Lycaon, and not to get caught up in Julian.

"She accepted it to help her mother." Lauren rested her head on his shoulder and stared into the darkness. She would've done anything to save her mother from the terrible death she'd endured. She would've taken her place if she could have. "Did Illia ever see her again?"

"No," Julian said in a solemn tone but the tension was still there, edging his voice. "Illia was not allowed to return to Olympus until her duty was done. She died before that happened. Selene watched over her when she was on Earth and continues to do so unto this day."

Lauren liked the idea of having a goddess watching over her, even though she didn't feel as though Selene was her mother. Would she feel different when she had awakened? Would she feel something for Selene?

"Julian... if Lycaon is growing stronger..."

"Lycaon is growing stronger. His curse no longer holds sway over him to the extent that it used to. He can now transform back to human form at will and doesn't obey the full moon's command to change. His offspring are stronger now too. They can change at will, but the full moon will still force them into wolf form." Julian's hand shifted against her arm, as though he wanted to draw her even closer. "The battle will not be easy Lauren. With the rise of Lycaon's strength, there has been a decline in the length of time Illia's incarnations are living."

Lauren swallowed. That was a nice way of telling her that she was likely to die quickly after going through the awakening. Her dream of living forever fractured but she held it together. She wasn't going to become a statistic in the decline of Illia and the rise of Lycaon. She wanted to live and she was going to give it everything to make sure that she survived the fight.

"Do not fear," Julian whispered and Lauren looked up at him. His breath washed over her face, warm in the cold darkness. She wanted to see him. "I will not allow anything to happen to you, Lauren."

Lauren could have sworn that he had said something after that, under his breath, so low that she might have imagined it. She thought he'd said 'not this time'. Perhaps her imagination was running away with her. First the Greek god of the sea and now this. Why would Julian want to protect her and see her survive more than he had with the others? Unless he really was attracted to her and that wasn't her imagination playing tricks too.

Julian drew a long breath and then tensed.

"Are you bleeding?" There was an angry edge to his tone. "You were not bleeding earlier. If Duke hurt you, I will kill him."

That warmed her from head to toe, even though she knew it shouldn't. The thought that he would go that far to protect her brought a smile to her face. She had only scraped her knuckles when banging on the container wall.

"It's nothing, really. I just... I was trying to get out." She raised her hands and then lowered them when it struck her that it was pointless to try to show them to him.

"Let me make them better." Julian took hold of her hands as though he could see them and raised them again. She gasped when something warm and wet touched her. His breath fanned over her skin, chilling the damp spots. He was licking her hands. She wasn't sure whether to take them away or let him continue. His hold on her was gentle, careful, and it added to the growing warmth inside her. "We have the ability to assist healing with our saliva. It helps ensure the survival of those we take blood from."

It sounded like a handy ability. She went to take her hand back but his fingers tightened against hers.

When he pressed a kiss to each knuckle, she swallowed hard and stared into the darkness in his general direction.

He released her hands, pulled the blanket around her, and held her shoulders.

Lauren wasn't sure what to do or say. She feared that if she opened her mouth, she would say something that would give her heart away, and she still wasn't ready. She still had to see with her own eyes what feelings he had in his, what he held in his heart, before she could offer her own without fear.

She touched her knuckles.

But if he didn't like her, what was that all about?

CHAPTER 13

The French landscape reminded Lauren a lot of England, so much that she found it hard to convince herself that they really were in another country. She sat beside Julian in the back of a large sleek silver Maserati Quattroporte, Duke behind the wheel and Astra next to him in the passenger seat. When Duke had driven it out of the shipping container at the dock, she had been sure that the elegant executive sports car wouldn't fit them all in, but it had. She had never been in such an expensive car before and couldn't picture herself ever owning anything as flamboyant and showy. It was powerful, sensual, and very luxurious. It suited Duke perfectly.

She smiled to herself and glanced at him and Astra.

They were talking business. Something about having to visit the Ghost headquarters when they arrived in Paris.

Paris.

She hoped it had snowed and was as romantic as she remembered it.

Sneaking a glance at Julian, she flashed a brief smile and then stared back out of the window when she found him looking at her.

Piper, Kuga and Leo were following in the black van behind them. When they had piled in, giggling and fooling around, they had reminded Lauren of the Scooby Gang. She'd wanted to go with them, where it looked more fun and relaxing, but Duke had insisted that she accompany them instead.

Julian hadn't said a word to her since they had left the container. He hadn't touched her and the only times that he'd looked at her, his expression had been emotionless, half hidden behind the funnel neck of his coat.

She'd never felt so confused. There were times when she honestly believed that he felt something for her, that whatever was happening between them, it wasn't one sided. Other times, she was convinced that he felt nothing, that over the centuries he'd lost all feeling.

With a sigh, she ran her gaze over the scenery. The sun was rising, burnishing the sky with gold and pink. A thin mist rolled down into valleys. The bare trees rising out of them were pale purple in the morning light. A strange warmth settled inside her and she turned to look at Julian.

"It's beautiful," Lauren whispered.

His eyes met hers. He'd been watching her the whole time, as though the sunrise didn't exist, or at least wasn't as beautiful to him as she found it. He seemed more interested in her, and although she felt that she should turn away and watch the sun come up, to absorb a rare moment of beauty, she couldn't. Her eyes wouldn't leave his.

He'd captivated her again, hypnotised her without trying.

The sun cast warm light on his skin, darkening the blue in his eyes and highlighting the tousled finger-length strands of his black hair with pure gold. He slowly reached up and unclipped his coat collar, revealing his face. The sunrise seemed pale compared to his masculine beauty. She could live a lifetime without seeing another one, but she didn't want to live a moment in which she couldn't see him, in which she couldn't take in the blush curves of his lips, the straight edge of his jaw and the noble line of his nose.

He removed his coat and placed it around her shoulders, carefully arranging it. His hands grazed her neck several times, sending sweeps of tingles through her body, and eventually settled on the collar. His thumbs framed her jaw and he stared into her eyes.

"Do you think the sunrise is beautiful?" Her question sounded stupid, pointless, but she couldn't just sit there staring at him without a reason. While he seemed perfectly comfortable with it, it made her blush.

"No." That answer made her frown. He glanced out of the window. "I curse the sun."

"Why?" she said and in an effort to lighten his mood, added, "Are you afraid you'll go poof?"

That's what vampires did. She wondered if he knew that, and then wondered if her facts on that matter were even right. Julian seemed to know about vampires—real vampires—while she only knew what happened in books and movies. Real vampires were probably a lot different from their fictional counterparts.

Julian gave her a wry look. "No. I am... weak... in daylight."

He'd put a lot of effort into saying the word 'weak', so much that Lauren couldn't help probing further.

"How weak? Kitten weak?" She couldn't imagine that.

He glared at her. "Human weak."

The way he said it made her realise that he didn't relish the thought of being as weak as a mortal again. He looked down at his hands. There was pinkish scarring on the one he had injured. Her eyes widened. It had been daylight when he'd saved her from the werewolf's basement. He'd come for her even though he'd only been as strong as a human and he'd been hurt.

"I am sorry," she whispered, feeling the need to apologise again. She'd lost count of the number of times she'd told him now.

"And there is still nothing to be sorry for," he said and she managed to smile at him. He took hold of her shoulder and turned her around so she was facing the window. "Come. It is a long way to Paris and you did not sleep on the boat."

Lauren noticed that he didn't mention the container. She also felt his eyes leave her for a moment and knew that he was looking at Duke. She ran her fingers over her knuckles. Whatever Julian had done to them, they were healing fast.

When Julian pulled her back so she was leaning with her head against his chest, his arm around her front, she sighed. She could get used to this. The feel of him against her made all her fears disappear. Even though he'd said that he was weak right now, he was strong to her—something solid and constant in her new ever-changing world, and someone who comforted and made her feel loved even in the darkest and most frightening times.

It felt so good when he held her.

She wished he would never let go.

CHAPTER 14

The only person in the room who didn't laugh at what Leo had said was Astra. She sat to one side of the huge ornately furnished living room, away from the group, and hadn't moved or said a word since arriving at dusk.

Lauren had passed most of the day sleeping in her bedroom. After showering, she'd felt so emotionally and physically drained that she hadn't been able to stop herself from crashing on the bed. She'd drifted away to a replay of everything that had happened, from the moment she had unmasked Julian to the drive to Paris in Julian's arms. So much had happened in that short period that she felt as though someone had put her life in a blender and turned it on, or that she had been caught up in an insane action movie. It had been one emotionally charged moment after another, each leaving her increasingly tired and each a struggle to overcome. She had never felt so frightened.

Julian had woken her at one point and had apologised, saying that he had only come to check on her. He had stayed a while and she'd tried to stay awake but it had been impossible. Late afternoon, she had woken alone in her room and had gone out to investigate the new office. She had found Leo, Kuga and Piper in this room and had been with them ever since. When night had fallen, Julian had arrived and announced that he was going out to scout. Lauren had offered to go with him and he'd told her to stay with the group where she was safe. The amount of emphasis he had placed on the word 'safe' made his concern clear. He was worried she would disappear again. She had no intention of it now. She'd learned her lesson and wasn't going anywhere without him.

The only person she hadn't seen all day was Duke. The moment they had arrived, Duke had gone out again, explaining that he had to drive across the city to report to his superiors and gather intelligence on the werewolf situation in Paris.

Paris.

Lauren looked around her at the bright warm room, with its lavish white marble fireplace that was almost as tall as her and three plush cream couches that formed a semi-circle in front of it. Large old paintings hung from the walls, pictures of people and landscapes, all of which looked expensive and as though they belonged in an art gallery. She had never stayed in such a fancy place. The London office was bigger than this building, but this one had serious style. She wasn't sure which one she preferred—the modern décor of London, or the antique air of Paris.

She pulled her knees to her chest, wriggling her toes as Leo continued to recount a fight against a demon that could shift like the wind. Even though

Lauren was sure that the battle had been difficult, one of life and death for Leo, he told it in such a way that it sounded like a comic farce.

Piper laughed along with her, but Astra remained silent, sitting on the end of an empty couch in a demure way with her legs crossed. The front of her black dress had slid away to reveal a milky thigh. The air she emitted reminded Lauren of a babysitter. Astra obviously didn't want to be with them. Had it been Duke or Julian who had told her to remain close? Lauren wouldn't put it past Julian. The thought that he might have was a little insulting, but her heart reasoned that he was only trying to protect her, and she had to regain his trust. Piper leaned her head on Lauren's shoulder.

Lauren placed her arm around her. The contrast in their clothing made her feel old. Piper was wearing a vivid pink jumper and pale blue jeans. Lauren was dressed in a black turtleneck and dark blue jeans. Piper's clothes made her look bright and cheerful. Lauren's made her look dull. She made a mental note to see if she had anything a little younger looking in her backpack.

Kuga sat on the couch to their left with his brother, both of them dressed in their usual revealing black clothing. When Lauren looked over at him, Kuga was watching Piper with a tender look of concern. Every time she'd seen him since the incident in the basement, he'd looked that way around Piper. Lauren smiled at him. She'd heard from Julian that Kuga had been the one to kill the werewolf. When she'd told Piper, the young woman had blushed, denying any knowledge of it. It seemed that Kuga wasn't one to shout about his victories.

Leo leapt from the couch, re-enacting his fight, tugging at the spiked red tips of his hair as he talked about the demon throwing him around.

The two brothers were so different sometimes.

"Have you been to Paris before?" Lauren said to Piper, hoping that Leo wouldn't think it was rude of her to talk during his glorious battle with an invisible foe.

Piper nodded, reached over the back of the couch and took a can of soda off the long mahogany side table that lined the length of the couch. "Several times. We never stay here long though. It's usually quieter than London, but I like it there and I think the others do too. London feels like home."

Lauren smiled when Piper looked at her.

"Have you been to Paris before?" Piper said.

"Once, when I was around your age."

A wistful look filled Piper's eyes. "Was it a gay carefree summer where you fell in love with a young French boy... all romance and flowers... long lazy days?"

Lauren laughed. "No, it was a school trip... it was summer though, and there might have been a boy that I liked but he certainly didn't like me."

"At least that's not the case this time." Piper grinned. "Paris might just be the city of romance after all."

Had Piper heard anything of the sort in Julian's head? Lauren wanted to ask but remembered that Piper had promised to keep Julian's thoughts secret.

Love Immortal

What was he concealing behind his ice-blue eyes? She wished that he would let her back in, would stop confusing her and finally show her how he really felt. He was showing her more feeling though. Perhaps he was letting her in by degrees, slowly opening the barrier around his heart to her.

The door opened behind them and Lauren looked over the back of the couch. It was Duke. He looked around at them all, a weary edge to his expression, and then walked out again. Lauren looked at Astra. She didn't make a move to follow him.

Smiling in apology to Piper, Lauren stood and went after him. He'd disappeared. She looked both ways along the quiet pale blue corridor. There was no sign of him. Light shone in through the bank of windows on the left side of the hallway to her right. The bedrooms were that way and she had the feeling that Duke wouldn't have gone to his room. She went left, trailing her hand over the white dado-rail that lined the wall at hip-height, and stopped at the corner when she heard a door close. She followed the noise. There were stairs leading downwards at the end of the hall and a broad double mahogany door to her right just before them. She pressed her ear against the door. Something moved inside the room. She knocked.

Silence.

"Come in, Lauren." Duke's voice was dim through the doors.

She opened them, not questioning how he'd known it was her. It was an office, with a large black desk to her left and another grand marble fireplace to her right. The room was smaller than Duke's office in London but far more luxurious. She looked around at the ebony bookcase that stood to her left against the same wall as the doors, mirrored by another on the wall opposite her. Taking up most of the wall behind the desk to her left was a huge oil painting of a pastoral scene. The warm colours were either those of sunset or sunrise and, now that she knew him better, she knew without a doubt that this wasn't Duke's office. Piper had mentioned that they never stayed long in Paris. London was clearly their base of operations, and they were borrowing another Ghost team's base while here.

Opposite her, two tall white-framed windows revealed the courtyard, a long black couch below them. Lauren spotted Duke outside. She closed the doors, went across the room to French doors to the left of the windows and out of them. Duke stood on a wide walkway that ran around the inside of the building. A few terracotta pots lined the wall to her left. The plants in them were long dead, glittering with frost. It hadn't snowed in Paris yet, but the weather was bitter.

Warm light came up from the courtyard below her, the lanterns on the wall by the arched entrance illuminating Duke's silver sports car. It took up most of the courtyard along with a black car. Another Ghost team were sharing the building with them but she hadn't seen any of them yet. They were staying on the floor above.

"Is something wrong?" Lauren leaned against the curved white wrought-iron railings.

Duke sighed and turned to face her. It was strange to see him wearing a dark suit, especially when the light from his office was struggling to illuminate the courtyard. He faded into the night, only his hands and face clearly visible. She pulled the back of her black turtleneck jumper down, closing the gap between it and her jeans. It was cold out tonight, worse than it had been in London. She chafed her hands together and waited for Duke to answer.

"I was hoping that Julian would be back by now," he said.

So was she. He'd been gone for hours. It was unsettling her but she'd been trying not to think about it. Wherever he was, she was sure that he was alright, yet she couldn't help worrying about him.

"Did something bad happen?" Lauren moved closer to Duke and he tilted his head to face her.

A flash of anger crossed his face and then he covered it with a smile and a wave of his hand. "The upper lot can be a pain at times. They are refusing to get involved."

It wasn't a convincing answer. There was more to it than he was letting on.

"What does that mean for us?"

"We just continue as we have been." He rifled around in his jacket pocket, produced a packet of cigarettes and held them up, his eyebrows raised in a question.

"Go ahead," she said. Normally she hated it when people smoked around her, but Duke looked as though he could use a fix to soothe both the worry and anger so evident in his voice and eyes.

"To be honest, they have been like this since we teamed up with Julian. It's nothing to worry about."

Her eyebrows rose and she waited to see if he was going to elaborate. Duke took a long time and a lot of effort to get a cigarette out of the packet, more than necessary. If he wanted to avoid talking about it without raising her suspicions, he should have tried a little harder to act normal.

What had his superiors told him that he was hiding from her? It was clear that he wasn't going to tell her without Julian present, but she was still tempted to push him until she found out what was wrong. She thought about it and then relented, not wanting to pry. Julian would return soon and she would find out then. In the mean time, she could take Duke's mind off it and get some answers to the other questions crowding her mind. "Duke?"

"Hmm?" He lit the cigarette, the flame bright in the night, lighting his handsome face but doing nothing to chase away the underlying sense of darkness that always lingered around him.

"How did you meet Julian?"

Duke took a drag of his cigarette, slow and thoughtful. A thin stream of smoke curled from his lips and then he exhaled, blowing a cloud out in a sigh. He ran a hand over his dark hair, his look pensive, and then tilted his head back and stared at the stars. Lauren looked up at the clear sky above and then tracked down the height of the building. The top floor was dark but there were lights on the next floor up and she could see people moving around. The other Ghost squad. She wondered what their mission was.

"We found Julian five years ago." He frowned, forming lines between his eyebrows and at the corner of his intense brown eyes.

"Found?"

Duke smoked, his expression remaining pensive, saying nothing. The length of time it took him to answer unnerved Lauren. He was putting a lot of thought into his reply, so much that it could only be bad. The creeping feeling of anxiety increased until she was close to shaking an answer out of him. He dropped the spent cigarette to the floor, crushed it under the toe of his black leather shoes, and then lit another.

"We had been looking for you." His tone was low and cautious, each word carefully measured.

"For me? Why?" She'd presumed that Duke had only started looking for her after meeting Julian.

"We'd thought you were a myth… a bedtime story told to young werewolves to frighten them… we weren't sure if you really existed… then we met Lycaon." Duke's expression turned grim. He took another long drag of his cigarette and then rubbed his nose on the back of his hand. "That was before Kuga, Leo and Piper joined us. Ghosts always work in teams of five. Back then, we had three others, all strong and experienced."

"Let me guess, Lycaon killed them."

"Butchered." The force behind that word sent a chill through Lauren. Duke frowned at the cigarette, a distant look in his eyes. "He butchered them before we could escape. If Astra hadn't been there, I would have been dead too."

Lauren hadn't been frightened of meeting Lycaon but now she was. If he'd easily killed three experienced Ghost operatives, and had almost killed Duke, what chance did she stand? She was going to wind up like all of Illia's past incarnations.

Dead.

She pushed that thought away and focused on Julian.

"And you met Julian?"

Julian didn't seem like the type who worked with others. He'd mentioned a delay. Maybe that was his reason for hooking up with Duke and his team—so he could find her before it was too late.

Duke nodded and then smiled. There was no trace of happiness in it.

"We went looking for you. It took us years and eventually we gained Leo, and Kuga, and then Piper, and we continued to look for you, giving them time to mature into their powers."

Lauren frowned and studied Duke. He couldn't be older than forty-five, but he was talking about raising Kuga and Leo, and then Piper. The twins had mentioned that Duke had come for them when they were six, and that was seventeen years ago. Had Duke fought Lycaon that long ago? By her estimation, allowing for a few years between losing his team and gaining the twins as children, he couldn't have been older than his early twenties when he had fought Lycaon and lost his men. She couldn't imagine someone that age leading a Ghost squad.

"Five years ago, we tracked you... or at least your predecessor... to a nice spot in Greece," he said. The pause made her stomach tense. She moved closer to Duke, holding his dark gaze. Greece? Had the previous reincarnation died there? Is that where they had met Julian? "The only thing there was rubble."

She frowned. "But you met Julian? I really don't follow—"

"We found him there, Lauren, buried under that building." His words were quick, piercing, and his look turned dark and disturbed. She blinked, not quite able to take in what he'd said. Duke's hand claimed her shoulder, holding it tight. He was shaking. "The whole thing must have collapsed on top of the basement... we dug him out."

Ice shot across her skin. "You what? He was trapped there?"

Duke nodded slowly.

Lauren couldn't believe it. It was too horrible, too painful to think of Julian trapped beneath a building, shut away like that. Alone.

She stared at the windows opposite her. Some of them had their shutters closed, leaving them dark in the night. Light streamed out of others, highlighting the courtyard. She tried to grasp what Duke was telling her but it seemed so unreal.

"That's terrible," she whispered and then met Duke's gaze. "How long was he trapped?"

Duke cast his gaze downwards and to the side, avoiding her again. "Lauren, you have to understand that when we found him... he... he wasn't like he is now."

Not like he was now? She wished that Duke would just spit it out. Dancing around the subject was only making her feel sick.

"He was in terrible shape... starved, emaciated... weak. He could barely stand and was wary of us, of the world around him. We offered to bring him a doctor but he refused. Astra knew right away that he was an immortal and that he had been trapped for some time. We didn't know who he was though, not until he asked what year it was." Duke shakily lit another cigarette and Lauren was tempted to ask if she could have one too. She'd never smoked before, but now seemed a good time to start. She needed a fix of something to steady her nerves. "We told him... and he said that it had been thirty years, but there was still time."

Lauren gasped and grabbed Duke's jacket to steady herself. "Christ!"

Julian had spent thirty years trapped in a basement. He'd only referred to it as a delay. She couldn't imagine what kind of damage it must have done to him. Her blood chilled when she remembered the shipping container and how dark it had been in that cramped space. The tension in his voice. The way he'd held her. Had he been reassuring himself, trying to calm himself and allay his fears?

"You bastard!" Lauren hit Duke on the arm. "You shut him in the dark!"

Duke caught her hand when she tried to hit him again. "It was his decision. It always is. Do you think I like doing that to him? Be thankful that this time he had you with him!"

Lauren's breath caught in her throat. Julian had travelled like that before? Did he always travel that way? The thought of Julian alone in the darkness made her heart ache. No wonder his eyes held such pain sometimes.

"Back then, when Piper found him and we dug him out, he asked about you," Duke said.

"He did?"

Duke released her hand.

"He said that he needed to find you. He was worried that he would be too late, and that you would be alone and Lycaon would come for you." Duke exhaled smoke into the still night air. "He wouldn't rest. It took him weeks to regain his full strength, to grow used to the outside world again, but even then he was relentless... he thought only of finding and protecting you."

Lauren didn't know what to say.

"I can't imagine what thirty years of isolation would do to a man." Duke dropped the cigarette to the floor and stubbed it out with the toe of his shoe. This time he didn't light another one. "Most men would have taken their life. He had his sword with him, Lauren. The silver in it would have killed him if he had punctured his heart... he endured it for you, Lauren... so you wouldn't be alone."

The strength in Lauren's legs failed and she stumbled into the office, collapsing onto the black couch below the windows. Her mind felt numb, her entire body cold as she tried to come to terms with everything that Duke had told her. Julian had gone to such lengths in order to find her and protect her from Lycaon. He'd endured thirty years alone in the dark, trapped with no hope of escape, so he could find her and so she wouldn't be alone. Tears filled her eyes. They were hot as they cascaded down her cheeks in a steady stream. She didn't cry. Julian wouldn't want her to cry for him. Instead, she let them flow freely and unrestrained as she thought about the horror Julian had been through for her, and his dedication to his duty. But more than that, she thought about how incredible he was, how beautiful what he'd done was, and how much she wanted to fight for him, so his nightmare wouldn't have been for nothing.

He deserved that.

She would do all in her power to take away his pain and suffering.

She would fight for him. Not only to defeat Lycaon, but also to be with him, so he would never be alone again.

CHAPTER 15

Julian stood on the edge of a building, eyes scanning the dark city streets far below, looking for a sign of demonic activity. The Eiffel Tower glittered in the distance, tall above the rooftops. Beyond it to the left was a bright spot marking the church of Sacré Coeur. The cold evening breeze blew against him. It was quiet tonight but that did nothing to quell his growing agitation.

The city stretching before him was dark and wretched, a hole unfit for human inhabitation, a festering pit of depravity and filth.

A desire to take Lauren away burned deep in his heart. He didn't want her here in this nefarious place. She belonged somewhere safer, somewhere clean and nice, somewhere far removed from here.

He knew there were werewolves here, hiding among the other things, living in an underworld that he would destroy if given the chance. He would cleanse this city one day. Purge all of the filth from it.

His lip curled in disgust.

He despised Paris.

A man passed by forty feet below, hands crammed in his jacket pockets and shoulders hunched as he hurried along the narrow alley. Julian's stomach tightened. His fangs itched. He dropped to the ground, landed silently behind the man, and grabbed him. He clamped one hand over the man's mouth and pulled the man's jacket collar aside with the other. Before the man could struggle, Julian bit down on his neck. He needed to feed and keep his strength up for Lauren. He had to protect her.

The blood was rich and warm, almost intoxicating as it slid down his throat. Its warmth spread through him, making him want to groan in pleasure. It had been too long since he'd fed like this, deep and without fear of a werewolf using his distraction to attack him. It felt good, revitalising him in a way that he needed. This city sucked the life out of him.

The man weakened. Julian stopped drinking and licked all trace of blood from the man's throat. The puncture marks would be nothing more than a series of scabs by the time the man woke and he wouldn't remember what had happened. Julian laid him down in the shadows and pulled his jacket closed to keep him warm. The man was a fool for being out in the small hours of morning anyway. It would teach him to be more careful in such a dangerous city. Others here wouldn't have spared his life.

Julian walked out into the wide open square. In the centre stood the Arc de Triomphe, unlit now that all of the tourists had gone to bed and the nightclubs had closed. Some cars still circled it, heading to destinations unknown and uncared about by Julian. He dashed across the road and then leapt up the monument, using statues and other decorative stonework as handholds.

Reaching the top, he turned and breathed out slowly. It did feel good to have some living blood in his veins again.

The wind whipped the tails of his coat around his legs. He stared out at the city and the distant Eiffel Tower. A city of romance. His eyes narrowed. A city of death.

Paris was rotten to the core, and he hated it with all his heart. He hated it and the predators that lurked in its shadows.

His eyes rose to the moon.

Selene.

"Guide your daughter's hand," he whispered, his hand resting on the hilt of his sword. He closed his eyes and his fingers trembled against his sword as the memory of waking in the pitch-black container assaulted him, shaking him to his core. Only Lauren's presence had kept him sane, had given him something other than the consuming darkness to focus on, and had given him a reason to endure the pain it brought him. He opened his eyes and stared at the moon again, tired of the weakness in his heart and the inescapable fear his imprisonment had created there. He swallowed and grasped his sword, determined to face his fears and become strong again, for Lauren. "Give me strength."

A scream punctured the night.

His senses sharpened.

Werewolves.

CHAPTER 16

Lauren looked through the two windows at the courtyard of the building. The sun was rising and Julian hadn't returned. She had spent the past thirty minutes pacing Duke's office, waiting for Julian with the others. Duke hadn't said anything since asking the others whether Julian was back.

Worry ate away at Lauren. She wanted, no, needed to see Julian. After Duke's revelation about how the Ghosts had met him, she needed to see him and do something to let him know that she was there for him. She didn't know what that was yet, but something would come to her. She had to show him that she would always be here with him, and that they were going to win this time. It didn't matter that the odds were probably stacked against her. They would defeat Lycaon.

She turned and paced back towards the windows. Kuga smiled at her from his seat on the couch beside Piper. Leo sat on the arm by the French doors. Piper sat Indian style between them. She smiled at Lauren too. Lauren tried to smile back at them but couldn't manage it. She turned, glancing at Astra where she stood the other side of the French doors by the bookcase, and then at Duke where he was leaning against the ebony desk in front of the oil painting.

The heavy double doors to Duke's office opened and Julian walked in. Lauren turned on the spot and was moving across the room the moment she saw the blood on his face.

"Julian," she whispered, her heart in her throat. A long gash marked his cheek, a thinner lighter one just below it. Her brow furrowed. When she reached him, she touched just below the cut and searched his eyes. "What happened?"

"Werewolves," he said and placed his hand over hers. She instantly felt more relaxed but her stomach didn't settle. If anything, the turbulent ache there grew worse.

Julian unclipped the two silver bands that held his coat collar closed and her eyes widened when it fell open. A deep bruise marked his jaw. She wanted to check him over, to make sure that the werewolves hadn't given him any more injuries, but everyone was watching her.

Including Julian.

There was an enormous amount of worry in his eyes and it unsettled her. He hadn't shown any emotion so strongly and clearly as he was right now. His hand closed around hers, holding it, and he looked over her head at Duke.

"My superiors are refusing to help," Duke said. Nothing new to Lauren, but everyone else in the room began to speak at once. Lauren could feel a sliver of their panic. It rippled through her. Her stomach twisted again.

"I feared that it would be this way." Julian lowered her hand but didn't relinquish it. "I slew three werewolves tonight."

Lauren moved to stand beside Julian so she could see Duke. He wore the same pensive and anxious look that he'd had when talking to her earlier. Her gaze shifted to Astra. She looked as concerned as Duke did.

"Is that bad?" Lauren said.

"It is very bad." Astra came to stand next to Duke. "Werewolves normally hunt alone. They are acting in packs, and packs have an alpha."

"A leader?" Lauren said. "Lycaon?"

"There is more." Julian's voice was calm but Lauren could sense that he was far from relaxed. "They lured me into a trap, used a female werewolf and pretended that she was a human under attack."

The room fell silent.

Leo announced what was clearly on everyone's mind. "Shit. They have to know that we're in Paris."

"How?" Piper looked worried. Kuga placed his hand on her shoulder, rubbing it and giving her a smile when she glanced up at him.

"I don't know." Duke frowned. He leaned against the desk and crossed his legs, staring at his shoes. "Perhaps he has an ally or it was pure luck or his senses have improved. It could be any number of reasons."

Lauren felt uneasy. Her stomach turned again, sending a twinge of pain through her chest. She rubbed it and looked at Julian.

"We are safe here. It is alright. There are other operatives in the building and I would sense Lycaon if he was close," Julian said.

Her insides flipped again. This time, her vision swam with them. Her hand went to her head and she told herself that she was pathetic for letting the stress get to her like this. She'd never been great at handling worry, but she hadn't been this bad before.

"What are we going to do about—" The world rushed past Lauren and suddenly she was staring at the ceiling.

"Lauren?" Julian appeared in view above her. She could feel his arms around her. He must have caught her.

She tried to stand but pain ripped through her, so intense that she doubled up and cried out. A sudden weakness washed over her and her chest felt empty. She couldn't breathe. It took all the energy she had to look at Julian. He lifted her, cradling her close.

"We are out of time." His expression was deadly serious.

Panic sent her heart beating erratically and made it harder to breathe. She tried to pull air into her lungs but they wheezed and she found she didn't have the strength no matter how hard she tried.

"Not... my... birthday... yet." Lauren forced the words out, desperate to convince herself that he was mistaken and she wasn't dying.

"What are you going to do?" The voice was distant and distorted. She couldn't tell who it was. All she could focus on was Julian and the fear in his eyes.

It changed to a look of resolve.

His arms tightened against her.

"I will not let you die," he whispered and, in a flash, they were in a different room.

Her room, she realised as he set her down on the bed. She was cold. She tried to pull the deep mauve coloured blankets around herself but Julian stopped her.

"Listen to me, Lauren," he said close to her ear and she nodded drowsily, barely able to move. "Do not be frightened. I will bring you back and you will be stronger than ever, I promise."

With that, he bit into his wrist. She trembled as she watched the blood break to the surface, beading there in great drops. It was death or life, and she chose life.

He brought his wrist to her mouth and she closed her lips around it, drinking deeply. It was hard to keep the blood down. She wanted to gag, but she kept swallowing, even when Julian took his wrist away. He moved close to her, his arm around her back supporting her.

A dark film covered her eyes. No matter how many times she managed to blink, it wouldn't go away. It only grew worse, until she couldn't make out anything other than Julian's beautiful face, looking down at her with such tender concern.

Her body felt slack and cold. She clung to Julian's arms but soon she didn't have the strength left in her hands to hold him. She tried to hold on, desperately fought the encroaching darkness, fearing what was on the other side, but it was relentless.

So this was what dying felt like.

She was too young to die.

"Don't... leave... me," Lauren whispered the words between slow shallow breaths. Her eyes sought Julian's. The darkness shrouded him too now. She could barely make out his face. "Stay... with me. I'm... scared."

He took hold of her hand. His was so warm against hers, so strong. Tears rolled down her cheeks.

"I will never leave you," he said and a flicker of warmth filled her.

That warmth turned to crippling pain. It hurt so much. She hadn't expected it to hurt this much.

"It will be over soon," he whispered and held her closer, pressing his cheek to her hair.

"Tired." She didn't have the energy left to speak anymore. Her breaths were too short, spaced out. She couldn't feel her hands or her legs. Her heart faltered.

Julian stroked her hair. "Go to sleep. When you wake, you will be fine and I will be here waiting."

Lauren closed her eyes.

CHAPTER 17

Julian held Lauren gently, watching her peaceful face. He stroked her deep red hair from her eyes and listened to her heart give its final beat. When she was silent, cold stole through him and fear swept up from below, engulfing his body. Compelled to hold her, he pulled Lauren close, pressing his cheek against hers, and closed his eyes.

It would be long hours before she awoke, reborn in her true form, and until then he could only wait and pray that she was strong enough. His blood could only fuel the change. Whether she survived the process was down to her and the Fates. He could do nothing to help her.

Twice she'd died shortly after the awakening, her body unable to cope with the change. Other times the Fates stopped her from crossing over.

He prayed that wouldn't happen to Lauren. She was strong but this time there was a complication that set his nerves on edge. The awakening had started early. It had never happened before and he wasn't sure what it meant. It was still over two weeks to her birthday. Was her early awakening significant or merely the result of the stress she'd been under and the threat of Lycaon?

It was times like these that he wished the gods would speak to him and answer his prayers. They had been silent since he'd crossed over, never coming to him. Only Selene would offer words to his heart through their connection, and even that was a rare occasion.

For a moment, he wondered if Selene had been the one to tell Lycaon of their movements and then discounted it. Selene had learned her lesson and had promised to protect her daughter and himself. He doubted that she would inform Lycaon of anything now.

Sitting back, Julian looked down at Lauren. Her skin held the ashen hue of death. He told himself that she would wake again. The sun was rising. When night fell, she would awaken and he would feed her. Everything would be alright. Lauren was strong—far stronger than she believed herself to be.

He lifted her up, one arm behind her back and the other under her legs, and carried her around the end of the bed to the large window. He placed her down on the long padded seat that lined the window alcove. When he was sure she was comfortable, he turned back to the bed and pulled the dark mauve covers across to reveal the white sheets beneath. He turned back to Lauren, picked her up, and lay her down on the bed. He removed her trainers and her thick zip-up turtleneck jumper, and then covered her. His eyes remained fixed on her face as he tucked her in so she would be warm when she woke.

The sun shone into the room through the tall window behind him, lighting the pale lilac walls and the door opposite him. Julian opened the window and closed the white wooden shutters, descending the room into darkness, and then turned on the lamp beside the bed. He rounded the foot of the bed, went to the door and locked it, and then returned to Lauren. She'd been more scared than usual. It had torn at him, making him feel weak and helpless. When she was dying, he could never soothe her or take away her pain, but for once, he'd wished that he could.

He'd wanted to stop her suffering. He couldn't bear to see it.

Julian looked at the window seat and then at the hard wicker chair in front of the antique dressing table in the right corner by the bathroom door, and then at the elegant white wrought-iron double bed to his left where Lauren lay under the dark mauve covers. He hesitated for a moment and then removed his coat, sword and boots.

He sat down on the right side of the bed and then lay beside her on top of the covers.

Waiting.

He would wait forever if it took that long.

He would never break a promise that he'd made to Lauren.

When she woke, he would be here, even though she wouldn't remember anything he'd told her, not at first.

Not until her instinct to live had released her.

Julian closed his eyes. The minutes passed slowly, the sands of time trickling down to gradually form an hour and then two. He lost track of time as he waited, monitoring Lauren with his senses, searching for a minute sign that she was awakening. The sun drifted overhead and then sank towards the horizon. Each heartbeat was loud in his chest. Every breath was drawn for her sake.

Just as he grew tired, something sparked in Lauren.

Julian pushed himself up and moved her so she was sitting leaned against the pillows of the bed. He knelt beside her, watching, waiting for her to give a stronger sign.

Her heart faltered and then began to beat. She gasped and shot forwards. Julian grabbed her as she thrashed around and whispered soothing words to her, reiterating his promise a thousand times over. She calmed down when he managed to move closer to her and her hands went to his black shirt, gathering fistfuls of it and pulling hard.

His heart leapt when she turned towards him and curled up. Her lips parted to reveal little white fangs. The sight of them warmed him and an intense sense of connection to her broke over him. He'd never experienced such a strong reaction to her before but he liked it—he liked how close he felt to her.

He moved her in his arms, keeping her close but needing her to be able to reach his wrist. Her side pressed against his, her knees drawn to her chest. She clung to him and he held her tighter. A smile curved his lips when she mumbled something and then fell asleep again.

He couldn't let her sleep, no matter how much she wanted to. Time was a critical factor right now. She needed blood to give her the strength to continue with the change and to bring her mind back.

"Lauren," he whispered and jostled her.

Her nose wrinkled and she moaned. She tried to burrow her face into his chest but he stopped her by taking hold of her cheek and drawing her away. He unbuttoned his shirtsleeve and offered his wrist. She rolled her eyes open a fraction, looked at it, and then hid her face against his chest.

He needed her to feed as soon as possible but he couldn't help savouring the feel of her against him and the fact that she was seeking comfort from him. He rubbed her back, continuing to whisper to her, and then tried again with his wrist.

He could sense her hunger. Why wouldn't she bite him?

He bit his wrist and offered it again. She sniffed and poked her head out a little. Julian supported her back and moved his wrist towards her, encouraging her to drink. She was still wary. He was used to this sort of behaviour from her when she first woke. Her movements were weak and instinctual, but she would soon regain her strength if he could make her drink. The blood ran down his bare arm. Her eyes were unfocused at first but they tracked the rivulet and then her pupils narrowed.

Her mouth opened. The sight of her small canines sent a jolt through him, as strong as the one he'd felt in the alley when her eyes had first met his. He watched with bated breath, waiting to see if she would drink now. Her eyes melted into silver. Tentatively, she leaned forwards and he brought his arm to her. The tip of her tongue poked out and she licked the trail of blood off his arm. A moment of hesitation and then she wrapped her mouth around the wound on his wrist and began drinking.

She drank deep, filling the room with hungry noises. Her hands came up and she grasped his arm, pulling hard on his blood. There was something deeply sensual about her suckling and the brush of her lips against his flesh. It filled him with hunger, passion. Affected him so much that his own teeth elongated against his will, drawn out of him by the sight and feel of her.

Her quiet mewls of supplication made his body harden. It called out for her touch. None of her predecessors had ever affected him like this, making him burn and hunger, dizzy with lust and need.

Julian wanted her to drink forever—to take all of him into her body so they could be one at last, him and Lauren. He ached to be inside her. The force of emotion she stirred in him was consuming, driving him out of his mind with a need to act.

Lauren deepened her feeding but he didn't care. It didn't matter if she weakened him dramatically. He would give her whatever she needed, would do whatever it took to help her awaken, even if she drained him near to death. He lived for her. Not just because it was his duty, at least not this time. Lauren was different. He believed in the feelings her eyes held for him. He believed in the feelings that she'd awoken in him.

Her teeth scraped his wrist but she didn't bite down. Instead, she lapped the wound, stroking his skin in a way that fanned the fire in his veins.

Julian tilted his head, closed his eyes and focused on her lips against his skin and her firm grip. His teeth sunk into his lower lip. Intense heat spread through him, radiating from the point where her mouth was against him. It had never been like this before. Never. It felt so good—so right—and he couldn't ignore the need pounding through his body.

He dipped his head towards her. Just as his forehead was close to touching her hair, she stopped feeding, pulled back and looked at him. Her eyes were wide, still distant and glassy. Instinct was driving her just as it always did when she awakened. She had so much to learn that it took over, suppressing her mind until she was ready and could control herself. It would be days before her consciousness resurfaced. That thought alone stopped him from acting on his feelings. She wasn't aware of what she was doing, of how she was making him feel. Until she was, he had to control himself.

His gaze fell to her lips. They were bright red and a single drop of blood ran down her chin from the corner of them. He wiped it away with his thumb and then licked his wrist to seal it. Lauren watched everything he did with interest and then looked up at him again. She was still pale. Her red lips were a stark contrast against her milky skin. She licked them.

Julian held the groan inside. It was hard enough to control himself when she wasn't doing things like that. When she did, it felt like torture. He'd already been aroused. Now he was close to bursting. Something about the sight of her fangs and her eagerness for his blood drove him crazy with desire.

Shutting down his emotions, he concentrated on Lauren. She would need feeding again soon, and that meant that he needed more blood.

He lay Lauren back down in the bed and covered her. She yawned, the sight of her tiny fangs sending another jolt through him, and curled up. When she had fallen asleep, he tucked her in and then put his boots on. He grabbed his coat but left his sword on the window seat. He wouldn't need it tonight.

Julian left the room, locking the door behind him. He walked along the pale blue hall, heading for Duke's office. Heartbeats sounded above him along with indistinct voices. The other Ghost team. He continued on, blocking them out, and turned a corner. The windows to his right allowed light to flood the corridor. Night. The cold, clear and crisp scent that crept in through gaps in the windows was refreshing and comforting. He always had enjoyed the smell of a winter's night.

His focus sharpened when he sensed someone in the corridor with him and then he relaxed when Astra fell into step beside him.

"How is the little princess?" Astra looked down as he tugged on his shirtsleeve to cover the new marks and her eyes narrowed. "Alive then. Is she well?"

Julian nodded, distracted by the marks. He brushed his thumb over them, the warm feeling her feeding had stirred still lingering inside him. They were his, but he'd made them for her, so they felt as though they were hers. He stared at them, using his senses to guide him around the building, and only covered his wrist when he finally reached Duke's office. He opened the double doors and walked straight in. Astra followed him.

Duke sat to his left behind the black desk. He looked up from his laptop and leaned back in the leather chair. The fire crackled in the grate, filling Julian's senses with the scent of burning wood and stealing the sense of connection he'd had to the night. He looked at the two windows opposite him. The night called to him to hunt.

"Everything well?" Duke said and Julian dragged his gaze away from the windows. Duke intimated the black chairs on the other side of the desk.

Julian declined the offer with a shake of his head.

The amount of concern in Duke's eyes surprised Julian. He'd thought that Piper, Kuga and Leo would grow close to Lauren, but hadn't anticipated that Duke would also come to care for her. He looked at the windows again. It was still hours until sunrise. Julian put his coat on and buttoned it.

"Lauren has come around and has fed." Julian tried not to think about how it had felt to have her feed from him. Just the thought of it made his blood burn and he didn't want Duke or Astra to see how deeply Lauren affected him. "She will take a few days to recover and then I will begin her training. Until then, I cannot leave her long. I must feed her constantly until her body has adjusted."

"Then you will also need to feed." Duke glanced at the windows. "We will protect her while you are gone."

Julian nodded his thanks.

"Or you could feed here." Astra touched her neck, a wide smile on her lips. Duke glared at her. Julian shook his head. Her smile became a frown.

"Dead blood is no use to me," Julian said.

Astra turned away and stared out of the windows. Duke's angry look melted away. Julian didn't know what game they were playing with each other, but it was as strange as Kuga and Piper's.

Seeing that neither were going to say anything and feeling out of place, Julian stepped back and left the room, closing the door behind him. He strode down the stairs to the ground floor, intent on his mission.

He would hunt and feed, and he would do it quickly.

He didn't want Lauren to wake without him.

He'd promised that he would be there for her, and he didn't intend to break that vow.

Not when she'd placed her trust in him.

CHAPTER 18

Julian stopped in front of Lauren's door. She would need to feed again soon. It had only taken him thirty minutes to hunt, but her feeds were always close together at this stage. When he grabbed the door handle, a barrage of feelings hit him.

Fear.
Panic.
A fast heartbeat.
Rapid breathing.
Lauren.

Julian unlocked the door and flung it open.

Something crunched beneath his boot. He looked down at the broken bedside lamp at his feet and then at the room. Someone had turned it over. The beat of his heart matched the frightened one that filled his mind.

"Lauren." He searched the debris for her and his gaze stopped on the dark corner to his right. Lauren was there, curled up beside the dressing table and trembling, her t-shirt and jeans ripped to shreds. He clenched his fists and cursed. It was obvious what had happened. She'd awoken without him and had panicked. He'd failed her.

Julian removed his coat and rolled his sleeve up. He looked at his scarred wrist. Blood. She needed to feed. It would calm and reassure her.

When he approached her, she looked up through the tangled strands of her red hair and snarled at him, exposing fangs. The feral look in her eyes and her defensive actions didn't scare him. She didn't know what she was doing. Instinct was forcing her to protect herself. Her fear was affecting her senses so she saw everyone as an enemy. If he remained calm, his scent would eventually reach through that fear and she would recognise him.

Lauren glared up at him through silver eyes, her little claws digging into her knees. She breathed hard, her heart still beating fast. As much as he wanted to reach out to her, he had to keep still and give her a chance to realise who he was. Holding her now wouldn't comfort her. It would only frighten her more.

Lauren's eyes darkened and narrowed.

She sprung at him and Julian let her take him down, wrapping his arms around her so he was sure that she would land on top. He didn't want her to hurt herself.

The air burst from his lungs when his back slammed into the floor. Small but firm hands pinned his shoulders. His eyes met hers. Was she back there behind those silver eyes, trapped by new feelings she didn't understand? That was how he'd felt during his awakening.

"I should not have left you for so long," he whispered, wanting to soothe her. He reached up and swept the hair that had fallen across her right cheek behind her ear. She bore her fangs at him and he stopped what he was doing in case it was scaring her.

Her knees tightened against his sides and she leaned over him, pushing more weight down onto his shoulders.

Her face came close to his, her eyes on his lips. They sparkled with interest. Julian swallowed hard when her soft lips parted and her breath fanned his mouth. Was she going to kiss him? That thought tightened his chest. His own lips parted in ridiculous anticipation. Lauren breathed in deep and her eyelids fell to half-mast.

Blood.

She could smell it on him.

Julian stiffened when she dipped her head and brushed her lips over his, tasting him. It was hard not to respond when everything in him cried out to. This was his chance. This tentative delicious sweep of her lips over his could easily become a kiss.

But Lauren wasn't in control. Her instincts were and they would make her do anything for blood.

Finding his strength, Julian placed his palm against her cheek. She closed her eyes when she leaned into his hand, turning her face towards it, and gave no warning. Her fangs sunk deep into his wrist. Her lips closed against his flesh. A thin dark line escaped the corner of her mouth and coursed down his arm.

Tremors of pleasure cascaded through him. He tipped his chin up and pressed the back of his head hard into the floor. It had never been like this before. None of her predecessors had stirred such feeling in him. Only Lauren gave him such painful pleasure, filled him with a burning desire to bite her in return and brought him to the very brink of ecstasy.

His body became fiercely aware of hers—the press of her knees into his side, the feel of her left hand against his shoulder and the fingers of her right around his forearm. The point where the apex of her thighs hovered above his. He ached and tightened with each pull on his blood, each caress of her tongue against his skin, until it became too much. His fists trembled with his fight for restraint.

With a gasping sigh, Lauren released his wrist and then licked it. She was learning. She must have picked up the way to seal the cut when he'd done it earlier. His eyes widened when she promptly settled her head on his chest. Her heart beat steady and strong against his. He closed his eyes for a moment and absorbed the feel of her body pressed into his, warm and soft, comforting. She was so different.

Julian placed his arms around her, holding her. She rubbed her face against him before tilting her head back. He craned his neck and looked down at her.

Love Immortal

This wasn't exactly a comfortable place for her to fall asleep. Being her bed had a strange appeal about it, but she would get cold sleeping out in the open.

Carefully moving her, he managed to get her into his arms and got to his feet. She burrowed into him, hiding her face against his chest. Her fingers closed around his shirt, holding him. No claws. The blood must have satisfied her instincts.

The room was a mess. He couldn't allow her to sleep here, not until he'd fixed it up again. He thought about taking her to one of the spare rooms and then thought the better of it. His room was the best choice. It was close to the others and his scent would make it familiar to her even when it wasn't.

He carried her up the hall to his room, trying not to wake her when he opened the door and then nudged it closed behind him with his foot. Lauren immediately sat up in his arms. She pushed against him and he put her down. He moved to the wooden bedside table on his right and turned on the lamp. At first, she just stood in one spot, staring at his room. The layout was different to hers. The dark wood double bed was to his right, against the same wall as the door. The white shutters were closed over the three windows opposite him, giving him some privacy from the courtyard. A dark brown couch below them left a narrow corridor between it and the foot of his bed. The bathroom door was white, bright in the low light, and far to their right beyond the bed.

Lauren took a few steps forwards and stopped. She looked at his bed and then at the couch.

His eyebrows rose when she picked up the black shirt draped over the arm of the couch, sniffed it, and then began to strip. He tried to avert his gaze but couldn't when she turned around and pulled her t-shirt off, revealing delicious curves and creamy skin. His body responded in an instant, hard against his trousers. Lauren bent over and pushed her jeans down her long legs, her luscious bottom round and firm in her pale blue knickers. His heartbeat accelerated. He told himself to turn away, that it was wrong to take advantage of her like this, but it was impossible. He stood transfixed by her and the desires that surged through him.

Confusion replaced that desire when she sniffed his shirt again, slipped her arms into it and started to fasten it over her chest.

"I have clean shirts," he said and took one out of the antique wooden dresser on his left. When he tried to hand it to her, she shied away and bared her fangs.

She pulled his worn shirt closer around her and closed her eyes, pressing her nose to the fabric and inhaling deeply. The smile that touched her lips stilled his heart. His scent. She wanted his scent on her. His insides warmed to melting. She crossed the room to his bed, crawled up to the pillows and curled up on it with the shirt still held to her nose.

A moment later, she frowned and emerged, and sniffed her way across the deep brown covers.

Julian was fascinated when she found the spot where he had slept, smiled, moved things around to make a nest, and settled down. He couldn't believe the way that she was acting, how she wanted to smell him even while she slept. Maybe she did like him. Maybe the feelings he'd seen in her weren't just his imagination.

"I must go and speak with Duke," he said, wanting to get her room fixed.

Lauren shot up into a sitting position, her eyes round.

Perhaps leaving her wasn't an option. He could send a message to Piper about the room. She would be listening for a report on Lauren. He'd been shutting her out so far but he could feel her probing, trying to hear his thoughts.

Julian sat down sideways on the bed beside Lauren so her head was near his knee, her legs tucked up behind his backside.

She took hold of his hand in both of hers and held it close to her chest. With his other hand, he stroked her cheek, trying to soothe her. He didn't understand everything that was happening, but he wasn't going to think too hard about things yet. Right now, he was going to stay here and enjoy this glimmer of need and affection that Lauren was showing him. This wasn't her new instincts. This was her old ones shining through.

"Sleep," he whispered and she curled up closer to him, so her hair brushed his legs. "I will be here when you wake this time."

CHAPTER 19

Lauren drifted along the corridor, following Julian's scent. Hunt. He'd mentioned hunting. She wanted to hunt too. There was pain in her stomach. Her teeth itched. Hunt meant blood. He'd told her that. Blood. She wanted blood too. Blood would make the pain go away.

Strange noises came and went, nothing more than a buzz in her head, unimportant. She floated along, her mind dazed and thick, heavy. Everything was numb and distant. Empty save for the gnawing in her stomach. Blood. Julian had gone to hunt. She wanted to hunt.

Two broad wooden panels blocked her way. She frowned at them, trying to recall what she'd done to the other one that had tried to stop her from getting to Julian.

Drawing her hand back, she rammed it forwards, sending one of the wooden panels flying off the little metal things that held it to the flat coloured part that she'd been following to find Julian. It landed near something bright and flickering in a box, which hissed and cracked at her. She bore her fangs at it.

Something warm and rich assaulted her senses. Blood.

She followed the smell inside. A room. Julian had told her to stay in the room. That was what he'd called it. And then he'd gone to hunt. She'd felt lonely. Hungry. But now there was blood. She could smell it. Someone had blood. She edged around the wooden panel on the floor, her eyes on the flickering thing in the box. It was emitting heat and her instincts said to keep away from it.

A heartbeat filled her ears.

She turned and looked in the direction it was coming from.

A man stood opposite her. His eyes raked down her and paused on her legs. She frowned and looked down at her bare legs and feet, and then at the material she wore that covered her from the hips up. A shirt. Julian had called it a shirt and had said he had clean ones. She didn't want a clean one. She liked his smell. His smell was warm and safe.

This man smelt wrong. He smelt dark and evil.

He smelt of death.

"Lauren?" His voice was dull in her ears.

Lauren? Julian had called her that. She nodded and blinked. She was Lauren. Did this man know her?

His blood smelt bad but she was so very tired after all the walking and she was hungry.

"Are you alright?" the man said. How could such a warm nice face have such bad blood? He smiled at her and looked at the wooden panel on the floor. "Don't worry about the door. I'll get someone to fix it."

She frowned, not understanding.

"The door?" He pointed at the panel.

Lauren looked at it. Door. She looked back at the man. Blood.

He held his hands out to her and she frowned at the death marks on his palms. A murderer. She instinctively stepped back. Images flashed through her mind, distorted and vague. She remembered those marks. She knew this man.

"Julian?" she said, hoping the man knew where he was.

He opened what looked like two very tall windows but reminded her of the wooden panels that she'd broken to reach this far. Doors.

Julian hadn't told her their name. He'd mentioned windows, and glass, and not to touch those things in case she hurt herself as she had in her room. Her room. It had been dark in there, and there had been no Julian. His scent had gone cold and she'd panicked when there had been no blood. The glass of the lamp had cut her hands. Then there had been blood but it had tasted stale. Nothing like Julian's blood. His was warm and intoxicating.

This man's was bad.

But she was so very hungry.

The man left the room. Lauren followed a few paces behind and edged out onto the walkway, keeping her distance from the man. The moon felt nice on her skin. Comforting. She raised her face to it and smiled.

"He went out for a while," the man said and she looked at him. He gave her a smile that Lauren didn't like. There was too much feeling in it. Julian had looked at her like that, and she'd liked it, but when this man did it, she wanted to kill him. "Do you need something?"

Lauren looked around. "Julian."

Yes. She needed Julian. Julian had blood. She wanted blood. Her gaze slid back to the man. He had blood too and the hunger was twisting her insides so much it hurt. She could have his blood. It might make the pain go away.

The man stepped towards her. She stood her ground.

"Are you hungry?" he whispered in a low seductive tone, his eyes sparkling with a promise that he could satisfy her needs.

Her eyes roamed down to his bare neck. The open collar of his shirt exposed it beautifully. The feel of her fangs extending further turned her stomach. It rumbled at the thought of blood. This man was so warm. He smelt rich and tempting but poisonous too.

"Julian might be a while." The man touched his neck, trailing fingertips over it. Her tongue ached to mimic that action. Her fangs itched with the desire to tear into his flesh. "If you are hungry... I would never refuse a lady."

Lauren licked her lips when the man stepped towards her, her eyes still fixed on his throat. She was so incredibly hungry. A sip would be enough. Only a sip. And he was offering so freely. His blood couldn't be that bad.

She reached out with both hands, intent on taking what she wanted.
A sudden shiver bolted down her spine.
She straightened, alert.

CHAPTER 20

Julian dropped from the roof and landed between Lauren and Duke. He turned on Duke, growling at him and baring his fangs as he offered his neck to Lauren, and pushed Lauren backwards away from him. Anger rippled through Julian, a desire to put Duke in his place, and he struggled to stop himself from ripping Duke to shreds. Whispered words of violence filled his mind, urging him on. Duke deserved pain as payment for what he had intended to make Lauren do. He couldn't allow it to go unchecked.

Lauren touched his arm and he found control, managing to tamp his feelings down. Her hand was warm and light on his arm, but it trembled. He had frightened her again, and fighting Duke would only scare her more. As much as he wanted to unleash his fury on Duke, he had to put Lauren first. It was his duty to look after her. No. It was so much more than duty.

He turned to Lauren, horrified that she'd left her room when she was barely conscious and hardly dressed. Fear clenched his heart and replaced his anger, worry that she might have been hurt. What had she been thinking? He removed his coat and placed it around her shoulders, gathering it closed so it covered her completely, dragging on the floor.

Her silver gaze slid to his wrist.

She grabbed it, yanked his shirtsleeve back and bit down hard. He flinched. Blood. She'd been hungry. Had she been looking for him? He'd told her to stay in the room where she would be safe. Perhaps he'd been gone longer than he'd thought and she'd panicked again.

His eyes slid across to Duke. Duke's gaze was fixed on Lauren. Julian could sense his intent.

"If you ever try to make her drink from you again... I will not hesitate," he said and Duke's attention fell to Julian's sword.

Julian gathered Lauren into his arms. She mewled when he took his wrist away and tried to get hold of it again. He wrapped his coat around her and picked her up, cradling her close. He glared at Duke before walking into the building.

Lauren wriggled in his arms.

"Wait," Julian said but she paid him no heed.

She turned her head away, twisting her body, and bit the arm he had behind her back. He could sense how deep her hunger for his blood ran and it rekindled the embers of his own desire. He needed her more than anything, but right now, she was off limits. He had to hold on until she had fully awoken and was conscious of her actions.

When they reached his room, he placed her down on his bed and took his wrist away. The loss of skin contact with her left him empty and aching to have her back against him.

Lauren sat on the deep brown bedcovers looking up at him, her large dark eyes showing an emotion that he hadn't expected.

Not fear. It looked like guilt.

"You should have stayed in the room," he said, testing his theory. She lowered her head. Her fingers traced invisible patterns on the dark bedclothes. Strands of hair fell down across her face. How could he be angry with her when she was already showing awareness? She was progressing far quicker than the others had done. Soon she would surface and her instincts would recede. She would regain control.

Then he would know her true feelings.

CHAPTER 21

Lauren woke with a frown and stared at the ceiling. The bright bedside lamp cast strange shadows across it. She reached a hand up and toyed with the strands of her hair that spread across the pillow. The sun was up. The shutters across the three windows blocked the light out, but she could feel it deep inside her, just as she felt the moon. She ignored it and listened to Julian's soft breathing as he slumbered beside her.

Her heart was still beating.

It felt as though she hadn't died and hadn't come back as an immortal. She didn't feel any different. Only the jumbled memories of the past few days made her believe that it had happened. Julian had given her blood. She had awoken. She was immortal.

Lauren turned her head to one side. Julian lay on his back on top of the deep brown covers, his black shirt half undone and his trousers riding up around his shins. He looked so tired and pale. She focused on him and smiled when she felt his fatigue. It was fascinating to be able to sense such things.

His lips parted and his brow relaxed. The black strands of his hair caressed his forehead in tousled waves, stark against his skin. She studied the subtleties of his face—the soft line of his cheekbones, his strong jaw, and straight nose. He was so handsome. More like a god than a mere immortal, and definitely beyond human. The only thing missing was his stunning pale blue eyes. She was tempted to wake him just to have him look at her, to be able to see those eyes and see if she could read anything in them. She could stare into them for eternity.

Eternity.

It was incredible to think that she now held that within her grasp. Julian had brought her back and given her eternity in which to live if she could defeat Lycaon. If. She still didn't feel strong enough. A part of her had expected to feel invincible when she regained her abilities, but she still felt weak and human.

She quietly left the bed, walked around it and went into the bathroom. She turned the light on, flinching as it reflected off the bright white tiles, and then closed the door so she didn't disturb Julian. She'd put him through so much since the night he'd first given her blood.

He'd given her so much, but she knew that if she'd needed more, he would have given her that too.

She stripped off Julian's shirt and held it a moment. His scent was comforting—a smell like a cold winter's night, crisp and metallic, but strong too. She couldn't tell what she smelt like. She remembered her encounter with

Duke. He'd smelt like death, and she'd known what his tattoos meant. He'd taken lives. Many of them.

Lauren removed her underwear, stepped into the cubicle and turned the shower on. The hot water felt good but it didn't satisfy the feeling inside her. It was strange—a mixture of need and emptiness. It didn't feel like hunger. That feeling had been one of pain. This was something else.

When she was done, she shut the shower off and dried. She stopped in front of the large gilt framed oval mirror and wiped the white towel across it to clear the image of her. She didn't look any different. Perhaps a little tired.

Lauren thought about blood.

Her eyes instantly turned silver and her vision sharpened. She gasped and then tensed when her teeth extended and altered. Every muscle in her tightened and her senses were instantly stronger. It hadn't hurt but she hadn't been expecting such a sudden change. She opened her mouth and prodded one of her canines. Her fangs were smaller than Julian's were but just as sharp.

Julian.

She could hear him breathing in the other room, loud in her ears, and could hear his heart beating. It felt as though it was beating in her chest, in her veins, and he was a part of her. She could smell his scent and almost taste his blood. He tasted so good. The memory of biting him warmed her skin in the places they had been against each other, until she could close her eyes and it was as though he was there with her. The feel of his hard body against hers had made her crave to be skin-on-skin with him, to have his hands moulded over her bare flesh, satisfying the deep hunger he stirred within her. It had been so long since she'd been close to a man, and no one had ever set her aflame as Julian did. He'd liked it when she'd pinned him to the floor. As mortifying as it had been to be a slave to her instincts, she'd enjoyed it too. It had been freeing and she had realised that she could take what she wanted, that she had the strength to seize the moment.

She licked her lips.

His had felt so good beneath hers. His breath had been so warm, trembling against her mouth. A part of her, even when her instincts were in control, had wanted to kiss him, and she knew he'd been close to kissing her.

When she'd touched her lips to his, she'd sensed his resistance, and she'd wanted to scream.

But then he'd been so sweet and kind that she'd felt satisfied in a different way. The way he'd looked after her had melted her heart and soothed her instincts.

She opened the door, looked at Julian where he lay sleeping on his bed and then back at herself in the mirror.

Her eyes were brown again. Her teeth normal. She smiled at the thought of Julian wanting to kiss her, wrapped the towel around herself and walked out into the bedroom. Some of her clothes were folded neatly on the brown couch.

Julian had thought of everything. She dressed quickly in the dark blue jeans and deep green turtleneck jumper and then walked over to him. The gnawing ache in her chest chased her own tiredness away. Now that she was up, and back in control, she wanted to stay awake. She glanced at the bedroom door. Julian needed his sleep. She would go for a little walk and come back before he woke. Lowering her hand, she carefully cleared the hair from his eyes and hesitated a moment before placing a chaste kiss to his lips. A thrill raced through her. She hoped that his dreams were good, and that she was in them.

Yawning, Lauren left the room, padding barefoot down the pale blue corridor. The dark blue carpet felt rough beneath her feet. All of her senses were sharper now, especially her vision, making her more aware of everything. The low light in the wide hall was tolerable but the small lamp in Julian's room had hurt her eyes. Would she adjust to her new senses? If light was always going to be this painful, she didn't ever want to go out in the sun.

The feeling inside her grew worse as she followed the corridor around a corner, gnawing at her stomach and her heart. Something said that she should return to the bedroom where it was safe but she walked on, aimlessly wandering. Bright sunlight streamed in through the windows to her right. She squinted at the courtyard and then covered her eyes, hurrying on.

A noise.

Lauren frowned, trying to focus on it, but while she'd been awake a moment ago, she now only felt half-aware of her surroundings. She followed the noise. It was coming from a set of white double doors to her left. She opened them and peered inside.

The lounge. The shutters on the four tall windows either side of the fireplace were open, allowing dazzling light to flood the already bright cream room. She squinted and raised her hand to shield her eyes. Someone had mounted a large flat-panel television above the white marble fireplace. The three plush cream couches formed a semi-circle around it and the low coffee table. On the long thin antique mahogany table behind the couch directly in front of the coffee table was an assortment of food and drink, empty wrappers, books and magazines. The place was a mess, and looked nothing like it had done the other night.

Someone was watching her.

Leo and Kuga were on the couch in front of her, both of them looking over the back of it. Tight black turtlenecks moulded to their muscled frames as they leaned against a couch in a way that made them look like a mirror image of each other. She looked at them, waiting to see if they were going to say anything to her. She wasn't sure how the others would react to her now that she had changed. She hoped things would continue the same as they had been before.

Kuga pressed a button on the black game controller in his hand and the sound died. Leo stared at her. A triangle of toast dangled from his mouth. They both sat there in silence, frozen with their eyes wide.

"Morning Lauren." Kuga stood at last, the game controller still in his hand, and looked past her and then back at her.

"Where's your shadow?" Leo said, resting an arm on the back of the couch, his toast now in his hand.

Lauren looked at her feet and then behind her at the floor. Shadow? It was right there where it had always been, stretching out into the corridor at her back.

"He means Julian. Ignore him, Lauren," Kuga said with a smile in his voice and a warm, welcoming expression. He ran his hand over the pointed red tips of his brown hair and then around the back of his neck. He motioned to the couch. "Will you join us? It's been a while since we've seen you."

Lauren blinked.

Nodded.

Leo shuffled across to make room for her. She walked around the couch and then sank down into the soft padded seat. Kuga sat to her left, completing the sandwich. He swung his heavy army boots up onto the antique coffee table between them and the television. They were both so close to her that she felt tiny, their broad frames taking up most of the couch either side of her. She pulled her shoulders in and settled her hands in her lap, making herself smaller. She wasn't sure what to say. It had been a long time since she'd used her voice. It felt as though it didn't work, and the buzz in her mind and the weird feeling in her chest made it hard to think.

"Wanna play?" Leo offered his game controller.

Lauren frowned at it and then at the television. Did she? Frozen in time on the screen were two soldiers with raised guns. A third man in front of them had his head blown open, blood spraying out. Blood.

She was suddenly aware of the hard steady beat of Kuga and Leo's hearts, and the hot pulsing rush of their blood. She took a deep breath and her eyebrows rose. Kuga and Leo smelt slightly different to each other. Kuga's scent was warmer, richer, and Leo's had more of a sharp edge to it. Both of them smelt strong and instinct told her their blood would easily satisfy the quiet hunger growing inside her.

Clamping her mouth shut as her teeth extended, Lauren fought for control over her instincts. The room brightened and she closed her eyes against the onslaught. She heard Kuga move, tracked his progress around the room, and listened as he opened each window to close the shutters.

"Is that better? Julian told us that you would be sensitive to light for a while." He sat back down beside her.

Julian. A voice deep inside said to return to him, to his room, where she was safe.

She told herself that she was safe here.

Lauren opened her eyes a fraction and snatched the controller from Leo. Her hands trembled as she struggled to calm herself and then her fangs slowly receded. Her vision dulled again and she looked around. Kuga had shut the sun out. Lamps lit the room now, soothing to her eyes. She thanked him with a smile.

He gave her a look that said it was no big deal and then picked up his controller from the arm of the couch.

"I warn you, he's damn good," Leo said with a wide grin and devoured another piece of toast.

Kuga smiled. "Shall we? It's head to head. Highest number of kills wins."

"Highest number of kills wins," Lauren echoed, glad that her voice was working.

Kuga started the game again and she watched his hands as he executed his first kill, following the motion he made with the small left joystick and which buttons he pressed on the right to fire. As the sound of battle reached her ears, she looked around at the screen and her senses sharpened. Her eyes darted about as she followed each enemy that appeared, watching Kuga kill them, and her hands moved of their own accord. She shot one of the men in the head, blowing it open. Something stirred inside her and she couldn't believe the speed of her reflexes as she killed one man after another.

The enemy moved in slow motion through the shattered buildings in front of her character, but her movements seemed quicker than normal. She shot another, and then another, growing dimly aware of Leo watching her. Her character moved forwards through the terrain of rubble and fallen walls. It moved as slowly as the enemy did, but she was getting faster on the buttons. She killed a man the moment he stepped out from behind a wall and then another before he'd even made it out all of the way. The sound of her kills racking up was like music to her ears, driving her on, and she focused on the screen, fascinated by how fast she was.

And then she started killing the men the second they appeared.

Kuga threw his hands up into the air and slouched back into the couch, his fingers still against his controller. "Incredible."

He said it with such force and awe that Lauren smiled. She impressed herself too. It was incredible.

Someone entered, pricking her senses, but she continued. It wasn't Julian. The smell of death and cigarettes was all over him. Duke.

"How is the little goddess today?" he said and she heard him lean against the door.

Lauren killed another two men the moment they appeared and pushed on, determined to see how far she could go.

"Fucking amazing," Leo responded and turned sideways on the couch beside her. "Have you seen what she's doing?"

There was awe in his voice too. She went to smile but the feeling in her chest grew worse and made her frown instead.

The dead tally on the screen hit treble figures. She wanted to keep going, was fascinated by how she could anticipate her enemy's movements, but she couldn't shake the weary, hollow tiredness inside her.

Love Immortal

Someone else entered the room. She felt their presence as a tripping of tingles up her spine and the hairs on the back of her neck rose.

Julian.

"What is going on here?" he said in a deep voice that held all of the weariness she was feeling.

"Lauren is amazing," Kuga said.

Julian's hands settled on her shoulders. "I asked Lauren."

Lauren paused the game and tilted her head back. He was upside down in her vision and stern, framed by the old paintings that lined the walls. There was no mistaking the disappointment and anger in his eyes. She furrowed her brow and tried to think of what she could say to make those feelings go away.

"I couldn't sleep," she whispered.

His look shifted, concern surfacing in his beautiful eyes. His black shirt was ruffled and half-undone. He hadn't changed before coming to find her. "You should have woken me."

"I didn't want to disturb you." Lauren toyed with the small joystick on the controller.

"You worried me." Those three words fell like lead on her chest, dragging her heart down into her stomach. His eyes showed all his anxiety, glittered with it.

She lowered her gaze away from his, unable to bear to see the hurt she'd caused. "I'm sorry. I was only here. I didn't go far."

"You went far enough." His tone was stern again, sharp edged and leaving her in no doubt of the anger that laced his worry for her.

"It wasn't far—"

"It was dangerous." His hands tightened against her shoulders. She fancied that they trembled a little but wasn't sure. "I told you not to go out of the room under any circumstance."

She tensed, anger coiling inside her at his controlling and commanding words. For a brief second, she wanted to turn on him and ask him what gave him the right to tell her what to do, to try to control her. The feeling passed when she saw the worry in his expression. He'd only wanted to keep her safe, just like last time. And just like that time, she'd gone against him and placed herself in danger. Only this time, she wasn't sure there was any danger.

Or was there?

Julian had threatened Duke more than once. It was clear that he didn't fully trust him. Did he doubt Kuga and Leo too?

Did he really not trust anyone where she was concerned?

"Cut her some slack, big man." Leo was treading on thin ice talking to Julian like that right now but Lauren appreciated the back up.

Julian glared at him and then his face softened when he looked back at her, right into her eyes.

"You are vulnerable in the hours of daylight," he said in a low voice and his thumbs brushed her neck, his hands firm against her shoulders. "Do you feel that?"

She did. She felt tired and weak, and her mind was foggy. Was this the reason why? Julian had mentioned that daylight made him weak. Was this how he felt too? As though something was gnawing at his insides and a voice kept telling him to find somewhere safe.

Only for him, there was worry too. She'd thought she was doing him a favour by letting him sleep, and instead she'd worried him. Her insides felt heavy. Her eyes darted between his, trying to read them. She wanted to apologise, wondered if he could feel that she did, would be able to sense it in her. He squeezed her shoulders.

"Do I have to go back?" She'd been enjoying the game and she would be safe now Julian was here with her. He didn't have his sword with him, but she knew he could protect her without it. She wanted to keep playing. If her responses were this fast during the day, what would they be like at night?

Julian dragged a hand over his face and she could see his fatigue. He pushed his hand back, fingers combing through the black strands of his hair, tousling it more than sleep had. He looked at the television and then at her.

"What are you playing?" he said with a softer look, all trace of anger gone from his eyes.

"Some war game," she said.

Julian looked at Leo. She heard him move to the other couch and then Julian sat beside her. There was a gap between them that Lauren wished didn't exist. He was sitting further from her than Leo had been. The space made her feel cold and made doubt creep back in. Now that she was almost back to normal, would Julian return to how he'd been before? Would he hide his emotions again and distance himself? Was he going to shut her out?

She shook the doubts away and focused on him, savouring his scent and the way she could feel a glimmer of his emotions. Even if he hid them behind his eyes, he couldn't hide them from her new senses.

"Show me what these men found so amazing," he said.

Lauren smiled at him, pushed the fatigue to the back of her mind and started to play the game again. She was slower at first, but then her senses sharpened and everything moved in slow motion while she moved faster. The dead tally kept rising. It was so easy.

When the figure on the television reached over two hundred, the thrumming of the four heartbeats in the room became impossible to ignore. The rich scent of Julian's blood overshadowed the tempting fragrance of Kuga, Leo and Duke's. She could taste it on her tongue. The memory of it sent trembles of pleasure through her and a sudden hunger twisted her stomach. She licked her lips, unable to concentrate on the game any longer. Enemy bullets tore her character to shreds. Blood covered the screen.

As if sensing her need, Julian raised the hand nearest her and turned his bare wrist upwards. Her gaze slid to it, to the deep pink marks of her fangs on his pale skin. Intense need rumbled through her. In a flash, she dropped the controller, grabbed his wrist and sunk her teeth into his flesh. A wave of bliss rocked her as the blood touched her tongue. Her eyes slipped shut and she slumped against Julian, boneless and sated as she fed.

The taste of blood no longer disturbed her. In fact, she craved the metallic tang and the buzz it gave her.

"That has to hurt." Kuga's comment sounded distant but she was aware of him.

She was aware of all of them watching her, but she didn't care, not when it felt so good.

"Julian doesn't seem to mind… looks like it's nice." Leo this time.

Lauren frowned at what he'd said.

She shifted away from Julian, not relinquishing his wrist, and looked at him out of the corner of her eye. He had his eyes closed, his teeth firmly pressed into his lower lip, his nostrils flared and his eyebrows tightly knitted together. It wasn't pain making him look that way. His eyes opened and fixed on her. Hunger filled their icy depths—visible passion that made her blush.

He did enjoy it. He liked it when she bit him. What did it feel like? A flicker of a thought chased through her mind and her blush deepened.

She wanted Julian to bite her too.

CHAPTER 22

Julian rubbed his thumb over the most recent set of marks on his arm. The hot water pounded down on his back, easing tired muscles but doing little to wake him. Daylight always made him tired, but while Lauren insisted on remaining awake, he couldn't give in to his need for sleep.

His thumb grazed the marks again. Each sweep sent a tremor through him, an echo of what it had felt like to have Lauren bite him. He had lost all awareness, even when he'd tried to retain his focus in case something happened while Lauren was feeding. It had frightened him to realise just how deeply Lauren affected him.

And it had made him think.

That thinking had brought him to this point, shut in the bathroom under the pretence of taking a shower but in reality needing some time apart from Lauren. He'd traced the progression of his feelings back to when he'd first met her but had found no point at which he'd dropped his guard. He had protected himself against her the moment he'd realised that she was different and that he was in danger of having his heart broken again.

Perhaps even then it had been too late. Maybe she had already worked her way into his heart. She had disarmed him with her shy glances and pretty blushes, with the way she smiled at him, her beautiful face lighting up with each one. Each one had seen her step a little closer, until she'd passed his defences and snatched his fragmented heart.

Now she held it in her hands. Now she had power over him as the others once had. With a single word or action, she could shatter him.

He buried his face in his hands, clawed his hair back, and dug his fingertips into his scalp. How could he be so weak and foolish? How could he believe even for a second that Lauren might love him? She could never love him. No one loved him.

No one but her.

And she was long gone. History itself had forgotten her, so why couldn't he?

She had cursed him to this life.

No, perhaps she had believed that she would be the same when she came back. Perhaps she hadn't realised how different she would be each time.

And how she would never love him again.

His hands shook against his scalp. He trembled on the precipice that Lauren had built him up to, pushing him ever onwards. It was still a long way down. Immortality wouldn't save him if he fell. It hadn't helped last time. It had only turned a quick death into a long painful torture.

He couldn't face that again.

But he couldn't push her away. If he did, she would take what little heart he had left, what spark of life she had ignited in him. He needed her too much. She was his life now. His precious Lauren. If he pushed her away, he would be dead again.

Since she had unmasked him on the rooftop, he had changed by degrees, convincing himself that she liked him. Duke hadn't helped, giving him a speech about Lauren and her feelings, making him believe that she could grow to love him. That she needed him and wanted to be close to him.

Her own behaviour had backed up Duke's theory, forcing Julian to face his own feelings and to discover the depth of them. It frightened him. The moment in the living room had been his breaking point. If he allowed things to continue unchecked, he faced an eternity of pain and misery stronger than he had endured before. He had to guard his feelings now before it was too late. He had to obey his orders, reinstating his sense of duty and his loyalty, not continue to push against them. He couldn't bend them anymore. They would break and so would he.

But he wouldn't push her away. No. He would distance himself again and guard his heart until he was certain of her feelings.

The water turned cold against his back.

Three thousand years of existence, of facing insurmountable odds and death, and he was scared of facing a woman.

But then death was a release from a painful existence. What Lauren could do to him would torture him for another three thousand years.

Lauren believed she wasn't strong enough and thought that he was. A mirthless laugh escaped Julian's lips. Strong? He'd never felt so weak. He had fought his heart, his feelings, and failed. He wasn't strong enough to overcome his love for Lauren. His heart had defeated him. He needed her. She was his weakness. Not Illia. For Lauren, he would do anything. If she ordered him to, he would leap from the precipice.

He would cut out his own heart and offer it to her.

"Julian?" Her voice was soft through the door, temptation personified. He shut the shower off and focused on her. She was worried.

Stepping out of the cubicle, Julian walked naked to the closed door and studied it. He could feel her on the other side, leaning against it. He placed his hand against the white wood, exactly where hers was on the other side. If only he were brave enough to take her hand like this, to hold it as he had before and let her see what she did to him. Would she understand the things that he'd been through? He'd hidden his pain from the others but each of them had contributed to it. Each of them had shattered his heart a little more. Illia had broken it in two. The next had smashed each of those two pieces into two again. And so it had continued. Each time she was reborn, the broken pieces of his heart doubled. Could Lauren piece it together? Would she do that only to break it all over again?

All he could do now was hold on until he could no longer bear it, until he could find the words and strength to make her understand what he had been through because of her, and until he was certain that she loved him.

"Julian?" she whispered.

Could she sense him standing here, so close but so far away?

Without a word, he stepped back from the door and turned around. He picked up a small white towel and rubbed his hair with it. The finger-length black strands turned fluffy. He ran a hand over them, tousling them back into long spikes that criss-crossed his forehead and stroked his neck. His reflection in the gilt framed oval mirror mocked him. Lauren wouldn't love him. She would take his heart and toss it into the abyss at his feet. She would make him follow it. She would never love him. No one did.

Julian cursed under his breath.

He would sooner face three hundred werewolves than such a moment.

He stared into his eyes, seeing himself as a commander, the soldier he'd once been. His fear of what a woman could do to him was shameful.

He reminded himself that it was a long time since he'd been human but the events that had occurred then had echoed in eternity with him. His love for Illia had paved the way for his eternal torture and this fear. It was painful enough without him allowing Lauren to make it worse. When you lived for forever, there was no such thing as taking chances and seizing the day. There was no definite end to the hurt if Lauren turned on him, if she didn't love him. He would carry that pain for centuries. It would be the end of him.

Julian drew a deep breath, wrapped the small towel around his waist, and stared at himself for a few seconds longer. He was stronger than this and he would overcome his fears. He would see if Lauren's feelings were real and weren't a figment of his imagination. He would test her and then he would make a decision about what to do.

Until then, he would keep the gates to his heart firmly closed. She might hold it in her hands, but she was still on the outside. Only he could let her in.

He opened the bathroom door and frowned when she wasn't standing there. She was sitting on edge of the bed facing him, her hands grasping the dark brown covers either side of her thighs. Her gaze immediately fixed on his face, and then steadily dropped to his bare torso. Her pupils dilated. Her cheeks turned crimson.

Aware of his almost nude state, Julian walked around the room, careful to make sure that her gaze was following him. He slowly gathered his clothes from the brown couch beneath the shuttered windows and made a fuss about cleaning lint off his coat whilst facing towards her. The way her gaze roamed shamelessly over his body made him burn but he didn't let his feelings touch the surface. She would be able to sense if she was affecting him, and, right now, he wanted to see if he affected her without his own feelings colouring her behaviour.

Julian's gaze shifted to her and her feet were suddenly fascinating. She stared at them, her face burning up, and wriggled on his bed. The smell of arousal was undeniable—a scent that he savoured because of the clear way it indicated her feelings. Did she want him? He could feel her heat, could sense her hunger and her desire. Did her feelings go beyond lust? Had he really not imagined the tenderness in her eyes sometimes and the warmth?

"Will I lose it again?" Lauren said and he frowned, trying to figure out what she was talking about. Slowly, her gaze came back to him. At first, it stayed fixed on his face but as he moved and pretended to take his attention away from her, it strayed down to his body. "I can remember the things I did."

Julian turned to face her and her eyes widened but didn't move away from his stomach. A few inches lower and he might have been convinced that she really did want him.

"I saw myself doing those things."

She was talking about the moment in her room when she'd pounced on him. Her hand came up and her fingers brushed her lips. An ache settled firmly in his chest, a dull throb echoing in his groin. He remembered it too. How could he forget the tempting sweep of her lips over his and the way her body had pressed against his?

Clearing his throat, he turned away, needing a moment to regain his composure so she didn't see exactly how much that moment had turned him on. If she'd been aware of it, then she would have been aware of his reaction, and possibly more.

He'd been so close to kissing her, to shattering the rules and taking the leap.

"You should retain control now." Part of him wished that she wouldn't. She was looking at him with such fierce hunger, the smell of it on her. He drew the fragrant scent deep into his lungs and savoured it again. His eyes slipped shut and then he opened them and turned to face her. "Are you hungry?"

She absently nodded, her eyes on his body, and then they widened as though she'd thought that he was talking about another kind of hunger. Had he been? The scent of it was all over her, a palpable need that echoed within him. He could so effortlessly give in and case both of her hungers—the one for blood and the one for sex. It had been a long time since he had been mortal and had been with a woman, but it wasn't something the body or mind forgot. Modern times had a quaint phrase for it. Like riding a bicycle. He couldn't ride a bicycle, but he could ride her.

He grimaced internally at his own thoughts and the disgusting manner of them. Three thousand years of being immortal and he still slipped back on his base mortal way of thinking when it came to sex.

Julian sat beside her on the bed, careful not to expose himself, and offered his wrist to her. She stared at it. Perhaps she really had been talking about another kind of hunger. She touched the marks on his arm, scorching his flesh with her fingertips and sending tingling heat chasing over his skin. He clenched his teeth and watched her fingers trail over his skin. Gods, her hands on him felt so good.

Something glittered in her eyes and then she looked up at him and snatched her hand back. "I can find my own blood."

Those words shook him. He grabbed her shoulders and stared into her eyes, trying to read them and hoping it was only guilt making her speak like this.

"No," he said, a little harsher than he'd wanted. His grip on her arms tightened. "I will not allow that."

"Why not?" she whispered and looked down at his hands. Strands of her short red hair fell forwards to obscure part of her face and he was tempted to brush them back behind her ears, was tempted to tell her exactly how beautiful she was and how the thought of her taking blood from another made him feel ill.

"I will not let you taint your mind by hunting humans."

Her head snapped up. Her eyes met his. Pure shock filled them. Her body trembled beneath his hands and her heart beat fast in his mind, a drumming that matched his own.

"Do you always insist on feeding me yourself?" The question was as probing as her eyes as they searched his.

He had no answer for her. Her look softened and he could see she'd found one for herself.

He didn't. He was protecting her in ways that he hadn't protected the others.

"You need living blood to survive, but I will feed and then feed you." The calm manner in which he spoke those words surprised him. For a moment, he'd been sure that his feelings would show in his tone.

Need and desire battled sense and duty in his heart. She couldn't always feed from him. It just wouldn't be possible. He would make it possible. He would remain always close to her, near so she would be able to feed whenever she desired. It would be his blood alone that sustained her. The thought of her touching another in such an intimate way choked him. He'd been close to tearing Duke's head off when he'd caught the man trying to lure Lauren into feeding from him. He couldn't bear the thought of her drinking from another.

"Will that work?" Lauren raised her head enough that her hair fell away from her face, revealing her beauty to him.

Julian stared deep into her dark eyes, captivated and lost in them. He nodded as absently as she'd done, having only half-heard the question. She could have asked him anything and his answer would have been the same. Her fingers closed around his wrist and he watched in quiet awe as she brought his hand away from her arm and then back towards her. She caressed the recent marks with her thumb, just as he'd done in the shower, and stared at them. When she was touching him, her feelings were clearer on his senses. He could catch a glimmer of them, and they were warm and delicious, comforting and quietening his soul, chasing away the fear that had settled in his heart.

Lauren lowered her head and did something that made his heart miss a beat. She kissed his wrist. He was convinced that he'd imagined it until she did it again, pressing a soft kiss to each mark that she'd made.

"I don't want to hurt you," she whispered against his skin, her warm breath teasing the sensitive flesh and sending tingles cascading up his arm.

Her words stole his voice so all he could do was look at her, trying to take in that she'd really said that she didn't want to hurt him and that he really wasn't imagining everything that was happening between them.

"It doesn't hurt." He wanted to place his hand over hers, to hold it against his skin and tell her to never let him go, to confess that he was falling for her and how delicate the object she held in her hands was. He wasn't strong. Not when it came to her. He drew a slow shuddering breath when she rested her cheek against his wrist and closed her eyes. It was too delicious, too divine. He wanted to tell her everything. He wanted to break all the rules. "I will feed you and you will get the blood that you need. It will be stronger because it is infused with your own blood."

How could he sit here and talk about such mundane things when she was touching him like this? It was all he could do to keep himself sane and stop himself from taking hold of her cheek, raising her eyes to his, and kissing her. The desire to have her lips against his pushed all sense from his mind. He didn't care about his orders. He took hold of her hand, trembled on the brink of going through with it, and then placed her hand in her lap and stood, distancing himself.

He couldn't go through with it. He still wasn't ready or sure that she understood. Until he found the strength to tell her what he'd been through, to confess things about his past that he'd hidden from her for millennia, then he couldn't act on his desires.

She had to know what she was getting into, what power she had over him, and how fragile his heart was. Her vision of him as a pillar of strength was nothing more than a cleverly constructed façade to protect himself. It wasn't strength. It was emptiness, a hollow desire to do his duty, all so he could avoid growing close to her again. All so the pain would continue to fade away.

Only she'd brought him back to life, had reignited the fire in him and restored his true sense of duty. With it, she'd brought back the pain, but this time it was new, and different, just like her.

He took his clothes from the couch and walked into the bathroom. When he reached the door, he looked back at her, found her watching him with the same confused look she wore each time he shut her out.

Only this time, her eyes reflected the pain he felt inside.

"We will begin your training immediately," he said and her face fell, all of the brightness disappearing.

He turned away, closed the door and leaned his back against it. He could feel her on the other side, waiting, watching, and hurting. There was no doubt that she felt something for him, and that his constant change of emotions was only causing her pain. He didn't want to hurt her, but he couldn't take it if she hurt him.

The precipice beneath his feet began to crumble.

He had to tell her.

As weak as he would make himself appear in her eyes, he had to tell her before they both wound up falling.

CHAPTER 23

The long curved blade caught the warm overhead lights and gleamed as Lauren tilted it towards her. Her eyes travelled over the length of the katana, studying the subtle shape and fine craftsmanship that had gone into its creation. Red and black threads covered the hilt, forming an intricate diamond pattern as they crossed over each other. A wavy line danced along the blade, defining the sharper edge. It wasn't a replica. Some of the men in her kendo class studied other Japanese martial arts and had katana. None of them had looked like this. This was old, real, and beautiful.

Julian walked in, closing the white double doors of the large ballroom behind him. The only furniture in the room were a few antique chairs that lined the pale yellow walls at intervals and the side table in front of her. Large elaborately framed mirrors hung between each tall window, almost spanning the gap between the floor and the high ceiling. Three faux-candle chandeliers hung in a row above her, evenly spaced so their warm light filled the whole room. She liked the glow they lent the ballroom as they reflected off the mirrors and the highly polished wooden floor. The light was low enough that it didn't hurt her eyes. Either that or she was growing used to her new abilities and senses.

It was four days into her training and she finally felt as though she was accustomed to herself. At first, she hadn't realised how different she was now, but Julian had soon begun to reveal the extent of the change that had happened during her awakening.

She was stronger, and more agile, and was faster. Julian had explained that there were two sides to her increased reaction time. She was quicker, but she also saw everything in more frames per second than a human did. Because of that, she could slow down her perception of things. She didn't have a clue how it worked, but it was amazing. She was amazing. And she'd never felt more alive.

Her years of kendo practice had given her a grounding in combat, enough to impress Julian. She'd been able to fight him right from the start, unafraid of attacking with a wooden katana.

Lauren ran the flat of her hand along Julian's katana, fascinated by how perfectly balanced and crafted it was.

Julian had told her that there was real silver worked into it and that it was toxic to them and werewolves. A deep wound made by a silver blade would take her weeks to heal. It would kill a young werewolf. They were more vulnerable to it than her or Julian.

Julian's reflection appeared in the silver blade.

She'd never felt closer to him either.

There had been moments with him that had infuriated her, where he'd given her tight-lipped smiles and hidden all of his feelings, but there had also been times that gave her a slender thread of hope to hold on to. Sometimes she caught him looking at her with a strange fire in his blue eyes, and sometimes his guard slipped. Yesterday she'd failed to block and his wooden katana had hit her across the right side of her head. He'd dropped the weapon in an instant and come to her. His fussing had felt like more than just guilt or normal friendly concern. There had been so much affection in his eyes. She was making progress. She only wished it were faster. At the moment, it felt like the old two steps forward and one back.

Lauren stared at him in the silver blade.

She remembered what Duke had told her. If this blade penetrated Julian's heart, it would kill him. That thought turned her stomach. Sometimes it was easy to forget that Julian wasn't without his vulnerabilities.

She shifted the blade and her own reflection appeared. It could kill her too. Lycaon had a silver sword. Every one of her predecessors had fallen to it. Lauren moved the blade across to her left and the intricately engraved Japanese characters that covered it near the guard broke her reflection.

"It's beautiful," she whispered, surprised that Julian was allowing her to continue her appraisal of his weapon. Until now, he'd kept it away from her, and she'd been scared that he would be angry if he found her holding it, but he didn't seem to mind.

She touched the cold metal, her fingertips tracing the characters.

"Where did you get it?" She looked at Julian.

His hair was wet, hanging in strands that framed his forehead. A flash of him in the small wisp of towel the other day filled her mind and she struggled to stop the blush that threatened to burn her cheeks. He had an incredible body, far more beautiful than any of the men in the club or any she'd seen period. It had been a constant fight to stop herself from just taking hold of him and seeing what his reaction would be. He'd been so tempting, especially when he'd sat next to her. When she'd kissed the marks she'd made on his wrist, she'd felt him trembling, felt the shift in his feelings, but then he'd changed on her again. Perhaps she'd pushed too far too fast.

Julian took the sword, shocking her back into the room as the weight of it disappeared from her hand. His fingers brushed hers in the process, sending a jolt through her.

He looked so devilish and sinful with his wet hair, his pale eyes fixed on her intently, and his lips curved into the faintest of smiles. His black shirt was open a few buttons, exposing delicious collarbones that she longed to run her fingers over. Lauren tried to focus on something other than how good he looked. It was impossible.

Each morning she returned to her room worn out from training and slipped into dreams of him, fantasies full of unbridled lust and hunger, visions so hot that she woke needing a cold shower just so she could face him in the training room. Each time she slept, they grew hotter, to the point that they now involved biting. She was itching to see if Julian's fangs in her would feel as good as they did in her dreams.

Julian studied the sword with an appreciative air and then brought it down in a swift arc at his side, his form perfect.

"We were given it in the seventeenth century when we saved a small village from Lycaon's men." He held the sword up, holding it blade down at head height to her. "The man who made it engraved these words on it and used one of our old silver blades in the process so we would be able to defeat any demon we met."

Lauren looked at the characters again and stroked a lone finger over them. "What do they mean?"

"There is no direct translation. It means something akin to 'strength to do what is right'." He ran a hand down the blade and then sheathed it.

"Was it mine?"

He shook his head. "You wanted me to have it because you believed that my skills were more worthy of such a weapon."

The pride in his eyes made her smile.

"It's too beautiful for me," Lauren said and stepped closer to him, placing her hand close to his on the hilt. She looked deep into his eyes, her heart trembling in her chest as she fought against her rising nerves, and then slid her hand a little closer to his, so they touched. "You have the form and grace worthy of such a weapon. I'm glad that whoever I had been back then, I had recognised that you were a superior swordsman... an incredible swordsman."

Nerves ate at her insides as he stared at her, his eyes wider than normal. His lips parted and her heart leapt up in her chest, anticipating his response. Her hand shook where it touched his. Why wasn't he saying anything? His silence was cutting, tearing at her, making panic surface and fear whisper dark words in her mind.

She'd overstepped the mark again. She'd made a fool of herself by letting all of her feelings show.

She'd thought that he would respond this time, had been sure that she wasn't wrong in her conclusion about his feelings.

Julian stepped back, causing her fingers to fall from the hilt of the sword. A dull ache settled in her chest when he turned his back on her. Shock replaced any nerves that she'd been feeling. He placed the sword down on the side table and paused before turning to face her. His eyes were empty again. Whatever feeling she might have stirred in him, he'd erased it.

She was such a fool.

He smiled his trademark tight-lipped smile. Forced.

No trace of emotion touched his eyes.

It was the final straw.

Her patience snapped.

"I don't understand," Lauren muttered and his expression shifted to confusion. She frowned, clenched her fists, and stared at him, feeling weak but strong at the same time. No more. It was now or never. Her heart couldn't take anymore. "What do I need to do to break through your armour?"

Tears began to fill her eyes. Her strength fell away. She swallowed and gazed deep into his eyes, hoping for a reaction. Something. Anything.

He stared back at her with empty eyes.

"I can't take this anymore, Julian. Don't push me away. I don't understand what I've done wrong." She stepped forwards to touch his arm but stopped herself. "Have I done something wrong?" An almost imperceptible shake of his head was her answer. She could only think of one other reason he was acting so distant. "If it was something they did... I'm not them... I don't remember them. I went through with this because I thought that if I did—"

Lauren turned her back to him and bit her lip to stop the words from leaving them. To tell him that she'd gone through with the awakening because she'd wanted them to be together would be to tear her heart from her chest and hand it to him to crush. A tear tracked down her cheek and she brushed it away, feeling foolish for crying over this. It hurt though, more than she cared to admit. If she did, the pain would be unbearable.

"Lauren," Julian said, his voice soft and laced with shock.

She heard him step closer to her. Her eyes slipped shut when his hand touched her shoulder. The silent order to face him went ignored. She didn't want to see him. Not when she was like this. He thought that she was strong but she was far from it. He made her weak, but for him, for the sake of his unswerving belief in her, she'd tried to be strong. She couldn't do it anymore. Not if he was going to continue to close his heart to her.

"Illia," he whispered.

Lauren jerked out of his grip and shoved him away. "Don't call me that!"

Fresh tears rolled down to her jaw.

"I'm not her... them. Don't try to make me be. Don't pretend that I am!" She stalked forwards, needing space. The room was massive but it felt too small. She could stand at one end with him at the other and he would still be too close to her.

She stopped when she felt him behind her, close, his proximity making her body quake.

"Lauren," Julian whispered into her ear. His warm breath caressed her cheek and she closed her eyes, relishing the nearness of him and the way his voice made her feel. She cursed the fact that she wasn't strong enough to move away, that even now she wanted to remain close to him where she felt safe and warm. His hands lightly claimed her upper arms, the touch thrilling her and tempting her to lean into him. "I am sorry. I did not mean to hurt you."

"Then why?" She opened her eyes and stared at the floor. It swam out of focus as tears filled her eyes again. After a moment, she turned her head slightly towards his. He was closer than she'd expected. Her cheek touched his and a sense of calm flowed through her.

"Because I am weak."

She didn't understand that answer. When she tried to turn to face him, he held her tight, not letting her move.

"I loved Illia." Those words hurt but she had suspected as much. He leaned his cheek against hers, giving her the reassurance she craved. He had said loved. A voice at the back of her mind reminded her that she was Illia. She wore Illia's face and had Illia's soul and Julian had fought so hard to convince her to go through with the awakening so she could continue Illia's duty. Had he just wanted Illia back? Did he do this with all of them? She tried to get free but he wouldn't let her go. "Listen to me."

Lauren stilled, not wanting to anger him. Whatever he had to say, it couldn't make her feel any worse than she already did.

"I loved Illia," he repeated and the pain in her heart renewed, a swift stab punctuating each word. "And she loved me."

Lauren stared at the far wall. Tears blurred her vision. Illia had loved Julian. She was Illia. Did that mean that her feelings were Illia's too? Julian had been familiar to her that night in the alley and her attraction to him had been fierce. Was it all because of Illia's soul? Was she just Illia? Weren't any of her feelings hers?

Was she even Lauren anymore?

Had she ever been?

Her head hurt and her heart felt as though it was breaking. Her whole life had been a lie. She'd never been Lauren. She was a carbon copy of a demigoddess, a fake, a shell born to house Illia's soul and everything that went with her.

Lauren stepped out of Julian's grasp and rubbed her head. It was all so confusing and painful. She'd tried to avoid thinking about the extent of Illia's hold over her but now that she'd started, she couldn't stop.

She turned to face Julian, anger and fear colliding inside her to make her brave. She had to know. His reaction would tell her everything.

"I'm just a copy of her, right? We've all been copies. Clones. So everything I feel..." She clutched at her chest and fought back her tears so she could continue. "They're not my feelings... I only feel this way because I am her... I only lov—"

She didn't want to say those words, not when Julian's grave expression had already given her an answer.

She couldn't take it.

Turning away, she ran from the room.

Julian didn't love her.

He loved Illia.

She wasn't Illia. She wasn't. She was Lauren.

Or was she?

CHAPTER 24

Julian flinched as the double doors slammed, one of them bouncing back open. It hadn't gone as well as he'd hoped. He closed his eyes and cursed himself. He'd never been good with these kinds of words, with speaking of his past. Perhaps he should have given more thought to how he was going to tell her. He should have practiced. Now he'd only made things worse.

Lauren was convinced that she was Illia. Her confession about her feelings had left him in no doubt that he hadn't imagined them, but it still didn't stop a part of him from being convinced that she didn't love him, couldn't love him. None but Illia had. He'd wanted to tell her that. It would have made her realise that she was wrong about herself. She wasn't Illia. None of them had been.

They were all different. The soul was the same but the heart changed.

His feelings for her weren't because of Illia. When he felt he loved her, it wasn't his love for Illia renewed but a new love completely.

Julian clenched his fists and cursed himself again. Now he'd hurt her. His pathetic confession had gone horribly wrong and he'd been silent when he should have explained to her that his love was for her, Lauren, not Illia. He needed to convince her of that.

He walked through the building, his senses fixed on Lauren's scent even though he knew where he would find her. Her bedroom.

He had to tell her everything, even if it meant setting himself up for a fall that would be more painful than the one he'd taken for Illia.

Seeing her repeatedly reborn and then die had hurt him deeply, as deeply as not being loved. His existence had been lonely even when he wasn't alone. Now Lauren was offering her heart to him, rekindling his lost emotions and his desire to do his duty and protect her so she would survive the fight against Lycaon. She deserved something in return.

As fragile as his heart was, he would offer it to her.

Reaching her door, Julian paused with his hand on the handle. The shower was running but it didn't mask the sound of her sobs or the hurt that he could sense. He leaned against the door and waited, giving her the space that she needed even though he wanted to go to her and ease her pain. It hurt to stand and listen to her crying when those tears were because of him. He had to tell her this time. He had to make it clear to her and let her in, regardless of the danger to himself.

The room fell quiet. He waited, listening. When it had been quiet for a few minutes, he knocked.

"Come in." Her voice was small and hoarse.

Julian opened the door and paused when he saw her sitting on the white wrought iron bed in front of him in a black satin slip, her damp hair twisted up and pinned. He'd never seen it so red or so short, or her so beautiful. Even Illia hadn't been so stunning. Lauren's warmth, her heart, added a new level to her beauty. She was beautiful inside and out.

He closed the door and tried to gather his thoughts so he said things right this time.

Lauren's eyes met his. In the warm light from the lamp on the bedside table, he could see that they were red. He hated that he'd hurt her, but loved it too because it made it perfectly clear that she did have feelings for him, and that there was hope for him yet.

After all the lonely years, it felt like an elixir, a sweet drug that she gave him with each stolen glance and secret smile. It had breathed life back into his tired body and rebuilt his heart. She'd made him whole again, and he couldn't thank her enough.

He could only offer himself and wait for her reaction.

He sat down on the edge of her bed, facing the door, leaned forward so his elbows rested on his knees, and let his hands dangle between his legs.

"I am sorry," he whispered on a sigh and looked at her. "I did not say things well. Will you allow me to speak now and I will try to... I will get it right this time?"

She made a small noise that he took as a yes and pulled her knees up to her chest, holding them with one arm and picking at the mauve bed cover with her other hand. Her slender legs were pale in contrast to the slip and the dark covers. He ran his gaze up them and then to her face. She was staring at the bed, her brown eyes still showing signs of tears and her cheeks flushed from crying.

Julian looked away at the carpet, not wanting to see what he had done to her, and then forced himself to face her again. She deserved that too, deserved to see in his eyes just how she made him feel and that he was telling her the truth.

"I loved Illia," he said and new tears threatened to spill over her lashes. He cursed them and himself, and quickly continued, hoping to ease her pain. "But that love has been fading since her original death, and since six centuries ago it has slowly died. I have been fooling myself since then, believing that I still loved her."

"But you don't." Those three words were a test.

He shook his head.

"When did you realise?"

Torn between wanting her to see his feelings and wanting to protect his heart, he flitted between looking into her eyes and looking away to his right at the shuttered window.

"Only recently," he whispered, not strong enough to fully voice those words or offer Lauren a better explanation.

Her eyebrows rose. She understood what he wasn't saying. She'd made him realise.

"You are not Illia, Lauren. None of you have ever been Illia. It has taken me three millennia to realise that while her soul was reborn in each of you, her heart was not. Her feelings for me died when she did. Each of you is shaped by your experiences, by your heart, and not by your soul, and each of you have been less and less like Illia." He took hold of her hand, wanting to reassure her and needing the reassurance that came from touching her too. His orders didn't matter right now, not when Lauren needed him.

Lauren gave him a look that stabbed him in the chest, her eyes full of pain and unshed tears. He longed to know what she was thinking, whether it was too late for him and he'd ruined everything. Had his confession done anything to make her see that he loved her and that his feelings had nothing to do with Illia or the others? Had he made it clear that she wasn't Illia?

"We are all different then?" she muttered into her knees, looking up at him now.

With a sigh, he reached over and stroked her cheek, looking deep into her eyes. "None as different as you."

A faint smile touched her rosy lips but it only lasted a second.

"You loved them all."

"I foolishly held on to a love that no longer existed, believing that they were Illia," he countered and tried to think of a way to explain to her what his life had been like. If she knew then she would understand him. He would have let her in and she would have complete power over him. It hurt, but he pushed the words out. "None of you have ever loved me."

He felt small and vulnerable as he sat beside her, waiting for her to say something.

Pain showed in her eyes. Her hand caught his, holding it tight, squeezing it so hard that it actually hurt.

In the blink of an eye, she was kneeling close to him, her arms around his neck and her forehead resting against his right cheek.

He didn't know what to do. His heart warmed as she clung to him, her breath soft against his throat. Lauren was so different. She was his salvation, his light in the darkness. While all others had forsaken him, had turned their back on him, she had embraced him.

"I'm sorry," she whispered against his skin.

He frowned and turned his head towards her, wondering if he'd heard her correctly.

"Why?" he said in a low voice, his hand coming up to rest on her arm. She was so warm and soft. Everything he'd ever wanted but never had.

"I don't know." There was a slight laugh to her tone, as though she really didn't know why she was apologising. "I just feel responsible. They're me and I'm them in a way."

"Only a small way." He took hold of her wrist and brought her hand away from his neck, causing her to sit back. Would she ever know exactly what she'd done for him, how she'd ended a painful existence and given him new hope and a new sense of duty? "You are so different to all of them."

Her fingers closed around his hand and she held it, her eyes still fixed on his. "I won't die. I won't put you through that again."

Placing his other hand over hers, he prayed that she could keep that promise because he didn't want to lose her. She averted her gaze. The atmosphere in the room turned heavy, stifling. Reaching up, Julian placed his hand against her cheek, cupping it and absorbing her warmth as she blushed. He raised her head and her eyes briefly met his before darting towards the window behind him. She was embarrassed. That reaction drew a smile from him, one that broadened when she moved closer and rested her head on his shoulder.

A quiet calm filled him, easing the tension from his body inch by inch. Only Lauren could make him feel this way—at one with the world and peaceful. When she was close to him, touching him, she made him warm and allayed his fears. She made him forget the world outside existed.

"You smell like blood," she whispered.

Fire swept through his veins when she tilted her head back, bringing her lips close to the right side of his neck.

"You need to feed." He offered his wrist.

"There are no scars on your neck." Her breath was warm against him but didn't compare to the heat of her touch as she lightly ran a finger down his throat.

He shuddered, barely able to take the way it felt to have her hands on him, caressing him, and her hungry gaze on his neck.

"Have I ever bitten here?"

"No."

"But vampires bite necks." She moved closer.

He tensed. It wasn't a reaction to what she'd said but to the feel of her breasts brushing his arm.

"We are not vampires." He might have sounded more convincing if he hadn't whispered those words on an exhale of sheer pleasure.

"I think we are." Her voice was sin and temptation, quietly spoken against his skin. "Why haven't I?"

"Because in the thirty incarnations since your first death, you have not loved me." He paused, steeled himself against the pain these words would cause him, and then said, "You forbade it."

His abrupt confession made her stop and draw back. She frowned into his eyes.

"And the first time?" she said and it was his turn to frown. "You said since my first death… meaning the first time was different. Illia was different."

"She died before she could bite me. She died in my arms that time and every time since then." It hurt to say that, to acknowledge it aloud for her to hear. Illia had wanted to bite him. When he'd come back, it had been too late to save her and too late for them. They had never had the chance to act on their feelings, but he had a chance with Lauren.

"But that time it was different, because I loved you too." Lauren knelt beside him, her hands in her lap and an aura of sorrow about her. She took hold of his hand and toyed with his fingers. "This time might be different too… if you want it to be, Julian."

With that, she leaned in close to his neck and breathed in deeply. She'd adapted quickly to her new life, to her new need for blood, proving herself strong even when she didn't believe that she was. He'd expected her to take longer to become comfortable with herself. She pulled the collar of his black shirt aside.

"I would like to, if that's okay?" she whispered against his skin.

A wave of warm desire surged through him.

He couldn't speak. All he could do was tilt his chin up in silent invitation.

Her lips brushed his neck, warm breath making him burn. She moved around in front of him, placing her knee between his legs so she was straddling his left thigh, her mouth against the left side of his neck. Her hands settled on his shoulders. His curled into fists in an effort to stop himself from reaching out and taking hold of her. He moved backwards on the bed, until his calves hit the mattress, giving her more room to kneel close to him.

The soft glide of her tongue over the side of his throat made him shiver and he leaned his head further to one side, desperately encouraging her to bite him, to give him everything he'd wanted for three millennia.

Connection.

Love.

An answer to his prayers.

Julian tensed when her small sharp fangs slowly punctured his skin and eased into his flesh. Her first shallow pull on his blood made him groan inside, the pleasure unbearable and so intense that it bordered on taking control, overpowering his mind and any shred of sense that remained.

She was so gentle, her suckling as soft as a kitten, tender and slow, as though she wanted to savour every drop of blood on her tongue. When her fangs left him, he mourned their loss and was sure that she would stop. Instead, she brushed her lips over his throat, licking and teasing, torturing him with the divine feeling of her feeding. It had never been like this.

The connection between them was incredible, giving him a glimpse of her feelings and what this moment meant to her. Her actions were so careful and measured, each caress of her tongue driving him a little further out of his mind. His lips parted as his own fangs extended without warning. He half-closed his eyes when she sunk her fangs back into his throat, drawing harder on his blood this time.

His breathing turned shallow.

He'd never imagined it would feel so intense, so beautiful, to have her do this. In fact, he was sure it was only because it was Lauren. She alone stirred the incredible passion inside him and the desperate need for her to continue. She could bleed him dry and he wouldn't care as long as she didn't let go of him until his heart had beat its last.

She moved closer and her body pressed against his—soft and light, warm and supple. His hands hovered close to her. He wanted to draw her near, so she was flush against him, her barely covered breasts on his chest and his groin against the apex of her thighs. He wanted to roll her over and nestle between those thighs.

Wanted to bite her and hear her cry his name as she climaxed.

Her slow drinking from his vein aroused him but he still retained the tiniest fragment of sense and control. He wished he didn't. Lost in the connection between them, her feelings and his own, it all seemed so possible. If he touched her, if he ran his hands over her bare thighs just as he needed to, she wouldn't resist. She would be his.

Back in the training room, she might have stopped herself but he knew what she'd been on the brink of saying.

She'd gone through the awakening to be with him.

That thought alone made him giddy. When combined with the feel of her lapping at his neck and her hands on him, it made him feel drunk.

Lauren drew back, licking the wound on his throat, light sensual brushes of her tongue—silk against his flesh. He inhaled deeply. He loved the smell of her skin, the scent of her blood and her arousal. It made him painfully hard. His eyes opened and zeroed in on her bare neck. He hadn't tasted her blood since the night she'd turned him. It was forbidden. She had forbade it. Now he wanted to taste her more than ever. He wanted to complete the connection and make her see just what she did to him.

Just how much he loved her.

His hands came to rest against her back and this time he couldn't pretend that there was no desire in his touch. This broke the rule she had once laid down but he didn't care. The material of her black slip caressed his skin, sliding easily with him as he lowered his hands towards her backside and then pulled them up again. Lauren sighed against his neck, the sound like music to his ears. She liked the feel of his hands on her. He raised them higher, aware that he was bringing the hem of her slip up with him, and peered downwards. Her backside was bare. The sight of the peachy round globes made him throb and ache. He grimaced and lowered her slip, unable to bear the torture.

Lauren licked his neck again with careful, sensual, and intentionally slow sweeps of her tongue.

Her movements stopped and she leaned her head on his shoulder, her hands lax against his arms. A long sigh escaped her lips.

She was tired.

He was about to burst.

"Thank you," she whispered and he trembled, fighting his desire to grab her and kiss her.

With a heavy sigh, Julian gently laid her down in the bed, covering her with the rich mauve blankets. It hurt to move. He couldn't remember a time when he'd been so aroused.

"Julian." Lauren caught hold of his hand and held it as though she feared he would leave. "I have a bad feeling I can't shake."

He frowned and brushed his fingers across her brow. When he smiled, she brightened, but the anxiety didn't leave her brown eyes.

"We're not safe here," she whispered.

That was enough to purge the lust from his mind. It wasn't good. He hadn't noticed anything, but her senses had always been more acute than his were, especially where Lycaon was concerned. He would have to go out and scout, to make sure that her bad feeling was only that and not something more sinister.

"We are safe here, Lauren. Rest now." His fingers paused against her cheek and she surprised him by smiling, leaning into his touch and closing her eyes.

"Where are you going?"

That surprised him too. None of her predecessors had been able to sense his intent so clearly.

He touched her cheek a moment longer, giving his hunger time to fade completely, watching her beautiful face as she fought her desire to sleep, and then stood.

"I will talk to Duke and see if anything has been reported. I will not let anything happen to you."

She smiled in her sleep and burrowed into the dark bedclothes. Julian pulled them up so they covered her shoulders and then touched his neck. It had felt so good to have her bite him there. He would never be the same again.

He stroked her cheek one last time and then left the room.

He would hunt for Lauren, so she would feel safe again.

He would keep her safe.

Not because it was his duty.

But because he loved her.

CHAPTER 25

Julian couldn't find Duke or Astra. He strode down the hallway back past the bedrooms, listening for a sign of the others. He filtered out the scents that he didn't recognise—those of the other Ghost team that was resident in the building and living on the floor above—and focused on Piper, Kuga and Leo's. A hint of a smile touched his lips when he turned the corner in the pale blue hall and sensed Piper.

She stepped out of the kitchen ahead, a plate of sandwiches in her hands. When she saw him, she smiled broadly and walked over to him with a bounce in her step. He couldn't remember what it had been like to be so young and full of life.

"Where's Lauren?" Piper said, the smile sticking, and peered around him as though Lauren might be hiding behind him.

He had kept Lauren busy with training since her awakening and the two women hadn't been able to spend time together.

It was clear that Piper missed Lauren. The two had grown close during their time together, with Lauren acting as a big sister. As far as he knew, none of Illia's reincarnations ever had siblings. Perhaps Lauren had wanted one and that was why she was so kind and protective towards Piper.

Or perhaps it was just Lauren being Lauren.

A smile threatened to curve his lips but he held it in, keeping it secret from Piper. Lauren was so incredibly warm and kind. She was nothing like the others.

She cared about him.

"Lauren is resting," he said and Piper's smile faltered. "She will be awake soon and I am sure that she would enjoy spending some time with everyone."

The smile returned, wider this time if possible. "I've been practicing with Kuga. I think Lauren would be impressed. I want to protect her too and help her."

The effect Lauren had on those around her amazed Julian. When Illia had been alive, she'd never inspired such loyalty from her men. She'd kept her distance from everyone, including him at first, and treated her Arcadians as inferior.

"Lauren would like that." It wasn't a lie to make Piper feel better. It was the truth. Julian was sure that Lauren would like to hear that the members of Duke's Ghost squad wanted to help her and protect her. They weren't alone this time. This time they might finally have a chance at defeating Lycaon.

Piper grinned and leaned forwards, peering up at him in a scrutinising way.

Her deep brown eyes darted between his, twinkling. "I like your thoughts today. They're warm and calmer than usual."

When her gaze fell to his neck, it caught on the marks that he hadn't bothered to hide. They were high on his neck, above the collar of his black shirt, visible to everyone. On display. He was oddly proud of them. He wanted to tell everyone about them.

And that she had feelings for him.

Clearing his throat, he ignored the knowing look that Piper gave him.

"I've never seen marks on your neck before," she said and peered closer. "Not even scars."

She grinned again. Was she happy for him? For Lauren? Or maybe for both of them.

"The others forbade it." He pulled his collar up a little, wanting to draw Piper's attention away from his neck now. He wasn't one for blushing but if she kept staring, he might start.

"Lauren is different." Piper set back on her heels and her gaze finally returned to his face. She ran her fingers around the edge of the large white plate in her hands, her expression thoughtful.

Was she reading his mind again? She'd told him once that she sometimes had difficulty reading him and he'd tried to keep his mind as open as possible because he liked Piper and he knew she liked his thoughts, but since Lauren's arrival, he'd guarded his thoughts more often.

"You weren't thinking it," Piper said. "You were feeling it, but sometimes it's the same to me."

Julian smiled this time when she did. Her youthful exuberance was infectious. He was convinced that the positive spin she put on their lives and her playful approach to everything was the reason that Kuga and Leo had not grown up at all in the five years that he'd known them. The three of them together was always a recipe for silly behaviour and an often dangerous lack of sense, yet they always scraped through somehow. He feared that one day they wouldn't. One day their games would cost them dearly. He didn't want that. He enjoyed their company, especially Piper's.

"Is Kuga around? If you have finished grilling me for information that is. I can feel you probing around and I will close my mind." It was a cruel ultimatum but it worked.

Piper immediately left his mind. She shook her head, sending her dark ponytail swishing side to side. Her large brown eyes pleaded him.

"I'm out," she said and he was sure that if she hadn't been holding the plate of sandwiches she would have held both of her hands up in a gesture of surrender. "Leo is out. Kuga is in the library."

Julian took the sandwiches from her. "Lead the way."

She bounced on ahead of him, pausing to look back sometimes. He strode along behind her, his pace leisurely as he thought about what had happened between him and Lauren, and what she'd said before drifting off to sleep. It wasn't good. He really needed to speak to Duke and find out what was happening in Paris.

He needed to go out and scout. While he was out, he could hunt for Lauren too. She hadn't taken much blood. She would be hungry again when she woke.

Piper opened a door and disappeared inside.

"I thought you were getting food?" Kuga's voice was loud. The anger in it was false but Julian felt Piper tense. She was blind if she didn't know that Kuga could never be angry with her. The boy loved her too much.

Julian rounded the corner and Kuga's eyes were immediately on him, and then the sandwiches. Kuga grinned and leaned back in the mahogany chair, closing the books in front of him and pushing them to one side of the large wooden table. The bookcases lining the walls were crammed with large tomes. One section behind Kuga was empty. Julian presumed those were the books now stacked on the table. He glanced at them. Shape shifters, lycanthropes, werewolves. All books about Lycaon's kind.

"Nice fang work," Kuga said without a second glance at him, and snatched the sandwiches the moment they were within his reach. Julian touched the marks on his neck. Kuga stuffed a sandwich into his mouth. Sometimes humans had no finesse. Kuga swallowed and frowned. "What's up, big man?"

"I need to speak with Duke. Do you know where he has gone?"

Piper drew out one of the seats on the opposite side of the table to Kuga and sat down in it with her knees drawn up to her chest. The blue stripes of her jumper blended into her pale blue jeans. Her bare toes wriggled. Julian could never understand why she would go to the length of wearing a jumper to keep herself warm but not wear socks.

Kuga leaned further back in his chair and stretched, yawning wide. His muscles rippled beneath his long-sleeved black t-shirt as it tightened across his body. He ran a hand over his dark hair and frowned as though thinking hard.

"Nope." Kuga yawned again. "What did you want to talk about... is something wrong?"

There was no point in lying to them. He didn't want to frighten Piper but they needed to know.

"There might be," Julian said and Piper's eyes were immediately on him. He sensed her tension rise. Kuga remained perfectly calm. "Lauren has a bad feeling, and that normally means that danger is close."

"Lycaon?" Piper whispered.

He nodded. "Possibly, but I do not want to scare Lauren by asking her. She is not ready yet. Is there any chance of reinforcements from Ghost?"

"I don't know." Kuga looked both pensive and worried. Julian knew both of those feelings well. He would give anything to have his army again.

"I do."

Both he and Kuga looked at Piper.

She buried her face in her knees and held them tighter. "There aren't any. HQ won't help. I heard Duke on the phone this morning and I knew Lauren would want to know so I snooped. It's bad."

"How bad?" Julian crouched down so he was eye-level with Piper. She looked worried, and felt scared.

Her dark eyes shifted to meet his.

"There's a lot of werewolves in Paris. Numbers have doubled this past week, and we're alone. It's just us, Julian."

He clenched his fists, cursing Lycaon and the leaders of Ghost for forcing his hand. The thought of what he was going to do disgusted him but he didn't have a choice. They couldn't go into battle against Lycaon with just the seven of them. They couldn't face him alone this time. Lycaon would slaughter them. He couldn't lose Lauren, and he needed an army if he was going to succeed in keeping her alive.

He had to do this to protect her.

He stood, his expression grim.

"I might be able to change that."

CHAPTER 26

Paris was nothing as Lauren remembered it. It was cold, dark, and had a smell of evil about it. She stayed close to Julian as they walked through the quiet streets, far away from any of the landmarks or tourist areas. Wrapping her arms about herself, she decided that she should have worn more layers than just her t-shirt, dark red turtleneck jumper, and brown combat jacket. It seemed that immortals still felt the cold. A glance at Julian warmed her. He didn't seem at all bothered by the frigid weather, but there was something on his mind. He'd been quiet all night, distant. The tall collar of his coat obscured part of his face but did nothing to hide his feelings from her. He was in a foul mood and she hoped it was nothing she'd done.

She was still trying to figure everything out. Shortly after Julian had left her, she'd awoken and hadn't been able to get back to sleep. She'd replayed everything that he'd said to her and rather than getting perspective and answers, she'd only ended up with more questions.

Julian had said that he no longer loved Illia and that he'd realised it recently. Had she really made him realise? He hadn't said as much but that was the impression she'd received from his words. He hadn't need words at all to convey his feelings when she had bitten his neck. He had enjoyed it and, deep in her heart, she knew it was because he had feelings for her.

When he'd come back to her room, he'd told her they were going out to see someone. His tone had been cold and harsh. Either she'd done something wrong, or he didn't like the person they were going to see.

A breeze blew up her back, entering through the gap the two short swords strapped to her back beneath her jacket caused.

She shivered and sighed. Her breath turned white in the cold air and then disappeared.

She'd always imagined that vampires didn't have body heat or heartbeats, but she had both. Julian had said that they weren't vampires. Were they so different to them?

"You still haven't told me who we're going to see," she whispered, a little afraid of asking any louder in case Julian's bad mood was because of her.

His pace slowed and he frowned, his expression pensive. The pale streetlights highlighted his face, turning his eyes a more vivid shade of blue and making her think about how good it had felt to bite his neck. The connection had been intense, the feel of his hands on her divine, and she'd been sure that he would do something more, something to ease both of their hunger. She'd tried to remain awake, but the taste of his blood had been too much, making her drowsy.

"In the fourteen hundreds, a man convinced you to share your blood with him." His voice was tight and strained, as though he didn't want to talk about it.

Lauren's eyebrows rose. She'd given her blood to someone other than Julian? He must have been dying too. A comrade of theirs perhaps.

"He had promised to join us, you, on your quest for Lycaon."

The way he said that made it perfectly clear that the man had lied. What reason could he have had for wanting her blood if he didn't want to help them? A voice at the back of her mind laughed at her. Her blood had made Julian immortal. What human wouldn't want to be immortal?

"He didn't?" The question felt redundant but she wanted to keep Julian talking so she knew more about the man they were going to meet.

Julian shook his head. "The moment the man had your blood and had been reborn, he changed."

"He's like us?" That could be useful in the fight against Lycaon.

Julian shook his head again. "No. He did not gain power like yours from your blood."

"But you did." Lauren could sense this was going to get confusing again. Why wouldn't the man have gained whatever Julian had?

"No, I did not." He looked heavenward at the clouds. "Selene favours me and Zeus lends me his strength so I may be a worthy servant to you."

"Oh." So her blood wasn't everything. "The man didn't know that, did he?"

Julian's eyes narrowed and she knew he was smiling behind his mask. Lauren got the feeling he was pleased and that this man was definitely the reason Julian was in a foul mood tonight. As much as that relieved her, it made her wonder just why he would take her to see such a man.

"He did not." Julian brought his eyes down from the heavens and stared straight ahead. "He embraced his life though, creating more like him, spreading his curse just as Lycaon has. Vampires."

Lauren gasped. Her blood had created vampires? She stared wide-eyed at Julian. Was this why he despised that name so much? Did he hate them because she'd given her blood to another? Because they were weaker than him, but shared a connection?

Thinking about it made her head spin.

She'd been responsible for a legend and she didn't even know anything about what she'd done or the creatures her blood had created.

Julian stopped in front of an old stone building. To say it had seen better days was an understatement. It was practically falling into ruin. She didn't like it. The sight of it made the hairs on the back of her neck stand on end and made her teeth itch to sharpen. She moved closer to Julian and he placed his hand on her arm. The touch soothed her but not enough. She wanted to leave, wanted to tell Julian to forget about this man because she could smell death and the scent of it choked her.

"Your blood runs in his veins," Julian said and Lauren's eyes met his. His steady gaze calmed her a little. "There is a chance you will be able to convince him to uphold his promise and help."

His eyes told her that he enjoyed the prospect of meeting this man as much as she did. If he was willing to go through with it, then so was she. Julian would remain close to her. They were both armed. If something bad happened, she would be safe. She had no doubt that Julian would protect her.

Julian pushed the door open. She wasn't surprised that it was unlocked. Vampires would probably welcome an easy meal in the form of a burglar. They entered the building. The interior was dark and as cold as the world outside. She followed close behind Julian, trusting him to lead the way.

A warm inviting glow crept out from beneath a closed door ahead of them. Julian opened the door and Lauren flinched at the sudden brightness, her eyes struggling to adjust.

He walked into the room and she continued to follow, remaining close and behind him. She could sense many people in the building, but there was only one in the room with her and Julian.

A person without a heartbeat.

Julian was right. Vampires were different to them. This person felt cold and empty. Dead. She had no sense of heat from him or any sign of life. He didn't breathe. His heart didn't beat. His blood didn't flow.

He was nothing like her and Julian.

Her gaze quickly scanned over the room. While the outside of the building had been decrepit, inside it was sumptuous and rich. Huge gilt-framed mirrors hung on the dark red walls, reflecting the opposite mirror into infinity. An expansive black marble fireplace stood to her right, flanked by two red velvet and gold framed couches.

On one of them, a man reclined, propped up in the corner furthest from the roaring fire, one arm on the back of the couch and the other on the arm. His long black-clad legs stretched out in front of him. As they approached, his attention shifted from the flames to Julian.

His eyebrows knit tight and his stormy grey eyes blackened into a scowl. The mussed tendrils of his dark hair made him look as though he'd been making wild love just a moment before they had entered the room. When she moved out from behind Julian, his gaze shifted to her and his bowed lips took on a decidedly seductive curve. He raked his gaze over her, heat following in its wake. His eyes hid nothing, revealing all his sordid and sensual thoughts. No, he didn't look as though he'd been making wild love. He wasn't the kind of man who knew how to make love. He looked like the type for raw dirty sex.

"Sonja," he whispered, his accent strong and definitely eastern European. He made no move to stand but his gaze tracked back up to her face. He smiled, confident and charming, even more so than Duke. "I knew you would return to me, my sweet."

Lauren frowned. Julian stepped between her and the man as he went to stand. The man paused, his hands gripping the back and arm of the couch, and eased himself back down.

"Ever the faithful guard dog, following her wherever she goes." The man's tone was lazy, his words drawled. He slouched back into the side of the couch and toyed with his hair whilst staring at her. He held his other hand out to her, his white skin a stark contrast to his black shirt and jacket. "Come, sweet Sonja."

She frowned at him again.

"I don't know that name. I'm sorry... I don't know you," she said and his eyes darkened, turning black. She hadn't imagined it. They looked as though his pupils had swallowed his irises.

His gaze shot to Julian.

Julian's eyes narrowed as though he was smiling. "Sonja died many centuries ago, and her love died with her."

Lauren's gaze darted to Julian. One of Illia's incarnations had loved another?

"He did not tell you?" the man said with a smirk. He didn't seem to care that the woman who had loved him was dead. "Wicked Julian."

A flash of silver crossed Julian's eyes. The vampire laughed.

"Still hurts does it?" He grinned from ear to ear and Lauren wanted to hit him. "While you gave her everything, there was only one thing that she wanted, and it was one that you couldn't give her... me."

The vampire's attention moved back to her, his gaze black and intent on her face. When it lowered to her body, Lauren moved closer to Julian. She didn't like his attention on her. She didn't like the edge of hurt that she could feel in Julian. And she definitely didn't like this place.

"Konstantin—" Julian started.

"Morgan," the man interrupted. "I go by Morgan now."

Lauren was glad that his eyes had moved off her and were again on Julian. The darkness in them lightened, melting away to reveal grey irises.

He smiled and she squirmed when his gaze came back to her. "And what name does my queen go by?"

Standing her ground, she glared at him, showing him that he wasn't going to fluster her. "Lauren."

"A beautiful name for a beautiful woman. I believe you look better now than ever. So young and nubile, flexible."

Lauren put her hands on her hips and refused to blush over the smouldering look he was tossing her way. He leaned back, his perusal of her languid and too familiar for her liking. Who was he to look at her as though he knew her intimately? She had an overwhelming urge to wipe the smirk off his face.

"Does your blood still taste sweet?" He licked sharp canines and dropped his gaze to her hips. "Do other parts of you?"

Her eyes widened. Arrogant bastard. He might be confident in his charms and his attractiveness, but he wasn't going to win her over. She hated his type. Smug, self-centred, and perverse.

She glanced at Julian. He was looking at her, his eyes silver and focused, sharp. The feel of them on her made heat touch her cheeks and made her heart pound. She bit her lip and looked away.

"Now that's disgusting," Morgan said with a disappointed edge to his tone. "I had thought my sweet queen had returned to me, but it seems she has other ideas. What would you want with a dog like him when you could have a king like me?"

Lauren had had enough. She stepped forwards, passing Julian, and stared at Morgan. He surprised her by leaning back and looking away for a split second, as though she'd unsettled him.

"What do you want?" Morgan snapped, all humour and light gone from his voice. His expression turned cold and dark. The change shocked her but she didn't let it show. "What does my precious queen want of me now?"

Lauren wondered just what kind of man he really was. Was he the laughing, frivolous one that had first greeted her, or this angry, bitter one before her now?

The only thing she could sense in him was intense hatred.

"I need your strength," she said with all the confidence that she could muster.

He laughed, hollow and empty, a mirthless sound. It filled the room, echoing around it. He wasn't going to help them. For some reason, he hated them.

"We are but shadows of you." Morgan stood and waved his hands theatrically around the room, as though indicating the others that she could sense. "What could you do with my strength?"

His eyes narrowed. A thin-lipped smile tugged at the corners of his mouth.

"Unless you have come to feed me again, my queen." He said his reference to her with such venom that Lauren took a step back, afraid of what he might do if he was close enough. "Have you missed the feel of me surging between your sweet thighs?"

Julian was beside her in an instant, his hand on his sword. Morgan laughed again.

"You really are pathetic, Guard Dog. Is it little wonder my queen didn't want you?"

Lauren placed her hand on Julian's, stopping him from drawing his sword. He looked down at her but she kept her focus on Morgan. She wasn't going to allow him to provoke Julian by playing on his past. That was over now. Whatever her previous incarnations had done to him, she wasn't going to hurt him. She was going to erase his pain little by little and show him that he was worthy of love and wasn't alone in the world anymore.

She would never betray him, not as Sonja had.

"Help us." She put more force into her words this time.

Morgan sneered at her. "I already do. All of my kin do. Your blood flows in our veins... compels us to war against the werewolves. We have slain many. Our thirst is never-ending. Our leash held tight. Our curse unbearable."

He placed his hand around his throat, as though it was a collar, and tightened it so his fingers dug into his flesh. The malice in his dark eyes unnerved her.

Julian was right. Morgan didn't have the same abilities as him, and he was angry because of it. He was bitter.

There was no way that he was going to help them. She wasn't even sure if they could trust him. It felt as though he would be more likely to side with their enemy in a fight.

Did they really need his help? Julian wouldn't have brought her here if they didn't. It was her duty to defeat Lycaon. To do that, she needed an army, and Morgan had men.

There had to be a way to make him help them.

It was hard to think when he was staring at her though, his dark look slowly melting back to one of seduction. He ran his hand over his hair, preening it back, and ran an appraising glance over her.

"My blood compels you to kill werewolves." Thinking on her feet had never been a strong point of hers. "Then surely you want to kill Lycaon?"

"He is of little concern to me. I can satisfy my hunger by killing his weak pups. Why would I risk myself to hunt the big dog?"

Lauren ground her teeth. Morgan was infuriating. She glanced out of the corner of her eye at Julian. He was staring at Morgan with murder in his eyes. She couldn't blame him. If Sonja had loved Morgan, had given her blood to him because of her feelings, then it must have hurt Julian deeply. Asking Morgan to help them now seemed ridiculous. If he did help them, which she doubted he would even if he promised to, then he would be a constant reminder of that betrayal whenever Julian saw him. Her gaze shifted back to Morgan. He was staring back at Julian now, an equally dark look in his eyes.

They wanted to kill each other.

It was hardly a good working relationship. In battle, it would be all too easy for Morgan to attack Julian without her noticing. Julian's plan placed himself in danger. Was the situation that desperate?

She wished she hadn't told Julian about her bad feeling now. It was clearly the reason they were standing here making a deal with the Devil himself.

"If Lycaon is dead, my duty dies with him. If my duty dies, then you will be free of your compulsion to kill werewolves." Lauren didn't know if it was true but Morgan didn't need to know that. His eyes brightened, returning to their normal grey colour, and he raised an eyebrow. He was interested at least.

"You will lose your hold over me?" he said and stepped closer. He tilted his head back a fraction and looked down the length of his nose at her, assessing her. He didn't believe her.

Love Immortal

"I never realised that I had one," she countered, intrigued now that he'd let slip that little fact. Julian had been right.

Morgan laughed. The sight of his fangs made her feel as though he was threatening her.

"You hold the leash, my queen."

She was beginning to hate it when he called her that. He bowed low and looked up at her. She ignored the fact that his half-undone shirt fell forwards with him, affording her a view of his pale torso—all hard packed muscle. The corner of his lips lifted.

"You hold both of them." His gaze slid to Julian.

Julian stepped forwards and drew his sword a few inches. Morgan laughed again.

"I dare you to try." Morgan's tone was flat and empty, but held a promise that there would be trouble if Julian attacked.

Lauren stepped between them and frowned at them both before looking at Morgan. "I hold no one's leash. The blood in your veins only compels you in the same way that it compels me."

"A slave to your own sweet blood? How delicious is that? It seems none of us can escape your destiny." Morgan sat down, ran his arms out along the back of the couch, and crossed his legs.

Sitting like that, with his black shirt open enough to reveal the contours of his pectorals, his long black-clad legs crossed, and his expensive leather shoes reflecting the firelight, he looked like Euro trash.

He smirked at her. "So you kill Lycaon and we're all free… only we're not all equal. If I'm going to help you, I want that as my boon."

"It is not possible." Julian sheathed his sword. "You can never be like us."

"Why not? Because you say so? How is it you came to be the way you are and I received this hollow curse?" Morgan stood so fast that Lauren felt the air shift.

The atmosphere in the room grew heavy and she took a step back, fearing the confrontation that she could sense coming. Morgan had issues that were six centuries in the making. Nothing she said would stop him from erupting.

"No life in my veins like yours. No heart in my chest like you have. No walks in the sunshine. No reflection to see myself like you have! How is it that you have what I do not?" Morgan growled and his eyes grew black. "No pretty silver to charm the ladies."

Julian moved to shield her. He was surprisingly calm, as though he'd been waiting for Morgan to explode.

"I don't feel her the way I know you can," Morgan hissed and glared at him. He pressed a hand to his bare chest and dug black claws into his flesh. "When she dies, I don't feel it. When she awakens, I don't feel it. I don't feel her… my queen… and I need to. I feel nothing. Nothing but pain and this need to kill. Nothing but this curse!"

"We are not the same." Julian held his arm out in front of her, his gaze fixed on Morgan. "I am favoured by Zeus, given this task of awakening and protecting Illia, and I was given her blood by the original, not a reincarnation. Her blood was stronger then. Each rebirth makes her weaker. Her blood can no longer sustain life."

"Life?" Another mirthless chuckle escaped Morgan's lips and he looked around the room as though searching for something. His hand tightened against his chest. "All I have is death. A need to taste the life in others, to drink it in the hope I may escape this eternal darkness and chill. If you cannot grant me life, I cannot help you."

"I can only drink blood too," Lauren said and Morgan frowned at her. "We both do. Didn't Sonja tell you that we can only feed on blood and need it to survive?"

The startled look in his eyes said that she hadn't.

"I can't give you a heartbeat, or a reflection, or 'life' as you put it, but I can free you of your constant war with werewolves. If you help me, I will do all I can for you."

Morgan sat back down, looking thoughtful as he stared at the fireplace.

The cracks and pops of the fire filled the silence. Lauren waited. At least he was thinking about it this time. It was more positive than her last attempts to convince him had been. Maybe her revelation about her blood drinking had made him see that they weren't so different. They shared that curse. If she could accept that side of her after only a few days then he should be able to accept it after centuries.

"I will think about it and give you my answer tomorrow night," Morgan said at last.

"This address." Julian handed Morgan a card.

Lauren nodded and turned around, wanting to leave straight away. She didn't want Julian in the presence of Morgan for any longer than was necessary and it was pointless to try to convince Morgan to commit to helping her tonight.

All she could do now was give him room and wait.

Tomorrow night she would hear his answer.

CHAPTER 27

Julian didn't say much on their way back to the Ghost office. He wasn't sure what to say. Lauren had discovered that one of her predecessors had been in a relationship with Konstantin. No. Morgan. Julian had almost laughed when he'd announced that he'd changed his name. Morgan sounded far less threatening than Konstantin. If he showed up tomorrow night, Julian had half a mind to tell him that just to see his reaction.

If he did that though, Lauren wouldn't be happy. She'd tried hard to keep the peace between them, clearly sensing that they hated each other. Hated? Far too light a word for the seething animosity that he felt towards the vampire. Despised. Julian despised the wretched creature. He despised Paris because that creature lived in it.

And he would free the city of its burden if Morgan dared to attempt to seduce Lauren again.

Gods, if she'd fallen for that vampire's charms, for his winsome smile and flirtatious air, it would have killed him. It was bad enough whenever Duke did it. But then he could forgive Duke. Not only did the man flirt on instinct but he was also making dire attempts to get Astra jealous.

The beauty of being three thousand years old was that he'd seen almost everything and could interpret almost every type of situation. Kuga loved Piper but was foolish enough to think that she was too young for him. Piper loved Kuga, but believed he only liked her in a brotherly way. Duke was insane for Astra and thought that making her jealous would somehow win her over. Astra secretly liked Duke but feared that her demonic status would one day see him leave her. It was all a complicated mess that he was gradually sinking in to.

He loved Lauren but was too afraid to tell her outright in case she threw it back in his face as the others had.

And Lauren?

She felt something, but was it enough?

Until one of them made a move, they would continue this dance, skirting their feelings, searching for the other's, waiting until the end of time.

They were all fools.

Lauren walked behind him as they entered the building, her silence a heavy weight around his neck. She had been thinking hard ever since they'd left Morgan's place. It concerned him. There was an air of confusion and hurt about her. He wanted to cheer her up, to see her smile again. Her smiles were his light. They made the darkness bearable. They made him feel alive. Each smile she gave him fixed another piece of his heart, fusing them, making it solid again.

"Are you hungry?" he said as an excuse to break the silence.

She looked up at him with weary eyes. The sun was rising. He felt it too—a heavy pull deep inside him that made him want to search for a safe place to rest.

She shook her head. "I'm not hungry."

He thought hard, searching for a way to break her doldrums and bring her back to him.

Opening his mind, he called out to Piper.

Piper would be able to cheer Lauren up.

They had barely reached the stairs to the first floor and Duke's office when Piper bounded down them, her bright purple knee length dress flowing with her movements. Hazardous black and grey horizontal striped tights made her look like a marionette or a sinister ballerina. She stopped at the foot of the stairs, her eyes wide and dark, sparkling, and smiled. For a moment, he wondered if she was going to hug him for calling her.

Instead, she went to Lauren, looped an arm through hers, and grinned.

"We need to catch up over ice cream," Piper said and hopped on the spot.

Lauren looked at him, her eyes a little brighter now. Julian nodded. If she needed his approval, she would have it, although he was hers to command and not the other way around.

"It will be safe. I must speak to Duke," he said when she didn't look sure.

"I don't eat," she said to Piper.

Piper's smile didn't falter. "I do. I can eat ice cream for both of us."

With that, she tugged Lauren towards the other set of stairs that led to the kitchen and library. Piper looked back when they reached them. He silently thanked her and watched them go up the stairs before heading up the set in front of him. He needed to find Duke.

When Julian reached the top of the stairs, the closed doors of the office did nothing to drown out the raised voices of Astra and Duke. Julian paused, unsure whether to disturb them. The argument grew heated and they sounded close to throttling each other. Duke mentioned something about a mission and leaving. Astra refused to go.

Julian knocked. The room fell silent. Cautiously, he opened the doors.

"I hope I am not disturbing you," he said.

Both Duke and Astra were red in the face. There was a flicker of bright blue in Astra's eyes. The atmosphere didn't clear as he walked in. If anything, it grew heavier as he waited for one of them to say something.

Duke huffed and leaned against the ebony desk to Julian's left. "Astra is refusing to go on a mission. If she does, we get the support we need."

Astra stood by the white fireplace opposite Duke, her arms folded across her chest. The glimmer of blue in her eyes increased, ringing her irises. Duke had to be pushing her to do something that she didn't want to do to get that sort of reaction from her.

Julian stepped back. He liked his soul just where it was. Duke gave him a look that asked him to say something. Julian shook his head. Astra was Duke's subordinate. If he wanted her to go, it was down to him to convince her.

"I don't want to leave," Astra said.

Julian had the impression that there should be a 'you' aimed at Duke on the end of that sentence.

In the past, he had tried speaking with Astra about her feelings for Duke but she always refused. She was nothing if not stubborn and Duke was getting a taste of that. If Astra didn't want to go on a mission, then she wasn't going to go, no matter who pushed her.

Both of them looked at him. Was he supposed to pick a side? Astra would suck his soul out if he chose Duke's, and Duke would probably kill him in the blink of an eye if he chose Astra's. It was a no win situation.

"Lauren has a bad feeling." Julian had his own reasoning to throw on the table. If they wanted to pick sides, he had one they could both choose. Lauren's. "Normally it means something terrible is going to happen. Now is not the time to send our strongest fighters off on petty missions. We went out tonight to see Morgan."

"Morgan?" Duke leaned against his desk. His inquisitive air didn't hide his anger.

"Vampire," Astra sneered.

Julian nodded, not surprised that Astra knew of him. "Morgan was once Konstantin, the first vampire… born of Illia's blood."

Duke stood sharply. "Her blood brought about the existence of vampires?"

"Astra has always believed me to be a vampire. Lauren and I have the same abilities to them to a degree, but a vampire is no match for us, and is not the same as us physically." Julian paced across the room and unclipped the collar of his jacket, letting it fall open.

He drew in a long steadying breath and sighed, trying to erase the way it had felt to see Morgan again and the anger his flirting with Lauren had stirred within him. Lauren was beautiful, far more so than Sonja had ever been. He had been a fool to take her to see Morgan and an idiot to sit back and let him get away with his advances. He should have put Morgan in his place and made it clear that Lauren was his. He wouldn't let anyone else have her. He would kill them for even trying.

Pinching the bridge of his nose, he closed his eyes and frowned, reining in his feelings so he could focus on his duty. It was hard when his head was full of Lauren. She made him believe that duty wasn't as important as he had grown to think it was and that rules didn't matter. She was changing him, making him more like the man he had once been and making him realise just how much he had changed over the centuries. His real self had faded as much as Illia had in her incarnations, until he almost didn't recognise himself. But now he was beginning to feel alive again, to feel like the man he had been, and he liked it.

And he wanted to ignore his orders and act as he would have, to take what he wanted, to show Lauren the extent of his feelings and desires.

It was difficult though. Whenever he came close, he remembered his duty and that he had followed his orders for millennia. Zeus had commanded him to obey her and obey her he would, no matter how much it hurt to, until she finally changed the rules as well as him. An urge to see her swept through him, a desire to tell her what the others had done so he could see if she would free him of the chains that bound him. In his heart, he knew that she would, and that she would understand the pain his orders had caused him.

He couldn't tell her now though, not straight after meeting Morgan. He would look weak in front of her and he needed to be strong, to keep her feeling as though he was her protector, the only man who could keep her safe and the only man she wanted to love.

Duke was staring at him.

"Is something wrong?" he said and Julian looked at him, shaking his head.

He dragged his focus away from Morgan and Lauren, and back to Duke and Astra.

"I wish that we did not, but we need strength and the vampires can offer us that," Julian said.

"Will they help?" Astra fidgeted with the black bracelet around her wrist. Her kind and the vampires had never got along. Their history was bloody and her kin's numbers had dwindled because of the vampires. He had considered not going to see Morgan because of Astra, but they needed more men. If he could bear Morgan's presence, then so could she.

"I am unsure. Morgan has offered us an answer tomorrow night. Lauren did all she could to convince him to help but he resents us both for what we have compared to what her blood gave him. There is a high chance that he only wanted us gone so lied to be rid of us."

Duke frowned and crossed the room to the windows. The sky was lightening, bright enough for Julian to make out the courtyard and the rooms opposite. The delicate white wrought-iron railings glittered with frost and a pale layer of ice covered the closed blue-grey shutters of his bedroom windows. The day would be cold, the clear sky lowering the temperature and stopping the ice from melting.

"No wonder you didn't like Astra's joke about you being a vampire."

"We cannot count on Morgan." Julian chose to ignore Duke's comment. "While I am sure he is compelled to help Lauren, and would do so, I am also certain that his hatred of me will stop him."

Duke stared out of the window. "Vampires. I had never imagined I would work with one."

Julian frowned at him and then looked at Astra. It had been a while since he had seen her so nervous. Neither of them were happy to be working with vampires. Only Duke seemed interested, although Julian suspected that Duke would have met vampires before.

Love Immortal

He remembered the way that Morgan had flirted with Lauren, his casual charm and seductive smile, and the way she had responded at times. Darkness filled his heart. He hoped that he wasn't making a mistake by asking the vampire to help them.

He couldn't bear it if she betrayed him, not this time, not Lauren.

He had to go to her and find out for certain how she felt about Morgan.

He had to know.

He needed to hear her say that she felt nothing for him.

CHAPTER 28

Piper took another huge scoop of chocolate fudge brownie ice cream from the half litre tub and stuffed it into her mouth, grinning the whole time. Lauren smiled, wishing that she could still enjoy such comfort food. She wished that she had eaten all of her favourite things before the awakening so she could remember the taste of them but everything had happened so fast. A hint of envy settled in her as she watched Piper eat the ice cream. She missed food.

She remembered how good it had felt to feed from Julian's neck. Perhaps it could be her new form of comfort food. A new and slightly strange one. It had been difficult for her at first to drink blood from him but now she had grown used to it, more than used to it in fact. She craved it.

"What's he thinking?" Lauren said, knowing that Piper would be able to guess who she was talking about. "Did he send for you?"

Piper hesitated and then nodded, swallowing her mouthful. "But I wanted to see you."

She chased ice cream around the tub, swirling it with her spoon, her deep brown eyes downcast and her fringe almost hiding them.

Lauren smiled and moved her chair back. The legs scraped on the slate tiled floor and squeaked. She flinched at how loud the noise was in the quiet room and then leaned one elbow on the well-worn wooden kitchen table. The small white room was chilly enough that she was tempted to light the stove to heat it a little but at least they could be alone here. She was thankful for that. Her heart felt heavy but whenever Piper smiled, Lauren felt brighter. She needed to talk and knew that Piper would listen to her with a kind smile and open heart.

"Julian thinks about you constantly." Piper fiddled with the spoon. Did she feel that she was breaking her promise to Julian by telling her?

"I won't tell him anything you say. I promise. And you don't have to tell me anything specific. I just need to know what's going on in his head. He's so hard to read sometimes." Lauren turned her arm so it was almost laying flat against the table and rested her head on her forearm. She was tired but she didn't want to sleep. Julian had gone to talk to Duke, probably about Morgan, and it had been so long since she'd seen Piper.

"He always did think about you constantly but he's different now. His thoughts have changed. They're warmer."

"Warmer how?" That perked Lauren up. Julian was thinking warm things about her. A little smile teased her lips. She thought warm things about him too. In fact, she couldn't get her mind off him.

Piper beamed. "Romantic."

Lauren shot bolt upright and leaned towards Piper. "Were they romantic before?"

Piper shook her head, sending her ponytail swishing, and toyed with another spoonful of ice cream.

"No... they were... solemn. I can see that now. I had thought that they were calm but they weren't." She placed the ice cream in her mouth and looked thoughtful as she ate it. "They were sad... dutiful. Now they're warm and tender... and they make me a little jealous that Kuga doesn't think about me like that."

Relieved, Lauren smiled at Piper and took hold of her hand. It was cold from holding the ice cream tub but soon warmed. Piper forced a smile, the pain in her eyes clear. She was thinking about Kuga. Lauren didn't have the heart to probe further about Julian's romantic thoughts when they upset Piper. Besides, she would rather have him tell her about them.

"It's your birthday soon," Lauren said and tried to remember when it was.

"In a couple of weeks... no... the end of next week. Which I suppose is a couple of weeks."

Was it? Her awakening was a blur and she'd lost track of time. She didn't even know what day it was.

Had her birthday passed yet? Not that it mattered now. She would always be thirty-four, which she supposed was better than being forever thirty-five.

"We should have a party." Lauren smiled.

"A double celebration!" Piper bounced on her chair. "My birthday and your awakening. I bet that was frightening."

"Not really. Only the part where I had no control over myself." Lauren frowned at the memory. "It's okay now though. I made the right decision and it isn't as bad as I thought it would be. Julian took care of me. But I want to talk about you and your birthday. You're turning eighteen. It's a big deal and we should make it one."

Piper grinned at her. "With a huge cake?"

"Perhaps we could convince Kuga to jump out of it."

"Naked?" Piper's look turned dreamy.

"I don't think most of the room would want to see that. Would you settle for a pair of shorts?"

Piper waved a hand and scrunched up her nose. "Seen it already. I'll be eighteen. I should be allowed to see eighteen rated stuff."

"I don't think full frontal nudity is eighteen rated. I think that's x-rated." Lauren laughed and then raised her eyebrows, falling silent. "If he's going to be nude, can I at least be standing behind him?"

Piper nodded and giggled.

"What if he switched with Leo?" Lauren said.

The smile fell straight off her face. "Ew. And I can tell the difference."

"You can? I couldn't before the awakening. They smell different you know." Lauren took a deep breath and wasn't surprised to find that Piper smelt sweet like candy and warm like sunshine. "What about Kuga?"

"What about him?"

"I mean, is he still going to take you out on your birthday? You said that he was going to take you on a trip out of the city and stuff. We're not in London anymore."

Piper picked up another spoon of ice cream and let it slide back into the tub.

"He's promised to take me out anyway. Somewhere he knows in Paris with a great view." Her look turned dreamy again and Lauren could tell that she was imagining the entirety of Paris stretched before them, all twinkling lights in the darkness, and Kuga beside her.

Piper was so smitten with Kuga that it was sweet. If Lauren were her age, she would be acting the same way about Julian.

"What does he think when he's around you?" Lauren said.

Piper rested her chin on her upturned palm. A blush stained her cheeks. "Sometimes it's romantic... other times he blocks me... or I just can't read him clearly."

"Can people block you whenever they want?" Lauren was surprised that Kuga would choose to block Piper, unless he didn't want her to know his thoughts about her. She thought of a very practical reason for blocking Piper. If Kuga was thinking about Piper in a more than romantic way, he would probably want to keep it private. A fantasy wasn't a fantasy when the person in it could read it all in your mind like a book.

"No." Piper pushed the ice cream away, their eyes meeting. "If someone is hurt it's easier to read their thoughts, to hear them, like when Julian was trapped."

A chill crept through Lauren at the reminder of what Julian had endured for her. She thanked God that Piper could read him. If she hadn't been able to, he might have been trapped still and Lauren would have died, either because of the werewolves or because of the awakening. It turned her stomach.

She tried not to think about it, pushed it to the back of her mind and focused on Piper.

"It must have been hard to find Julian," she said.

"He kept shutting me out but once I made it clear that I didn't want to hurt him, only help him, he opened his mind again and told me where he was."

"He can do that? Do people feel it when you read them?"

Piper shook her head. "Only Julian can feel it. He can tell when I'm probing about in his mind. If I try to go too deep, he shuts me out. I've learned to stick with the surface thoughts that he lets me read."

"Why would you want to go deeper?"

"Duke wanted me to at first. He thought Julian would have valuable information and made me try to go deep and find out what he knew about you and Lycaon so we could find you. Duke has wanted to prove your existence for years, ever since he first heard of your legend. I think when he found Julian, his mission changed. He wanted to help Julian. Julian shut me out before I could even get close to reading anything. It was the first time I realised that he had total control over his mind and could sense me." Piper sat back and stretched. She smiled as though something had amused her. "I promised Julian that night that I wouldn't do it again and I told Duke that I couldn't read Julian anymore. He still believes me."

"You lied to Duke?"

"Don't get me wrong. I love Duke and Ghost, but it was wrong of him to try to use Julian like that when he was still weak."

Lauren couldn't agree more.

What reason could Duke have for treating Julian that way? Piper had mentioned wanting to find her. Had he been gunning for glory by proving her existence? Had he expected her to join Ghost? Neither of those were an important enough reason to hurt Julian.

She stifled a yawn.

"I'm keeping you up… I'm sorry," Piper said and Lauren shook her head, smiling.

"I don't want to sleep today. There's too much on my mind and I'd rather do something constructive." Talking to Piper had sent the bad feeling to the back of her mind but if she went to her room, she would start thinking again, trying to figure out why she felt as though something was going to happen. She needed to keep her mind off it, Morgan and everything else. "Have you been practicing?"

Piper nodded. Nerves flickered in her eyes.

"There might be a fight coming, but you already knew that didn't you?" Lauren said and Piper nodded again. "I can feel it. It would be good for us to practice."

"Practice?" Piper squeaked. "With you?"

"Come on, I'll go easy on you." Lauren grabbed her two short swords from the table and took hold of Piper's hand. She led her down the hall past the bedrooms to the ballroom.

She wanted Piper to grow more confident with her powers, to see that she could control them and that she wasn't going to hurt anyone. At the heart of her fear had to be the thought that she might kill someone close to her again. She had to make Piper see that it was pointless fearing something that might never happen.

The ballroom was empty. Lauren left the door open. She placed her swords down on the lone side table and removed her jacket and jumper, so she was only wearing a black short-sleeved t-shirt and her jeans. Piper's gaze darted about the room, constantly going back to the open door.

"It's okay. I always train here with Julian." Lauren rolled her shoulders and warmed up.

Piper still looked wary. She toyed with the skirt of her short purple dress. "What am I supposed to do?" she said.

Lauren paused. "Throw things at me and I'll cut them down?"

"What like... chairs? I think they're antiques."

Lauren could see the flaw in her plan now. There was nothing for Piper to push or throw at her. Duke would definitely be upset if she cut the furniture to pieces. She glanced at the wooden training katana, and then thought the better of it. Julian had given her plenty of practice with those weapons and it wouldn't help her or Piper get better. She needed something different and Piper needed to practice with her skills not a sword. If Piper hurled things at her using her powers then she could throw them from all angles, keeping Lauren on her toes. It would help her in a real battle where the enemy could come at her from behind or the side.

"It is not good news." The sudden sound of Julian's voice made her jump.

She pressed her hand to her chest, cursing him for sneaking up on her.

He frowned when she looked at him. Her heart beat a little quicker when she saw that he'd removed his coat, carrying it slung over his arm. How did a man get to be so damn good looking? His ice blue eyes held hers, narrowing slightly. Strands of his black hair fell down across them and she was tempted to brush them away so she could see them clearer, to caress his forehead and cheek, and lure him in for a kiss.

Embarrassed, she dropped her gaze. It stopped on the marks on his neck and her cheeks burned to see them and then blazed when she remembered how good it had felt to be pressed against, his hands sliding over her. She was sure that he had raised the hem of her slip enough to see her backside and she was sure she'd felt him sneak a peek at it. Her whole face burned. Julian raised an eyebrow, a sparkle in his eyes that told her he had noticed her racing heart and the desire spiralling through her. She wondered how he could sound so casual when he spoke.

"Ghosts have reported another increase in werewolf sightings. They killed eight last night but suffered casualties. The werewolves are moving. I am going out to scout."

Those last six words made her stomach drop. She was across the room in an instant, standing in front of him.

"No. It's daylight out there. You said it yourself. We're weak in the day. Look at what that other werewolf did to you when I—" Lauren held her hand out when he didn't look as though he was going to heed her words. "Give me your sword."

His eyes darkened and his hand went to the weapon hanging at his side. He frowned but handed it to her. She held it behind her back.

If she'd thought that it would stop him, she'd been mistaken.

"I will return before nightfall."

Lauren grabbed his wrist with her other hand. "You can't go out. I won't let you. It's too dangerous. Morgan will come and then we can go out."

He gave her a thunderous look. It had been another mistake to mention Morgan.

"You really believe that he will come?" Julian's tone was as black as his look.

"No. But I have to hope that he will. You said that we needed him. If you're willing to put yourself through this, through working with him, then we must really need help."

"Who's Morgan?" Piper said.

Neither Lauren nor Julian looked over. Lauren tightened her grip on Julian's wrist when he tried to move again and lowered her head, staring at his boots.

She couldn't say what she needed to when she was looking at him, not without tripping on the words or giving up.

"Please don't go out. I want you to stay with me. I'll feel safer if you stay. I need you, Julian... I don't want anything to happen to you. Don't go out, not today, not without me." She swallowed and closed her eyes when he removed her hand from his wrist. He was going to leave. "Please."

Her heart jumped when he touched her cheek, his hand sliding over her skin until he was cupping it, holding it gently and raising her head. She opened her eyes and stared straight into his, losing herself in the affection in their icy blue depths. The heat in his gaze made her want to look away but he held her steady, as though forcing her to see all his feelings and the effect her words had had on him. She hadn't said them to provoke feelings of tenderness in him. They had spilled out of her, words straight from her heart to his, a plea for him to stay because she needed him more than air and couldn't bear the thought of losing him.

"You looked as though you were going to train," he said but her heart heard different words in the tenderness of his tone. Her display of affection had touched him, pleased him, and he was happy.

She nodded.

He reached around her. His body pressed into hers, their eyes still locked. Her breathing hitched. His hand grazed hers and he took hold of his sword. A faint smile teased his lips and made her insides flutter. She released the sword and Julian stayed a moment, staring into her eyes with his body against hers, and then stepped back. He held the sword out to her.

"You could use practice with a long sword. I will watch."

Lauren took the sword, unsure of what to say. She felt giddy from the feel of him touching her and overwhelmed by the fact he was allowing her to use his katana. It showed his trust in her more than anything he might have said.

With a smile, she unsheathed the sword and held it in both hands. It really was a magnificent weapon.

"That's a scene for an erotic anime if ever I saw one," Leo said as he leaned against the doorframe and raked his gaze over her. "In fact, I think I own one like it."

Leo stumbled forwards past Julian when Kuga pushed him. "Pervert. Still, katana-wielding woman is always going to be a popular image. It suits you."

"I'm just borrowing it," Lauren said, heat scorching her cheeks. "We were going to practice."

"You and Julian?" Leo propped himself up against the wall.

"No. Piper and I."

Kuga's eyes widened but then he smiled.

"Only I have nothing to throw." Piper's tone held a note of emphasis. Lauren hadn't forgotten that they were lacking missiles. Kuga stepped forwards.

"I think I can help." With a flick of his wrist, he produced a bright blue crackling ball. He turned his grin on Piper. "I make them, you throw them. They won't hurt if they hit her."

"Who said they're going to hit me?" Lauren readied herself.

As Piper hurled the first energy ball at her, Lauren ducked to one side and turned swiftly to cut it in two. It disappeared on contact with the sword.

Lauren grinned at Julian. He was watching her, a smile curving his beautiful lips and a new light in his eyes. She'd made him happy. Her chest warmed and she attacked the second ball with glee, throwing everything into it. All her worries melted away and she couldn't stop smiling when Piper started getting into it too, attacking her from different angles as though looking for a weak spot. Kuga started laughing and it wasn't long before Leo was cracking jokes and Lauren was missing balls. Each one that struck her gave her a tiny jolt but she didn't care.

It had been too long since she'd had this much fun.

She only wished she could shake the feeling that something terrible was about to happen.

CHAPTER 29

The sun was still up. Lauren trudged through the pale blue corridors, weary and trying to ignore the voice inside her that was telling her to return to her room where it was safe. She didn't want to. The moment Julian had left her alone, she'd started thinking about the bad feeling in the pit of her stomach and it had grown worse. She'd tried to sleep but it had evaded her. A few minutes ago, she had given up her fight and gone to Julian's room. It had taken her a while to build up the courage to open his door and when she had, she had found that the bedside lamp was on but Julian was sound asleep. She had stood there for a long minute, taking in the sight of him as he slumbered, his black hair messy and his chest bare. The brown duvet had covered him from the waist down and Lauren had wondered if he slept naked.

Some part of her was still wondering it.

She hadn't had the heart to wake him. He needed his rest and it was selfish of her to wake him just to have some company. She'd snuck forwards instead and had stolen a kiss, pressing her lips lightly against his. He had moved when their mouths had met and her stomach had flipped with anticipation, light from the thought that he might return the kiss. He had murmured something, smiled and fallen still again.

Now she was searching for someone else to talk to. Was Kuga awake? The training session with Piper last night had only been a success because he had shown up. She wanted to thank him. She tried to think where he would be in the afternoon if he were awake.

The first place she checked was the living room. Kuga wasn't there. Duke was. She could smell him and hear his heart beating but couldn't see him. She walked forwards into the low-lit room, the shutters blocking out the sun, and peered over the back of the cream couch directly in front of her. Duke was sprawled out on it, his white shirt half-undone and one shoe off, that leg dangling over the edge. Her eyebrows rose and she watched his fingers twitching. It wasn't a usual sleep twitch. There was something wrong about the way his fingers were tensing, making his hands look like an eagle's claws. She jumped when he flung an arm out to his right. It slammed into the coffee table but he didn't wake. Lauren looked at his hand, resting palm up on the coffee table. The roses on it were moving, shifting as though in a breeze. Her eyes widened when one of them changed colour, brightening from black to red. Duke muttered something, words she didn't understand but she felt the power in them. A chill descended on the room. Lauren stepped back, instinct telling her to leave before she was hurt. Duke would never consciously hurt her, but she doubted he would know he was doing it when he was asleep.

She closed the living room door and continued along the corridor, past the closed double doors of Duke's office, down the stairs to the ground floor and back up the other set towards the kitchen. The gym door was open. She smiled when she saw one of the twins inside and walked in. He didn't stop what he was doing and he didn't notice her. He stood with his back to her, raining hell and fury down on a full-length punch bag in the middle of the white room. All of the other gym equipment lined the sides, leaving an open space in the centre covered with black mats. A sickening sense of anger curled around her, shrouding her in a dark haze. His scent came through it along with other feelings, all negative and all strong.

Leo.

And he was in a bad mood.

She went to back out of the room but he caught the punch bag and turned towards her. The scowl on his face made him ugly, his usually bright brown eyes so dark they were almost black. When he noticed her, his look shifted and his feelings lightened.

"Lauren," he said with a smile that she knew was fake. His emotions might have changed slightly, but they hadn't changed completely. He was angry about something and the punch bag was paying for it.

He wiped the black sweatband around his wrist across his forehead and breathed hard. Sweat beaded over his bare muscular shoulders and arms, and the black tank top he wore was drenched in a V down the front and back. He smiled again. This time there was genuine feeling in it.

"Couldn't sleep?" he said, still out of breath.

She nodded, hesitated, and then said, "I was looking for Kuga."

Leo's look darkened, all of the anger coming back stronger than it had been before. It left her feeling queasy. She remembered what Piper had said about the brothers and how they fought sometimes. Had Kuga done something to upset Leo? Perhaps she should have left without mentioning his brother.

Leo turned back to the punch bag and started hitting it again, harder this time, so it swung violently back and forth. She hadn't meant to upset him more but clearly she had. She didn't know what to do so she stood there, waiting to see if he would tell her were Kuga was and unsure whether to just leave. Part of her wanted to ask Leo what was wrong, to try to comfort him and lessen his anger. She didn't want to leave him alone to wallow in his feelings. She wanted to make him feel better.

He sneered and punched the bag again, so hard that the chain rattled and she looked at the metal plate that fixed it to the ceiling, fearing it was going to break.

"Kuga?" Leo snarled and hit the bag. Lauren swallowed, her guard rising and her whole body tensing, readying for a fight that she didn't want to happen. Leo laughed. "Kuga, Kuga, bloody Kuga… everyone loves the golden boy."

Bright white sparks of electricity arced along his fingers and he hit the punch bag again. It almost hit the ceiling and swung back fast at Leo. He hit it with his other fist, the electricity there making it a white blur, and the punch bag broke away from the ceiling and flew across the room, slamming into the far wall. Lauren stepped back. Leo turned on her, anger shining in his eyes and written in the thin line of his lips. His fingers curled into fists again and twisted ribbons of electricity chased around them. She didn't want to be on the receiving end of a punch powered like the one the bag had fallen to. Immortal as she was, she was sure it would hurt like a bitch.

The darkness in Leo's eyes lightened and he drew a deep breath. Lauren was relieved to hear his heart steadying and sense his feelings settling down.

"Kuga is out," he said from between clenched teeth.

"I'm out?"

Lauren tensed on hearing Kuga behind her. He walked into the room and she wanted to turn to him, to tell him to get the hell back because his brother was about to explode, but couldn't move. Leo stared past her, the darkness back in his eyes.

"Well, now that you're back, maybe you'd care to join me?" Leo's voice was tight with the rising anger Lauren could feel in him.

She turned to Kuga. He stood by the door, dressed in his usual black jeans and a black jacket. He removed it to reveal a long sleeve black turtleneck. Piper stood behind him, her shiny blue bomber jacket open to reveal clothing that surprised Lauren. It was more provocative than her usual attire—a small dark purple low-cut top that exposed some cleavage and tight deep blue jeans. If Piper had been out on a mission with Kuga, it wasn't the only reason she was dressed more seductively. She wanted Kuga's attention. It was written in the way Piper's brown gaze was fixed steadily on Kuga, so much so that she seemed oblivious to the tension between the brothers.

Kuga stepped forwards. Lauren wanted to tell him to leave, to not train with his brother because something bad was likely to happen. Leo was out for blood and Lauren had a feeling she knew why. Piper had mentioned before that Kuga was stronger than Leo, and Leo probably didn't like it.

Kuga handed his black jacket to Piper, who hugged it to her chest, her gaze now on Leo. The worry in her eyes and the hint of fear lacing her scent told Lauren that she'd realised something was up with Leo.

Lauren stepped back, towards the wall, as Kuga passed her. She held her breath, struggling to say something that would stop the fight she could sense coming. Kuga pushed his sleeves up.

The moment he readied himself, Lauren opened her mouth to speak but it was too late.

Leo unleashed a tremendous bright white bolt of electricity with both hands. It slammed into Kuga's chest and flung him across the room. He hit the wall, fracturing the plaster, and then fell to the floor, lying face down on the mats and very still. Piper was kneeling beside Kuga in an instant, her glare directed at Leo.

"Jesus, Leo! What the hell is wrong with you?" Piper scowled at him and then placed her hands on Kuga's shoulders and pulled him over.

Lauren could hear his heartbeat. It was fast but stable. She was surprised that Kuga could take such a shock without serious injury. Did their power render them resistant to attacks by electricity?

Leo left without even looking at Kuga.

Lauren looked down at Piper and Kuga. Kuga opened his eyes and smiled dazedly up at Piper as she stroked his forehead, tears lining her eyes. He raised a trembling hand and wiped her tears away before they could fall. Lauren glanced at the door again and considered leaving quietly so Piper could be alone with Kuga, but Kuga pushed himself up and then stood. He dusted the plaster from his backside and frowned at the open door.

"What was that all about?" Lauren said and he looked at her.

"Remember that sibling rivalry I mentioned?" Piper answered and sighed. "I said it could get nasty."

"Why?" Lauren tried to sense Leo. He was distant but she could still feel his anger flowing through the building, lacing the air. What had happened to make him so mad?

Kuga rubbed his head and then flinched when a spark leapt from his fingertips and hit his forehead. He flicked his hand, shaking off the threads of electricity crackling along them.

"Leo always gets touchy when Kuga is chosen for a mission over him." Piper went to Kuga and placed her hand on his arm.

He smiled again. "I'll be alright. He caught me off guard, that's all."

Kuga's gaze dropped to Piper's chest and then shifted back to the door. It didn't surprise Lauren that Piper was proving a distraction for Kuga. The way she was dressed was bound to get his attention when she normally wore clothes that covered her up.

"Duke chose you for a mission rather than Leo?" Lauren said.

Kuga nodded. "He called us both into his office and selected me for a solo mission."

"Only you asked me to come along," Piper whispered and Lauren could sense that she felt guilty that Kuga had asked her to go with him, again leaving Leo out.

"I needed your power and we look better as a couple than I would with my brother. It's less conspicuous for us to be seen together." Kuga's tone was blasé but there was an underlying thread of nerves in his heartbeat. He glanced at Piper.

Her cheeks were beetroot red and her smile was ear to ear.

Lauren held her smile inside, glad that Kuga and Piper were growing closer. They still didn't look as though anything was official yet, but she knew it wouldn't be long before they really were a couple.

How would Leo feel then?

She reached out again with her senses, searching for him. The anger was still there. She couldn't blame him for being upset about having his younger brother chosen over him, especially if it happened often. In fact, she could sympathise with him. She'd spent her whole life being picked last and overlooked, only it was probably a lot worse when it was your own twin chosen over you.

"You want to train?" Kuga said and Lauren shook her head.

"Actually, I just wanted to thank you for helping out last night."

He shrugged. "No problem. Pip needs the practice."

Piper frowned and pushed his arm, sending him stumbling to the side. She gasped and rushed to him, her hands fluttering about him and her eyebrows furrowed. Lauren smiled.

"I'm sorry. It was only a little shove," Piper said with guilt in her eyes again.

Kuga laughed and rubbed the back of his head. "Guess he must have hit me harder than I thought, or you're stronger than you look."

Piper grinned, her cheeks bright red.

Lauren took a step back towards the door and both of them looked at her.

"You sure you don't want to practice?" Piper said and Lauren shook her head again.

"I need to get some rest before tonight but you two should practice." Lauren looked at them both in turn and then settled on Piper. She smiled. "In fact, I think it would be good for you to practice together."

Piper blushed again and then tensed when Kuga placed his hand on her shoulder.

"'Night." Lauren waved and then walked to the door. She glanced back at Piper, smiling again when she saw her looking up into Kuga's eyes.

Maybe soon they would take the next step. Piper's birthday was drawing close now and she was sure that Kuga wasn't just going to show her the city that night. She was sure he would tell her about his feelings.

Lauren walked down the hall, the weariness returning as her mind emptied. She slowed when she neared Julian's door and then stopped outside it. His heart was beating steady and strong, his breathing soft. He was still sleeping.

She didn't hesitate this time before opening the door. She peeked inside and smiled when she saw Julian sprawled out beneath the bedcovers. He looked fantastic. She thought about waking him and then decided against it. He needed rest as much as she did and she couldn't disturb him just because she was scared of being alone in her room with her bad feeling.

She stepped back to leave and he stirred, rolling onto his side. He frowned and then his eyes snapped open and he was suddenly sitting up, staring right at her, one hand reaching towards his sword where it rested propped against the wall between the bed and the side table.

"Lauren," he whispered, an air of confusion about him, and he brought his hand away from his katana. "Is something wrong?"

"I didn't mean to wake you." She closed the door to give them some privacy, walked over to the bed and sat down on the edge, facing Julian. He moved backwards, sitting with his back against the headboard and the covers tucked in around his waist. She tried to keep her eyes off his chest and stomach. "I couldn't sleep."

"Do you still have the sensation that something will happen?"

She nodded.

Julian pushed his fingers through his black hair, pulling the strands out of his face, and sighed. He dragged his hand down over his face, closed his eyes and leaned his head back. He was tired. She could feel it in him and it made her feel terrible for waking him.

Lauren looked at the marks on his neck. Her marks. They were dark pink and tempting. He swallowed, sending his Adam's apple bobbing, and she wanted to lick the length of his jugular and kiss every inch of his throat before sinking her teeth into it. She swallowed too and then stared at the brown bedcovers when Julian looked at her.

"How do you feel now?" he said and she glanced at him. His pale blue eyes were dark in the low light from the bedside lamp.

"Better." She found the courage to look him in the eye. "I feel better when I'm around you."

He smiled and her heart fluttered. "Better enough to sleep?"

She nodded again.

"Would you like me to come to your room?" he asked and her eyes widened. He swallowed again and then quickly said, "I could sleep in the chair."

She shook her head, heat creeping onto her cheeks as she thought about what he'd said and what she wanted to say. She could do this. All she had to do was open her mouth and let the words spill out, just as she had last night in the ballroom, only this time she was going to look him in the eye and say it.

"Julian," she whispered and her gaze met his. A jolt rocked her, as strong as it had the first time she'd looked into his eyes. She cleared her throat and picked at the bedcovers. Her heart settled and she stared into his eyes. The shine in them fascinated her, just as it had last night. He was happy again. Was it because he knew what she wanted to say? If he knew, then she could just say it. "Can I stay here with you?"

Her pulse set off at an alarming rate and doubled when Julian nodded.

"I can take the sofa," he said and went to leave the bed. Lauren caught a flash of the waistband of his black boxers and then reached out to him.

"No," she said and he stopped and looked back at her. Her hands trembled and her heart skittered about in her chest. "I can sleep on the... Julian... I... can I... I want to stay close to you."

He looked down at the empty space in the bed beside him, his eyes wide. His heart rate picked up until it almost matched the speed of hers.

"I can sleep on top of the covers," she said hurriedly, hoping he wasn't going to turn her away. She wasn't crazy. He had feelings for her. She knew it. Just as she had feelings for him. All she wanted was to be close to him, to feel him beside her, so she would feel safe and could sleep.

"Lauren." He stopped and frowned, staring at her now. His eyes darted between hers and she could sense his feelings were in disarray. She'd triggered another internal battle and she wished she knew what was wrong and what he was thinking. She wanted to ask him to tell her, to order him if she had to, but she couldn't find her voice. "You really wish to remain here... with me?"

She nodded and swallowed her trembling heart, knowing that he was asking about more than just sleeping in his bed. He wanted to know if she was serious about him, if she had feelings for him and if she wanted to be with him. "I want to stay with you."

He surprised her by drawing the covers back, revealing the white sheet beneath, and looked at her.

It felt like a challenge.

If she wanted to be with him, she had to make the first move to prove it. She stood, removed her trainers with shaky fingers, and then froze. She looked down at her jeans. She wanted to take them off but wasn't sure how Julian would react. Her fingers skimmed over the belt and she looked at Julian. His gaze was tracking her hand, his pupils wide and dark. Perhaps he wouldn't run if she undressed. Perhaps this was the push they both needed to leap the first hurdle and stop skirting around their feelings.

She undid her jeans, pushed them down her legs, kicked them off, ran around the bed while sensing Julian's gaze on her, leapt into bed, rolled onto her side with her back to Julian, dragged the covers over herself and hid.

That wasn't so hard.

The bed was warm.

Her heart was thundering.

She swallowed again and switched her focus to Julian. He was still sitting up behind her. She tensed when he lay down and then closed her eyes when his hand came to rest on her arm.

"You can come closer if you wish," he said in a low voice that sent a delightful shiver down her spine. "I shall not bite you."

Lauren rolled over into his arms, feeling as though she was dreaming as they wrapped around her and held her close. She settled her head against his bare chest and closed her eyes, savouring how it felt to be in his arms.

After a few minutes had passed, Julian's heart was slow and steady again in her ear and his breathing was soft. Lauren relaxed and smiled. It hadn't been so difficult after all and the reward for her bravery was incredible. Sleeping like this with him made her feel warm and loved, and most of all safe.

Lauren looked up at Julian. His lips parted as he slept, revealing blunt teeth. She blushed.

She wished he would bite her.

CHAPTER 30

"And he said that he would give you his answer tonight?" Duke's expression was stern but thoughtful.

Lauren had spent the past hour standing in Duke's office explaining about their meeting with Morgan. Everyone had a different opinion about working with a vampire. None as strong as Astra's. She didn't want to. Duke had bore the brunt of her anger but Lauren knew that she was angry with her too. Astra wasn't happy that her blood had created the first vampire. Julian had explained that it had been Sonja's blood and not hers, but Astra didn't care. Both of them were a reincarnation of Illia. To Astra, they were the same.

Kuga and Leo seemed to be back on talking terms. It was almost as though the incident in the gym had never happened. They had both voiced concerns about working with a demon that they couldn't trust. Piper didn't like the fact that Julian and Morgan hated each other. She didn't want to see anyone get hurt. Lauren could understand that. If Morgan joined them, he was likely to try to hurt Julian.

Duke seemed to enjoy the idea of a vampire joining them.

And Lauren didn't think it was because of the number of men that he would bring.

"He did. The night is still pretty young so there's plenty of time for him to—" Lauren's blood turned to ice and she stiffened as the feeling of danger in her increased a hundredfold.

Piper touched her shoulder. "What's wrong?"

"I feel him," Lauren whispered.

The lights went out, plunging them into darkness.

Her eyes automatically adjusted, her canines sharpening with them and her senses on high alert.

Julian grabbed her hands and shoved her two short katana into them.

A moment later, two glowing pale blue balls appeared, punctuating the black and chasing it back. They illuminated Kuga and Leo's faces.

Lauren stared wide-eyed straight ahead, ice creeping up her spine. She didn't want to know how she could feel him at such a distance or how she knew it was Lycaon, but she could and she did. She blinked. "Courtyard."

"Damn," Duke muttered from the shadows.

Lauren looked over at him. The broad hairy frame of a werewolf filled one of the windows, towering over Duke. It turned its deadly yellow gaze from Duke to her and opened its jaw. Saliva oozed down its long teeth. It threw its head back and howled.

Before she could turn to Julian, he was out of the French doors and on the balcony, cutting the werewolf down mid-howl.

Another howl sounded in the night.

And then another, until it was a cacophony in her ears. She covered them, her heart pounding. They had found them.

He had found them.

Two more werewolves appeared on the balcony and then there were shouts from below. It had to be the other Ghost squad. They had returned a few minutes ago and had been unloading gear from their car in the courtyard. Lauren moved immediately. She had to help them. The werewolves were here because of her.

"Damn!" Duke cursed again and grabbed his guns from the desk. He shot through the window at one of the werewolves. The glass shattered. The bullet buried deep in the werewolf's chest and it exploded, showering blood and flesh down on the courtyard.

Lauren made a mental note to avoid those bullets.

He rushed out onto the balcony and disappeared.

Astra's eyes turned violent blue, lighting the darkness. In a flash, she was gone, leapt through the broken window and into the fight. Kuga and Leo patted Lauren on the shoulder, gave her a wink, and followed Astra out into the fray. Piper went after them.

Without a second thought, Lauren ran out into the fight. She'd never killed before. The thought of taking a life, even a werewolf one, made her hands shake. It was a fight just to steady them enough to unsheathe her two short katana, but it wasn't time to be scared. It was time to fight. Julian had taught her well and he would be close to her. It was time to prove how strong she was. She would defeat Lycaon.

"How the hell did they know we were here?" Duke reappeared close by her elbow, looking a little tired and firing off another shot at a werewolf that was coming in from above.

They were attacking from all angles. The courtyard below was crawling with them, the Ghosts there fighting for their lives. Lauren noticed that Duke's car was gone and looked at him. He smiled and shrugged. Was that where he'd gone, to teleport his car to safety? Before she could ask him, she spotted Astra across the balcony with Leo. Werewolves surrounded them and they were fighting like wildcats.

"Someone must have told them!" Leo shouted, firing off bright bolts of electricity that lit the pale stone walls of the courtyard and sent werewolves flying across it.

"Your new vampire friend perhaps?" Astra grabbed a werewolf around the throat. Lauren grimaced when Astra bit it on the neck, striking like a cobra, and the werewolf convulsed and died, returning to human form. It had been a woman.

"No." Lauren couldn't believe that Morgan would do such a thing. He was compelled to kill werewolves just as she and Julian were, and he had seemed as though he needed her. He wouldn't send Lycaon after them. It didn't make sense.

The hairs on the back of her neck rose and she stiffened.

She turned on a pinhead to face the werewolf behind her. Her heart thundered and she backed away a step. It snarled and swiped at her, its claws cutting through the sleeve of her green jumper as she raised her arm to defend herself. Lauren leapt back a step and readied her swords for a fight. The panic she'd expected didn't come. Nothing but calm filled her. When the werewolf lunged for her, she crossed her two swords across its throat, beheading it. It slumped to the floor and she stared at it.

That had been too easy.

A growl.

Lauren spun on the spot and stared up at the second werewolf. It towered over her, much larger and fiercer than the one she'd just killed, radiating strength that made her tremble. She tried to back away but stepped on one of the terracotta plant pots and stumbled, almost losing her footing completely. The werewolf stalked after her, treading on the plant pot that had tripped her and smashing it. Her heart raced and she fumbled with her swords as its paw came crashing towards her, razor-sharp claws shining in the moonlight. She flinched away and brought her swords up in a desperate attempt to block the attack.

The tip of a blade appeared through the werewolf's chest. It snarled and tried to pull the silver sword out. The blade disappeared into the werewolf's chest and it stumbled forwards. Lauren stepped to the side and pressed herself against the wall to avoid the swipe the werewolf took at her. It growled, clawed at the bleeding wound in its chest and fell over the balcony into the fight below.

Julian stood before her, half of his face hidden behind the tall funnel collar of his long black coat. The hard look in his eyes quickly changed to one of concern and she knew he was silently asking her to be more careful. She nodded and readied her swords, sucking in a deep breath to calm herself. It was just like a big kendo match, only she had to be the victor this time. Julian had taught her well. She could do this. She could fight the werewolves and protect her friends.

"Morgan would gain nothing from betraying our location," Julian said loud enough for everyone to hear over the din of battle. "They must have followed us."

"Agreed," Duke said, firing two more rounds from his position across the balcony. This time the werewolves they struck didn't explode. They simply dropped dead, shifting back into their human shapes.

There was a garbled scream from below. Lauren raced to the railings and then turned sharply away when she saw one of the werewolves mauling a member of the other Ghost squad.

She still had her eyes closed when she sensed another werewolf near her. She blocked its attack with one sword and then opened her eyes and struck at it with the other, slicing down its chest. It howled and she spun on the spot, bringing both swords around together and cutting it in half across the midriff. It toppled to the ground, spilling blood across the balcony that ran over the edge to the courtyard below. Lauren looked around, forcing herself to see what was happening. This was all because of her. Lycaon was trying to get to her. These people were trying to help her and she had to do something to give them a chance. There were only four Ghosts down below, most of them young, and at least nine werewolves.

"Leo! Astra!" Both of them looked over at her. "Get down there and help!"

Leo nodded and clambered down the metalwork of the balcony before she could say another word. Astra gave her a cold look and then disappeared, reappearing in the fray. She scowled up at Duke. Duke grinned and winked, evidently amused at teleporting Astra somewhere she hadn't wanted to go.

"Kuga, Duke, Piper, I need you to keep them out of the building up here," Lauren said and didn't wait for a response. "More are coming."

Another six werewolves dropped down from the roof, using their claws against the walls to control their descent. Lauren readied herself, intent on fighting and winning the battle. She wasn't going to fail her friends and the other Ghosts.

Duke appeared amidst the werewolves when they landed on the balcony, shooting with wild abandon and shifting whenever a werewolf struck at him. Their attacks passed straight through as he seemingly jumped from werewolf to werewolf, appearing only briefly enough to shoot them and then disappearing again.

The powers the Ghosts held were amazing.

She had amazing power too. She had killed that last werewolf without even trying. Instinct had guided her movements and it had been incredible.

As she realised that, a mighty howl sounded above her. Her head snapped up, her gaze immediately fixed on the owner of it. A man silhouetted against the crescent moon. His long hair and coattail flowed in the frigid wind.

She knew him.

Her blood chilled.

The man drew a sword.

Lycaon.

Lauren was moving in an instant, heading towards the man who had killed her parents, intent on having her vengeance.

"No!" Julian shouted from behind her. "Wait... I need to tell you something!"

She cut her way through the werewolves that blocked her path, not stopping to hear what Julian had to say. She had to get to Lycaon and end the fight before anyone else was hurt. The werewolves fell in slow motion, some dead and others injured, and she pressed on, her eyes never leaving her target.

Two floors above her.

Lauren sprung at the wall and ran along it, heading upwards, using the deep windowsills and shutters to help her. Her focus remained fixed on Lycaon. She leapt onto a small balcony on the floor below the roof and jumped the gap to the next, working her way around the square courtyard of the building, back towards her enemy. The sound of the battle grew distant.

When she ran out of balconies, Lauren ran up the wall, using all of her speed and dragging one of her swords along behind her. Orange sparks showered down onto the world below. Still her focus stayed on Lycaon. He'd moved to face her. He was waiting. She could feel it.

He was calling to her.

The moon was low and bright. It lit his face when he turned to her with open arms. Lauren gripped her swords, sped up the slate incline of the roof and hit the flat top, sprinting towards him. He was larger than she'd expected from his silhouette, his build broader than Kuga or Leo's, but she had faced bigger werewolves. Her gaze fixed on his face. He looked barely the same age as her but she wasn't going to let that deceive her. The closer she got to him, the clearer she could sense his strength, and he was far more powerful than she was. It added to her fear, making her feel as though she was doomed to failure. She wasn't. She could do this. She could defeat him.

She would defeat him.

A smile curved his thin lips and the breeze toyed with his hair. Grey streaked the long dark waves and the silver-blue thread that held it back in a ponytail glinted in the light, as though made from the moon itself. His eyes narrowed, empty pools of black in the low light, and he tilted his chin up.

With a yell, Lauren launched herself at him, bringing both swords down. He grinned, amusement lighting up his dark eyes, and stepped to one side, easily evading her attack. She stumbled past him, through the flowing tail of his long black coat, and struggled to regain her footing.

The moment she did, she turned and attacked again. He didn't move this time. He simply blocked with his sword and pushed her back. She almost fell on her backside.

She hadn't expected him to be so strong, or that she would have to fight him in human form. It made it difficult for her. The others she had killed had been monsters. Abominations. Now she felt as though she was fighting a human even when she knew that he wasn't.

His sword came down fast. Lauren quickly crossed her two shorter ones in front of her. His blade struck the left one of hers and slid down to the V she'd formed. Her arms trembled as he surged forwards, a sneer twisting his lips and narrowing his eyes, and she pushed back, desperate to stop him from cutting her.

Shoving forwards, she managed to gain enough room to leap backwards. She breathed hard and clutched her swords, readying herself again. Her hands trembled. Nothing she did steadied them.

Lycaon held his sword out to one side. It wasn't a katana. It looked European, like a broadsword. He straightened and smiled. He was mocking her. That thought made her stand tall, made anger rush through her. She frowned, focusing on him and her abilities. She clenched her teeth and her fangs cut into her gums below. With a cry, she ran at him, raising her swords at the last minute. Her attacks were rough and unfocused. She searched for an opening but everywhere she struck, he blocked her with little effort. She'd underestimated him but she wasn't going to back down now.

If Lycaon died, she would be free. They would be free. She and Julian could be together and nothing would hurt them ever again.

Lauren used all of her speed to pass Lycaon and attacked from behind. He whirled to face her and something flashed in his eyes. Victory. His sword came at her so fast that she couldn't block it. She threw herself forwards and cried out when the tip of his sword caught her shin. Rolling onto her feet, she clutched her leg and tried to stifle the wave of panic that crashed over her when blood trickled down her leg. Stark reality sunk in. He was trying to kill her. This wasn't pretend as it was in the movies or harmless combat as it was in her kendo classes. This was a real fight. This was life and death. It chilled her to the bone, but she refused to surrender.

Gripping her swords, she assumed a fighting stance and glared at Lycaon. He wouldn't be the victor. She was going to defeat him.

She growled and thrust one of her swords at him, forcing him to block. He struck that sword away, but she brought the other one down. He shifted in an instant, so fast that she didn't see him move. Her eyes widened when she sensed him behind her and she spun on the spot, bringing both of her swords up in a blind attempt to defend herself.

A foot in her stomach knocked the breath from her and she fell backwards, hitting the flat top of the roof and skidding dangerously close to the angled section. One of her swords fell from her hand, tumbling down the roof and catching in the gutter.

"It was too easy this time." Lycaon's voice was deep, laced with both amusement and a hint of disappointment. The moon shone on his face. It was one she would never forget, covered with small scars and rough-hewn, a face that had seen many battles. A familiar face. A cruel smile tugged at the corner of his lips.

Before she could move, his blade was closing in on her throat.

Lauren's heart stopped.

She stared up into his eyes. Their dark irises melted to yellow.

It was over.

A black blur shot past her and the sound of metal clashing rang through the night. Julian stood over her, his feet planted either side of her thighs, and his sword blocking Lycaon's.

"Go," Julian said without looking at her.

Lauren scrambled backwards. He didn't need to tell her twice to move but she wasn't going to leave him here to fight Lycaon alone. Together they could defeat him. Her arm stung when she tried to lift her sword. Lycaon had cut her again at some point and she hadn't realised. The warm burning sensation soon gave way to a cold numb feeling when the chill breeze blew against her. She moved her sword to her left hand and struggled to calm herself. It was her weaker one but she'd developed good strength in it during her years doing kendo. She would still be able to fight.

"I will not let you hurt her," Julian said.

Lauren could only watch as he and Lycaon fought. It was fast and violent, both moving at speeds that made it hard to keep up with them even with her new senses. Was this how Lycaon had expected her to fight?

Lauren realised with disappointment and confusion that Lycaon had been going easy on her. Why? He could have easily defeated her. She pushed herself up onto her feet. Pain shot up her leg and she hopped on her other one and looked down at it. Blood. It shone in the moonlight.

Her gaze returned to the fierce fight between Julian and Lycaon. The night was full of the sound of their swords clashing, one ring after another. A symphony of violence. She could never fight like that. She couldn't even come close.

Julian dropped back so he was near to her again. He was protecting her and for some reason it didn't make her feel warm this time. It made her feel weak. Without Julian around, she didn't stand a chance against Lycaon. She wasn't strong enough yet.

Lycaon glared at her and then at Julian, and then attacked again. He was relentless, but wherever he moved to, Julian was there to block his path.

Lycaon laughed.

"What are you going to do?" His tone was as mocking as his smile.

He didn't block Julian's next attack and Lauren gasped as the blade struck his shoulder, expecting it to slice through him. Julian stepped back, removing the sword and bringing it up to defend himself. There was a slash in Lycaon's coat but no blood on Julian's sword. Lycaon touched his shoulder and brought his hand away clean.

"You cannot cut me." Lycaon's smile became a grin. He struck hard and Lauren screamed as the sword hit Julian across the shoulder, mirroring the area that he'd hit Lycaon.

Julian stood there, the lower half of his face masked by his coat collar. The black spikes of his hair shifted in the breeze. He showed no hint of pain, not even when he took hold of Lycaon's blade with his bare hand and removed it.

"A stalemate." Julian thrust Lycaon's blade back at him. "You can attack forever, and I will not let you hurt her."

Lauren moved forwards. Julian looked back at her. Her eyes widened when someone else appeared beside Lycaon. It was a slim young man, no older than the twins, with eyes as yellow as Lycaon's and blond hair cut close to his head. He sneered at her, revealing sharp teeth, and Lycaon raised his hand. The man shot past him, the flared tails of his long dark military coat flowing out behind him, and drew the katana strapped to his back. Before Lauren could call out to Julian, the young man had cut across Julian's chest and was standing beside her.

Julian's eyes filled with pain and disbelief. He looked down at his chest, touching the long gash there, and then at Lycaon.

"Who said I would attack? I might not be able to hurt you… but my boy could cause you more pain than you could bear."

Julian shot around to face her.

Lauren screamed as he fell to his knees, his hand held out in front of him, blood staining his fingers. She rushed towards him. The sound of battle and the stench of blood came up from the courtyard below. Her hands shook but she readied her one remaining sword and ran straight past Julian, heading for Lycaon. Her heart was surprisingly steady. Her hands became firm, her grip sure, and she let the feel of battle flow through her. When she didn't fight her instincts, her reactions were fast and her attacks strong and graceful, exactly as they had been when she'd trained with Julian. She could do this. She wouldn't be weak. She could fight.

Lycaon blocked her attacks but she was pushing him back, each strike of her sword forcing him towards the corner of the building. Lauren yelled and brought her sword up from below, knocking Lycaon's sword out of the way. The tip of her blade sliced across his stomach and up his chest. Payback.

He snarled and leapt backwards, distancing himself.

She turned the moment she heard swords clashing. The young man was back, attacking Julian. Lauren couldn't believe her eyes. Julian was on his feet, fighting again, as strong and violent as before, and Lauren knew in her heart that he was doing it for her. He wouldn't give up, no matter how much he was hurting himself, not until she was safe again. His strength and power, his determination to protect her, touched her beyond words. Not even a mortal wound was stopping him. Seeing him fight for her gave her the resolve to fight for him in return, to use every last shred of her strength and skill to defeat Lycaon and the young werewolf.

She brought her sword up and Lycaon attacked, faster than she could defend. She half-blocked his attack but had to dive to the side to avoid his blade. He struck again but halted mid-way, his sword held still in the air. He scowled over her head.

"Lauren!" Piper's voice echoed across the roof.

Lauren turned to see her running towards them, her hands held up in the air.

She was stopping Lycaon. Lauren saw her chance and took it.

"Hurry, he's too strong to hold," Piper shouted.

Lauren brought her sword around and ran at Lycaon.

"Not so fast," he said.

Lauren's blood froze when Piper screamed.

She turned to see the young man heading for Piper, his blade held ready to attack. Lauren changed direction, going as fast as she could to protect Piper. Kuga reached her before she could, sending a blast of electricity into the young man that hurled him backwards. He tumbled down the roof and out of sight.

Her senses pricked and she whirled around, bringing her sword up to block the attack. Lycaon swung hard and the impact sent her backwards. She blocked repeatedly, but each one forced her towards the edge of the flat roof.

Losing her footing on the sloped side of the roof, Lauren skidded down the slates until her feet hit the low wall that edged it. The cut on her leg stung and she gritted her teeth.

Lycaon towered above her on the flat section of the roof. She went to move up the roof but stopped when Lycaon signalled and the young man appeared again, attacking Julian with glee. Her heart ached as Julian fought one handed against the man, his other arm across his injured chest.

Lauren could sense how weary Julian was. The smell of his blood made the air heavy. He couldn't hold out much longer, not fighting one handed against that sort of barrage. If she didn't intervene, the young man might defeat him. She had to do something to protect Julian. She ran up the slope of the roof. Julian leapt backwards, flipping over high in the air, and landed on his feet. A second later, he collapsed onto one knee, his hand against the slates.

Fuelled by anger, Lauren attacked the young man. He wouldn't fight back. He smiled at her as he dodged her blade, not even bothering to use his sword to block, and then disappeared, moving quickly past her. She turned and went after him, intent on making him pay. Lycaon signalled again and the man retreated, disappearing over the edge of the roof. Lauren cursed and attacked Lycaon instead.

He smiled as her blade zoomed towards him.

Wasn't he going to block?

She put all of her strength into the swing, using her body weight to propel the sword, and smiled right back at him.

If he didn't want to block, she wasn't going to complain. Her sword was going straight for his neck. She would cut his head off.

His smile widened, narrowing his eyes, and a hint of warmth touched them.

"This is the strength I expected from my daughter."

Her blade stopped, frozen in time by those words. A chill tumbled down her spine, spreading along her limbs. She stared at him, struggling to understand what he'd just said. Something deep inside her responded, calling out to him. His look softened for a split second, his dark eyes widening and becoming just like hers. Lauren reached out without thinking.

Someone moved behind her.

With a grin, Lycaon was gone.

Silence descended and reality came crashing back.

Daughter?

All of her strength left her and she collapsed to her knees. The sword fell from her hand, clattering across the bloodied rooftop.

She blinked. Her ears rang. Her insides numbed.

Daughter?

CHAPTER 31

Awareness finally began to dawn on Lauren. The night was quiet. Peaceful. The moon shone down, its light warm on her skin and soothing, a caress that she felt deep in her heart. Her cheeks were damp. She raised a hand but it shook. Her fingers trembled, stained red by the blood of her enemy.

No. The pain slowly crept back in, stinging her arm and leg. Stained by her own blood. Nothing more than a handful of words had snatched victory from her.

A painful revelation that had halted her attack and cut her more deeply than if Lycaon had used his sword.

His daughter?

A bitter laugh left her lips. Mirthless. Hollow.

She stared into the distance, over the rooftops of the city. Numb. Blood crept down her arm. It felt as though her life was flowing out of her.

"Are you okay?" Piper.

Lauren didn't have the strength to look at her. She just kept looking ahead, as though the answers to her questions lay there. They did. They lay with the man who had called himself her father.

Her father?

She frowned. She'd had parents. That man had taken her real parents from her and now he was claiming to be her father. None of it made sense and she didn't know why it was shaking her up so badly. She'd had a father. Her father had raised her, had loved her, and had taught her to do what was right. Lycaon wasn't her father.

If he wasn't, why would he say such a thing? His words hadn't halted her attack. It was the fact that she'd known the truth in them. Something inside her had responded to his claim. A glimmer of a memory had surfaced in the darkness of her soul.

Now he was gone and her answers were gone with him.

Confused and hurt, Lauren pushed herself up onto her feet. Piper went to take hold of her arm but she shook her off, not wanting anyone near her. She needed some space. Kuga and Piper stared at her as though she'd gone insane. She needed them away from her. None of this made sense but she knew that he'd been telling her the truth. He hadn't lied to her.

Her gaze settled on Julian where he knelt on the rooftop a short distance away, his arm still across his chest.

He'd once told her that her mother, Selene, old goddess of the moon, had favoured Lycaon.

He'd lied.

Her mother hadn't merely favoured Lycaon. She'd taken him into her bed.

Julian stared at her. She could smell the blood on him, see it glistening in the moonlight, covering the front of his long black coat. His collar was open. His guilty eyes confirmed her fear. He'd known. He'd lied to her. A voice at the back of her mind reasoned with her. Julian had tried to stop her from attacking Lycaon. He had wanted to tell her something and she had ignored him. Perhaps he had wanted to warn her about this. She pushed it away, too hurt to listen to reason, and hobbled over to him. Her vision blurred with hot tears but she ignored them, tried to push the pain away as it engulfed her heart, breaking her from the inside out.

She stood over Julian, looking down into his eyes and cursing him for doing this to her. She'd never felt so betrayed. She'd thought that he liked her, and that he was honest with her, having her best interest at heart. She'd been wrong. Lycaon might have killed her because of this. Why hadn't Julian told her before?

Casting her gaze downwards so she didn't have to see the pain she caused, she hesitated a moment and then slapped him. He slumped, sitting back on his heels. Lauren hobbled past him, intent on getting away.

Duke, Astra and Leo appeared from the roof door. They ran towards her and then called after her when she walked past them, not stopping. She didn't want to see anyone. She wanted to be alone.

The lights were back on in the building. She'd made it down the steps and halfway along the empty quiet corridor of the top floor when she realised that she wasn't alone anymore. Julian. She cursed him for following her. She wanted to hate him, wanted to take out all the confusion and anger burning inside her on him, but at the same time, she wanted to throw herself into his arms and cry.

"You are injured. You must feed to heal."

Ignoring his words, Lauren kept walking. He wasn't in any position to heal her. He was bleeding worse than she was.

Her heart hurt. She rubbed her chest, hoping to soothe it. Lycaon wasn't her real father. The man who had raised her was her father, the man who Lycaon had killed. It still hurt though. It hurt that the man she loved hadn't told her.

Her arm ached and throbbed, and she pressed her hand against it. The blood was sticky and warm on her palm. It made her want to retch.

"Lauren, please stop," Julian said.

She focused on him.

He felt weak and that scared her more than anything did. She wanted to be angry with him, or wanted him to be angry with her, or something insane like that. She didn't know why. Someone deserved punishment. Her or him? Lycaon? He was gone and she'd failed. Her moment had slipped through her fingers because Julian had kept things from her.

Did he trust her? Did he want to protect her? Lycaon should have killed her in that moment. She wouldn't have been able to stop him.

"Lauren, please?"

Lauren stopped and clenched her fists, staring at the floor. This wasn't just Julian's fault. She hadn't stopped to listen to him. It was her fault too. If she had stopped for a moment, perhaps he would have told her about Lycaon. All of this could have been avoided. They might have succeeded in killing Lycaon.

She tried to get everything straight in her head. Lycaon was her father. She'd frozen because she'd been about to kill him. Her father. What kind of person killed their parents?

No. She shook her head, screwing her eyes shut. He wasn't her real father. She didn't even know him, hadn't met him before tonight, and he wanted to kill her. Whatever he was to her, he wasn't her real father. A father wouldn't want to kill their daughter. A father would want to protect their daughter.

"You need blood." Julian's voice was weak.

Lauren looked over her shoulder at him. Guilt stabbed her heart when she saw him resting against the pale blue wall. A long red smear marked where he'd been leaning into it while walking.

Her brow furrowed and tears filled her eyes.

"You lied to me," she whispered. He reached a bloodied hand out to her. She shook her head and stood her ground. As much as she wanted, needed, to go to him, she needed to say this even more. "When you said that my mother had favoured Lycaon, you meant that she had slept with him… that she had a child… Illia… me."

His silence made the pain worse. She wanted him to tell her that she wasn't Illia. That it didn't matter because she was Lauren and she was different. She wanted him to say that he hadn't known about Lycaon being her father. She just wanted to hear his voice and have him tell her than none of it mattered, because he loved her, and together they would defeat the man who had killed her parents and be free.

"Why didn't you tell me?" Tears ran down her cheeks, hot against her skin.

Julian licked his lips and swallowed hard. He pressed a hand against his chest and it was hard to stop herself from going to him. He needed her help, but she needed answers.

She needed to know why.

"You asked me not to." He leaned his head against the wall. "But I tried to this time… I tried… I went against your order."

She took a step towards him, unable to stop herself when he paled.

"No, I didn't. I never asked you to."

He nodded. "After you had given me your blood… when Lycaon… had defeated you… you made me promise… ordered me… to never tell you."

Lauren gasped when Julian slid down the wall, leaving a red smear, and collapsed to his knees. She ran over to him, her knees hitting the blue carpet close to his, and her hand going straight to his shoulder to hold him up. His dull eyes swam with pain. She felt it deep in her chest, each sorry glance a shard of glass in her heart. She cupped his cheek and cursed him for following her, for weakening himself by moving. Her fingers traced the line of his jaw as he struggled for breath.

"You could not bear... the pain... knowing that you... had to kill him... your father. He exploited... that weakness. With your dying... breath... you made me promise." His eyebrows furrowed and he touched her cheek, his thumb wiping away her tears. His ice-blue eyes held hers, shining with unshed tears now, and his hand shook against her face. She covered it with hers, holding it tight as fear gripped her. Julian had to be alright. He was the strong one—her pillar. She couldn't do this without him. "So you would... never... be weak again. I have... kept that promise... upheld that order... but with you... I could not."

Her breath shuddered with each sob and she closed her eyes, holding Julian's hand against her face.

He had tried to tell her. He, a man of such incredible loyalty, a man who placed such great importance on his duty, had gone against an order and tried to tell her about Lycaon. Guilt settled firmly in her stomach, heavy and sickening. She'd struck Julian for what he'd done, when in reality he had done more for her than for any other. He had gone against his nature and tried to tell her. She hadn't listened.

"I'm sorry," Lauren whispered, not knowing what else to say to him, and looked at his chest. Had it been a silver blade that had cut him? Tight fingers squeezed her heart. "You need blood..."

"Not yet," he said and closed his eyes.

"Don't leave me, Julian!" She let go of his hand and took hold of his shoulders.

A tight smile curved his lips.

"Leave?" he whispered and slowly opened his eyes, looking at her. "Not so easy to die. Just need... a moment. Will heal... with blood."

He sighed heavily and closed his eyes again.

Lauren dragged the sleeve of her green jumper back and, without hesitating, bit into her wrist. It hurt more than she'd expected. Julian sniffed and then frowned. Before he could open his eyes, she'd pressed her bloodied wrist against his lips. He pushed it away.

"You need blood." She offered her wrist again. If it had been a silver blade, he needed strong blood to heal. She wasn't sure if hers was strong, but it was blood. "Drink."

He didn't move. Seconds ticked by and a trail of blood crept down her forearm and soaked into her jumper. His warm breath tickled her wrist. She moved it forwards so it touched his lips and her heart jumped when his mouth moved against her and then his tongue poked out. It caressed her, sending fire chasing over her skin, and she bit her lip. The slow smooth glide of his tongue over her flesh was divine. Heat pooled at the apex of her thighs when he closed his lips around her wrist and began to suck. She trembled with each pull he made on her blood and watched him through hooded eyes. He held her arm in both of his hands, gently cradling it, the black tendrils of his hair falling forwards to mask his face. Everything about the moment made Lauren feel as though he was awed, worshipping her blood, savouring it in the same way that she savoured his.

Her eyes widened when the gash on his chest, visible through his ruined coat and shirt, started knitting back together. By the time he had finished drinking, he had completely healed.

Lauren reached out and ran her fingers over his chest, fascinated by how quickly he'd healed, leaving nothing but a thin pale scar. He paused with his lips against her wrist as she stroked his skin. A flush of heat washed over her when she traced the line between his pectoral muscles and felt his eyes on her. Getting the better of herself, she took her hand back and gave him a shy smile.

"Sorry... it was just... incredible." Lauren wondered if she could sound any more lame than she did. Her arm ached as she took her other hand back from him and she struggled to hide the pain.

Julian gave her an odd look and then dragged her into his arms. He crushed her against his chest, until her eyes went round as saucers. His heart beat hard against her ear and his arms were like warm steel around her, holding her fast. As if she wanted to leave. She closed her eyes and melted into his embrace as the shock subsided. Being in his arms felt better now than ever, because now there was something behind it, feelings that she'd been longing to sense in him and had since sleeping in his embrace this afternoon. Her moment of bravery had changed everything. Julian had been warmer tonight, closer to her than ever, and she believed it was only a matter of time now. Soon things between them would change again and they would no longer hide their feelings.

"I am sorry," he whispered into her hair and held her close. "I should have told you. I should have made you wait. I should not have left you vulnerable."

Lauren smiled and sighed. The pain in her arm and leg felt distant as she absorbed his words and the affection in his tone. She felt warm and calm, peaceful.

Tired.

She could just go to sleep.

"Lauren?"

Lauren nuzzled his chest and leaned into him, too weak to hold herself up.

"Come, you need blood," Julian said.

Before she could form a protest, he'd slipped his arm beneath her knees and picked her up. She lay cradled close to his body, her hands in her lap. She wanted to sleep here safe in his arms.

"Why didn't he kill me?" she mumbled and tried to open her eyes but her eyelids felt too heavy.

Julian began to walk. She could feel each step but didn't have the energy to ask where they were going.

"Lycaon is playing with you. It is his way." Julian's arms tightened against her. Lauren smiled when she realised that it was his desire to protect her showing. "He relishes defeating you, has done for many centuries now. He no longer sees you as his daughter. Now you are just an enemy to be toyed with and defeated. I will not let that happen this time. I promise you, Lauren. I will protect you."

He held her closer and her smile widened.

"I am truly sorry," he whispered.

"I know." She was too tired to be angry with anyone right now. She just wanted to sleep for a few days and then think about things when her head didn't feel so heavy. She lazily stroked the patch of his chest visible through the cut in his clothes. "I'm sorry that he hurt you."

"I am already healed thanks to your blood." There was a hint of warmth in his voice that Lauren liked. It sounded as though he was smiling. She leaned her head back into his arm, wanting to see if he was. He was beautiful when he smiled, even more so when it was because of her.

"Does it always heal you instantly?" Her eyebrows rose as she looked up at him and saw that he was smiling, his gaze fixed straight ahead as he carried her.

His eyes dropped to meet hers and he stopped.

"I do not know," he said with a frown. "I have never fed from you since you first gave me your blood."

Lauren smiled into his eyes. "Don't tell me... I forbade it?"

He nodded. All of her predecessors had to have been insane not to love this man.

With a wave of her hand, Lauren said, "I lift all my stupid rules."

Julian smiled, dipped his head and kissed her. Warmth instantly spread through her, chasing away her fatigue. She closed her eyes and began to return the kiss, a little dizzy from the suddenness of the moment. His mouth was warm against hers, claiming her lips, dominating her with fierce and desperate passion that made her giddy. She relaxed into him, letting him take control.

She could feel his need, his passion, as he poured it into his kiss. His tongue glided over hers, teasing and hot, demanding a response. She met him, stroking his tongue with her own, eliciting a groan of pure pleasure from him that rippled through her. The kiss turned rough, short bursts that had her craning her neck to reach him, to kiss him harder. The hunger he showed her, the desire that she felt in him, made her feel as though he couldn't get enough of her. It was thrilling and passionate and she didn't want him to stop. She wanted it to go on forever.

His lips left hers and he kissed down her throat, his mouth hard against her, each kiss pressing deep into her flesh as though he wanted, no, needed, to taste her.

A thrill bolted through her when he pressed his teeth against her neck. Her heart missed a beat at the thought that he would bite her. He held her closer and she leaned her head back, silently begging him to do it. She wanted more, needed it as badly as he did.

His fingers closed over her arm and she flinched when her wound stung. Julian immediately drew back. Lauren cursed under her breath.

He leaned his forehead against her cheek, his breathing as choppy and fast as hers was. She could feel him trembling, could sense his need.

"I am sorry," he whispered gently against her.

Lauren closed her eyes and leaned her head against his. "Don't apologise... I liked it."

She felt him smile. She smiled too, still floating from the kiss. She couldn't believe that someone had forbidden such a thing, but she was glad that they had, because it had saved Julian for her and she liked it that way.

Voices came down the hall. Lauren buried her face in Julian's neck when he turned, revealing that everyone had managed to find them. She didn't want to see anyone right now.

She didn't want to deal with the questions when she didn't have the answers herself. Piper and Kuga had been on the roof. They would have heard Lycaon. They would know that she was his daughter.

The voices stopped and a cacophony of heartbeats filled the silence. Lauren refused to come out from Julian's arms.

"Lauren needs some time," Julian said and she wanted to look up at him, but didn't dare poke her head out.

"She's hurt. She needs blood," Duke replied.

Julian held her possessively against his chest. She liked this side of him. It made his feelings for her clearer and made her a little braver.

"I will take care of Lauren," he said and her cheeks burned when she thought about exactly how he could take care of her.

She told herself to get a grip. She was still bleeding. She was hardly in a position to live out her fantasies with the object of them, regardless of the temptation and the desire his kiss had stirred within her. As painful as it sounded, she needed to rest and think about what Lycaon had said so she could clear the confusion from her mind.

"I need to be alone with you now," Lauren whispered, knowing that Julian would hear her. "Please."

His hands tightened against her. A silent reply.

"Contact us in a few hours with a damage report. Until then, no one is to disturb us."

Silence.

"Will Lauren be okay?" Piper again. Lauren smiled against Julian's chest, Piper's concern warming her heart.

Julian stepped back with her, his arms tight around her and his heart drumming steadily in her ear.

"I will not let anything happen to her. I will always take care of Lauren."

Always? He turned and started walking. Lauren looked up at him. He had his gaze fixed straight ahead, his jaw set firm in a look of sheer determination. When she moved back a little, he looked down at her. The hard set of his eyes softened to reveal concern and affection.

Would he always take care of her?

Always.

She liked the sound of that.

Lauren smiled at Julian when he carried her into her bedroom and placed her down on the edge of her bed. She reached over to her right and switched on the lamp on the bedside table. Julian turned around and closed her bedroom door, and then came to stand in front of her. He stood over her, assessing her wounds with concern in his eyes. When his gaze fell to her wrist, he paused. His pupils dilated. That reaction made her wonder what he was thinking. He licked his lips. That one made her want to kiss him again.

Their first kiss had been everything she'd dreamed of—passionate, rough, and full of need.

She wanted him to kiss her like that again.

Julian dropped to his knees on the lilac carpet and lifted her leg. He frowned and checked the wound on it through the cut in her jeans. It stung when he touched it and she sucked in a sharp breath, gaining an apologetic look from him. She smiled again, hoping to alleviate his guilt, and he continued to check her over.

Her gaze slid to her right, to the photograph beside her bed. Her parents.

Julian's hands paused against her shoulders. She slowly shifted her eyes to him. He was watching her closely. The concern was back in his eyes, stronger than ever, and she could feel it in him.

"Lycaon always uses this against you." Julian brushed the hair from her face. His touch was gentle, slow, and full of hidden meaning and care. He was trying to calm her, to make her feel better, treating her as though she was fragile. Was he afraid that she would break down again?

The tears hadn't been because of Lycaon. They had been tears for Julian, because for a moment she'd believed that he'd kept things from her. Illia had banned him from telling her. How many of her predecessors had he lost because of this alone? Yet he'd kept his promise, he had obeyed her order, and not told them for three millennia. But he had tried to tell her. Was she really so different to them? Did he care about her that much that he was willing to go against his orders? It didn't matter now. She had broken them for him, released him from the chains that had bound him for millennia, and she was glad that she had.

"It still feels weird." Lauren reached over to her right and took hold of the picture of her parents, setting it on her lap. Lycaon had killed them. He wasn't her father so why did she still feel that he was? There had to be a way to convince herself that he wasn't. He was the enemy. If she didn't kill him, then he would kill her.

"There is always a connection to him and Selene that is reborn with your soul." Julian's hands appeared in view and settled over hers. His firm grip comforted her. "Your heart does not affect it. He is not your father but you will feel a connection to him."

"I had parents," she whispered and blinked back her tears when she thought about them and what Lycaon had done. "Lycaon isn't my father. I don't even know him, hadn't met him before tonight… I don't have any feelings for him other than hatred."

The realisation of that lightened her heart and cleared her head. She'd gone through with the awakening, had severed ties with her friends and the outside world, because she'd wanted to avenge her parents. And wanted to be with Julian. Lauren raised her head and gazed into his eyes. Their cool blue depths warmed her. She'd gone through with everything, had trained so hard, so she could defeat Lycaon and be with Julian.

Lycaon was nothing to her. He was playing games just as Julian had said. It had worked once but it wasn't going to work again.

Julian squeezed her hands. "I will not let Lycaon hurt you. I cannot hurt him, but I can still protect you."

Heat flushed her cheeks and she couldn't stop the smile that touched her lips. His look was so earnest, so beautifully affectionate and determined that she knew he wasn't making shallow promises. He was making a solemn vow, one that he would keep even if it meant his death.

She wasn't about to let that happen.

She was stronger now, had survived her first fight and knew what she had to do. She would train hard and do all that she could to be ready for the next battle. She wouldn't let anything happen to Julian.

She wanted him to live up to what he'd told Piper.

She wanted to be with him always.

CHAPTER 32

"Thank you," Lauren whispered and then hesitated a moment before adding, "I'm sorry I hit you."

Julian smiled at her, wondering where her sudden apology had come from. "You have done worse in the past."

"I can imagine." She looked down at their joined hands. It felt so comfortable. Did it feel comfortable to her too? They had never held hands like this before, as though they were lovers.

Her red hair slipped out from behind her right ear and covered half of her face. She didn't make a move to push it back. Her gaze remained fixed on their hands and a faint smile teased her soft dusky lips. Ever since she had come to his room this afternoon and had slept in his bed beside him, things had been different between them. They both knew they had feelings for each other and he was sure it wouldn't be long before their relationship progressed. She had been so confident when he had asked her whether she wanted to stay with him. The surety in her eyes had surprised him, but it was a welcome one, and it had strengthened his resolve to bring her completely into his life so he would no longer be alone. Lauren would be his and he would see to it that they were together for eternity.

Julian sat back on his heels, his knees pressing hard into the carpet, and looked up at her. Fatigue laced her round brown eyes and her normally rosy cheeks were pale. She blinked slowly, her long black lashes caressing her cheeks, and then looked up at him. She needed to feed, but he knew without asking that she would refuse his blood if he offered it right now. The taste of her blood and their kiss lingered in his mouth, teasing him, stirring his feelings. He'd wanted to kiss her more, longer, deeper, but didn't want to frighten her away. Three thousand years had probably robbed him of any skill he'd ever had when it came to kissing. That kiss had felt as though it was his first.

He was sure that she'd thought it was terrible. He would show her that he was better than that, that if she wanted to be with him, it would be worth it.

When she'd lifted her ban, he'd reacted without thinking, seizing the one thing he'd been aching to do for weeks now, and then the fear had set in. He'd never felt such crushing nerves. They had controlled him, made him stutter and stammer his way through what he had hoped would be a mind-blowing kiss.

He would do better next time.

"Which incarnation banned feeding from me?" she said, dragging him out of his thoughts.

Julian looked at her with a blank expression and then frowned.

"The second. She banned feeding and touching." It hurt to admit that but the sympathy in Lauren's beautiful brown eyes was worth the pain. It soothed his aching heart. He laughed. "Imagine my surprise when I found her and awakened her, and then when I went to kiss her, thinking she would remember me, she made me swear to never touch her... to keep away."

His throat felt tight. His gaze dropped. Saying that had hurt more than he'd expected. It had been millennia since he'd thought about it and he'd thought he was over it. The humiliation and shock that he'd experienced in that moment three thousand years ago had tortured him all of his life. She'd turned on him with such fierce cold eyes, rebuked him with her glare and sharp-edged words. It had imprinted itself on his mind and his heart. Never touch her. Never take her blood. Never feel alive ever again. A sentence that had felt it would last eternity.

And then Lauren had come along.

"They were crazy not to love you."

Julian stiffened. Her hand tightened against his. He could feel her nerves and fear, and he knew why she was scared. Was she saying that she loved him? His heart pounded to a fast rhythm that made him nauseas. He told himself not to read into her words, that her fear made it obvious that she hadn't meant them in that way, or that she wasn't sure about the depth of her feelings. As tempted as he was to push her for an answer, now wasn't the time. In pushing her, he might push her away. After so many millennia alone, he didn't want to ruin this one chance.

"You need to feed," he said, as though she hadn't spoken at all. "And we need to heal your wounds."

Hadn't said that she loved him.

She loved him.

His heart warmed. His fragile heart that she'd carefully rebuilt piece by piece, and breathed life back into. It was hers if she wanted it. She only had to claim it.

She sat there, watching him, a touch of crimson colouring her cheeks.

Julian glanced at her arm and then her leg, trying to distract himself from his thoughts. He would need to remove her clothes so he could get to her properly. He wasn't sure how to ask her. It had been hard enough to control himself this morning when she had lain close to him, dressed in only her underwear and a t-shirt. The very thought of her stripping off now, of running his tongue over her satin skin, stirred his desire back to boiling point. He cleared his throat and looked into her eyes. She was watching him, wide pupils stealing the brown from her eyes and telling him that she had sensed the spike in his feelings.

"We should seal those cuts," he said and she nodded. He swallowed when she stood right in front of him and removed her jeans. He couldn't look away. She pushed them down to reveal black knickers and then sat on the edge of the bed, her creamy skin a contrast to the mauve covers. His groin throbbed. This was going to be impossible. There was no way that he could control himself as he needed to, not now that she had erased all the rules. He wanted her.

Julian clenched his teeth and focused on removing her trainers and jeans. Lauren was injured. This wasn't the time to be thinking about such things. His gaze shifted to her thighs when she lifted her leg to help him remove her shoe. Gods, he wanted to settle himself between those thighs. He swallowed again and closed his eyes.

"Is something wrong?" Lauren said.

He shook his head, reined his feelings in and removed her other trainer and then her jeans. The wound on her leg wasn't too deep but Lycaon's sword was silver. It would heal slowly without help. Julian hesitated a moment and then took hold of her leg. He raised it towards him and blinked, staring at the cut and trying not to let the soft warm feel of her skin affect him. He closed his eyes the moment his lips touched her leg and breathed in deep. The smell of her blood was divine, rekindling the intense feelings of hunger and need that feeding from her had evoked. He savoured the taste of her as he licked the gash clean and then held in a groan when he sucked to draw any silver out of it and his mouth filled with her sweet blood.

Lauren didn't hold back.

She moaned and he immediately looked up at her. He ached and cursed when he saw that she was lying on the bed, propped up on her elbows, her eyes closed and head tilted back.

Julian sucked again to make sure the wound was clean, eliciting another moan from Lauren, his gaze fixed intently on her. If she kept on like that, it was going to become impossible to control himself. Her blood was intoxicating, fuelling his desire and stripping away his restraint. It was only a matter of time before he lost control and acted on his need. When he released her leg, Lauren looked disappointed. She sat up and her eyes locked with his.

"We need to clean your arm," he said.

She removed her green jumper. It pulled her camisole with it when she tugged it over her head, flashing the smooth skin of her stomach. An urge to pull her to him and pepper her stomach with kisses filled him. He cast his gaze back down to her leg. He would have to bandage it. Seeing his chance to escape torture, he went to the bathroom. There were bandages in the cabinet. He took them out and glanced at the window on his way back to Lauren. The shutters were closed. He looked at the door. No one would disturb them. That thought stirred desire in his veins. He was alone with her. Lauren looked over at him, her eyes wide and lips parted. She couldn't have looked more inviting if she had tried. He reminded himself that he was supposed to be healing her, not seducing her, and kneeled in front of her. She kept still as he bandaged her leg, split the end in two, and tied it off.

"Ready," she said and he looked up. Her cheeks were dark, her eyes still round. She ran her fingers through her hair and smiled. Sitting on the edge of the bed in nothing but her knickers and a dark red camisole, she was irresistible. Temptress. He needed her so much. Everything about her said to come and get her, and everything in him begged him to comply. He pushed away his own need and focused again on hers—not the one for fulfilment, but her need to heal, feed and rest.

Julian took hold of her upper arm and frowned at the cut. It was shallow but he still needed to clean it. Lauren needed to heal fast in case Lycaon returned.

He steeled himself and then quickly cleaned the wound and bandaged it. Lauren played with the frayed ends of the bandage when he was done, her cheeks still flushed.

"You must feed." He offered his wrist to her and she glanced at his neck. A jolt shook him, rocking him to his core at the thought that she again wanted to feed from there. It had felt too good last time. He'd never ached for a woman as fiercely as he had for her. This time it might be too much. He was already balancing on the fine line between retaining control and surrendering to his desire. She blinked slowly and licked her lips. It was no use. He could never refuse her. He didn't want to.

Julian removed his coat and focused on the damage done to it and his shirt to distract himself and claw back some control. The shirt was ruined but he would repair his coat. It was his only one and bore the scars of many battles. He'd quickly learned to repair it after acquiring it several centuries ago. He liked the air of mystery it gave him and the fact it made him instantly recognisable to most demons. Humans also had a tendency to blank him out when he was wearing it. It added to the danger that they could sense whenever they looked at him and steered them away, their instincts telling them to avoid him and forget they ever saw him.

He was folding his coat when Lauren undid the top button of his shirt, causing him to pause and watch her slender fingers working surely and steadily. No hint of nerves in her now. She was in command. She knew what she wanted and was going to take it.

If only she knew how willingly he offered it, needed to feel it again, dreamed of it. When she drank from his wrist, it thrilled him. When she fed from his neck, it was heaven. The gods couldn't create an elixir sweeter and more seductive than the feel of her fangs in his throat and her tongue on his skin.

He didn't even have time to place his coat down before she'd claimed his shoulders, pulled him up to kneel between her sweet bare thighs, and had bitten down on his neck. He shook as her fangs penetrated his flesh and bit back a moan as she drew on his blood. The sense of connection ran deep, their feelings mingling until he couldn't tell where his ended and hers began. He wanted to. He wanted to know what this meant to her and whether it felt as good to her as it did to him.

He wanted to know if she loved him.

His claws extended and he clutched his coat tightly when she withdrew her fangs and licked at the wound, the tip of her tongue caressing each hole in turn, teasing his blood out.

More cuts in his coat that he would have to repair but he didn't mind. There was nothing quite like this, having her at his neck, feeding from his vein with her hands on him. Her grip was sure against his shoulders but soon moved down, skimming across the front of his shirt. She pressed her palms against his chest and her thumbs stroked his bare skin through the rip in the material, torturing him.

He wasn't sure how much more he could endure without wanting to touch her too. The desire to clutch her to his throat was overpowering. His lips ached to whisper words into the soft shell of her ear, encouraging her to keep drinking because this was his heaven, this made everything he'd been through worth it. She made it all worth it.

She moaned softly into his throat and Julian's gaze shifted to her neck. His whole body trembled at the thought of biting her. He needed her. He needed to feel her against him, to taste her again. Her blood was incredible. He needed another taste.

Her mouth left his neck and she sat back, licking crimson-stained lips with a look of sheer pleasure on her face.

"You should rest in case Lycaon returns." His heart told her something different. He didn't want her to rest. He wanted her to stay awake and talk to him, to spend time with him, to pass the hours in idle conversation and light touches, as lovers would.

"You had so little blood from me," Lauren said and his heart started at a rapid pace, his mind racing forwards to imagine what she would say next. His gaze tried to stray from hers, to drop to the delicate curve of her throat, but he held it steady. His fangs itched to extend.

"It empowers me." It wasn't a lie. He'd never healed as quickly as he had tonight and the wound had been severe. Only a drop of her blood had given him his strength back, and more. It had been a long time since he'd felt so strong. But his desire for her blood went beyond that. He craved the sweet taste and the connection to her.

"Take more then." Lauren's gaze remained fixed on his, showing no sign of fear. Her pupils were wide. He could smell a hint of arousal on her, a scent that he loved. He wasn't the only one who enjoyed it when she fed from his neck. "So you'll be strong."

Julian went to take her wrist. She drew her hand back, away from him.

"No," she said.

His heart fell. She'd changed her mind.

"Not there. You deserve more than that," Lauren whispered and his gaze shot up to meet hers. Was she saying what he thought she was? She touched her throat. "Here."

His eyes zeroed in on her neck, following the sensual trail her fingertips took as they traced a line down it. His heart thundered in his ears, beating so hard that he felt dizzy. Her neck? Gods, he would die if he fed from there. It would push at the limit of his control, shove him past it and over the edge into oblivion. What if he couldn't stop himself? How would Lauren react if he acted on his desires?

"Come," she whispered and held her hand out to him.

She moved to kneel in the centre of the mauve bedspread. Julian stared at her, at the smooth expanses of milky skin that her fragments of clothing left exposed. He longed to caress them, to let his fingers wander in absorbed fascination across the planes of her body while he kissed every inch of her.

Temptress.

Julian followed in a dream, her willing slave, unable to resist this chance she offered him. He wanted this and he was going to take it, just as she took what she wanted from him. He would be a fool to turn her down.

Not when she so clearly wanted it too.

He knelt on the bed, moving close to her, and blinked languidly as she cleared her short red hair from her throat. Her left side. The same side she'd bitten him. Duke was bound to make comments about matching marks.

Piper would think it was fantastic.

He didn't care about any of it. All that mattered was this moment and what Lauren was offering him. It was more than blood. It was the connection he felt when she bit him but in reverse. It was trust, and love, and everything he'd craved all of his life. She wanted to bear his marks. She wanted others to see what he'd done to her and what they had shared.

When he reached her, he shifted his focus to Lauren's feelings, needing to know what this meant to her. Her heart was beating fast, a butterfly in her chest, its rapid pace matching his own.

Julian licked his lips and moved closer, until her left leg was between his and he could feel her trembling. His fangs extended, the world sharpening as his eyes changed. Everything blurred after that. The moment his lips touched her throat, she hissed and arched into him. His fangs sunk deep into her flesh and warm sweet blood burst onto his tongue. It intoxicated him, satiating his craving but bringing his desire back to boiling point. Her hands clutched the back of his head in the way he had wanted to with her, her fingers threading through his hair and holding him tight against his neck. Her silent plea didn't go unanswered. He wouldn't let her go, not now that he had her. His body responded in an instant, erection hard against his black trousers, painful and throbbing as Lauren moaned into his ear.

Julian frowned, closed his eyes and bit down harder, needing more. Lauren groaned and her fingers dug into his scalp, sharp points telling him that she'd changed too and her nails were now claws. The taste of her blood was divine, but the connection was so much more. It was more sensual and erotic than he'd expected. She clung to him, her feelings those of passion and desire. She wanted him. The thought of that sent him spiralling downwards, deeper into the bond that sharing blood evoked between them, until he was lost in it, teetering on the brink of losing control. He bit deeper and she moaned hotly into his ear, her breath tickling his throat. Anticipation sent the hairs on the back of his neck rising. He willed her to bite him too, to go through with the intent that he could sense in her.

Lauren writhed against him, forcing him to rise to his knees with her. Her hip pressed against his groin and he grasped her waist, desperate to stop her in case she noticed what this was doing to him. He was so hard against his trousers. Each pull on her blood made him throb, made his restraint weaken, but he wouldn't surrender to his hunger, no matter how strong the temptation.

He couldn't overstep that mark.

She moved again and he pulled back. It was too much. He licked her throat once and then sat back on his heels, shifting so his shirttail fell across his lap, concealing his erection.

He went to leave the bed.

Her hand on his wrist stopped him and he looked down at it, and then up into her eyes. They were large and soft with understanding, pupils wide with her own arousal.

Her cheeks darkened, stained as red as her lips, and her gaze darted away and then back, flittering around the room.

"Stay," she whispered and shifted closer. She looked at his knees and then her hand where it held his wrist. "Let me ease you."

Julian swallowed hard as those four words hit him. He couldn't find his voice to tell her that it wasn't necessary, that it would pass, not when he wanted it more than anything.

Her hand left his and he could only watch as she moved his shirt aside, exposing the bulge in his trousers. She undid his belt with trembling hands and then went to work on his trousers. Julian swallowed again, his throat suddenly dry. His erection ached with anticipation. Lauren tugged his open trousers down a little and something told him to move, to help, but he was frozen to the spot, lost in the moment and afraid to move in case it made her realise what she was doing.

What they were doing.

Her hand slid inside his trousers and he breathed in sharply when she wrapped her fingers around his length and took him out. He couldn't stop himself from jerking forwards, pushing him through the ring of her soft hand, and his teeth sunk into his lip. The pain was the only thing that stopped him from coming undone right that moment. His eyelids dropped and he struggled to breathe.

Lauren's breathing was a light steady sound in the darkness of his closed eyes. Her heart beat at a rhythm half his own and it soothed him, reassuring him that this was something she wanted to do. She'd offered to touch him, to place her delicate warm hands on his flesh and ease his aching hunger.

She moved and he bit back his groan. Swift strokes of her hand on his shaft made his thighs quiver and tense. It wasn't going to take long to find release. The feel of her touching him, caressing his sensitive flesh, was too divine to handle, too wonderful. He'd dreamt of this, thought that he would never experience such a thing again, and now she was offering it to him, pleasuring him in so many more ways than just one. It was more than giving him relief—it was a sign that she wanted more, wanted to be with him, and had truly gone through with the awakening so they might be together.

That thought alone sent him spiralling over the edge.

Julian screwed his eyes shut. The tight coiling heat in his abdomen became too much, seizing control of him as he neared his climax. His hips pumped, thrusting him through the circle of her fingers, primal male instinct taking control, and Lauren's grip on him mercifully tightened. He grunted, hungry and desperate to find release, aware of Lauren's eyes on him and the scent of her growing arousal. She was enjoying this. The fluttering of her heart, her rapid breathing, and the smooth hard strokes of her hand on him were testament to that.

With a mighty shudder and moan, he bucked his hips forwards and exploded, throbbing in her hand.

His heartbeat slowly steadied again and his breathing returned to normal, and he became painfully aware of what he'd done. He should have stopped her. Her hand left his softening length and he opened his eyes, looking down at the mess he'd made on his trousers and then her hand. He couldn't look at her. Fear claimed his heart, icy fingers squeezing it when she moved off the bed and walked away.

He lowered his head and closed his eyes, breathing deep to settle the ache in his chest. What had he done?

The mattress depressed again and Lauren's knees appeared in view in front of his. She reached over, cleaned him with a damp washcloth, and then rubbed the mess off his trousers.

Her heart was steady. Her breathing normal. Her touch was light and caring.

"We can wash these tomorrow." Her hands disappeared from view.

He braved it and looked up at her. She smiled and then leaned over and kissed his cheek. His eyes fixed on the bathroom door on the opposite wall, unfocused. She kissed down to his neck, each brush of her lips feather-light and warming his heart, and pressed a solitary kiss to the marks she'd made on his throat, before kissing back up and along his jaw until she reached his mouth.

She hovered there a moment, her breath mingling with his, tickling his lips as he waited with his heart in his mouth, and then she kissed him.

It was tentative and slow, a tender exploration of his lips with hers, as though she was trying to memorise each subtle curve of them. Her tongue caressed the seam of his mouth and he opened to her. Heat washed down his spine as their tongues met. The soft glide of hers against his was enthralling, the warm taste of her making him want to deepen the kiss. He restrained himself, keeping it light and letting her remain in control. This was more than a kiss. This was her way of telling him without words that what they had done was only the beginning—she wanted to be with him.

He wanted nothing more than that too.

Her lips barely brushed his, stirring a light warm feeling inside him. He could kiss her like this forever. He had never realised how wonderful a bare meeting of lips could be. It spoke so much of her feelings that his heart was made whole again.

She sat back and he looked at her, fascinated by her crimson-stained cheeks and the shy glimmer in her eyes. Her kiss had been far better than his. There was no reason for her to be embarrassed.

"It's dawn. Come to bed," Lauren whispered.

Julian's eyes widened. The kiss hadn't made her awkward. It had been the thought of saying those words. Inviting him into her bed. He had felt nervous this afternoon when she had come to his room and had slept beside him, and he knew she had too, but that feeling didn't compare with how he felt now. This time she wasn't asking him merely to sleep beside her. Her nervousness told him that this time there was a possibility of it being more than that, that they would kiss again and sleep more intimately entwined.

She unhooked her bra, shimmied out of it with her camisole still on and then slid under the dark mauve covers. He remained motionless in the middle of the bed, trying to come to terms with what was happening. Everything had moved so quickly that he felt left behind somewhere. She'd changed so much between them in only a short hour. She'd seized his heart with both hands.

He waited for her ask him again, so he knew that he wasn't dreaming.

Lauren pulled the cover back by his feet. "Stay with me."

Julian moved backwards off the bed, tucked himself away in his boxers and stared at the empty space in front of him beside Lauren. Her hand lingered there, the same hand that had tangled in his hair as he'd fed from her neck and wrapped around his flesh as she'd brought him to climax.

Turning away, he walked around the bed to the door.

A rustle of material behind him made him look back at Lauren. She now sat on the edge of the bed, eyes showing the panic that he could hear in her heartbeat. They filled with relief when he locked the door and came back to her.

He wasn't going to leave. She was offering him his elusive dream—someone to love him, and someone he could love. He was no longer alone.

Julian stripped off, aware of her eyes on him as he removed his shirt and trousers. When he was only wearing his black boxer shorts, he rounded the bed again. Lauren shuffled back to make room for him on the left side of the bed.

He settled beside her on his back and Lauren threw the covers over him. He stared up at the ceiling, wondering just how he'd got there all of a sudden. He was still trying to catch up, but he was sure of one thing—Lauren wouldn't break his heart. She would protect it as fiercely as he protected her.

He smiled when she sidled up to him, pressing the length of her front against his side and hooking her knee over his legs. She rested her head on his chest and he wrapped his arm around her, holding her close. She felt so perfect tangled up with him, bare flesh against his. Everything he'd ever wanted was in his arms. She belonged there. Close to his heart—the heart that belonged to her. Not Illia, but Lauren. He felt complete at last.

He closed his eyes and breathed her in, smiling.

Lauren pushed herself up onto her elbow and leaned away. A flash of panic lanced through Julian when he realised that she was going to turn off the bedside lamp and his hand shot up, catching her wrist tightly enough that she gasped. He instantly released her, ashamed that he'd hurt her and that he'd shown such weakness in front of her, and looked away.

"Sorry," she whispered and pressed a kiss to his chest. Her hand lightly cupped his cheek, bringing his head around to face her. He didn't resist. She sighed and stroked her fingers across his brow, concern shining in her eyes. "I forgot."

Julian silently cursed Duke for telling her and closed his eyes. He didn't want to see her pity.

Lauren's head came back to rest on his chest and she sighed again.

"Thank you." Her breath tickled him and he frowned when he felt her sorrow. "Thank you for doing that for me."

Julian pressed a kiss to her forehead, relieved that she didn't see his fear as a weakness and touched that she worried about him.

No one had ever made him feel like this. Not even Illia.

"You are my light, Lauren. For you I would endure eternal darkness."

CHAPTER 33

Julian looked down into Lauren's eyes to see what her reaction would be. She smiled up at him and her feelings were warm. This close to her, he could sense them clearly. She was happy about something. Was it because of what he'd said? If saying such things made her happy, he would say them all the time.

"Julian," she whispered and he raised his eyebrows at her, inviting her to ask the question he could sense in her. "Do you want to talk about it?"

He frowned. Did he? He had never really spoken to anyone about what had happened to him. If he started, he feared that he would tell her other things, such as what her predecessors had done to him and how he had died. He stared into her eyes. Did she want to know such things? He wanted to know more about her. Perhaps she wasn't just asking him to tell her about his time trapped in the basement. Perhaps she wanted him to speak about himself and let her in. It was difficult. Since becoming immortal, he had kept everyone shut out and at a distance. He wasn't sure where to start.

"You don't have to," Lauren said and he shook his head a fraction, drew a deep breath, and sighed.

"No doubt it was Duke who told you?"

She nodded.

"Lycaon led Illia's last incarnation back to Greece. He ambushed us and made sure we were divided. I was lured into the old villa and she was outside. Lycaon…" Julian swallowed and stared at the ceiling, trying to get a grip on his feelings so Lauren wouldn't think he was weak. There was no darkness now and he wasn't trapped. It didn't soothe the tight feeling in his chest or ease his breathing. He could still smell the dust as it clogged his lungs. He could still remember every moment he had passed, every heartbeat and breath that had carried him through the years, waiting. "I… it was—"

Lauren rolled onto her front, propping herself up on her elbows beside him. He couldn't look at her. Didn't want to see the shame in her eyes. Her commander wasn't strong. He was weak.

"You don't have to tell me," she whispered and then her hand was on his chest, stroking it lightly in a soothing caress. The motion of her fingers was as constant and steady as her heartbeat, easing his fears enough that he could look at her. There was only worry in her eyes. She brought her hand up and brushed the hair from his forehead, and then trailed her fingertips down his cheek. They paused at his jaw, warm against his skin. He raised his hand and caught hold of hers, needing the comfort it gave him and the feeling of connection.

"Lycaon blew the foundations of the villa. It collapsed on top of me," he said in a tight voice that didn't sound like his own. He stretched, trying to ease the tension from his body, and swallowed. Nothing he did relaxed him. Only the constant feel of Lauren's hand in his was grounding him and helping him maintain an element of control over his emotions. They were whirling inside him, turning his stomach. The darkness and fear pushed at the edge of his mind but he wouldn't give in. He would fight it. He would face it so it would never control him again. "I waited for you."

"I know," she said and tears lined her eyes, sparkling in the lamplight. She smiled but there was sadness in it now. Sorrow for him. As much as he hated to see it, he loved it too. No one had ever shown him such compassion and tenderness. "I know."

"I did not want you to be alone."

"You endured it for me, and I can't imagine how horrible it must have been, but I'm glad that you did, that you came to me and that we met."

He smiled at her, touched by her words, and squeezed her hand. "When I saw you, I knew you were worth the wait."

She blushed and her gaze fell to his chest. He wanted to raise her head and have her look at him, to see in his eyes that he meant what he'd said. She was worth waiting three millennia for.

"None of them even compare to you, not even Illia," he whispered and she looked at him now, her eyes enormous and lips parted. He could feel her shock. He stroked her cheek with the backs of his fingers. It was blazing hot. "It is the truth, Lauren. You are so beautiful. I have never met a woman like you and I am thankful I endured so many lonely years so I could have this time with you at last and no longer be alone."

Tears rolled down her cheek. This time he knew they were tears of happiness, not sorrow. He had never been good with words when it came to romance, had never had much practice, but he must have said something right to get such a reaction from Lauren.

"Julian... you said that they ordered you to do things... that they made you stay away and banned things... whatever they did to you, I'll never do that."

"I know," he said and closed his eyes. Every one of her incarnations passed through his mind. He remembered the things they had done and how each of them had contributed to the pain that Lauren had healed. They had pushed him away, closing him off from any form of connection by ordering him to refrain from touching her in any way, from taking her blood, from even healing her. They had each bound his hands a little more, stealing away part of his duty until even helping her awaken had felt as though he was breaking the rules. He hadn't realised the extent of what they had done to him until Lauren had come along. His prison had been invisible to him and then she had made him see the bars her predecessors had constructed, and he had wanted to break free.

"You've been alone since she died, haven't you?" Lauren's tone was quiet and solemn, as though she didn't want to ask that question but had felt compelled to. She was talking about Illia now, about the last person who had cared about him.

He nodded and swallowed.

"I'm sorry."

"It is not your fault." He looked at her. The tears were back in her eyes again, lining her wet lashes and threatening to fall. He swept them away with his thumb, not wanting to see her cry for him. It hurt him to think about the life he had led and how hollow it had been without any physical contact with another. The pain was still raw, his heart cut deep by the things the others had done to him, but he knew Lauren could heal even that hurt in time. "They had their reasons, each of them different, but I cannot deny that it was difficult for me to exist in such a way."

"Live," she said and he frowned. "You said exist... but you're alive... unless... was it that bad?"

The spike in her emotions made his heart miss a beat and his breath left him in a gasp when she threw herself at him, covering his chest with hers and pressing her cheek to his.

"I hate them all. I hate them for what they did to you. You didn't deserve such treatment when you only wanted to protect them. You didn't do anything wrong," she whispered and ran her fingers through his hair. She kissed his cheek, her lips resting against it, warming the spot they touched. He wrapped his arms around her and held her close, absorbing her warmth and affection, and the love she was showing him.

"You made me live again," he breathed into her ear and she drew back, her eyes wide.

They narrowed as she smiled and then her lips were against his, dancing soft and slow, a sensual bare meeting of their mouths that stilled his heart. Love. He could feel it in her and it echoed in him. He loved her more than anything, needed her more than anything, and couldn't live without her. If he told her that, how would she react? He wanted to find the right words again, to say something that could convey the depth of his feelings for her. He trembled inside, a voice at the back of his mind telling him that she could turn on him as the others had and it would be the end of him if she did, if he said the words he wanted to say and she rebuked him.

His heart said that Lauren wouldn't do such a thing to him. She had been telling the truth when she'd said that she would never treat him as the others had. He believed her, and he would risk the pain to let her know his feelings.

"I waited for you and when I saw you... I would have waited more than those thirty years. I would have waited for eternity to meet you and it would still have been worth it." He frowned when she looked away and this time he caught her cheek and made her look at him. His hand shook against her face, his nerves rising now that he had stopped speaking. Her eyes met his. The endless depths of warmth in them gave him the strength to continue. "You breathed life into me, Lauren. You gave me a new reason to live. You. I live for you. You are the blood in my veins and the air in my lungs. You gave me life and ended my empty existence."

Love Immortal

Her lips were instantly back against his, slow still and steady. Their tongues met, softly tangling, and she moaned into his mouth. He smiled against her lips and held her close, savouring the way she felt against him and this moment. It was hard for him to tell her his innermost feelings but he trusted her now. She wouldn't betray him. She loved him. Facing his fears and saying things that left him vulnerable was worth it when she kissed him like this.

"Julian," she whispered against his mouth and then pulled back, her eyes immediately locking with his again. "I… I really don't deserve a man like you, but I do love the things you say."

He smiled wide, pleased that his words had meant so much to her.

"I am certain all my talk must have made you tired," he said and she shook her head. "No?"

Another shake.

She looked more awake than ever now, her eyes bright and twinkling and her smile wide. It felt good to see her so happy and relaxed. It made him feel the same way. He kept his arms around her, wondering what she would like to know about next. He could tell her more about the others, or he could tell her more about himself.

"Would you like to hear about ancient Arcadia?" he said and her face lit up. She nodded and moved closer, so her breasts pressed against his chest. He groaned inside at the feel of her warm body on his and slid his hands downwards to settle in the arch of her back. There was a bare patch of skin between her camisole and knickers. He caressed it, enjoying the softness of her skin, and thought about what to say.

"Did you wear a loin cloth?" she said and he laughed. It came out before he could stop himself, pushed from him by her ridiculous question and the spark of expectation in her eyes. It had been a long time since he had properly laughed, and it felt good.

"No, not exactly." He smiled and ran his fingers through her red hair, twisting the tips of it where it flipped outwards. She really was beautiful. Dark lashes rimmed her large brown eyes and her rosy lips promised kisses that would make his head and heart spin. She was beautiful and she was his, and he was never letting her go.

"But you didn't wear much."

He laughed again. What exactly had she been imagining him wearing?

"I am not wearing much now either," he said and crimson stained her cheeks. Her fingers tensed against his chest. "We wore armour for battle and dressed in little else. Surely you would like to know other things more interesting than this?"

She shook her head. "I'm trying to picture you back then."

"My hair was longer, and lighter. It tends to get wild when I let it grow."

She raised an eyebrow and brushed her fingers over his hair. "It's pretty wild now."

"I used to tie it back. Other than that, I look very much the same."

She frowned and he knew it wasn't the answer she had wanted. What did he tell her? He did look the same and he was beginning to act the same as he had as a human. Besides drawing her a picture of his armour and clothing, he wasn't sure what else he could say or do to make her see him as he had been back then.

"Were you a good man?"

"I was a poor man," he said with a smile and she frowned again. "Soldiers of my rank were rarely from rich backgrounds. I was raised to be a soldier so I would have food to eat and wine to drink, and could serve my purpose and die on the battlefield."

"Which you did." The solemn edge was back in her voice. "Do you remember what happened?"

He nodded. How could he forget?

"It is hazy now, but I do remember the night that I died. The moon was full and we were fighting on the slopes of Mount Lyceum in Arcadia. Lycaon and his army were forcing us back and I had lost the last of my men. I refused to retreat as Illia had ordered me to and fought a werewolf. He had been in human form, which was rare in those days when the werewolves had little control over themselves under the full moon." Julian frowned and stared at the ceiling, trying to remember what had happened that night.

It had been dark even with the bright light of moon and the smell of olive trees had hung in the still warm air. Summer. He remembered the scent of earth and heat, a smell he had long forgotten but now it came back so strong it was as though he was there again. When the last of his men had fallen, Illia had told him to fall back. He had fought on, refusing to leave her side and desiring to carry out his duty to protect her. He and his men were expendable, born to serve her mother and in turn her. If he died protecting her, it was a good death. He closed his eyes and could see the battle again, the dead spread over the mountainside, the dusty earth drenched in their blood. He could see Lycaon and his men, and could hear Illia. He wouldn't fall back.

"Was he the one who killed you?" Lauren whispered.

He nodded and tried to remember what had happened. He recalled the man and their fight but it was fuzzy. He couldn't picture it clearly.

"I fought him while Illia attacked the others, trying to get to Lycaon. He was faster but not stronger than me, or at least that was what I had thought. A young man. I do not remember him well but I do remember I underestimated him and that was my downfall. Fighting him in human form made me believe that he was as young as he appeared, and it would be an easy fight." He could still recall the moment he had realised his mistake and even then it had been too late. The werewolf had seized the chance. Julian looked at Lauren, his chest tight and painful with the memory of what had happened to him. He had been trained for death but when it had come, it had been frightening and cold, and he had felt as though he was going somewhere dark, not journeying into the afterlife to a hero's welcome. Lauren placed her hand against his face and her thumb caressed his cheek, soft and gentle as always, soothing his pain. "I realised too late that he was hiding his full strength, and the extent of his abilities. I tried to stop him but I... he... it was a blur. One moment he was at a distance and the next his sword was through my chest."

Julian pressed his hand to his chest, seeing the sword there and feeling everything he had in that moment—the fear, the pain, and the threat of endless darkness. He tried to blink away the image of the bright blade puncturing his heart. It wouldn't go. Lauren's hand covered his, her fingers curling around to press against his palm, holding it tight and chasing away the sword. The scar on his left pectoral burned and his heart missed a beat. He screwed his eyes shut and drew in a long shuddering breath. He wasn't there again. That moment had long passed. It was only the pain of remembering it, of thinking about it for the first time in centuries.

"Illia came to me then, drove the young man away and saved me." He wasn't sure what else to tell Lauren and whether he would even be able to speak if she did ask more. His throat felt too tight and dry.

"I'd thought it was Lycaon who had killed you," she said and a little frown creased her brow.

"Lycaon would not stoop to kill someone inferior to him. He is only interested in Illia, in you, Lauren. My men all died at the teeth and claws of his children."

"I'm his child," she whispered with a pained look in her eyes. He caressed her cheek and she looked at him.

"You are not his child, Lauren. It has been millennia since Lycaon has felt any attachment to Illia or her incarnations. With each reincarnation, he showed less and less compassion and guilt on taking her life, and more and more cruelty and pleasure at drawing out their death. Toying with them."

"Because we changed. You said that we became less like Illia each time, and more like ourselves."

He nodded. "None as much as you. You are nothing like Illia."

"We're just an enemy to him. A strong opponent to play games with... but I don't want to play his games... and he's just an enemy to me too. I won't hesitate again. Next time I meet him, I will kill him." The resolve in her eyes made Julian smile. It was a world apart from how she had looked on the rooftop, shaken by the revelation that Lycaon had been Illia's father. Now she had found her feet again and he knew that she wouldn't falter. He would see to it that she grew stronger and was ready to fight Lycaon again.

He wouldn't fail her.

"Come," he whispered and drew her up so she was level with him.

Her hands claimed his shoulders and she smiled as he brought her down for a kiss.

He was gentle this time, trying to keep it as a light meeting of lips just as she had done. He felt weightless and warm as their lips and tongues brushed sensually against each other in a slow dance that built heat inside him. He slid his arms around her back and held her tight, losing himself in how it felt to be with her. Too good. He loved the feel of her body on his, the way her hands burned against his flesh and the way her soft lips teased his. He loved everything about her and he would do anything to keep her safe.

Anything.

Her tongue traced his lower lip and then she pulled back, looking at him with wide pupils full of desire. He was tempted to take her silent offer and to take this beyond kissing, but he could sense the underlying fatigue in her and her need for rest, even if she was unaware of it. He stroked her cheek again and then slid his hand around the back of her head and lured her down, so her cheek rested against his chest. She sighed, her warm breath chasing over his bare skin.

Holding her close, Julian thought about the fight to come. He had trained her well so far, but he needed to do more this time, he needed to help her hone her skills to perfection because he was sure it wouldn't be long before they faced Lycaon again.

Something was different this time.

He had the terrible feeling that Lycaon had only been passing the time by killing Illia's incarnations and that he had only been doing so when they had gotten too close. Lycaon had never come after them before. He had always led the dance, making them chase him.

This time, he was chasing them.

Both of them.

Lycaon wasn't only after Illia now. He was after Julian too. He had never attempted to kill him before, only to distract him long enough to kill Illia. Something was wrong.

Julian held Lauren closer.

Lycaon wanted them both dead.

And Julian wanted to know why.

CHAPTER 34

Julian snapped awake at the second knock. He sharpened his senses and frowned. Duke. Relaxing back into the bed, Julian toyed with the idea of turning Duke away and focused on Lauren where she slept in his arms. This was too good to give up. He didn't want to go back to the world, not yet. Just a few more hours of having Lauren sleeping softly against him.

The sun was high. He could feel it glaring down on him, reproaching him and stealing his strength. It was approaching mid-day. Their altercations in the past should have taught Duke not to wake him during daylight unless it was a life or death situation.

But he'd said a few hours.

He should have said to wait until nightfall.

The knock came again.

Julian rubbed his eyes and sighed. Craning his neck, he kissed Lauren's forehead and she mumbled as she woke. Her eyes were full of sleep when they opened.

"I must speak with Duke," he said softly and cleared the hair from her eyes. She frowned and nodded. "I shall not be long."

She tilted her head back and he smiled when he realised what she wanted. Dipping his head, he pressed a gentle kiss to her lips. She responded by clutching his arms and deepening the kiss, sweeping her tongue over his lips and teeth. He couldn't resist tackling her tongue with his own, slanting his head at the same time so their mouths fused together in a passionate embrace. Lauren moaned and Julian frowned. Now he really didn't want to leave. He moved back so his mouth left hers, severing the connection before he gave in to temptation.

She sighed and snuggled back down into the bed when he left it. He pulled the mauve covers over her, tucking her in, and stared at her a moment.

Julian cringed when he remembered that he couldn't wear his trousers. He thought about putting his coat on or just his shirt, and then decided that there wasn't much point. It was only a short walk from Lauren's room to his one. His boxer shorts would suffice. Duke would just have to put up with his state of undress.

Reluctantly, he walked around the bed to the door and opened it. Duke stood in the pale blue hall, hand raised as though he'd been about to knock again.

"Follow me." Julian stepped out into the hall and closed the door behind him.

He could feel Duke's eyes on him as they walked.

"Is this your new look or did you get lucky?" There was a grin in Duke's voice.

Julian threw him a black look.

"You're right. It's none of my business." Duke held his hands up, exposing the roses on his palms. Death. Duke stank of it.

Entering his room, Julian went straight to the dresser against the left wall and took out a fresh pair of trousers and a new black shirt. He dressed without ceremony and then remembered that he'd left his boots in Lauren's room. He didn't want to go back and wake her again. He could go without for now. Duke wouldn't be stupid enough to ask him to head out anywhere during the day.

Duke waved a hand towards the door when Julian glanced at him.

"I have something interesting to report. My office would be the best place for it."

Julian nodded and followed him through the corridors to his office. The whole building was quiet. There was at least one less heartbeat than before. Lycaon hadn't been the only one to lose men.

His fists clenched when he thought about Lycaon and how close he had come to losing Lauren. He should have stopped her and told her that Lycaon had been Illia's father. His foolish clinging to duty had almost got her killed. It wouldn't happen again. From now on, his old duty was over, replaced by his new duty to protect Lauren at any cost. He would fight harder next time. She would never have to fear Lycaon again.

Duke's office wasn't empty.

Leo and Astra talked beside the white marble fireplace to his right, and Kuga and Piper were looking out of the broken window, up towards the roof. Lauren's two short katana and his own sword lay on the ebony desk to his left. In his haste to follow Lauren, Julian had forgotten to take their weapons from the roof.

"I did not realise that everyone would be here." Julian went to his sword and gently laid his hand on the flat of the blade. It was reassuring to have it close when the sun was making him weak.

"Where's Lauren?" Piper said with her usual bright smile. He could feel her probing around in his mind but gave her only surface thoughts. The ones that she wanted to read about her friend were his alone to know.

"She is resting."

"I'll cut to the chase." Duke leaned against the desk, looked around the room and then ran a hand over his rich brown hair and frowned. His dark eyes held a hint of anger. "The other Ghost squad lost two members in the fight… which means the backup I had been negotiating isn't going to happen."

Julian hated what he was going to say, but it seemed to be the only option. "I may be able to convince Morgan, but I still have my doubts that the vampire will help."

There was a clatter from his right and everyone looked there. The fire irons lay on their side on the hearth near Astra's feet. She glared at him.

"We do not need the help of vampires." Her words held a sneer that he'd expected.

"We need all the help we can get." Duke's harsh tone softened as he turned to Piper. "Perhaps it would be best to wake Lauren and bring her to us."

Julian nodded.

Lauren needed to rest but she needed to know what was happening more.

CHAPTER 35

Lauren pulled her black zip up jumper on over her head just as someone knocked on the door. She quickly smoothed her red hair out. It couldn't be Julian. He wouldn't have knocked, not after last night. They were past such formalities now. She smiled.

She opened the door and her smile became a grin when she saw Piper on the other side, toying with the sleeves of her pink jumper.

"Duke asked me to bring you to his office," Piper said and the moment Lauren stepped out into the hall, the younger woman slipped her arm through hers and started walking. Lauren winced when Piper knocked the cut on her arm. The one on her leg was still sore too. Julian had told her that they would take at least a day to heal because Lycaon's blade was silver.

"Thanks for last night... holding Lycaon for me." Lauren straightened out her jumper and tried to push the fog of sleep from her mind. Being awake during the day was a struggle. Her head felt groggy and heavy.

Still, the closer she got to Julian, the better she began to feel. The moment he'd left her, the bad feeling had returned. It compelled her to go to Julian where she would feel safe and could sleep.

"It was nothing," Piper said, still smiling. "Did you have a breakthrough with Julian? Duke sent me a thought that said Julian left your room in just his underwear."

Julian had? With a blush, Lauren remembered what had happened to his trousers.

"Oh, erm... yeah. We kissed." Amongst other things that she wasn't about to go into detail about with Piper. Julian wouldn't appreciate her broadcasting every sordid thing that had happened.

"And this?" Piper poked her neck.

Lauren placed her hand over the mark there and her cheeks felt as though they were going to catch fire. She tugged the collar of her jumper up to cover it.

"That too," she mumbled and hoped her answer would satisfy Piper.

Piper released her arm, hopped a few paces ahead and then turned to face her. "I had a breakthrough too!"

Lauren smiled when she saw how happy that made Piper. "What happened?"

"I was practicing with Kuga and I hurt myself." She held her arm up and pulled the sleeve of her pink striped jumper back, revealing a bandage on her wrist and hand. "I heard Kuga's thoughts... his worry when I hurt myself... his sweet thoughts when he checked me over."

Piper bounced on the spot, grinning so wide that Lauren couldn't help laughing. Piper had never looked so excited or happy. Lauren thought about her time with Julian and the breakthrough they had made. She knew him so much better now and he had finally let her into his heart. Her smile widened again. Piper wasn't the only one feeling happy.

"I can't wait for my birthday!" Piper looped her arm around Lauren's again and tugged on it. Lauren tried not to grimace so Piper wouldn't feel bad for hurting her.

"I'm so happy for you too. It's nice that you and Julian are becoming closer. We could double date!" Piper said and then pouted. "Julian won't let me in today though."

"Really?" Lauren blushed again, knowing exactly why that was.

"Yeah. But now I've seen these." Piper pulled Lauren's collar down and prodded the marks. She grinned. "It's no wonder he's being private today!"

Lauren was beetroot red by the time Piper pushed the doors to Duke's office open and they walked in. Julian immediately turned to face her and frowned when he saw her. He strode over to her and touched her cheeks.

"What is the matter?" he whispered and his concern washed through her.

Lauren looked askance at Piper. Piper grinned. Julian looked away. A hint of colour blossomed on his cheeks.

"I understand." He took hold of Lauren's hand, leading her away from Piper and towards the others.

Piper moved across the room to Kuga and her expression turned serious. Lauren looked around.

Everyone's expressions were serious.

"Is something wrong?" Lauren said. They had been talking without her. She knew that she should have got out of bed quicker and followed Julian.

"The other Ghost squad lost some men," Duke said. "We need to find Lycaon and attack before he can regroup."

Lauren didn't like the sound of that. She wrapped her arms around one of Julian's and leaned her head against it. The desire to sleep was almost too strong to resist as the sun edged higher, stealing all of her energy.

"He was injured." Lauren tried to think of how they could find him. By now, he would be miles away, if not out of the country entirely. "Does he heal as fast as we do?"

Julian shook his head. "Werewolves do not heal as quickly, just as vampires do not."

"Will Morgan help?"

Julian frowned. It was all the answer she needed. Morgan had been a no show. He wasn't going to help them.

"Piper can help," Kuga said and all eyes were on him.

He looked at Piper. Lauren did too. Piper's round eyes showed a trace of the fear Lauren sensed in her.

Lauren walked over to her and took hold of her hands. "Can you help us?"

Piper nodded and tried to smile. Her hands shook and her heart pounded out a nervous rhythm in Lauren's mind.

"It was when I was practicing this morning with Kuga," Piper said in a small quiet voice and then raised her head, growing a little more confident. "It suddenly all fell into place, just like Duke said it would."

"What did?" Lauren said.

"I'm not afraid anymore, Lauren. I can do this… I can control my power. I can help."

Suddenly everyone was crowding around them and Lauren had to fight to keep her place in front of Piper. Kuga ruffled Piper's hair and received an annoyed look for it. Duke patted her shoulder and said something about being pleased. Leo gave her a little jab on the arm. Even Julian came closer. He placed his hand on Lauren's shoulder and she looked up at him. She was glad that Piper had finally found the ability to control her power and had faced her fears.

"This is big, man," Leo said and Lauren looked at him as he spoke to his brother. He didn't seem happy as he took hold of Kuga's shoulder. "You didn't mention it."

"It wasn't my place. Piper wanted everyone around when she announced it." Kuga shrugged and pushed his brother's arm away, knocking his hand from his shoulder.

Lauren frowned. She didn't like it when there was tension between the twins. Normally they and Piper were full of laughter and jokes, but now all three looked so deadly serious. Lauren leaned back into Julian, seeking his embrace and the comfort there. She wanted everyone to get along again but could understand how being left out must have hurt Leo, especially after seeing him after his brother had been chosen for a mission over him.

"You can control it?" Lauren said to Piper, wanting to be sure.

Piper nodded. "And there's more. Lycaon is weak and when I halted his attack, I could read him. If I concentrate hard, I can still faintly hear his thoughts. He's gone to ground but… he isn't too far away… I think that I can find him… like I found Julian. He isn't guarding his thoughts."

"Then we're leaving immediately." Lauren ducked under Julian's arm, went to the desk and picked up her two katana.

She turned back to face the others. Julian nodded at the same time as Duke. If both of them were in agreement with her, then it was the right thing to do. They couldn't give Lycaon time to heal and escape. If Piper could hear his thoughts, he couldn't be too far away.

"We should wait," Leo said and everyone's attention was with him. He threw a nervous glance around the room. "If Lycaon is out there, his goons are with him. We should wait and see if the vampire shows or at least wait until it's dark and you guys are stronger."

Lauren paused. Leo did have a point. She and Julian were weak right now. They would be no good in a fight against Lycaon. They would have to rely on Duke and the others to give them an opening in which to kill Lycaon.

"No." Julian retrieved his katana from the desk behind Lauren. He held it point down at his side. "We will track Lycaon now while we have the advantage."

"He's right. If Lycaon heals, we lose that advantage." Duke came forwards, his frown heavy. He looked at Piper. "Although we will be outnumbered of the rest of the werewolves are with him."

Lauren thought hard and then went to Piper. The younger woman was looking nervous again but Lauren could sense that she was determined to prove herself and repay Ghost for its faith in her.

"Do you think he's alone?" Lauren said.

Piper frowned and closed her eyes.

"Yes," she whispered after a few minutes had passed. "I think so."

Lauren looked around the room at everyone. Her eyes settled last on Julian and stayed there. He stood tall, his head and shoulders tilted back, his sword held firm at his side. Her Arcadian. Her commander. Ready for battle if she gave the word.

"We leave now."

CHAPTER 36

Clouds marred the night sky. Preparations had taken longer than expected and they hadn't left the Ghost office until late afternoon. Now the sun had set and they stood shrouded in darkness, out in the countryside where Piper had led them. The city lights were a glow in the distance. It was further away than Lauren had expected. Duke seemed surprised too. Piper's ability was obviously stronger than anyone had suspected.

Piper had announced a mile back that they were going the wrong way and had pointed across the open fields. With no roads to take them that way, Julian had decided that they would walk. Piper had said they were close. Lauren wondered how close.

Lauren flinched when Duke clicked on a torch. She brought her hand up to shield her eyes from the brilliant white light and turned away.

"Sorry." Duke lowered the torch to point at his feet. His husky voice reminded her of Morgan, always seductive sounding.

She didn't want to think about the vampire. They had needed him last night and he hadn't shown. Julian had been right about him. He wouldn't help them.

"How are you feeling?" Lauren looked at Piper. It was hard to see her in the low light from the torches that Leo, Duke and Kuga held but Lauren didn't want to frighten her by changing her eyes so she could see better. If she did that, her fangs would also extend. She didn't want Piper to have that image of her and see her as a monster to fear. She was a friend, and right now, she was concerned that tracking Lycaon was taking its toll on Piper.

Piper shrugged. Her skin was so pale that she almost glowed in the torchlight. "I'll cope… I think."

Lauren wanted to tell her that they could stop if it was becoming too much but she couldn't surrender this chance to find Lycaon while he was still injured. She wanted to finish their battle while he was alone and didn't have the other man with him. Only she could kill Lycaon, but Julian could help her defeat him by protecting her.

A blush touched Lauren's cheeks when she focused on Julian and felt him close by, his eyes on her. Whenever she thought about what they had done, the marks on her neck tingled and she couldn't help blushing. It had felt so good. She longed to be back in his arms and tangled in the sheets of her bed with him. They started across the fields. Piper was right. He was incredible—handsome, loving, strong. He was everything a man should be and he was hers at last.

Piper stopped when they reached the crest of a hill and rubbed her temples.

"What's up, Pippin?" Leo shone the torch on Piper's feet.

Piper frowned. Evidently she didn't like that nickname of his either. She brushed her straight across fringe away from her eyebrows and looked into the distance, her gaze unfocused.

"He's clearer," she whispered and Lauren came forwards to stand beside her. Julian flanked her.

Lauren placed her hand on Piper's shoulder and rubbed it lightly, hoping to reassure Piper that she wasn't alone out here in the darkness. They were together and they would protect her when they found Lycaon. She'd done her part by tracking him. She didn't have to fight him. Piper looked at her and smiled. Lauren detected a sense of happiness deep inside her. She saw Kuga standing on the other side of Piper, his hand on her other shoulder. Lauren smiled. She was glad that they were finally making some headway with their relationship. By the time Piper's birthday had passed, she was sure they would be together.

"There's less static now. His thoughts are louder. Just like Julian's were when we were close," Piper said.

"Let's keep moving then." Duke drew one of his guns and started down the other side of the hill.

Piper and Kuga followed.

Lauren walked behind them with Julian. She couldn't feel Lycaon yet, but she was sure that she would when they were close enough.

Julian's hand brushed hers. She looked up at him. His eyes narrowed. The tall funnel collar of his coat hid the lower half of his face but she was sure that he was smiling. She reached over and ran her fingers across his chest, following the line where Lycaon's man had cut. When Julian had been sewing his coat, she'd noticed all the other areas where he'd repaired it. She'd asked him how long he'd had the coat and he'd only said 'a long time'. To mortals that would mean a decade or two. To Julian, that was centuries.

Piper gasped, wrapped her arms around herself and lowered her head. Lauren ran over to her.

Fear radiated from her friend.

"He has no good feelings," Piper mumbled. Kuga drew her into his arms, rubbing her back and whispering to her. Piper shuddered. "I saw his mind. He's planning something terrible… evil… wants revenge for something… the world will suffer his wrath."

"We won't let that happen," Kuga said, his arms tightening around her. He pressed a kiss to her dark hair. "I won't let Lycaon near you."

Lauren glanced at Julian. He was watching her. His eyes were dark in the low light but they were telling her the same thing. He would protect her at any cost—even his life. What would happen if he died and she died? Her reincarnation wouldn't awaken.

No. She couldn't let him sacrifice himself. As noble as it would be, it would place the world in danger.

But if she died and was reborn, it would be nothing but torture to Julian because she would no longer love him.

She loved him.

"We must keep moving." Duke startled her.

Lauren continued to stare into Julian's eyes.

"Is something wrong?" Julian said as the others moved on.

She shook her head and smiled. "No. In fact, everything is good. I just realised something, that's all."

She walked on but when she realised that he wasn't following, she turned back to face him and crooked her finger. He gave her a questioning look but followed, falling in line beside her. With her heart fluttering in her throat, she looked at his hand, and then slowly reached across and slipped her fingers into his. They closed around hers, tightly holding her hand.

She looked ahead of her. Her smile widened when she saw that Kuga was holding Piper's hand. Piper was probably trying to read him and Lycaon at the same time now.

A short distance on, Piper stopped again.

"We're close," she whispered, as though afraid that Lycaon would hear her. "Very close."

Julian's hand left hers and Lauren sensed him change. She followed suit, shifting so her vision was sharper. She scanned the countryside around them. There were no obvious hiding places—no vehicles or buildings. She couldn't feel Lycaon. Back at the Ghost office, she'd sensed his arrival. Out here, she could sense nothing but a glimmer of everyone's feelings and could hear nothing but their heartbeats. Julian's and Duke's were steadiest.

Astra didn't seem to have one at all.

She stood close to Duke, her eyes occasionally flickering blue. Could she see better when she was in her demon guise?

"We must move." Piper's voice trembled. "He must be near here. His thoughts are so clear. No static."

They had crossed over another fence when there was a cry from behind them. Lauren turned on a pinpoint along with Julian. It was Leo. He was standing in the other field clutching his ankle.

"You alright?" Kuga shouted, earning a glare from Duke and Julian. The sound carried in the still cold air. Kuga gave her a guilty look and she smiled. He hadn't meant to give away their position. Hopefully Lycaon would just think it was a human working in the fields.

Leo continued to rub his leg and shouted back. "I think I sprained it."

Piper walked past Lauren and she caught her arm. The younger woman smiled at her. "He's always getting cramp in his calf. It's probably just that. He's such a big baby. I'll make sure he's okay. I'm getting used to playing physio to him. He tells me that no one but me has the magic touch that cures him."

Lauren let her go and looked over her shoulder at Kuga. He didn't seem bothered.

He shrugged and smiled. "She's right. Sometimes he makes mountains out of grains of sand."

Lauren turned to Julian, secretly thankful for the break. She needed a rest. Being awake during the day had drained her and, at times, it was a struggle to keep going.

Julian touched her hand again, his face still too dark for her to read. She wished the clouds would clear so the moon would light the world and she could see him. Kuga and Duke were a few metres away and the light of their torches didn't reach them. Astra was still close to Duke but outside the circle of light. The only other torch was with Leo.

The night was silent. Lauren couldn't even hear a car. It was too cold for insects and small animals, although she didn't feel the chill through her thick black jumper and brown combat jacket. Julian didn't seem bothered by the cold either. His hands were still warm. They chased the cold from hers as he brushed his thumb over the backs of her fingers.

"Why?" The voice was distant. Trembling. Weak. Confused. Afraid.

All emotions that hit Lauren like a tidal wave.

Piper.

Lauren whirled on the spot and her heart stopped when she saw Piper and Leo in the other field.

Leo stood facing Piper, his hand spread over the top of her head. Piper was looking up at him. Lauren could feel her fear as though it was her own. Lights were immediately on them.

"You should have remained defective," Leo said in a voice laced with disappointment. "We can't risk letting you live now."

"No!" Lauren was moving before she even thought about running. She sprinted across the field towards them, her own fear stealing her strength now and slowing her down.

"Piper!" Kuga was running beside her, his muscles visibly straining as he raced to reach her.

Lauren vaulted the fence at the same time as him.

Piper turned to face them and reached a hand out. There was so much fear in her eyes. Lauren reached for her, begging her legs to go faster. She couldn't let this happen. She'd promised to protect Piper.

A sad smile touched Piper's lips.

Her whole body jerked and then she dropped to the ground in a heap.

Cold emptiness filled Lauren but she kept running, pushing herself to reach her friend. She begged the gods to let Piper survive. She couldn't hear Piper's heart though or sense her feelings. Tears blurred Lauren's vision as reality began to sink in but she refused to believe it. Piper couldn't be dead. Leo couldn't have killed her.

Leo turned to face her and dropped his torch. It hit the ground near Piper.

Lauren drew one of her swords and screamed at him. There wasn't even a hint of guilt in him. Not one sign of regret over what he'd done.

"Piper!" Kuga yelled, his voice cracking under the rage and sorrow that Lauren could feel in him. Those feelings ran through her, fuelling her into readying herself for a fight. She would make Leo pay for what he had done.

Leo drew his arms back and pushed them forwards.

A bright white shockwave of electricity rushed towards them. Kuga grabbed her and swept his other arm out, sending his own shockwave back at Leo. The collision sent them flying. Lauren hit the ground hard. She tumbled along, head over heels, losing her sword along the way. When she came to a halt, she lay in the dirt breathing hard, trying to get her mind to stop spinning. She could taste blood.

Kuga was on his feet first and racing back towards Piper. Lauren pushed herself up and followed as fast as she could.

Leo was gone.

Kuga's knees hit the dirt hard beside Piper and he pulled her straight into his arms, cradling her close to his chest.

Tears obscured Lauren's vision when she reached them and saw Piper. Her knees gave way and a jolt bolted up her spine when they slammed into the frozen ground. There was no happiness in the smile on Piper's face. It was the same sad smile that she'd given them as they had tried to save her.

Lauren blinked and the tears rolled down her cheeks. She reached out with her senses but the only thing that came to her was Piper's warm scent and Kuga's strong emotions and heartbeat. He was furious but breaking too. His sorrow and pain too much for her to bear, she tried to shut down her senses, but couldn't shut off her own emotions. They swallowed her, turning the still emptiness inside into a sea of sadness and hurt, of heartbreak and misery, all laced with anger. She didn't want Piper to be gone. She couldn't be gone.

Lauren stared at her friend, cold to the bone and aching inside.

It was so unfair. Piper had been looking forward to her birthday, to being with Kuga, and to her future now that she was comfortable with her power. She'd worked so hard to master her ability and it had cost her life. Leo had said it himself. If Piper had remained unable to control her power, she would have lived.

"Why?" Lauren whispered, trying to understand what had made Leo turn on them, and stared at Piper with wide eyes rimmed with tears. They blurred her vision but she didn't blink them away. She kept staring at Piper, some part of her expecting her friend to open her eyes and be alive again. She'd died and come back. Why couldn't Piper do that too? Why did she have to go?

Kuga didn't respond. He clutched Piper close to his chest, trembling, and buried his face in her hair. His hurt mingled with Lauren's, making her shake and clutch at her chest as it burned with fierce raw pain.

She couldn't let Piper go like this.

Lauren grabbed Piper's arm and tried to pull her free of Kuga. His grip on her tightened and he held her closer.

"I won't let her go!" he said in a muffled voice, tight with his tears, but Lauren wouldn't give up. She tried to prise his arms off Piper, desperate to get her free so she could bring her back. She would bring her back. She wasn't going to let her friend die.

"I won't either!" Lauren countered.

Kuga looked up at her, his wet lashes reflecting the light of the torch on the grass a short distance away.

"Please," Lauren whispered and pulled on Piper's arm again.

Kuga released her and then frowned when Lauren laid her down and knelt over her. Lauren opened Piper's jacket and measured down to the point over her heart. She locked her hands together and started frantically pumping, counting just as she'd been taught in school.

"Come on, Piper," Lauren said and tipped Piper's chin up. She pinched Piper's nose and covered her mouth with her own, breathing into her. "Don't give up on me."

Lauren pumped her chest again, holding back her strength in case she accidentally broke a bone. She didn't want to hurt Piper. When Piper woke up, she wouldn't forgive her if she'd broken one of her ribs. It would take a lot of chocolate ice cream to make up for it. Lauren breathed into her again and then listened to her chest. Nothing.

"Damn it, Piper, come on," she said and pumped her chest harder, desperately searching for a sign of life with her senses. Tears streamed down her cheeks and she hiccupped on a sob and then tried to hold them in. She couldn't. They came on too strong, pushing out of her as she saw Piper's solemn face and kept pumping her chest. She couldn't be dead. If anyone was listening to her, if a goddess was really watching over her, they wouldn't let this happen. She couldn't let Piper go. She couldn't. "Please, Piper!"

She listened for a heartbeat. Nothing. She tried harder, breathing into her again and then pumping her chest, unwilling to give up. She needed Piper back with her. She needed to see her smile as Kuga reluctantly jumped out of a cake on her birthday and see her happiness when she came back from her night out with him. Piper had to live because she had so much to live for. She had done nothing wrong. She'd only wanted to help. She didn't deserve to die.

She'd been so afraid.

She'd been so happy.

Now all of that was gone, stolen in the space of a breath.

Kuga sniffed.

Lauren froze and looked at him, her eyes wide and wild. Electricity. Electricity had caused this and it could undo it.

He was motionless, hollow eyes staring down at Piper's pale face.

"Do something!" Lauren screamed at him and he looked at her, his expression remaining blank. She grabbed his hands and pressed them against Piper's chest. "Defibrillate her!"

He snatched his hands back.

"It's no use." He held his hands close to his chest. They were shaking as much as the rest of him. When he looked at her, the torchlight shone on the tear tracks down his face. "Leo shocked her mind. It won't work. I can't bring her back!"

His voice hitched on the last word and he pulled Piper into his arms, burying his face in her hair again and crying. His breaking down was Lauren's cue. She wrapped one arm around both him and Piper, pressing her forehead against his shoulder, and grasped Piper's cooling hand with her other. She sobbed against it, crying so hard that her lungs burnt with each breath she dragged in. Hot tears stung her eyes. She clung to Piper and Kuga, angry, distraught, too numb to face a world so cruel and unjust. Flinging her head back, she screamed at the night sky, cursing Lycaon and cursing Leo.

Why had he done this to them? They had trusted him. He had been a part of their group, family to Piper and Kuga. They'd believed in him. She'd believed in him. Her sobs came harder as she looked at Piper, great gasping ones that made her head spin. Why?

Piper had done nothing wrong.

Her parents had done nothing wrong.

Lycaon had killed all of them. She hated him. He took everything from her.

He took everything that she loved.

Strong warm hands against her ribs made her cry harder. They lifted her off the frozen ground, away from Kuga and Piper, and turned her. She buried her face in Julian's neck when he wrapped his arms around her, holding her so tight and close that she threw her arms about his waist and clung to him as she sobbed.

Fear made her heart ache and tremble.

What if he was next?

What if Lycaon took him too?

She couldn't bear it. Just the thought of it robbed her of her strength to live.

"Duke?" Astra's tone was questioning, searching.

"No." Duke's voice was tight and harsh. Whatever Astra meant by her unspoken question, he didn't like it. "I won't."

Lauren took deep breaths to halt her tears. Julian's hands worked lightly against her back. It comforted her and gave her back her strength. When he held her like this, he made her want to be strong so they could be together.

Lycaon would pay for what he'd done.

Leo would pay.

She didn't care that he was Kuga's brother. He'd deceived them all. He'd taken Piper's life.

Now she knew why he'd been so upset that Kuga hadn't told him about Piper mastering her power, and why he'd wanted to wait for Morgan to show. He'd wanted to buy Lycaon time to escape. By persisting in going after Lycaon right away, Lauren had forced Leo into a corner. She'd given him no choice but to kill Piper to protect Lycaon.

Damn him.

Damn him straight to Hell.

"You must have known about this." Duke and he wasn't happy. Lauren didn't come out of her hiding place Julian's arms. If he was talking to her, then he wasn't going to get a reply.

"I didn't," Kuga said and she heard him stand, heard his heart beat a little harder, and felt his emotions change towards anger. He was gearing up for a fight. This wasn't the time for it.

"You expect us to believe you did not know that your brother was up to something?" Astra this time. The malice in her was palpable. It sickened Lauren.

Kuga tensed.

"She's right. You must have known something," Duke said.

"Perhaps you are also a part of this conspiracy—"

"I'm not!" Kuga cut Astra off and Lauren felt the spike in his emotions. He was on the verge of snapping. What were they playing at? Couldn't they see how devastated he was by Piper's death and Leo's betrayal? It wasn't an act. This had hurt him more than anyone.

"You must have noticed that your own blood was a Lycaon lapdog!"

Lauren pushed out of Julian's arms and turned on Astra. "Shut the hell up!"

Duke and Astra stared at her. Kuga stood to one side by Piper, his eyes downcast.

"He didn't know!" Lauren stepped forwards. Even if it was blind rage at Piper's death making them react in such a manner, it was wrong and she wasn't going to stand by and let them hurt Kuga like this. "I saw it in his eyes… he was as surprised as we all were… it was his brother for God's sake… his own brother!"

Astra turned away and Duke's dark expression switched to one of regret. Kuga glanced at her and then walked away into the darkness.

Lauren removed her jacket and placed it over Piper, covering her head and sniffing back her tears. She couldn't cry now. She had to be strong. She threw an angry glare at Astra and Duke and then went after Kuga. With her night vision, he wasn't difficult to find. He was standing by a copse of trees in the middle of the field, staring up at the cloudy sky.

"I'm sorry," she whispered. Her apology felt feeble, far from enough to make up for how his friends had treated him, and for what Leo had done. It was all her fault. She would rather Lycaon had escaped than had this happen. She looked back towards Piper where Julian stood sentinel over her body. It wasn't sinking in that Piper was gone but it did feel as though a light had disappeared from the world.

From this point forward, it would be a darker place. Piper had brought them so many smiles and so much laughter, and she'd offered Lauren so much comfort and support. She had found a friend in her, a wonderful young woman full of hopes and dreams that had made Lauren want to be a better person and had made her feel accepted even after her awakening. She had felt as though she'd had a family again, a sister and brothers, people she had quickly grown to love, and now all that was gone. She didn't want to believe that Piper was dead or that Leo had betrayed them, but she was and he had, and nothing she could do would change that. All she could do now was fight harder to protect those she loved and to avenge Piper. She wouldn't fail her. She would become stronger so she could save the world.

"What do we do now?" Kuga whispered and she knew that he meant more than just this moment. He was asking how they went on in a world without Piper.

She didn't have an answer to that question, but she could answer the surface one.

She looked back across the field at Piper. In her heart, she knew what Piper would have wanted.

"We take her home."

CHAPTER 37

London seemed different. Or perhaps it was her. Lauren felt different returning to the city that had raised her. Stronger, as though she finally knew herself. She only wished that she'd made the discovery under better circumstances.

The sun beat down on her, stealing her energy along with the ceremony. She stared at the coffin in front of her, hollow and drained, so tired that she could barely stand. She had to go on but didn't know if she could. It felt as though Lycaon, Leo, had taken her life from her, leaving her nothing but a shell. She had felt nothing these past few days and she wanted to feel. She wanted to cry. She wanted to scream and beg the gods to tell her why they were doing this, why Piper had died and why her parents were gone. She wanted to be stronger so she could avenge her parents and Piper. She had been born to fight and she had filled the past few days with nothing but that, with an endless fight to become strong enough. She still wasn't and she owed it to Piper to be strong.

She owed it to everyone, even herself.

She had to become stronger so she could protect those that she loved.

Duke stepped up to the wooden lectern at the head of the coffin. Each sentence was hard to hear as she listened to him speak about Piper. Her friend was gone because of her. She'd had so many chances to stop it from happening. She should have defeated Lycaon that night. She should have said to wait until they were stronger rather than going after Lycaon right away. She should have been faster and reached Piper before Leo had shocked her.

She blinked back her tears when Duke moved away from the lectern and Kuga left her side. Her gaze followed him and the endless pain returned to her heart when he stood behind the lectern, staring at the grave. He hadn't spoken since the night Piper had died. She had barely seen him. Duke had told her that he wasn't eating or sleeping. She guessed they were both the same in that respect. Kuga's words were quiet, spoken with a soft reverence that touched Lauren and brought more tears to her eyes. His fingers clutched the edges of the lectern, knuckles white, and his voice hitched and cracked. She didn't need her senses in order to detect his fight to control his emotions and hold himself together. He frowned down at the microphone and then closed his eyes and swallowed hard. When he opened them again, he looked at Duke and shook his head. Duke nodded. Lauren's heart ached for him as he left the stand. He couldn't say anymore. Duke looked at her. She shook her head. She didn't want to speak, didn't want to announce her farewell to Piper to the world.

Lauren leaned into Julian and closed her eyes briefly when he placed his arm around her shoulders, drawing her close. His proximity was a comfort, quietening the instinct inside her that said to go somewhere safe and sleep. She couldn't sleep—hadn't slept since that night.

Kuga returned to his place beside her, his eyes on the open grave and the mahogany coffin suspended above it. Piper was too young to be put in the dirt. Her whole life had been ahead of her. It was her fault that Piper had died. She should have been the one in that coffin.

Leo should have killed her instead. He'd had plenty of chances. He could have killed her when she'd still been human and they had gone out to see her friends.

She realised what had happened that night. Leo had gone for cigarettes to give the werewolf a chance to attack.

And he must have told Lycaon they were in Paris.

That was how they had found them so quickly.

Rage burned fierce in her heart when she thought about how long he'd been deceiving them but quickly faded, leaving her empty again.

They lowered Piper into the ground and began to cover her.

Lauren glanced at Kuga. If she'd made these connections, then he must have too. He had to know exactly how involved his brother had been in Lycaon's attacks.

She couldn't imagine how much this had hurt him.

She couldn't imagine how much it had hurt everyone.

Lauren went to reach across to Kuga but Julian's arm around her tightened, keeping her close. She touched the hand that grasped her shoulder. She knew that he didn't like being out here without weapons when they were both weak from the sunlight. Both of them hoped that Lycaon wouldn't expect them to return to London. They all needed some time to regroup now.

She looked at Duke where he stood on the other side of the coffin, dressed all in black just like the rest of them, a single white rose in his buttonhole. Duke wanted them to move as soon as possible to somewhere unknown to Leo. Perhaps he was right.

She wanted everyone to be safe too. She needed time to grow stronger so she could face Lycaon. Right now, she was drained and weak, too tired to face anything.

Her gaze moved over Astra and Duke, and then finally settled on Kuga. She could feel all of their pain. Even Astra and Julian were hurting because of Piper's death. Because of her.

A part of her heart told her to give up before she caused any more pain. She would never be strong enough to defeat Lycaon. He had already taken her parents and Piper, and had almost taken Julian, and she had been powerless to stop him. She didn't want anyone else to die and she was afraid that they would if it continued, but she couldn't ask them to give up, not after everything they had been through. She couldn't belittle Piper's death and their sacrifice by asking them to do that. They had to continue. They would want to avenge Piper and face Leo, just as she did.

When Lauren reached for Kuga's hand this time, Julian didn't stop her. She slipped her hand into Kuga's, feeling it tremble beneath her fingers with sorrow and anger. His warm brown eyes held tears that never fell. They coated his lashes, glittering in the bright sunlight. He was so much stronger than she was. She'd cried to the point where she couldn't anymore. The tears came but they didn't fall. Was Kuga the same as her, had he cried to his limit, or was he holding them back?

She wished her tears would come. Without them, the hollow pain in her heart wouldn't ease.

Lauren squeezed Kuga's hand and was surprised when he squeezed back, his eyes still fixed on the grave where Piper lay shrouded in cold earth.

His hand left hers when they placed the last of the dirt on the grave. He stepped forwards, laid a single white arum lily on the mound, and walked away from them, heading down among the gravestones.

Duke went to go after him and Julian was there in an instant, blocking his path, his hand on Duke's chest.

"Let him go," Lauren whispered, her voice hoarse. Her body shook from fatigue, her head heavy and fuzzy. "He'll come back when he's ready."

Her gaze shifted to Julian. He nodded.

Lauren kneeled by the grave and placed her lily down, laying it beside Kuga's one. Kuga had chosen them. Duke had told her afterwards that it was Piper's favourite flower.

"I'll miss you, Piper." Lauren laid her hand over the two flowers and reached out through the soil, wishing she could feel Piper one last time, could smell her scent of sunshine and sweet happiness. She closed her eyes and tried to find the words but couldn't bring herself to say goodbye. "Be at peace."

When she went to stand, her head spun. She tried to walk but her legs were unsteady, weak as the world wavered in front of her eyes. They gave out and she was falling forwards, the grass a green blur. Something struck her across the ribs below her breasts and then she could see the blue sky. Julian. He lifted her, wrapping her in his arms, and set her down on her feet, holding her steady. She tried to smile for him when he dipped his head and looked into her eyes.

He looked different in a suit. Handsome but out of place. His ice blue eyes searched hers. The concern in them brought fresh tears but they weren't for Piper. They were for Julian now. She was so afraid that he would be next. Lycaon was taking everything that she loved from her and she loved Julian more than anything.

"You are still not strong enough to be out in the sun." Julian's soft tone echoed his concern.

Lauren didn't protest when he scooped her up into his arms. She sunk into him, barely finding the strength to wrap her arms around his neck. Her head came to rest against his shoulder. She'd never felt so bone-deep tired before. There wasn't an ounce of energy left in her. Her eyes slipped shut.

She wanted to stay here forever in Julian's embrace, safe and warm, shut away from the dark world.

She wanted to run with him so they didn't have to face Lycaon, because she couldn't shake the feeling that when all this ended, she would be alone.

CHAPTER 38

Julian held Lauren close, carrying her down the gentle slope to the black Mercedes waiting on the gravel drive, away from the open site of the grave. She felt frail in his arms, the sun stripping her remaining strength and leaving her vulnerable. They were both vulnerable. He'd wanted to bring his sword but Lauren had insisted that they did this one thing without weapons. She'd wanted Piper's send off to be different from the short life that she'd lived. She'd wanted all trace of violence gone.

Lauren sighed and Julian looked down at her.

He could sense her weariness. She hadn't slept or fed since Piper's death. He'd tried to feed her before the funeral but she'd refused. They were both growing weak. If they continued without feeding, they would be no match for Lycaon even at night. He needed to hunt for Lauren. He was reluctant to leave her when she was so weak, but he had to. She needed blood and it was his duty to feed her.

When the wake was over, he would ask Duke to keep Lauren safe. Duke was strong enough to protect her while he went out to hunt.

The driver opened the car door for them and Julian carefully placed Lauren down on the back seat. He went to move away but Lauren grabbed his black jacket, her knuckles white as she held him fast. With a nod to the driver, Julian stepped into the car. Lauren moved across to make room for him. She was weak if her instincts were making her stop him from leaving her side. He'd only intended to go to the other side of the car to enter.

The moment he was settled, Lauren turned on the seat to face him, hooked her legs over his right thigh so her knees pressed against the inside of his left, and curled up against him with her hand on his chest. He placed his arm around her shoulders and took hold of her hand. She didn't need to fear the day. As weak as he was, he would still defend her should anyone attack.

It wasn't far into their journey back to the London office that he realised that Lauren had finally succumbed to sleep. He caressed her fingers with his thumb, memorising their softness as he listened to her light breathing and her steady heart. Tilting his head back, he stared at the black roof of the car and asked the gods to give her good dreams. Lauren needed her rest. She hadn't stopped training since the night that Piper had died. She couldn't go on the way she had, not without hurting herself.

She needed her sleep so much that he was loath to wake her when they reached the old warehouse.

Julian quietly opened the door and stepped out, leaning back in again to manoeuvre Lauren into his arms. She stirred, her nose wrinkling and a frown creasing her brow, but didn't wake. He nodded his thanks to the driver and then carried her into the building, moving swiftly but silently up to her bedroom.

It was difficult to close the door without waking her but he managed it. He turned to his left, where the wooden double bed stood against the same wall as the door. When he set her down on the Wedgewood blue bedcovers, she woke and blinked sleepily at him. Her gaze tracked over everything in the room and then settled on him. He went to the three windows opposite the bed and closed the blue curtains to shut out the day. The room looked cold and stark in the low light from the lamp on the bedside table.

"We're back?" Her voice was still hoarse from her crying. He'd hated to feel her pain, to hold her as she wept for her friend. It had sounded as though her heart had been breaking.

He sat down beside her on the double bed, loosened his tie and then undid the top button of his black shirt. During the ceremony, it had felt as though it was choking him. They had never worked with others before, not in all the millennia that he'd been assisting Illia's reincarnations. Other than Lauren's predecessors, the last graves he'd attended had been those of his men in Illia's army. Three thousand years ago. He hadn't cried back then, not even for his closest friends or those who had turned to werewolves, the creatures they despised most, but tears had filled his eyes today when he'd said his silent goodbye to Piper.

He would never forget her. As long as he remembered her, she lived on, and he could go on for another three millennia. He would tend to her grave, replacing the headstone when it weathered and her name faded. He would never let her die.

And he knew that Lauren wouldn't either.

She wouldn't forget any of the Ghosts who had become her friends. Not Piper. Not Duke or Kuga. Not even Astra. Even though the two women didn't like each other, Lauren would still mourn the demon's death.

Her heart was so warm and loving, so full of tender concern for those she met in life.

"You fell asleep," he said.

"I did?" Lauren looked at her knees and picked at the black trousers she wore. The dark formal clothing didn't suit her.

Julian reached across and undid the single button on her black jacket. She didn't move as he removed it and placed it on the bed beside her. Even the white pin-tuck shirt was too stark against her pale skin, making her look drawn and deathlike. He'd seen too much death for an eternity.

As if sensing the fact that he didn't like such sombre clothing on her, Lauren undid her shirt, revealing the small pale grey camisole she wore beneath it. She took the shirt off and laid it down on top of the jacket. Julian took them both, rounded the foot of the bed, and laid them over the back of the white armchair in the corner by the bathroom. He removed his own jacket and carried it back to her.

"This place reminds me of her," Lauren whispered and drew her knees up to her chest. She rested her chin on them, her short dark red hair falling forwards to obscure her face, and sighed. "I'm afraid that Kuga won't return."

It was a valid fear, but one which wouldn't come true.

"He will return."

Lauren looked up at him through the tangled threads of her hair. "Really?"

Julian nodded. She was looking to him for strength and he would give her all that he had, every last drop of it, so she might be able to find some peace in her heart and sleep again.

"Come." He held his hand out.

Her fingers were warm in his and he drew her towards him, making her stand. He pulled the mid-blue covers back on her bed. Her sweet scent filled his senses and he closed his eyes, remembering how lonely it had been to sleep in his own bed the past few days. Lauren had insisted that he rested. Whenever she'd needed time alone, he'd gone back to his room and tried to sleep. It had been impossible. He'd been able to feel a glimmer of her sorrow and pain as she had trained alone on the floor below, practicing her moves until she was near to collapsing. Feeling that in her and not being able to go to her had been torture.

"You need to rest," he said.

Lauren stared at the bed and shook her head. He frowned, heart aching as he saw the look in her eyes and sensed what she was going to say.

"I can't." She removed her trousers, took the grey marl jogging bottoms from the end of her bed and slipped them on. Her shoulders slumped and she rubbed her hand across her face, as though trying to erase the fatigue he could feel in her. She was hurting herself by doing this, by never sleeping and always training, and he couldn't bear it.

"Lauren, you must rest."

She shook her head again. "Not yet."

Before he could stop her, she had left the room and was walking down the corridor towards the stairs.

He followed her, quickly catching her up and striding along beside her. When they reached the gym on the floor below, she picked up two of the wooden katana from the stack leaning against the mirrored wall and took a deep breath. Julian picked one up too and Lauren looked at him. Tears lined her eyes. She moved into a fighting stance in the middle of the black floor, holding the wooden swords out in front of her, clutched tightly. Her hands trembled. She wasn't strong enough to train right now but nothing Julian could say would stop her. She had been like this since Piper had died.

"Doing this will not bring her back." He moved to stand opposite her, his single training sword held out in front of him.

"I know," she whispered and met his gaze, her brown eyes sparkling with tears but dull with fatigue.

"Then rest a while."

She shook her head. "I can't."

He clenched his fingers around the hilt of the sword and frowned. Nothing he said had stopped her so far. The only thing he could do was let her practice until she was too tired to do anything but sleep. The way she was trembling said that wouldn't be long now. She had fallen asleep on him in the car. She was close to reaching the point where she would have to sleep, regardless of what she wanted to do.

She attacked while he was still thinking but he easily blocked it. He knew her moves now. At first, she had been harder to predict and her attacks had been random. As her energy had drained away, she had begun to go through the motions of a single routine. She was so tired that she probably hadn't realised that she was doing it. He blocked her swords, forcing her backwards, wanting to change her routine and make her live again. She was relentless, hacking at him with both swords, her fury breaking through the dullness in her eyes to bring back the shine.

It broke his heart to see what she was doing to herself. Her push to become stronger was only hurting her. She could pretend all she wanted that she was all right but he could hear her heart crying out and could feel her pain. He blocked her when she brought both of her swords down overhead and leapt back when she attacked again. She stumbled forwards and he reached out to steady her but she pushed him away.

She straightened, moved back into a fighting stance, and stared at him.

He moved back to stand before her and then lowered his sword when she attacked. Her sword stopped a hair's breadth from his face. She jumped back, frowned at him, and then attacked again. He dodged it, stepping to the side. She tripped forwards a few paces, made a frustrated noise, and attacked again.

He didn't want to fight her anymore. He wanted to stop her. He wanted her to give up and take his strength again, to be as she was before, not weak but someone who felt they didn't have to be strong, not when they were breaking inside.

Lauren yelled and attacked with both swords. The whole of her was crying out to him, screaming of her pain and her tiredness. Julian blocked her and she didn't stop, she drove him backwards, growling as she shoved her swords against his. He put his foot out behind him to stop him and she wobbled and then collapsed.

Julian dropped his sword and caught her, wrapping his arms around her waist and lowering her gently to the ground. He kneeled beside her. She breathed hard, leaning heavily against his chest, and the swords fell from her hands. He held her close, stroking her arm and then her back, trying to soothe her.

"I have you," he whispered and she curled up against him and cried. "Shh, it is alright, Lauren."

"No." She tried to push him away and stand. Her legs gave out before she could manage it and she was on his lap, leaning into him again. "I don't want to cry. I have to be strong."

He held her tightly when she tried to get up again, not letting her. He'd had enough. He wouldn't stand by and let her kill herself. He loved her too much. Even if she ordered him to, he wasn't going to let her go. He wasn't going to let this continue.

"No, Lauren, you do not have to be strong. Let me be strong for you," he whispered and she drew back and looked at him. Tears streaked her cheeks. Her eyebrows furrowed tightly and she searched his eyes. He cupped her cheek with one hand and held her around the waist with his other. "You do not have to be strong around me. You do not need to push yourself like this."

"I do." She frowned at him, wiped her tears away with the back of her hand and sniffed. "I do. I owe it to everyone to see them through this."

He smiled and caught her hand, holding it gently in his. It was damp with her tears. "Everyone here chose to be a part of this. They are strong, Lauren. You do not need to bear the weight of this alone. Let me bear it with you."

Tears filled her eyes and her brow furrowed again. "Why?"

"Because I need to." He captured her tears with the pad of his thumb before they could fall. "I want to. I need you to see that you are not alone in this. I am here with you and I will be your strength until you are strong again. Your sword. Your shield."

"Because I'm your commander?" Her eyes searched his deeply and he knew what she wanted to hear.

"No..." He choked on the words that he needed to say, the ones she was expecting. He couldn't voice them but others came that he hoped would please her. "No... not because you are my commander, but because... I need you, Lauren. I cannot bear to see you hurt, and to see you hurt yourself. I do not want to see it. I want to take away that pain and make you smile again. I want to make you feel safe and make you feel you are no longer alone. I want to make you believe that I will never leave you. I cannot."

"Why?" she whispered again, her eyes wide now, glittering with tears. The corners of her lips shifted into the faintest of smiles and he could feel the threads of her happiness. She brought her hands up and placed them against his chest.

"You are my everything, Lauren." He stroked her cheek, staring into her eyes and meaning every word with all of his heart. "Without you, there is no reason to go on... there is no colour in this world or life in my heart. I would bear anything for you, do anything. I feel helpless—"

Her fingers against his cheek silenced him. She smiled weakly.

"I've worried you again." Her smile faded. "I'm sorry."

Julian reached up, took hold of her hand, and brought it to his lips. He kissed her palm and she smiled again.

"I'll rest now... if you'll stay with me," she whispered.

He nodded, placed his arm under her knees and the other around her back, and stood with her. She leaned against him, her forehead resting on his neck.

"I will never leave your side," he said and she looked up at him.

She rewarded him with a brief kiss that warmed his heart.

He waited for her to settle again and carried her upstairs to her room.

When he set her down in her room, she smiled at him and then walked to the bed. He closed the door and locked it.

"The wake is in a few hours. We can sleep until then."

She nodded wearily and stripped down to her underwear, again shimmying out of her bra under the cover of her camisole. He tried to keep his eyes off her. Tried. The sight of her made that impossible. His gaze traced the beautiful curve of her body, the way she dipped in at the waist and then came out into full hips that sent all manner of sordid thoughts racing through his mind.

He shook them away. Now wasn't the time for succumbing to lustful thoughts.

Lauren moved onto the bed, slid under the blue covers and then held her hand out to him.

He swallowed. Always the temptress. If she knew how little control he had when she was close, she wouldn't offer to have him in her bed at all. Deep inside, he burned with the fierce desire to touch her, to slide his hand under the hem of her camisole and cup her breasts, and to slide that same hand down to the elastic of her knickers and lazily trace the line of them, silently begging for an invitation.

Refusing her was impossible though. She'd asked him into her bed again, and he would be a fool to turn her away when she so clearly needed him. He stripped down to his underwear. Her gaze appraised him in a slow sensual way, igniting his passion. He yearned to act on it.

One day.

But not right now.

Lauren needed her rest, they both did, and neither of them would be able to fight their fatigue long enough for anything to happen. For now, he would settle for sleeping with her back in his arms, because that was what they needed most—the connection, the love, and the feeling of being together.

When he slid into bed beside her, she shuffled close to him as she had done before, tangling her legs with his and resting her head against his chest. She breathed a contented sigh and he focused on her, trying to sense her feelings. She seemed more relaxed now. With a little blood, she would be tired enough to sleep.

He looked at his wrist. He didn't have anything to give her other than his own, and there wasn't a trace of living blood in it now. It had been too many days since he'd fed. His blood wouldn't give her sustenance but it would restore some of her strength.

"Lauren," he whispered and she tilted her head back, her eyes meeting his. "You must feed."

She shook her head, her deep brown eyes fixed on his. He lifted his hand and carefully swept strands of her hair back, out of her face, making sure that he brushed her skin at the same time. Her eyelids fell to half-mast and she smiled at him. The tenderness and happiness in it made his heart beat harder.

"Please, Lauren. Feed for me?" He wasn't below begging if it got him what he wanted. She was so weak. It was important that she kept up her strength and slept.

Her gaze shifted to his wrist and he paused with his fingers against her cheek. He could see that she wasn't going to go through with it. His fangs extended. She gasped when he bit into his wrist and then looked ashamed when he offered it to her. He didn't understand.

"What is wrong?" he said.

"You haven't fed." She ran her fingers in circles on his chest, staring at them as though they were the most fascinating thing in the world. A drop of blood ran down his forearm. He licked it up, not wanting to stain the sheets. "You'll get weak."

"I will hunt tonight," Julian said, touched that she worried about him. He would be strong enough to hunt when night fell. "Feed. You will not weaken me."

"Liar," she said but took his wrist anyway. She drank slowly, barely taking a sip from him. Was she really so afraid of weakening him? Did she fear that someone would be able to defeat him when he was hunting if she took too much?

He knew Lycaon well. He wouldn't expect them to return to London to bury Piper. He didn't understand or care about such things. He left his men where they fell and had no sense of attachment to them. His focus now would be on recovering and recruiting more men. Until he had regrouped, he would leave them alone.

Lycaon would make himself known soon enough, but it wouldn't be tonight and it wouldn't be in London.

Lauren licked Julian's wrist, her tongue sliding sensually over the marks that he'd made, cleaning and sealing them. He savoured the feel of her hands on him and her body pressing into his. This truly was his heaven. If only she knew.

With a sleepy smile, Lauren kissed his wrist and then settled down with her head on his chest. Her fingertips swirled over his skin, following the line of his stomach muscles. He resisted the urge to tense when she reached his navel and closed his eyes. It was torture to have her touch him like this, but one he could endure forever. A pleasant kind of torture.

"Why didn't Lycaon have Leo kill me?" she whispered.

"Because that is not his way. He will not allow another to take your life." Julian held her close, hating the cold feeling of dread that seized his heart whenever he thought about Lauren fighting Lycaon. He stroked the scar on her upper arm, remembering how close he had been to losing her. Never again. "I will not let him harm you, Lauren. Sleep now. Good dreams will come to you."

"Mmm… because I'm in your arms."

Julian smiled at that. It was actually because the gods were looking down on her and would grant his request, but he preferred her reason more. If she believed that she would have good dreams purely because she was in his arms, he wasn't going to tell her different.

Before long, she halted her exploration of his body and rested more heavily against him. He ran his fingertips up and down her bare arm, listening to her sleeping. It had been a long day for her, one that she would never forget, not even if she lived to be his age.

And he would see to it that she lived forever, with him.

CHAPTER 39

Lauren stood by the roof exit, hidden in the shadow of the small structure. Her senses had led her here when she'd begun to worry about Kuga. The wake was over and he hadn't returned.

But he had in a way.

He was sitting on a raised section at the other end of the flat roof with his back to her, staring up at the moon and the stars that glittered above them. She'd been intent on finding him so he wouldn't be alone, but now that she was here, she wasn't sure whether to go through with it. He probably didn't want company. If he did, he would have come down to see everyone.

Julian had gone out half an hour ago, telling her to remain indoors where it was safe. The roof wasn't indoors, but she knew that he wouldn't be upset with her for being out here so Kuga wasn't alone.

No one should be alone.

Lauren quietly approached Kuga, still torn between disturbing him and leaving. When she reached him, he roughly wiped the heels of his hands across his eyes, keeping his head turned away from her.

"Is Julian with you?" Kuga hunched over and ran his fingers into his hair, locking them behind his head. His elbows rested on his knees.

Lauren could feel a glimmer of his pain. She waited a moment to see if he would say anything else, do anything that would give her reason to believe that he wanted to be alone. He remained motionless, curled up in a defensive position, but didn't push her away.

"No," she said and sat close to him, crossing her legs and looking out over the differing roofs of the city buildings. It was beautiful up here, so much to keep the eye entertained but it couldn't keep her thoughts off Piper. The whole of London stretched out in front of her. She remembered how excited Piper had been about going out with Kuga on her birthday to see Paris laid out at her feet and the dull ache returned to her heart. "Are you okay?"

Kuga snorted. Bloodshot eyes met hers when he turned his head to the side. The smile he gave her faltered and trembled. The incredible hurt in him echoed in her chest.

"I keep thinking about that moment... what I could have done different. How I could have saved her."

Lauren didn't think he could have helped Piper but she kept that to herself. He didn't need to hear her say it. The look of loss and hopelessness in his eyes said that he already knew.

"He was my brother." His voice cracked. "How could he do that to Piper... to me?"

Lauren's brow furrowed. Her insides felt heavy when she replayed the night Piper had died and tried to find an answer to Kuga's question.

"I don't know." She honestly didn't. Since meeting them, she'd watched the brothers. They might have had their moments, but Leo loved Kuga, so much and so openly that Lauren had grown more than a little envious of their relationship. She'd always wished that she'd had a sister.

And she'd thought that she'd found one in Piper.

But now Piper was gone.

And Leo had turned on them.

Lauren placed her arm around Kuga, barely able to reach across his broad shoulders. The sight of him still in mourning attire made her want to cry. Everyone else had changed back into their normal clothes. Changing out of the suit and back into her jeans and jumper had made her feel better. She was sure that it would be the same for Kuga.

No. What was she thinking? Even if Kuga changed out of the black suit, he couldn't change his appearance. Leo was his twin. Who did Kuga see when he looked into the mirror? She hadn't thought about it before. Kuga would never be able to escape what his brother had done, not when they looked the same. His own face would be an eternal reminder of his brother's betrayal.

"I miss her," he whispered in a hoarse voice, as though he was barely holding back his tears. "I miss him… I wish he'd killed me."

"Don't say that." Lauren took hold of his hand and pressed her fingers tight into his palm.

"No one trusts me… and for the first time in my life, I'm alone… I don't… I hate that he killed her, but I can't hate him. Why?" His eyes searched hers.

She didn't have an answer for him. The only words that came to her were ones of bitterness and hatred. She wanted to tell Kuga that he should hate his brother, that he should want to kill him for what he'd done, and that she would kill Leo for him if he couldn't, but she held her tongue. Kuga didn't need to hear her anger—he needed her comfort. In time, he would find an answer to his question for himself. All she could do was hold his hand until he did.

She sighed and squeezed his hand, not quite sure what to say to him and finding it difficult to keep her tone warm and full of the affection she felt for Kuga. "No one hates you, Kuga. It was a knee jerk reaction. Everyone is worried about you."

"Is that the truth, or are you just telling me what I want to hear?" The edge to his voice startled her but she didn't relinquish her grip on his hand. It trembled in hers, betraying his pain as much as his eyes did.

He didn't want to be alone. She couldn't imagine how hard this was for him, not only to lose Piper but to lose his brother too. They had been together all their lives, and now they were enemies. It was impossible for her to understand the burden that Kuga's heart had to bear, the pain he would have to endure for the rest of his life. No wonder he'd wanted Leo to kill him instead. He probably felt as though he was dying inside.

"It's the truth," Lauren said and his look softened. The moonlight made him pale and made the tears in his eyes shine like diamonds. "I need you with me on this, Kuga. I'll make Lycaon pay for taking Piper from us. I promise. But I need your strength. We all do."

Kuga tilted his head back and stared at the stars. When had she gotten so good at the pep talks and speeches? She'd never been a strong person, but, somewhere along the line, she'd found some source of inner strength that made her want to lead these people to victory. She wanted everyone to survive this. She'd seen too much death already. Lycaon wouldn't take anyone else from her.

She wouldn't let him.

"It's her birthday tomorrow, you know?" A single tear slid down Kuga's cheek.

A little smile touched his lips and then faded, as though he'd remembered something nice but then realised it was gone now too.

"She would have been eighteen. I was going to tell her—" His voice cracked again and he coughed, as though trying to cover the fact that he was crying when she could plainly see his tears. "I wanted to tell her that I'm in love with her."

"Oh, Kuga." Lauren squeezed his hand. Her heart ached for him and for Piper. They had been so close to being together but time had been against them. It made her realise that she couldn't waste time with Julian. She couldn't wait and tell herself that it would happen in time, always delaying making things more serious between them. Who knew what tomorrow held? She didn't want to end up like Kuga and Piper, on the verge of a relationship and revealing their feelings only for it to be taken away from them. "I know you both loved each other."

His gaze snapped down to meet hers. "She loved me?"

Lauren nodded, feeling awful when she sensed his pain increase.

"It wasn't me that she reached out to when—it was you, Kuga. She reached out to you." It hurt to say that, to tell him something that was only going to cause him more pain. In the long term though, he would come to cherish the fact that Piper had wanted him until the very end and that she'd reached out to him that night because she'd loved him.

Kuga turned away, his shoulders heaving. Damn. Now she'd made a grown man cry. It wasn't something she'd ever wanted to do, and she certainly hadn't wanted to upset Kuga this much. Rubbing her hand in a soothing circle on his shoulders, she stared at the back of his head.

"I shouldn't have said that. I'm sorry. I didn't mean to—"

"No," he said surprisingly firm and steady. "Thank you... I didn't know. I'm glad that I do now... that I can imagine what her reaction would have been."

Lauren looked out across the city, remembering the times she'd talked to Piper about the birthday trip Kuga had planned for them. The location hadn't excited her. It had been the fact that she would be alone with Kuga and that it had been his idea. Piper had been so happy when she'd read Kuga's feelings about her. Lauren was glad that Piper had at least had that moment with him.

"She was excited about the trip," Lauren said and Kuga turned back so he sitting beside her again. "She said that you'd been practicing something for her."

Kuga nodded and then frowned at his hands. A spark, sky blue in the darkness, flickered above his left palm and then grew until it was the shape of a heart. Not a heart like Duke had produced, human and beating, but a cartoon-style heart. A love heart. It glowed white-blue, the size of a tennis ball above Kuga's upturned hand.

"It's low voltage so it takes a lot of effort to make it keep its shape. You can touch it."

She did. It was warm and tickled. Her fingers went straight through it but the shape held. She looked at Kuga.

"She would have loved it." New tears filled her eyes.

Kuga looked so lost.

Fear threatened to squeeze the air from her lungs. Lycaon had taken her parents and Piper. Who was next? Julian was out there alone, hunting for her. She didn't want to think about that but couldn't stop. She wanted him back with her, called to him with all her heart. He'd been gone too long.

"Kuga," Lauren whispered and he closed his hand. The heart shattered, leaving them in near-darkness again. "I need you with me on this, please? You're not alone. You have us... we all believe in you and we need you now more than ever. Together we will defeat Lycaon. We will face Leo and avenge Piper."

Kuga nodded and took hold of her hand. "I wouldn't miss it for the world. I want to see Leo and beat the shit out of him."

Lauren smiled at last. That was the Kuga she knew. Brash, confident and strong. She only hoped that she didn't lose him too.

She didn't want to worry, it distracted and weakened her, but she couldn't help it. She couldn't bear the thought of losing Julian, or any of the remaining Ghosts. She wasn't going to lose them.

Kuga stood and helped her to her feet. "Come on, we'd better go in. They're probably worrying about you."

"Us," she corrected him. "They're worried about us."

She went to follow him into the building and then paused. Kuga stopped a short distance ahead of her. Lauren gazed at the three quarters full moon, feeling the warmth of its rays on her skin and the comforting way it soothed her heart whenever she looked at it. Selene. Illia's mother. Her mother in a way.

The reason she was here, fighting Lycaon, losing her friends and her family one by one.

Lauren opened her heart and mind to the moon.

"Protect us both, all," she whispered, feeling foolish for thinking that Selene was up there listening to her, watching over her, but willing to place her faith in her plea all the same, willing to believe that her mother could hear her and would do as she asked. "Please. Don't side with the enemy."

Turning away, she followed Kuga into the building, leaving her heart and mind focused on the moon until its light no longer touched her.

She had to believe that Selene was listening.

She needed all the help she could get.

CHAPTER 40

Julian didn't listen to a word that Astra was saying, or any of Duke's responses. He'd felt an urge to return and when he had, he'd found that Lauren was outside. He'd gone to see her but she'd been with Kuga. Not wanting to interrupt their conversation, and knowing that only Lauren could convince Kuga to continue their mission, he'd left them. Kuga would protect her should something happen.

He would join them again in the fight against Lycaon.

The young man had loved Piper. He would want to avenge her death.

Julian brushed the long tail of his black coat aside and rested his hand on the hilt of his sword. His fingers flexed around it. Anger filled his heart but he didn't hold onto it and it quickly faded again. Piper's death had been pointless, like many he'd seen when he'd been a commander. She'd had so much to live for.

He missed her.

He missed the way she'd offered him quiet company, especially when Ghost had rescued him, and even missed her nosy probing of his mind. Her lively air had given life to the group, always cheering everyone up. They all needed that most now, when she could no longer give it. He had owed her a lot. He should have saved her life as she'd saved his.

He paced across the large room towards the gun collection that took up most of one of the walls. When he reached it, he turned back towards Duke where he leaned against the huge mahogany desk with his left foot up on one of the dark red leather armchairs. Duke glanced at him, the pain visible in his eyes. Duke had hidden it well so far, but Julian knew that losing Piper had hurt him deeply. He had felt responsible for her and now she was gone.

The door to the office opened and Kuga entered. He stopped in the corner near one of the large bookcases. Julian couldn't blame him for keeping his distance after the way that Astra and Duke had treated him.

Lauren followed a short distance behind, her expression troubled. A wave of hurt swept through the room when she closed the door. It cut short the sense of relief he'd had on seeing her return safe.

She came straight over and stood toe-to-toe with him, looking up into his eyes.

He opened his arms and she stepped into his embrace. When she settled against him, he felt whole again, the missing part of him returned and back in place. He wished they were alone, wished the tall funnel collar of his coat wasn't masking his face, because he wanted to press a kiss to her hair and give her the comfort she sought. She turned in his arms so they were hip to hip, her by his side with his arm around her shoulders.

"What's happening?" she said.

"I have spoken to headquarters. As you probably expect… it is the worst kind of news." Duke pushed away from the mahogany desk and paced the room, toying with an unlit cigarette. Julian had quickly noticed that whenever things went badly with the leaders of Ghost, Duke gained a dependence on nicotine. "They told me to disband the group."

"Why?" Lauren stepped out of Julian's arms, her look one of confusion.

Julian knew why.

"We are exposing the whole organisation to danger," Julian said and she looked at him, still frowning.

It melted away and she looked at Duke, Astra and Kuga.

"I can't make you help me," she said. "I understand if you don't want to. Julian and I have faced Lycaon alone before."

He nodded when she glanced at him. They had. And she'd died every time. This had been their best chance. Even though there were only five of them now, it was still three more than they normally had, and the Ghosts' powers were invaluable.

"I'm in," Kuga said in a firm voice and stepped forwards, joining the group. No one questioned him. It was clear that he'd made his decision the night that Piper had died and that he was going to see this through to the end. A vendetta was a strong reason for continuing.

"I've come this far," Duke said and flipped the cigarette over in his fingers. "Piper was my ward. I will fight."

Everyone looked at Astra. She was a powerful ally and one they needed. Astra leaned against the cream wall between the two mahogany bookshelves and stared at him, and then Lauren, and then finally Duke.

She pushed the long waves of her black hair from her face and blinked languidly. "I go where he goes since we are going to be tied to each other."

Julian stepped forwards, shocked that Duke had made such a decision.

"We need more fire power." Duke smiled but Julian could see the strain in it. The man was worried about what he'd proposed to do with Astra and with good reason. Although she was immortal, Astra could die as easily as himself. It was a dangerous path to take, even if it did gain them more power and a better chance of defeating Lycaon. "I am going to hand my soul to Astra for protection."

"Is that wise?" Julian said. He'd grown to like Duke, although they had their differences, and he didn't want to risk losing him. "If the procedure goes wrong—"

"I die." Duke cut him off. "Astra has done it before. She knows what she's doing."

"I don't like it. I don't want any more death on my hands," Lauren said.

"It isn't your decision." Duke placed the cigarette in his mouth, walked to one of the three tall arched windows and opened the sash. He lit the cigarette and took a long drag on it. "And it isn't for you. It's for Piper. It's not as though I haven't died before… to fight an immortal, I need to become immortal."

"Can it be reversed? Can she give your soul back?"

Duke said nothing.

"I will take good care of it." Astra's gaze lingered on Duke and then she looked down at her feet and frowned. It wasn't like Astra to show emotion. It gave Julian the feeling that she didn't want to go through with this, but Duke had forced her hand. "As long as I live, Duke will live. When I die, he might regain his soul."

"Don't speak like that!" Duke's voice was loud in the room, startling the group into facing him. His expression was as dark as midnight, his eyes black. An aura of darkness grew around him, sucking the light from the room until it grew dim. Ribbons of black smoke curled around Duke's tense twitching fingers. Astra had provoked a response from Duke's true nature.

Lauren's eyes were as round as saucers. Julian stepped closer to her. He was no match for Duke but he would do his best to protect Lauren if something happened.

Duke closed his eyes and the room brightened again as he regained control. He looked at the roses on his palms and his brow furrowed. "I have had enough of death."

"Take my soul too." Kuga moved forwards again.

Astra shook her head. "We cannot risk that. You may lose your powers. Duke's are already of death. They would cross over."

"Even if the procedure is a success, we are still vulnerable." Julian placed his hand on the hilt of his sword again. It was a comfort to feel it beneath his fingers. There if he needed it. "Leo spied on us. He knows everyone's strengths and weaknesses."

"Then we go somewhere Leo doesn't know, somewhere safe, and prepare." Duke took another long drag on his cigarette and blew the grey smoke out of the window into the night.

"It's hopeless."

Julian hadn't wanted to hear those words coming from Lauren. He touched her shoulder but her gaze remained downcast, her expression unchanged. She looked so lost. She couldn't give up now. He wouldn't let her. Whatever pain she was feeling, he would bear it for her. He would carry it all if he could—her fear, her pain, her burden. He would be strong for her, because he knew deep in his heart that when he was, it made her strong too.

"Training won't give us the advantage. It will only hone skills that Leo and Lycaon have seen firsthand. I know that now. It won't give us the element of surprise that we need," she said.

Julian tensed. She wanted an element of surprise. She could have one if she fought hard enough. Last time they had failed, but Lauren was so much stronger now. She could convince him.

"We need to return to Paris," Julian said.

Lauren turned to face him, her expression incredulous. "Morgan? He was a no show, remember?"

"We must try again. You know my feelings for Morgan, but it is better than nothing." He took hold of both her shoulders, keeping her facing him, and stooped so he was looking straight into her eyes. "I am sure you can convince him this time. You are their queen and you are strong enough now to lead him. We will not fail again."

"It's worth a go," Duke said.

Lauren didn't look convinced but she nodded.

"Take the van and go to Paris." Duke turned to Kuga. "You'll have to hide Lauren and Julian in the compartment in the back."

"I will hide and you can ride up front with Kuga. You will look like a couple." Julian's hand slipped from her arm.

Both Kuga and Lauren frowned at him. He didn't understand why they were so upset. He was going to be the one trapped in the back.

Lauren grabbed his hand. "I'll go with you."

"No." He shook his head and placed his other hand over hers. "I will have a light and it will only be a few hours while we are crossing the channel."

"I don't want you to be alone."

The honesty in those words and the worry in her eyes touched him, but not as much as the fact that she'd said them in front of everyone, openly declaring her growing attachment to him. Duke had been right that day at the docks. Lauren did want to be with him. She didn't want him to be alone.

"I will be fine," he said with a smile and unclipped the collar of his long coat so she could see it. "Just make sure Kuga drives carefully."

"I can knock you out." Duke grinned. Regardless of his denials, Duke took too much pleasure from knocking him unconscious. Julian shook his head. Although it was tempting, it was better that he remained awake in case something happened.

"We should leave tonight," Julian said and everyone murmured in agreement.

"We will meet you in two nights at the Arc de Triomphe." Duke stubbed out his cigarette and glanced at Astra. "We'll arrange a new base of operation."

Julian knew that he had other reasons for staying. He was going to go through with giving his soul to Astra to protect and he didn't want anyone around when it happened. Julian didn't know much about the process, but he knew it would take time for Duke to recover, just as it had taken Lauren time to adjust when she'd awoken.

Julian still wasn't sure that Duke was making the right decision.

He clipped his collar shut again and then smiled. Astra would see to it that Duke lived though. She wouldn't want to be in a world without him.

Julian took hold of Lauren's hand.

By tomorrow night, they would be back in Paris.

Morgan.

Could Lauren really convince the vampire to help them?

A part of him wasn't sure she was ready to command such creatures, especially someone as wily and self-centred as Morgan, but he was certain of one thing.

Morgan wouldn't help them unless they gave him something in return.

Julian just had to wait and see what that thing was.

And he had a long journey in which to think of the many ways he would kill Morgan if it had anything to do with Lauren.

CHAPTER 41

Julian glared at the dark decrepit building. He wanted to turn around and leave, but that wouldn't solve anything. They had to approach Morgan again whether he liked it or not. If he didn't go in with Lauren, then she would have to go alone.

Or go with Kuga.

Julian trusted Kuga to protect her, but he didn't want her to face Morgan with him. Lauren needed him now more than ever, and he needed to make sure that Morgan didn't overstep the mark that he'd firmly drawn fifty feet around Lauren. Jealousy coiled in his heart, occasionally striking at his deepest fears. He tried to ignore them but it was difficult now that he had grown closer to Lauren and let her in.

He couldn't bear it if she betrayed him.

Her hand slid into his, fingers intertwining and warm palm pressing against his own. He looked down at her hand. It was more than a simple gesture of comfort. It was a symbol of how far they had come. What had once been infrequent and fleeting was now almost permanent between them. Lauren would seek his hand whenever they were close enough to touch. Her gaze would often linger on his, warm and affectionate, full of emotions that made his heart sing and beat stronger. She would often find reason to touch his face, to kiss him or be close to him. It was all evidence of her love for him. That night she'd told him the truth by accident. She'd admitted her feelings before she'd even realised what they were.

They were clear to him now.

Just as his were.

"Stay here," Lauren said to Kuga as he went to exit the black van.

Julian shuddered when he thought about the cramped compartment in the back. It had felt like a coffin. The small torch he'd taken with him had done nothing to ease his fears. Only the sound of Lauren's voice and the steady beat of her heart had kept him going. If they were ever to travel together, he needed to find a better way of getting around. Perhaps Duke had connections of the criminal sort that could get him a fake passport. As far as he knew, he could be photographed.

"I want to go with you." Kuga remained half out of the van, holding the door.

"I need you here, so we can get away quickly if we need to." When Lauren smiled, Kuga nodded and got back into the van.

Julian rolled his shoulders and took a deep breath. Even on the outside, the building smelt like death. He knew Lauren could smell it too. Stale blood and earth. Ashes and flowers. Death had a strange smell.

Julian walked into the building, locking part of his senses on Lauren so he could make sure she was close to him, and using the rest to track down Morgan. The place was crawling with vampires. He could detect over forty on the floors above. Only one ahead. It had to be Morgan. Someone would have told him of their arrival. He would be waiting for them in the same room as last time.

Julian only hoped it went better this time.

A sudden need seized his heart. He grabbed Lauren, pulled her flush against him, tugged his collar down and kissed her. Her hands were immediately on his chest, her lips moving against his, sending a wave of hunger through him. He crushed her mouth under his and backed her into the wall of the corridor, lifting her. She wrapped her legs around his hips and a deeper shiver of need bolted through him. The feel of them around him was as sweet as he had imagined it would be. One hand tightened around her waist and the other pressed against the wall. He slanted his mouth over hers, kissing her rough and hard, pinning her between the wall and himself. Lauren moaned and raked her fingers through his hair, scoring his scalp with her nails. He breathed in deep and kissed her harder, his tongue dancing against hers in an act of sheer possession. She was his and his alone, and he wanted her to know that.

Lauren pushed him back, gasping for air. He kissed along her jaw, tasting her skin, savouring the scent of her blood as it rushed close to the surface. She was his.

He smiled against her throat when she melted into him, relaxing again, and twirled his hair around her fingers.

"Where did that come from?" Her whispered words broke the silence.

Julian narrowed his eyes on hers. Her lips were blush and swollen from the kiss, luring him in. He wanted to kiss her again. He wanted to kiss her until she knew without a doubt that he was never going to let her go. He needed her too much, couldn't bear the thought of Morgan looking at her, thinking things that he had no right to. Lauren was his. He was never going to give her up.

Lauren smiled at him and ran the backs of her fingers down his cheek. Her legs tightened around him, drawing him closer, and he frowned at how good it felt to be between her thighs. Deep in his heart, he wanted to leave this place and find somewhere quiet with her, somewhere he could make slow hungry love to her.

"I've come to love that look on you." She pushed her fingers into his hair and pulled his mouth back to hers.

He kissed her again, letting her lead the dance this time. It was fierce and hungry, showing all her passion for him, reinforcing his desire to take her somewhere private far away. She moaned into his mouth, smashing her lips against his and licking his teeth. His fangs began to extend and he pulled back. If she cut herself, if he tasted her blood, all hope of him remaining here would be shattered. He would leave with her in an instant. He would forsake Morgan and even Kuga in his need to have her.

Julian took a deep breath and reluctantly lowered Lauren to her feet. She placed her fingers against his jaw and her thumb swept over his lower lip, warm and sending a shiver through him.

"Maybe we shouldn't keep him waiting." Lauren glanced towards the door at the end of the corridor.

She was right. Julian could feel Morgan too. He was waiting and he would be able to feel them standing out in the hall. He would know what they had been doing. Good. He wanted Morgan to know. Julian gave himself a moment longer to regain his composure. Lauren straightened her clothes out, smiling broadly the whole time. He liked feeling how happy she felt when he kissed her.

He moved his sword to one side, pulled his collar up and then walked to the door and pushed it open. He entered with Lauren tucked close behind him, just as she had done last time. Only this time, she immediately moved out and fell into line beside him. She really was stronger now, even if she didn't see it.

"Morgan," she said, her tone commanding and confident.

Morgan preened his black hair back and ran his grey gaze over Lauren. It lingered too long on her hips and breasts, and her face. She'd chosen to wear clothes that covered her but a loose black hooded sweatshirt and jeans weren't going to stop Morgan's imagination. He knew Lauren's body in ways that even Julian didn't. Julian clenched his fists and corrected himself. Morgan didn't know Lauren's body. He knew Sonja's. Lauren and Sonja were two different people.

"My queen and her guard dog," Morgan greeted with a theatrical and regal wave of his hand. He bowed his head and the mussed tendrils of his dark hair fell forwards. He sat back, raising his head again, and brushed them from his forehead. With a broad smile, he stretched his arms out along the back of the red velvet couch. "I have missed you, my queen. Did you miss me too?"

Lauren shook her head and her eyes narrowed on him. "No. But I am disappointed. If you missed me so much, why didn't you come to see me?"

Morgan laughed and idly traced the gold woodwork that edged the couch, his focus on his fingers. "I thought my queen deserved to learn a lesson. Patience is a virtue apparently, but not one I have ever entertained. I do not like virtues. I much prefer vices."

His gaze slid back to Lauren although he remained facing the fire. The flames were high, dancing merrily in the ornate black marble fireplace. The wood crackled and popped, filling the tense silence. So far, Morgan hadn't overstepped the mark. Idle banter didn't bother Julian. If Morgan showed a hint of desire though, he was going to lose his head. Lauren might be able to command the vampires herself.

Julian's fingers twitched against the hilt of his sword.

"Tsk, tsk." Morgan waggled a finger at him. "I am sure our queen would not like you to get ideas above your station. Stay perfectly still like a good dog and I will grant you an audience."

Lauren looked at him. Julian lowered his hand away from his sword and nodded.

"You promised me once that you would help us." Lauren stepped forwards, nearing the back of the couch opposite Morgan. The vampire smiled at her. His eyes narrowed seductively.

"I do not remember promising you anything." He raked his gaze over Lauren. "You are not Sonja."

"Our souls are the same."

"You have a soul? It must be nice. Like a heartbeat… like breathing… or being able to see yourself." Morgan's tone was snide. Lauren was going to lose him if she didn't do something to soothe his temper. Six centuries hadn't eased his anger in the slightest. It had only given it time to fester and grow.

"You seem to get along without a mirror," she said with a sweet smile and then glanced at Julian. It was a sign that she hadn't meant her words but they hurt all the same. Julian cast his gaze downwards, studying the old wooden floorboards. His jaw tensed.

"Your guard dog doesn't like to hear such words towards another man. You play a dangerous game, my queen." Morgan laughed, hollow and empty, and then stood. He went to the fire and prodded it with an iron, causing the log to split and shower sparks. "Are you so desperate for me to help you that you would risk upsetting him? How far are you willing to go?"

Lauren tilted her chin up. "Remember your place. I hold the leash. That's what you told me. My blood has power over you… power which you believe in. When you call me your queen, you do so because you revere me… you need me." She smiled as though remembering something. "You said that too. You need to feel me and you can't."

Morgan's eyes turned black.

"You can sense me when I'm close, can't you? Even if you can't see me," she said.

He nodded.

"You like me being here, on your terms." She paused and Morgan nodded again, his gaze fixed on her, holding a hint of fascination. "You missed me. If you work with me, you'll always be close… you'll be able to feel me."

"It isn't enough." Morgan tossed the fire iron back into the rack and crossed the room to her. Julian didn't move. Morgan would be watching him and he couldn't wreck Lauren's chance of convincing Morgan by breaking his rule. He wanted to protect her and to do that he needed Morgan to help them. "I need more."

Julian didn't like the sound of that. It seemed Lauren didn't either because she stepped backwards towards him.

Morgan looked as though he was going to lose his calm edge and then smiled. It was tight and forced. He wasn't happy. The last time they had come to see him, Morgan had demanded the impossible as payment for helping. He would have something else in mind now, and instinct told Julian it would be something to do with Lauren.

"The werewolves." Lauren's sudden change in topic wasn't going to stop Morgan. He would wait, biding his time until he could mention his price for helping them.

"What of them?" Morgan sat back down on the couch, crossing his black-clad legs. He casually straightened out his dark red shirt. "They are crawling all over my city, infesting it because of you."

He leaned his head back and stared at the ceiling.

"This city used to be peaceful. I came here because no werewolves did. I was free here… free of this compulsion."

"And you can be again," Lauren said and Morgan's chin dropped and he stared at her. She stood tall, head held high and radiating confidence. Her gaze didn't stray from Morgan's. She stared right back at him, commanding and in control. Like a queen.

There was something alluring about her when she was like this, displaying her inner strength. It made all sorts of wicked thoughts cross Julian's mind. Lauren could command him all she wanted and he would do whatever she bid. He looked away from her, struggling to regain composure and drive his lustful thoughts from his head. He had to focus on Morgan and the situation. His gaze snuck back to her. It was hard when Lauren looked so beautiful.

She placed her hands on her hips and frowned at Morgan. "It can be peaceful again if you help. If Lycaon dies, you'll be free of your compulsion to kill the werewolves."

"And what of my city?"

A lot rested on that question. Morgan wanted Paris to be peaceful again. Julian had never realised just how much Morgan hated his need to do the bidding of Illia's blood. Lauren looked uncertain now, her confidence ebbing away. She glanced at him out of the corner of her eye, as though asking him what to do. There was only one thing they could do.

"When Lycaon is dead, we will return to Paris and help you clear the city of werewolves. A fair exchange," Julian said and Morgan's black eyes melted back to stormy grey. His dark eyebrows knitted and seconds ticked by. Julian wasn't going to rush him. The less they pushed right now, the more chance they had of convincing him.

Lauren moved closer to Julian but wisely kept a gap between them. Julian could sense her growing fear and unease. Her gaze shifted to his hand and then away. For a moment, he'd thought that she would take hold of his hand. He would have to stop her if she tried. Morgan was watching them closely, searching for a reason to grow angry again. They had to tread carefully. Any sign from Lauren that they might be together would wreck their chances.

Morgan had shown his jealousy the last time they were here and it had probably been that which had kept him away.

Morgan hated seeing Illia's incarnation with another man, just as he did.

Now Morgan knew how he'd felt all those centuries ago.

"I want to hear it from her." Morgan's dark grey eyes settled on Lauren. There was nothing seductive about his look now. It was open, expectant.

Lauren took a deep breath and stood tall again. "You will help us, and then we will help you."

Julian smiled inside. Very commanding, even if he could sense the smallest trace of nerves in her.

She jumped when Morgan slammed his hands down on the seat of the couch and stood.

"I will do it then, my queen." He bowed low and smiled up at her. "I will help you and your little dog."

Julian frowned at him. Morgan was more of a dog than he was.

"If you're serious then meet us tomorrow night," Lauren said with a frown, clearly not believing him.

"Where?" Morgan moved around the couch, his gaze fixed on Lauren. He was up to something. It would take more than just an offer to rid Paris of werewolves and an order to make him help them. There would be a bigger price to pay.

"The Arc de Triomphe." Lauren didn't look up at Morgan as he came to a halt in front of her, standing at least six inches taller. She tilted her head back and looked down at him. Very regal. Very queen-like. Exactly the way that Sonja and Illia had treated those below her. Even him.

Morgan took hold of her hand, raised it as he smiled at her, and then kissed the back of it.

Julian's fingers flexed with an urge to grab his sword. Instead, he took Lauren's hand from Morgan. The vampire fixed him with a dark glare. Julian's eyes shifted to silver.

"Until tomorrow, my queen," Morgan said and turned his back on them.

Lauren was the first to move, heading straight for the door. The moment it closed behind her, she wiped the back of her hand on her jeans and breathed a long sigh.

"What are you doing?" Julian said as they walked through the building. "Making him meet us while we wait for Duke?"

"It's better than giving him our new location when we have it. If he is going to tell him, I would rather Lycaon attack us at the Arc de Triomphe than discover our new hideout." She paused near the entrance of the building and turned to face him. It was dark in the hall. He had to use his heightened vision to see her and he could see that she was too. Her irises shimmered silver, as beautiful and beguiling as the moon. "I have to be sure that I can trust Morgan."

"Morgan would not betray you. He lives to serve you. He is merely fighting his blood."

Lauren frowned and stepped closer to him, looking up into his eyes. "Do you only serve me because of my blood—"

"No!" Julian interjected. How could she think such a thing after everything they had shared? "I serve you because I love you."

His heart pounded so hard he was sure it would break again. Lauren stared at him, lips parted in shock, her own heart thundering in his ears. He wished she would speak, would say something to put him out of his misery. This wasn't how he'd imagined it would go. In his fantasies, in all the times he'd played out this moment in his head, she'd been happy and had returned his feelings. A cold sense of doubt crept through him, turning his blood to ice, slowly edging towards his heart.

Her eyes searched his. Didn't she believe him?

"Me?" she whispered with furrowed eyebrows. "Not Illia?"

He had expected that question. It was understandable that she needed to be sure.

Julian undid the collar of his coat, letting it fall open so she could see the whole of his face and read in his expression that he was telling the truth. He had wanted to tell her so many times but the words had eluded him. Now they were out in the open and he felt he could say them again. With a smile, he swept his fingers up her soft cheeks and into her hair, brushing it back. His gaze held hers.

"You." He caressed the top curve of her ear with his fingers and her cheek with his thumbs. "I love you, not Illia."

A smile grew on her lips. It turned the ice in his heart to fire.

Lowering his head, Julian slowly kissed her. Her lips moved so lightly against his that his insides flipped over, turning with each brush of her mouth. He loved it when she kissed him like this. She tiptoed, her hands pressing into his chest to steady her. Julian claimed her waist, holding her so she couldn't break the kiss. One hand slid around her back as he angled his head towards her and the other threaded itself into her hair as their tongues met. He pulled her closer and her fingers tensed against his chest, the tips of them pressing in. Their hearts beat hard against each other, the rhythm of his almost matching hers. His surroundings melted away, his focus so fixed on her and his senses so full of her that he lost awareness of everything else. Her tongue stroked his and he closed his eyes, absorbing the delicious feel of them intimately entwined. The kisses grew short, bursts of lips and tongues, a sensual mix of light brushes and hard strokes. His blood burned and his breath shortened. Her heart pounded in his mind, her warm breath filling his mouth.

The feel of her against him was divine. He couldn't get enough of it, of her touching him. He craved it like a drug. Needed it more than anything. More than her blood.

His senses spiked. Lauren tensed. He cursed.

Two vampires were directly above them on the first floor, a reminder that this wasn't a good place to lose track of their surroundings.

"We should…" Lauren said and shifted her gaze to the side when he looked at her. In the low light, he could still see her cheeks darken. Was it his confession or the kiss that made her blush?

He did love her. Just as she loved him. She bit her lip and smiled. She didn't have to tell him right now. He could wait. He'd been waiting for eternity after all.

"We should return to Kuga," he said and she nodded.

Taking her hand, he walked with her.

"It's best that Kuga isn't alone too long," Lauren whispered in the near-darkness. "Leo's betrayal and Piper's death have hit him hard. He feels alone."

"I know how that feels," Julian said, trying not to think about how long he'd spent alone, even when he wasn't. "But I know that you will be there for him, just as you have been for me and the others. We will not let him be alone."

Lauren smiled.

Julian opened the door for her.

Kuga was leaning against the van glaring at them. "Where the hell have you been?"

"Talking to Morgan," Lauren said, unflustered.

The young man folded his arms across his chest, his muscles bulging under the thin layer of black he wore.

"I've had no less than five male vampires checking me out as their next meal. I swear they thought I was hanging around for some fang action."

Lauren looked as though she had been going to laugh but thought the better of it. "Sorry."

Julian could imagine the shocking reception those vampires had received from Kuga and could tell by the tone of Kuga's voice that he wasn't impressed that they had thought he was into men.

"Duke called." Kuga pushed off from the black van. He opened the door for Lauren. She pulled herself up into the van and shifted across to the middle seat. Julian got in beside her and closed the door. Kuga opened the driver's side and settled himself behind the wheel, sandwiching Lauren between them. He started the engine. "They're en route."

"How did Duke sound?" Julian already knew what his answer would be. He was glad the procedure had gone well though.

"Like hell." Kuga left it at that.

Exactly as Julian had expected.

Lauren leaned her head against his shoulder. He shifted on the seat so his arm was around her shoulders and held her close.

It would take Duke more than just the journey to Paris to recover from what Astra had done. He hoped they knew what they were doing and that Duke's powers had remained with him.

"Head out of the city." Julian leaned back into the seat as Kuga pulled away.

The more distance they placed between him and Morgan, the better he felt, until he was calm again and could think clearly.

"Where are we going?" Lauren muttered. Her eyes closed and he could sense that she was still exhausted. Things were only going to get harder from here on. He hoped that she was strong enough to see it through.

"We need to find somewhere safe to pass the day."

"Do you think Morgan will come tomorrow night?" Lauren looked over the back of the seat.

A part of Julian wished that he wouldn't. As much as they needed Morgan and his men, they didn't need the tension his presence would bring. Julian wasn't the only one who would be on edge when they were around.

He would grin and bear it though, for Lauren's sake.

He just didn't know if Astra would.

Julian nodded.

"He will show, if only to tell us his true price."

CHAPTER 42

It was colder tonight. The wind blew the long tails of Julian's coat around, making it dance in the darkness as he stood on the rooftop overlooking the square. His gaze scanned over the city spread out before him, searching for a sign of trouble. Cold but quiet. Nights like this he could get used to. The air was crisp and fresh. The stars were bright and clear. The moon was growing fat. The lights of Paris twinkled, a myriad of colours when combined with the taillights of the cars zooming around the golden Arc de Triomphe below him. For once, he didn't hate the city. Being here with Lauren now, knowing that she loved him, made some of his loathing for Paris fade away. Standing high above it, watching the cars and the Arc de Triomphe, and the people walking around it, he could see why they called it the city of romance. He wanted to bring Lauren up here and show it to her, and then kiss her and hold her close, and tell her again that he loved her.

While his hatred of Paris had eased, his hatred of Morgan hadn't. Nothing would change that.

Julian stared at the brightly lit arch.

He'd left Lauren there with Kuga. The two of them would look like tourists as they waited for Duke and Astra to show up. Lauren hadn't liked his idea of keeping an eye on things from up here but she had reluctantly let him go when he'd told her that it was better this way. A sword wielding man would have police in the area in an instant. He wouldn't surrender his weapon tonight. They were in too much danger to risk being unarmed. Lauren's short katana were back in the van. Kuga would protect her and, if something happened, Julian would be there in an instant.

Two policemen walked past Lauren. She tensed. Police in France carried guns. It was probably unsettling for her when she was unarmed and unused to seeing people with guns. Julian willed the police to leave, not only for Lauren's sake. Their presence wouldn't stop Duke but it would deter Morgan. The vampire was wary of humans with weapons. It would only take an officer to shoot him and see that he didn't die from the bullet and Morgan wouldn't be able to show his face in Paris for a long time. Humans tended to get jittery about people who could take a bullet in the head and survive.

Julian had learnt that almost a century ago in Russia.

He paced across the rooftop, his eyes on Lauren. Where was Duke? Julian didn't want Lauren exposed any longer than necessary. By now, Lycaon would have recovered. He would be after them again.

Julian rubbed his arm. The ache in it reminded him that Lauren could take care of herself.

When they had found a quiet place in the country to wait out the day, she'd insisted that they practiced rather than sleep. The little rest she'd had in London and during their journey seemed to have restored enough of her strength for her to alter her routine. Her moves were faster, stronger, and she had been more aware of any opening he had given her. She'd bested him at one point, bringing him to his knees, a place he was willing to go for her. He loved her and would do anything that she commanded. Anything. He would fight Hades himself for her soul so he could bring her back should she die.

Not that he feared that happening anymore. She'd proven today just how much stronger she was. Her skills had been exceptional, even during the peak of the day, and he'd seen her resolve and determination to defeat Lycaon. It had been centuries since he'd seen one so strong, possibly not since Illia herself.

Could Lauren survive when even Illia had died?

His fists clenched.

He would make sure that she did. Now that she loved him, he wasn't letting her go.

Not even Hades could separate them.

"You seem rather resolved too, young Julian."

Julian turned, sword unsheathed and raised, and attacked the man standing a few feet behind him. He hadn't sensed him, hadn't heard him. The middle-aged man just smiled and held his hand up, stopping Julian's blade mid-swing without touching it and holding it there. Dark curls caressed the man's olive skin. His vivid blue eyes shone in the moonlight. It was a face that Julian knew. One he had seen during death.

He dropped to one knee, laying his sword out before him, and bowed his head.

Zeus laughed heartily. "Stand, young Julian."

Julian did as instructed but kept his head bowed as a mark of respect. Zeus hadn't visited him since he'd taken on the task of awakening Illia's incarnations.

Zeus's hand clapped down hard on his shoulder. Power reverberated within Julian. The power of a god. A power beyond his grasp. If he had that, he could easily protect Lauren. She was worth fighting for. Even worth sacrificing himself if he was sure that in doing so he wouldn't destroy her.

"Do not worry about Hades. My brother has no interest in separating you from Illia's soul. He brought Illia back to you early this time."

"Lauren," Julian said, surprised that he'd dared to correct Zeus, and sheathed his sword. He looked at Zeus to judge whether he would reprimand him for his actions. Zeus's expression remained fixed in a smile. The feel of his power overwhelmed Julian. Even without physical contact between them, he could sense Zeus's strength. It pressed down on Julian so hard that it was a constant fight to remain standing. His knees threatened to give but he stood firm, unwilling to surrender to such a superior force. The world shimmered around Zeus, a visible distortion of their surroundings that was like a heat haze haloing him. His power affected the entire world. Julian tilted his chin up, struggling to maintain his stature and refusing to show his weakness to Zeus. He was strong, a worthy protector of Lauren, and he needed Zeus to see that he deserved the trust he had placed in him millennia ago. "Forgive my questions, but why are you here and why did Lauren awaken early?"

Zeus laughed again but when he spoke, his tone was grave. "We have uncovered a plot against the gods. Lycaon plans to overthrow us. He is in league with the Titans."

Julian frowned. That wasn't good. Selene was a Titan, one of the old gods. He stared at the moon, wondering what she was up to and whether she was truly watching over her child.

"Has she betrayed you again?" he said.

"No, not this time." Zeus's grim expression matched his tone. "She fears for Illia's... Lauren's... safety and begged Hades to awaken her so she would be strong against Lycaon. Selene is still on our side. She still lights your path and holds your destiny."

Julian was thankful for that. Selene had always watched over him, especially in the periods when he was searching for the next incarnation of Illia.

"What must be done?" A car horn sounded far below them and another responded. The still night air carried the scent of snow. Julian looked down at Lauren and Kuga. They were still alone under the bright golden arch. It towered over Lauren, making her look small. He balled his hands into fists and clenched them tight. "We are few but are willing to fight."

"Lycaon cannot be allowed to restore the old powers." Zeus sat down on the edge of the roof, his legs dangling over the side, and frowned at the arch. It wavered in the halo around Zeus and then became clear. A weight lifted off Julian, the oppressive feel of Zeus's power disappearing enough that he could bear it. "He contacted Selene."

Julian's stomach twisted at those words. He sat down beside Zeus on the low wall. He could still sense Zeus's power but it was quieter now, a subtle sensation rather than an overwhelming presence. Zeus must have realised the effect it was having on him. Julian wasn't sure whether to be grateful for it or not. In a way, it made him feel weak.

"He beseeched her, desired an audience which she granted. When she appeared, Lycaon sought to convince her to continue their original plan to overthrow me and my kin."

"And?" Julian said.

"She refused."

He was relieved to hear it but it didn't alleviate the tight feeling inside him. Lycaon was on the move and Zeus had come to Earth. The gods had long vowed not to interfere in the lives of men or appear before them. It had to be bad if Zeus had come to him.

"Lycaon grew angry and struck her. He confessed that he had never loved her. It has wounded her deeply. Her maidens received no response from her for days." Zeus sighed, his shoulders heaving with it. "She came to me and told me everything, the whole plan, and that she has broken her vow but has not told Lycaon of it."

Julian frowned. "Vow?"

Zeus didn't look pleased. "I did not know of it but Selene granted Lycaon more than simple love and her blessing. She had gifted him protection while under the full moon, rendering him invulnerable when it shines."

Julian sat in silence, shocked as he remembered all the final battles that Illia's incarnations had faced and realised that one thing had always remained constant. The moon had been full. A chill swept over him. Lycaon had won because he'd been invulnerable. Illia's incarnations hadn't stood a chance. How could Selene do this to her daughter? Julian glared at the black velvet sky.

"Do not be angry with Selene, young Julian. She had believed you and Illia capable of defeating Lycaon during the times when the moon was not full, and tried to help as she could. It caused her great pain to even speak of her vow to another, and took incredible effort on her part to break such a strong and long-standing spell. It has left her very weak, and yet she still watches over you and this new incarnation of Illia."

Lauren. Julian looked down at the arch. Selene had broken her vow for Lauren's sake. She too wanted to protect her. She had given them the advantage that they needed to survive. This time when they fought Lycaon, they would be able to defeat him.

"I will tell Lauren to fight him then, under a full moon, when he cannot die."

"Only this time he can," Zeus said with a knowing smile. "Selene has kept it secret. He will not know until it is too late."

Julian smiled too. "It is exactly the opening that I have been looking for."

"Lycaon will move fast now. The moon is full in only a handful of days. He will make himself known so he can put his plan in motion."

Julian nodded. "I will tell her and her alone. One of our men has betrayed us. I cannot risk telling everyone Lycaon's new vulnerability."

"Ah, one of the twins. The younger is the more powerful. It has been foreseen that he will be the victor."

"Thank you," Julian said with all his heart, grateful that the gods were indeed watching over them. He paused, unsure whether to ask Zeus such an impertinent question, and then said, "Can you not send us someone to help?"

Zeus shook his head. "We gods cannot interfere. It was part of the original curse. If I change the curse, Illia's soul will pass over and she will die. I could not even correct my mistake and make her invulnerable to all but Lycaon without risking her death. Selene has made it clear that if her daughter dies because I changed the curse, she will protect Lycaon again and side with the Titans. Our hope rests on Illia."

"Lauren," Julian whispered and looked at her. Duke and Astra had arrived. Lauren seemed so small in the distance. Too small to hold the weight of the world, and Olympus, on her shoulders. He would do all that he could to bear the weight for her, to help her through this. He couldn't harm Lycaon, but he could lessen his forces and clear the path for her. He could be her shield.

"Julian."

Julian looked at Zeus, amazed to see something akin to concern in his rich blue eyes.

"Tread carefully. Lycaon wants to end it this time. He told Selene that he will not only take Illia's life but yours too. If he does that—"

"I will not let that happen." Julian wrapped his fingers around the hilt of his sword. The knowledge that Lycaon was targeting him too this time unsettled him but it wasn't unexpected. Lycaon had never bothered to try to kill him before. There had never been a werewolf strong enough. Julian thought about the young man that had been with Lycaon. He had been strong, and familiar somehow. "I will not fail her. Even if I fall, I will ensure that Lycaon falls too this time, and that Lauren survives."

"Go. I have stayed too long already. Artemis demands my return." Zeus stood and brushed the back of his trousers down. "My daughter watches over you too. She finds human love intriguing and none more so than yours for this incarnation of Illia. Lauren. This world has forgotten the old gods but we have not forgotten you. We will be watching and will help in any way that we can. Although, you have new allies awaiting you."

Julian looked across at the Arc de Triomphe. Three new people stood near Lauren.

His hand tightened around his sword.

Morgan.

CHAPTER 43

Lauren fidgeted. Being out in the open was making her nervous. Police kept walking past them. Whenever they did, Kuga fired off another photograph of the arch or of her, acting the tourist with the small digital camera they had bought. By now, he probably had about sixty pictures of the arch and countless ones of her. She'd even taken a few of him.

A nice couple had taken a picture of them together in front of the Arc de Triomphe. Lauren had wished it had been Julian with her. She would like a picture of them together.

She paced a short distance from Kuga and then came back again, her gaze repeatedly straying to the side street where he'd parked the van. She wanted her swords. She no longer felt safe without a weapon when Julian wasn't around.

"Relax," Kuga said with a soft look. She'd never really seen him concerned about her before. "No one will get near us."

"You need to take heed of your own advice," Lauren whispered, sensing his tension and seeing the spark in his eyes. He was as on edge as she was, but then he'd been like that since Piper's death. He'd been different since then—suddenly so serious and grown up. Gone were the jokes and the laughter. Would Kuga ever be the same? He barely smiled these days.

He was right about one thing though. No one would get near them. When they had been out in the countryside today, Kuga had revealed the depth of his power and it had been devastating. The man was a living weapon.

"Boo." Someone breathed the word into her ear.

Lauren jumped, her heart lodging itself firmly in her throat, and turned on a pinhead to face her attacker at the same time as Kuga raised his hands, sparks flickering around his fingers.

Duke grinned at her.

He looked like hell but clearly his sense of humour was still as dire as ever. He couldn't have snuck up on her. She would have smelt him. He must have appeared out of thin air as he had done during their fight with the werewolves.

"Bastard," she grumbled and glared at him. If she'd had her swords, one of them would have been against his throat by now.

He scratched his dark stubbly jaw and raised his eyebrows. His bloodshot eyes shifted to Kuga. Lauren noticed Astra walking across the square towards them.

"You look like shit," Kuga muttered and lowered his hands, the threads of electricity disappearing.

"You don't look much better," Duke retorted with a wide smile. He turned his smile on her, raking a quick glance over her.

"You still have a heartbeat," she said, unsure what she had expected. He didn't seem different at all. Only his appearance had changed. He looked as though he'd spent a few nights drinking and hadn't slept for a week. Duke scratched at his chest now, frowning as he stared at his fingers.

"I didn't know what to expect either." His hand paused and he spread his fingers out across his chest.

"I did say that it would not change you," Astra said as she finally finished walking over to them.

Lauren stood a little taller. As usual, she was dressed in casual wear while Astra looked like a billion dollars in her long flowing black dress, her hair a shimmering wave of black and her face as beautiful as a geisha's. That kind of clothing had never suited Lauren, and it certainly wasn't any good for fighting in. Maybe when all this was over, she could go out somewhere with Julian and see the sights. She could dress up then. He gave her hungry looks when she was only wearing a jumper and jeans. She couldn't imagine what his reaction would be if she wore a dress of Astra's style.

Her cheeks burned at the thought.

"Where's Julian?" Duke gave her a smile that said he knew she was thinking about him.

Her blush deepened. "He's watching from a rooftop somewhere."

"I found a good secure base. Is this man of yours joining us?"

"Possibly," she said, still not certain whether Morgan was going to show or not. "I told him to meet us here tonight if he's going to help us. Julian thinks that he will."

"Then he will. Julian isn't normally wrong about things." Astra's words surprised Lauren. She'd never heard the woman talk kindly about anyone.

Duke's smile said that he was surprised to hear Astra speaking nicely about someone too. Astra scowled at him. When Duke rapped his knuckles against his chest, Astra's frown became a wicked smile. There was a hint of seduction in it that left Lauren wondering just what the procedure for Astra taking Duke's soul into protection had entailed.

"I'll give him until Julian returns." Lauren paced over to Kuga.

Even with Duke and Astra around, her nerves weren't getting any better. She wanted Julian to come back.

The hairs on the back of her neck rose and a cold prickly feeling edged down her spine. Someone was watching her. Someone was coming.

Lauren turned slowly, trying to pinpoint the direction the feeling was coming from, and stopped when she saw Morgan striding towards them, clad head to toe in black, his shirt half undone and exposing his pale chest. Flanking him were two broad men, also in black, who had murder in their eyes.

Morgan came to a halt in front of her and gave her a cocksure smile as he dramatically brushed the hair from his forehead. His gaze raked over her in a way that she was becoming oddly accustomed to, and then settled on her face. He bit his lip, teasing the lower one with his teeth.

Correction.

Fangs.

"Filth!" Astra hurled the word with such venom that it startled Lauren. The air around them grew colder and then Astra was storming towards her. Duke grabbed Astra's arms, holding her back. Lauren wouldn't have swapped places with him for all the money in the world. Astra looked ready to kill someone. "Dirty despicable filth! Let me go... I'll rip you to shreds!"

Morgan apparently.

Lauren looked at Morgan. His grey irises melted to black and he sniffed at the air. He grinned, revealing his extended canines.

Astra's eyes turned a dark sapphire and then began to glow. The sight of them still made Lauren wary and gave her chills. Astra hurled a string of foul words in Morgan's direction, struggling against Duke's hold.

Lauren placed herself between Morgan and Astra when he looked as though he might retaliate. Whatever had Astra's knickers in a twist, this wasn't the place for it. Police patrolled the area regularly. A fight was going to draw the wrong kind of attention.

"I will not let the vampires near you," Duke said in a low voice, his tone light and soothing.

Astra looked at Duke and her eyes shifted back to their normal dark colour. Lauren wondered how she hadn't noticed it before. They had feelings for each other.

"The filthy vampire wants my blood." Astra glared in Morgan's direction.

"Morgan won't lay a finger on you." Lauren didn't know whether she could really stop Morgan from doing anything, but she had to say something to calm the situation down.

Lauren tensed when someone behind her placed their hands on her shoulders.

"I would love to lay a few fingers on you," Morgan whispered into her ear.

She ducked out of his grip and slammed the flat of her hand against his chest. He stumbled backwards and laughed.

"You are feistier than she was." He licked his fangs and Lauren pulled a disgusted face. If he thought that he was going to charm her then he had another thing coming. She wasn't interested in anything he had to offer in that way. She only wanted his help.

"Did you just come here to piss me off?" Lauren glared at him, wishing that she had her swords so she could put him in his place.

"I have men willing to follow him... you... my queen." His smile was sweet now, dripping charm. He certainly knew how to win himself back into her good book.

"Thank you."

The air shifted and Julian was suddenly between her and Morgan, his sword drawn and aimed at the vampire. He undid the tall funnel collar of his coat and looked back over his shoulder at her. Morgan's gaze fell to Julian's neck. His eyes darkened to black, a look of pure disgust and hatred turning him ugly. He looked at her neck and she instinctively touched it. His sneer and show of fangs said that he realised what had happened between her and Julian and he wasn't happy.

"We should move," Lauren said, hoping to distract Morgan from whatever dark thoughts were crossing his mind.

She hesitated when everyone broke away, leaving her alone with Morgan and Julian. The vampire hadn't moved. She hoped he wasn't having second thoughts about helping her. She couldn't lose him now. They needed his men. She swallowed. They needed him. As much as she hated that, it was the truth. Without Morgan and his men, she didn't think they would win the fight against Lycaon.

She moved past Julian, touching his hand so he sheathed his sword, and held her hand out to Morgan.

Morgan stared at it for a moment and then took it. His skin was cold against hers. He had no body heat. Without flowing blood and a heart to beat, he was the walking dead. A living corpse. It was little wonder he was upset about what had happened to him. If she'd ended up like this instead of becoming like Julian, she would have been bitter too.

"Thank you for helping us," she said with a smile.

It faltered when he frowned. She had the terrible feeling that he was going to walk away so she tightened her grip on his hand.

"I'll keep my promise if you keep yours. Help us kill Lycaon and we'll rid your city of werewolves."

After a short pause, Morgan nodded. She went to take her hand back but he raised it to his lips again, kissing the back of it.

"Whatever my queen desires, my queen receives... I am at your service." His lips brushed her skin as he spoke.

When he straightened and finally released her hand, he was staring at Julian. With a smile, he signalled his men and went in the direction that Duke and the others had gone. Lauren turned to Julian. He was frowning but it melted away as she approached. He took hold of her hand and wiped the back of it with his coat sleeve, a dark look in his eyes.

Lauren sighed and caught his hand, stopping him. "I was worried about you. You were gone so long."

Julian smiled and she was glad to see it. He was so handsome when he smiled, his pale blue eyes narrowing with it. The warm golden light of the arch lit his face, highlighting the finger length strands of his black hair.

"I met an old friend. I will tell you about it later," he said and she frowned now. Her curiosity was piqued. She wanted to know what had happened, but

Julian's look said that he wouldn't tell her yet. He looked over at the others. Didn't he want to mention it in front of them?

They walked together to the others. Duke and Astra got into his curvy silver Maserati Quattroporte. Julian looked as though he was going to suggest going with them but she glanced at Kuga, directing his attention there. Kuga was toying with his keys, waiting by his black van. She didn't want him to be alone and she really did prefer the van to Duke's fancy car.

"A van? How distasteful." Morgan looked it over. The two men with him said nothing. They opened the sliding door on the side of the van and Morgan stepped in. Kuga scowled at all three of them.

She hadn't expected Morgan to be catching a lift with them.

Lauren definitely wanted to go in the van with Kuga now. Someone had to keep an eye on the vampires. Who better than their queen?

Julian opened the passenger door for her and she got in, sliding over to the middle seat next to Kuga. Julian sat beside her with his sword across his lap and closed the door. Kuga drove the van in silence, following the Maserati in front of them. Morgan talked to his men but Lauren didn't listen. She settled her head against Julian's arm. Who had he met?

Their new place was far from the sights and the centre of the city. The area was residential, filled with white Parisian style townhouses with tall lead-grey roofs. Duke stopped the car in front of one, an elegant pale stone building with black framed windows and a black door. They gathered in front of it and Duke held his hand out and closed his eyes. Up the entire height of the building, symbols sparked into existence. They shifted and twinkled, interlocking circles and strange signs. Duke muttered something and the markers disappeared.

"We can enter now," he said and everyone followed him.

Everyone except Morgan. He'd taken a step back and was warily watching Duke. When she caught Morgan's eye, he casually walked towards her, as though nothing was bothering him. He'd been fine with Duke earlier. Was it the magic that he didn't like?

They entered the building. Duke closed the door, held his hand out and said something. Through the rectangular window above the black door, Lauren saw the symbols flash into existence and then disappear again.

"No one can come or go without me lifting the barrier. It will keep us hidden from our enemies," Duke said.

Morgan looked uncomfortable. Lauren didn't like the thought of being trapped in the building either but if Duke thought it was a necessary precaution, it was one she could live with. When Morgan looked at her, she smiled briefly, finding herself wanting to reassure him.

His eyes turned black. "Why do you need me?"

"I don't understand." It was the truth. She thought that she'd made it clear why they needed him. Without him, they were only five people. That wasn't enough to defeat Lycaon.

He pointed at Duke but kept his gaze fixed on her, an accusing glare in his eyes. "You expect me to believe that you need me when you have a necromancer among you?"

"I don't raise the dead," Duke coolly replied.

Lauren turned to look at Duke but Kuga shot forwards, catching her attention. Her hand was against Kuga's chest before he could pass her. There was so much pain in his eyes when he looked at her. She knew what he was thinking because she'd thought it too, but then she had remembered Astra's unspoken question that night and Duke's reply.

"It isn't the answer, Kuga," Lauren whispered and he looked as though his heart was breaking. "I miss her too, but it isn't the answer. If it was possible, Duke would have done it that night."

"When you raise the dead," Duke said and they both looked at him, "you raise a demon, a foul and fetid creature that is mindless. I don't raise the dead... not anymore."

Morgan snickered. "Rich words coming from you."

Did Morgan know Duke somehow? Duke's expression said it all—he wasn't happy. Whatever Morgan knew about him, it was something he'd wanted to remain hidden.

"I didn't recognise you without your soul." Morgan's lips were a thin line of pure hatred. "Did you have fun back then... hunting... entertaining yourself? My kin didn't stand a chance... the humans didn't stand a chance... and neither did her kin."

Morgan nodded towards Astra. She looked away, shame written across her face. Duke's past wasn't news to Astra. Lauren glanced at Julian. He was calm and composed as usual, his pale eyes emotionless. He knew too.

"What's he talking about?" Lauren said to Duke, growing tired of always being the one who didn't know what was going on. "He isn't just talking about when you hunt demons now, is he? It's something else. Morgan knows you and I want to know why."

The smile on Morgan's face held a hint of amusement. He was enjoying bringing this up, making her feel left out and making Duke squirm.

Duke reached for his pocket. Cigarettes. She'd put him in a tight spot then. She grabbed his hand and held it fast, not letting him get what he wanted. He would have to face her without his comfort.

"Tell me..."

His gaze fell anywhere but her, as though she didn't exist.

"Ghost formed one hundred years ago... and I was one of the first members."

Lauren snatched her hand back. "How is that possible? You're human."

"Because he's not as young as he looks, my queen. This pawn has deceived you." Morgan wasn't helping her temper and she knew that was his intention. He wanted to make her angry.

"I have not," Duke said, then sighed and rubbed the bridge of his nose. "I was mortal before Astra took my soul... but I am over four hundred years old... and I am a necromancer. You know it in your heart. You can smell death on me. Julian told me as much when he first met me."

She nodded. He did smell of a strange concoction of flowers and ashes. A scent that she somehow recognised as death.

"I joined Ghost to atone for my sins and forget my past. I did not think that my past would come back to haunt me." His gaze shifted to Morgan and then back to her. "I admit that I once revelled in death. I carelessly raised the dead or took the lives of demons to make them... fight... to entertain me..."

"Don't leave out the good part." Morgan moved forwards. Lauren shot him a glare and he stopped. His eyes were still black, murderously fixed on Duke. His hands curled into tight fists. "Do tell her all, old man."

Duke looked even more uncomfortable. The tension in the air was palpable and choking. It tightened her insides.

Julian stepped up close behind her. His presence was comforting, his aura wrapping itself around her like a warm cocoon.

"I raised them for mere entertainment... uncaring of the fact that the human mind and spirit is also revived and the zombies feel... experience... everything against their will." Duke didn't look proud of what he'd done. His sombre and grim expression said that he now regretted the things he'd done back then. He wanted to atone. She had no right to stand in his way, even if it was difficult to step aside and accept what he was. All of the Ghosts had their reasons for being with the organisation. His was just a little darker than she'd expected, and Morgan was trying to upset her.

"What—"

"Shut up," Lauren said, cutting Morgan off before he could provoke Duke. Morgan glared at her. She glared back. Duke was already explaining. He didn't need Morgan to help.

"He was going to ask what happened to them on death." Duke rubbed a hand through his hair, tousling the short dark strands, and gave her a hopeful look when he patted his pocket. She nodded. He could have his comfort now that she knew some of his story and no longer felt lost. He reached into his pocket and took out the crumpled pack of cigarettes. Removing one, he toyed with it as he had done in his office in London. It seemed just holding it and knowing that relief would come was enough for Duke. "On death they are taken to a hellish dimension... I have seen it... I never realised where they went."

"How have you seen it?" There was so much fear in his eyes that she had to ask. Her eyes widened. "You died once. You said that."

A smile tugged at the corner of his lips but there wasn't a trace of happiness in it. "I can cheat death with great effort and my powers slow my aging... but sometimes things don't go the way we plan, do they?"

Lauren shook her head. She'd made so many plans in her life. Over half of them hadn't come to fruition. Dying and becoming immortal hadn't even factored in them.

"I died once." He looked down at his palms. She knew what those roses meant. Death. "I saw where I sent the souls of those I had... used. I revived myself, using every shred of my power to bring myself back, and vowed never to raise the dead again."

He held his hands out to her, palms facing, and frowned. She remembered the roses so vividly, how they were only scattered ink outlines on his forearms, and how close together they were on his hands, a multitude of different shades of red.

"Each rose is a life that I sent there... one which I must atone for. The empty ones I have saved and they have passed over to a better place. The red ones are still waiting."

"The black ones?" she said, touching one of the tiny roses on his fingers. Some of them were smaller than her little finger's nail.

"Lost," he whispered. The pain in his eyes spoke of regret and she believed that he truly felt it in his heart. He'd wanted to save them all and now he couldn't. "They have been swallowed by the darkness where I sent them... they are evil now."

"You can't save them." It wasn't a question. They were lost forever. She took hold of his hands, interlocking their fingers and pressing her palms against his. He looked at her with raised eyebrows but the pain in his eyes wasn't going anywhere. Everyone made mistakes and Duke had realised his and seen what kind of man he had become. He wanted to change and she honestly believed that he was trying to atone for his sins. She smiled. "I wish I could help you."

"You already do," he said.

Lauren released his hands and stepped back towards Julian. Morgan didn't look pleased. He'd clearly expected better entertainment and she'd foiled his plans. She frowned at him. They would have to keep an eye on the vampire. He was proving himself trouble and they had only just begun working together. He was always calling her his queen. Perhaps it was time she assumed that role and kept him on a tight leash.

Duke looked at Kuga. "I don't want to go to the other side but I might be able to find a way to contact Piper so you can tell her whatever you need to. It will take time though, months perhaps."

Kuga nodded and turned away. Lauren had seen the tears in his eyes. She could feel how happy Duke's offer of help had made him. It made her happy too. Piper deserved to know just how Kuga felt about her. He loved her and Lauren knew that he always would.

"Choose a room and rest. They are all furnished and have the necessities. We will meet tomorrow night to discuss what to do." Duke waved a hand around the corridor. Kuga was the first to move, heading up the stairs. Lauren

Love Immortal

let him go. He needed to be alone. Astra looked at Duke. Lauren wondered if they were going to head for the same room.

She looked at Julian. Her heart missed a beat. Would he share a room with her?

"What about blood?" Morgan said, breaking into her pleasant thoughts. "We didn't feed tonight. Perhaps the pretty soul sucker could oblige. A man could go all night on blood like that."

Astra sneered at Morgan. He smiled at her, his eyes narrowed into a heated look.

"It isn't going to happen." Duke's tone was flat. "There's blood in the refrigerators."

Morgan gave him a look of sheer disgust. "Dead blood?"

"It's fresh enough to sustain you and your bodyguards." Duke should have chosen better words. A spot just below Morgan's left eye twitched.

She'd thought it too but had decided not to mention it. Morgan's goons certainly didn't look like anything other than heavy hands. She couldn't blame him for bringing protection when he hadn't known what he was walking into, but he should have expected someone to mention it. She was surprised that Julian hadn't. The two of them seemed to love to rub each other up the wrong way.

Morgan's sensual gaze slid her way. "Who will feed the queen... her knight or her king?"

CHAPTER 44

Julian bared his fangs at Morgan. If the vampire wanted a fight, he was looking in the right place. Lauren stepped close to him. Her scent soothed the raging fire inside him, the burning desire to make Morgan pay for every glance he'd dared to throw Lauren's way and every touch he'd stolen.

"There's only one man I will ever take blood from," Lauren said and turned to look up at him. Her round dark eyes sparkled as she stared deep into his and her hand came to rest against his chest. "The man I love."

A jolt rocked Julian. Had he heard her right? She smiled, confirming it. He really needed to be alone with her now. He needed to hear her say those words again as he peeled the layers of clothing from her inch by agonising inch and kissed her. Hunger flashed in her eyes. Julian was about to reach for her when Morgan spoke.

"I want something in return for helping you."

Julian glared at him and his jaw tensed. He'd known there would be a price.

"What?" Lauren turned to face Morgan. Julian could sense her nerves. They travelled through her hand where it rested against his chest, flowing straight into his heart.

"Blood." Morgan smiled. "Your blood."

Anger flooded Julian's veins at the thought of Morgan touching her and taking that from her.

"No," Julian snapped and glared at Morgan. He wasn't going to share Lauren with anyone, especially Morgan.

"It's okay." Lauren's hand stroked Julian's chest. He looked down at her. Her expression was soft and warm, her eyes full of reassuring affection. He wanted to say no again but it was her decision and he had to trust her not to betray him. She smiled and then faced Morgan. "When you help, I'll give you a drop of blood as a reward."

With that, she walked away, heading up the stairs. Julian followed her. As soon as they were out of earshot, he caught hold of her arm and stopped her.

"Did you mean it?" His grip on her tightened. She flinched and he released her, giving her an apologetic look. He hadn't meant to hurt her, but the thought of her letting Morgan drink from her disturbed him and was mixing him up inside. She was his now. Wasn't she? If she was, he wasn't willing to share her.

"It's only a drop of blood. I'll put it in a glass."

"No," Julian said with a frown. He should have made himself clearer in the first place. Grabbing her had probably given her the impression that he was angry. "Not the blood. What you said. Do you love me?"

She toyed with her fingers a moment and then nodded. "Yes."

Julian grabbed her around the waist and crushed her lips under a fierce kiss. He backed her into the wall of the corridor, pinning her there with his body as his tongue plundered her mouth, tangling with hers. The thought that she loved him, hearing those words, sparked a hunger in him stronger than he'd ever felt before. He needed her.

A door down the hall opened.

Julian released her, his hands trembling with the need to touch her, to feel her bare skin beneath them. Lauren blushed deeply, twisting her fingers together.

The door closed.

A little smile curved Lauren's delicious lips.

"Maybe we should continue this in our bedroom?" she whispered and looked at him through her lashes.

Their bedroom?

His heart thudded hard against his ribs. Her look was shy but her eyes were dark with passion.

Not wanting to waste a second, he swept Lauren into his arms and sped along the hall and up the stairs to the second floor. He stopped in front of the door furthest from any heartbeats and opened it. Lauren pushed away from him and dropped down, landing softly on the wooden floorboards. She turned the light on to reveal a large white room with two blue armchairs and a couch in front of a white marble fireplace.

To their right were an open set of white double doors. Beyond them was a bedroom. Lauren smiled, took hold of his hand, and led him into the room. He pulled away from her, slamming the door shut and locking it. The last thing he wanted was someone walking in on them.

Lauren's hand was gentle and warm in his as she led him towards the bedroom. Layers of rich blue covers swathed the large bed, making it look soft and inviting. He imagined sinking into it with Lauren, her bare legs wrapped around him as their bodies moved as one. Gods, it had been eternity since he'd had a woman.

Back in his day, for his level in society, sex was primal and dirty, a satisfaction of lust and urges. He'd never made love to someone. He'd never taken the time to learn a woman's body intimately and discover the places that satisfied her most. He wanted to do all that with Lauren. He wanted to spend the rest of his life learning about her.

"What's wrong?" Lauren said and he realised that he'd stopped walking just short of the bedroom and was staring at the bed.

"Nothing." His lie was fruitless. When she smiled, he knew that she'd seen straight through it. "It..."

Julian cursed under his breath. If he continued like this, her only memory of this moment would be how pathetic he'd been. He wasn't a virgin. Three thousand years was a long period of abstinence but he hadn't forgotten how things worked. The fantasies he'd had of Lauren were testament to that. He only had to take command and live out those dreams in the flesh. Hunger surged through him at that thought. Lauren, skin to skin with him, moaning his name as she had done in his fantasies. He could make that happen. He would make this a moment she would never forget.

He pulled her into his arms so her chest pressed against his, and kissed her.

CHAPTER 45

Lauren's heart raced. She placed her hands on Julian's waist as his mouth slanted against hers, their tongues caressing, turning the flicker of heat in her stomach into flames that licked her skin. She tilted her head back and tiptoed, wanting to get closer to him, to kiss him harder and pour out the passion growing inside her. She wanted him. She loved him. It was all out in the open now, both of their hearts on display, handed to the other with a few simple words that meant the world.

Her hands moved to Julian's chest to steady her and she ached at the feel of his tensed muscles beneath her fingers. The man had the body of a god. He was a god. Ancient Greek perfection. She corrected herself. Arcadian. He'd never once referred to himself as Greek. Her Arcadian protector. Her commander. Her Julian.

Feeling a little bolder, she slid her hands across to the buttons of his coat. The thick material was stopping her from touching him, hindering her desire to run her hands over every inch of his body and explore it at last. Sleeping next to him when he had only been wearing underwear had been torture but she had been too afraid to take the next step after touching him that night.

The memory of him biting her neck made her skin prickly and hot. She rubbed her thighs together, tensing her muscles to make the most of the sudden bolt of arousal. Julian took a deep breath and groaned.

"You do not know what you do to me," he whispered, each word punctuated by a hungry kiss.

When he kissed her like that, his hands pulling her firmly against him, she knew exactly what she did to him. She wrestled free of his embrace so she could continue with her plan to get him naked. This time she wasn't going to chicken out. This time she would take their relationship past the point of no return. They were in love and she wanted to show him that she was his and his alone. He had no need to fear Morgan's hungry stare or Duke's flirting. It affected her less than just a glance from Julian did.

"You don't know what you do to me," she countered and undid the buttons on his jacket. "How long I waited for you to take this damn thing off and show me what you looked like." It dropped to the ground and the urge that crossed Julian's face amused her. He wanted to pick it up and place it somewhere, didn't want to leave it on the floor. She held his gaze and he relaxed, his pale blue eyes intent on her. "You are damn gorgeous."

A hint of colour touched his cheeks. She reached up and ran her hands through the finger-length strands of his black hair, her gaze studying his handsome face. His pupils widened when she swept her fingers along his jaw and then caressed his lower lip with her thumb.

"Both sides of you are gorgeous," she whispered and his eyes changed, the blue turning to liquid silver. His lips parted, revealing fangs. A thrill ran through her, anticipation burning in her stomach, making her bite her lip. She gave him a coy look, tilting her head to one side. His eyes shifted to her neck and her heart beat harder. She willed him to bite her again. It had been nothing short of exquisite and she craved it, needed to feel his fangs in her again.

Wanted to feel him in her too.

She needed him inside her, claiming her as his at last.

"Temptress," he muttered and dragged her back up against him.

Instead of kissing her as she'd expected, he tugged her jumper and t-shirt off in one fell swoop. His hands covered her bra-clad breasts and she arched her back, pressing them into his palms. He groaned again and his eyes narrowed into a look so full of raw passion and need that she grabbed his shirt and kissed him hard. His teeth caught her lip. A metal scent flooded her mouth, and he kissed the breath from her. Blood. She'd never thought that it would make a passionate moment more intense, but it did. The taste of it drove her out of her mind with desire, sending her arousal spiralling upwards until she ached to satisfy it.

Her own teeth shifted, growing long and sharp. Her fingernails changed to pointed claws. In a fit of desperate need, she ran them down the join of his shirt, slicing it open. Julian hissed and leaned back, facing the ceiling as he tensed. She pushed his shirt open and saw that she'd caught his skin with her claws in a few places. The long red scratches followed the line between his pectorals and between the two sides of his abdominal muscles. She wet her lips, moved in and carefully licked each cut. The taste of his blood stirred hers, making her squirm as new heat flooded her knickers. She writhed as she slowly savoured the tiny drop of blood each cut gave her, working her way downwards.

When she was kneeling before him, licking the cut above his navel, he placed his hands on her shoulders. They trembled. He wasn't alone. Inside, she quivered too, partly out of excitement but mostly because of nerves. She didn't deserve someone as perfect as Julian.

"Is something wrong?" Julian said, coming to kneel before her. He looked worried.

She shook her head.

Julian's fingers were gentle against her jaw, raising her head so her eyes met his. "I can sense you, remember?"

Lauren sighed and looked away. What did he expect her to say to him? She only had questions. What did he see when he looked at her? Why wasn't he with someone more beautiful? Did he really love her? Was all of this real or just make believe? A dark voice at the back of her mind said that he could do this with all of Illia's reincarnations, making them believe that he loved them and not Illia, so he could have his way with them.

No. She knew Julian. He'd kept his distance and his eyes had held such pain. Pain that she'd felt in him. It wasn't a lie.

Her eyes met his and she searched them deeply, looking for a glimmer of love in them. They were blue again, filled to the brim with tender concern and affection. When she'd met him, his eyes had been so cold and empty.

"Lauren?" he whispered and lightly cupped her cheek. His fingers were still trembling. She could feel his nerves as though they were her own. "Speak to me. You look so upset and I... did I do something wrong?"

The pained look he gave her went straight through her, cutting her deep. God, now she'd hurt him. His hand left her cheek and he looked away. When he looked back at her, his eyes held fear. She'd never seen a man look so vulnerable.

"If I did... I apologise. I have waited so long for someone like you. I had thought that I loved Illia but she is nothing compared to you... this feeling I have is so much more than the one I had for her ever was. I love you, Lauren." He looked deep into her eyes and then down at his knees. "Do not speak. Not yet. Let me say this. You are so warm and beautiful, so very kind. I have never met a woman like you, one which I wanted to protect with my own life... with the life that you gave back to me. I was dead these past millennia, empty inside with nothing but my duty to sustain me and I am glad that it did because it brought you to me. You..." He looked up at her through his lashes and Lauren didn't think that her silence could last. His beautiful words were making her want to cry. She wanted to tell him that she loved him too. That she wanted to spend eternity with him. "I was broken inside and you fixed me. You breathed life back into me. You gave me new purpose and new feelings, and I have never felt so alive... and I have never feared anything as much as I fear losing you."

Lauren threw her arms around his neck, holding him tight. Foolish man. His pretty speech had been all because he was afraid that she was going to leave him.

"You'll never lose me," she whispered against his skin, her warm breath bouncing back at her. "Never. I'll be with you so long that you'll want rid of me. Centuries. Millennia. If you'll have me that is."

She was sure that her last sentence was definitely something a man should say. It made her think of marriage proposals. She didn't think immortals could get married, but she would marry Julian in a heartbeat.

"I have not done this since I was mortal... but let me show you how much I love you... my beautiful precious Lauren." He kissed her cheek and smoothed her hair with one hand, holding her tight around the back with the other.

She struggled to hold her tears back. Damn him for being so sweet.

She pressed a kiss to his neck and stilled when she felt his pulse against her lips. A desire to bite him filled her. She hadn't fed on living blood in a long time and Julian smelt of it, warm and enticing. He moaned when she licked the length of his artery, pressing her tongue in hard.

"Feed," he urged, his voice strained and as tense as his body. His fingers pressed into her back, his grip on her firm. He wanted her to bite him. The thought of blood, of biting Julian and feeling the connection between them, made her fangs extend and her eyes switch.

She closed them and kissed his neck, searching for the place where she'd bitten him before. It was the wrong side of his throat. She thought about moving to the other side and then thought the better of it. If he wore her marks on both sides, no one could doubt their relationship. It would annoy the hell out of Morgan but she didn't care. She wanted Julian to be hers and hers alone.

He hissed out his breath in a sigh of sheer pleasure when she sank her teeth into his throat. His hands tensed against her and then relaxed, drawing her closer. She moved so her knee was between his, her breasts brushing his chest, and bit deeper. A burst of blood was her reward, rich and warm, sending her out of her mind.

Julian kissed her neck and she wanted to release him and tell him to bite her too but didn't want to leave his throat. She drank deep, satisfying one of her hungers while feeding the other. Julian whispered soft affectionate words into her ear, encouraging her to keep going, to take all of him into her.

She wanted to. She wanted him inside.

Lauren pushed all of her weight against Julian's shoulders. He fell backwards, hitting the wooden floor hard, his body trapped beneath hers. Her lips didn't leave his throat. She kept drinking even as she moved to straddle his hips. He groaned and his hands slid down to her backside. Her eyes widened when he thrust up against her.

The moment her mouth left his neck, he rolled her over, nestling himself between her thighs. He came to a stop above her, his hungry gaze burning into hers. It told her everything. He wanted her and he was going to have her. She relaxed into the cold wooden floor and licked the blood off her lips. He could have her. She was his.

He lowered a hand, his claws extending, and cut the band between the cups of her black bra. It tickled when he traced his fingers over her ribs and she wriggled. Julian smiled, pushed one cup of her bra aside, and then lowered his mouth. Her eyes rolled closed and her hands went straight to the back of his head when he wrapped his lips around her nipple and suckled, teasing the bud into hardness. She groaned and rubbed her hips against his, eager to get out of her clothes and be skin-to-skin with him.

Julian's hands eased downwards to her hips and then across. He undid her belt as he sucked her nipple, swirling his tongue around the sensitive peak and sending sparks shooting out over her body. She shivered as he blew on it and then moved away, heading towards her other breast. He pushed the other cup of her bra aside and licked her nipple, torturing her with the too-light contact. She needed more.

Pushing his shirt off his shoulders, she smiled when he sat back and removed it. A blush blazed through her entire body when she looked down the length of herself. He'd managed to undo her jeans. Blue knickers. She cursed the gods for letting her wear odd underwear on today of all days.

Julian didn't seem to care. When he was done stripping his shirt off, he tugged her trainers and socks off, and then her jeans, leaving her lying exposed on the floor in her offending unmatched underwear. He smiled and hooked his fingers into the hem of her knickers. Lauren swallowed but before she could say anything, he'd whipped them off her and tossed them away.

She frowned and was about to protest about the fact it was freezing and he was still half dressed when he stood, pulled her up off the floor and then up into his arms. She felt like a princess, light and petite, as he carried her effortlessly to the bed and placed her down. She sat on the edge, a little shy over being naked around him. All sense of awkwardness disappeared when he undid his belt and his trousers, kicked off his boots, and stripped in front of her. Unabashed, she raked her gaze over him. Every flex of his muscles as he moved was torture, sending her temperature up a notch. The smooth, pale planes of his body were beautiful, perfect. Tight skin barely hid the taut honed muscles, making them always visible enough to tempt her into touching. Boy did she want to touch.

He removed his underwear and her eyes were immediately on his hard length. She ached to feel it inside her, to have their bodies as one. When he moved towards her, she shuffled backwards up the bed towards the headboard, removing her bra as she went. Her heart skittered about in her chest, thumping erratically as she waited to feel him against her.

She didn't have to wait long. Within seconds, his body was on hers, the length of him pressing into her side as he settled there. She relaxed into the bed, intent on letting him lead the way. It felt as though he was worshipping her as he kissed every inch of her, starting at her neck and moving downwards. His tongue teased her nipples, bringing them back to stiff peaks, and then he continued down over her stomach. He licked around her navel and she tried not to tense when she realised where he was going next.

Her eyes closed when he moved her knees, parting her thighs. She trembled with anticipation and stifled her moan when he kissed her inner thigh and moved up it towards the apex of them. Her breath hitched when he licked the length of her, from her slick opening to her clit. She bucked her hips, eager to feel his tongue on her. He pressed it hard into her pert nub and flicked it. She gasped as heat spread outwards from her thighs and bit her lip. If it had really been millennia since he had done this, she couldn't tell.

When she was close to climax, he moved away, kissing back up the length of her body. His hips settled between hers, the hard length of his erection pressing against her. She rubbed herself against it and he groaned. His lips claimed her nipple again and he thrust against her, grinding his length into her clit and making her ache with need.

"Julian," she whispered and he looked up at her. She swallowed and lost the words she'd been going to say. She'd never been forward during sex. She wanted to blush when she thought about commanding him to enter her now, to take her, to make love with her.

A smile tugged at the corners of his lips. He shifted his hips back and took hold of himself, guiding himself into her. She bit her lip, staring up into his eyes as he filled her, joining them as one. His eyes narrowed on hers, all of his feelings there for her to read, nothing hidden.

Lauren tilted her head back and moaned when he drew back and thrust all the way in, deep enough to sate her hunger to feel him. She wrapped her legs around his, entwining them together as he leaned down on one elbow. He cradled the back of her neck and lifted her head off the pillow, bringing her lips to his. His other hand slid around her back, settling in the arch and holding her as he moved inside her, plunging slow and deep into her core. Their combined breathing filled the silence, as fast as the beating of her heart.

Julian buried his head in the crook of her neck, kissing it between breaths, nipping occasionally. She curled her fingers into his hair, holding him against her, loving the way his body moulded perfectly to hers.

Nothing had ever felt this right.

She couldn't remember a time when being with someone had ever felt this good, touching her deep in her soul and her heart, making her want to tell him how much she loved him. Julian shifted and thrust deeper, moaning softly against her throat each time their hips met. She tensed around him and then relaxed, torn between wanting release and wanting it to go on.

He kissed up her neck and along her jaw until his lips found hers. She poured all of her energy into kissing him, teasing his lips with the barest caress of her tongue and making him groan. When their mouths met again, a deep sense of connection ignited in her chest, a strange heady feeling that made her giddy. She could sense him. Every emotion he felt reflected within her, every breath he took matched hers and every beat of his heart echoed in her chest. It was as though they were one—one body, one heart and one soul. Being with someone had never felt like this. It had never felt so intense and perfect. It made her realise something. This was making love, and no one had ever done this with her before.

Julian drew back and looked down into her eyes, his clear blue ones full of a single question. Was she feeling what he was? She smiled at him, telling him without words that every emotion he felt, every ounce of love and affection, of hope and happiness, was in her heart too. She loved him and she never wanted to let him go. She would never let him go. They were together now. They were no longer alone and they never would be again.

He smiled, a beautiful one that stole her heart all over again, and pressed his forehead against hers. Their warm breath mingled and Lauren closed her eyes, focusing on his emotions and the feel of his body rocking against hers. His lips met hers again and this time the kiss was slower, softer, like the way he was moving inside her. It felt beautiful. She arched into him, wanting to be closer still, and his hand tightened against her back.

Her breath left her in a sigh when he kissed back down her jaw, his breathing loud in her ear. His heart beat hard against her chest, drumming steadily in her mind and her veins. She lifted her legs and wrapped them around his waist, moaning when the change in position allowed him deeper inside her and caused his pelvis to brush her clit with each thrust. Julian moaned too, nipping at her neck as the pace of his thrusts increased. He tensed and she could feel he was close, that he was going to find release before her. She wanted this moment to be perfect, and it would be.

Lowering her hand, she nicked the cuts on his neck with her nails and they began to bleed again. She pulled him over to her so she could taste his blood. The angle was awkward, forcing him to lessen the depth of his movements, but it was worth it when she wrapped her lips around the marks and then sunk her fangs into his flesh. He shuddered and groaned, coming completely to a halt. After her first, long pull on his blood, she pressed her feet into his backside, encouraging him to continue. He did, filling her over and over, making her abdomen painfully tight and hot with need. She brought his mouth down to her neck.

It seemed he didn't need any encouragement. His lips didn't even touch her neck before his teeth were in her. It was divine. The connection between them was incredible, so deep that she could feel everything that he was and this time it went beyond his surface feelings. She could feel his tenderness, his love, his gratitude, his desire and his passion for her. She could sense it all, and she knew that he could sense the depth of her feelings for him.

One pull on her blood and his hips jerked forwards, sending him deep within her, tipping her over the edge. Hazy bliss ran in her veins, warm and sedating, her entire body throbbing in time with his as he spilled himself inside her. His hands clamped tight against her back and her neck, holding her still as he remained inside her and drank from her. She fed deep too, her head fuzzy from the combination of her climax and his blood. She didn't want to let him go, and she wouldn't.

Not now.

Not ever.

They were in this forever.

All they had to do was defeat Lycaon.

CHAPTER 46

Lauren smiled lazily when she woke and stretched, her body pleasantly sore from the day's bedroom activities. Julian lie on his back beside her, sound asleep, his dark hair tousled and messy, a little smile on his face. The deep blue duvet barely covered his hips and wrapped around his legs as well as hers. The sight of him sprawled out across the blue sheets was incredible, as was the thought that he was definitely hers now. His neck bore no less than three new sets of her marks and several scratches. Most of them were scars now thanks to the blood he had taken from her. Any bites and scratches she had made after his last feed remained as scabs though. It had interested them both to see just how her blood affected him. While the strength it gave him lasted hours, the healing ability only worked on cuts he had sustained before drinking her blood.

She looked down at herself with raised eyebrows. He wasn't the only one looking worse for wear this evening. Things had turned a touch naughty somewhere along the line and she'd ended up with a bite mark on her thigh, several nicks on her stomach, and a few marks on her neck too. The sting of each cut as it healed only added to the amazing sense of satisfaction that filled every inch of her. She was so relaxed that she didn't even care that the blanket only covered her legs, leaving her bare torso exposed.

Rolling onto her front, Lauren studied Julian's face as he slept. The lamp beside the bed threw warm light over his skin, making his hair an even starker contrast to his pale complexion. She traced the line of his lips with her fingertip and his nose wriggled. It didn't stop her. She brushed it along the curve of his strong jaw and around his earlobe, teasing the tiny sensitive hairs on it, and then ran her hands through his hair.

"Stop that," he muttered and sleepily caught her wrist, his eyes still closed. "Go back to sleep."

He pulled her over to him, so she was lying with her breasts against his stomach and her head on his chest, and then threw a heavy arm around her shoulders, turned his head to one side, and sighed. Lauren reached up with her other hand and stroked the line of his collarbones. When she touched one of the bite marks on his neck, he smiled. What goddess was watching over her to give her such a man?

"Julian," Lauren whispered and he frowned but opened his eyes and looked at her. She smiled. "I love you."

His smile widened and he pulled her up, rewarding her with a long slow kiss that threatened to restart their sordid Olympic sex-athon.

She pushed against his shoulders and he reluctantly released her. He looked around the large white room and then back at her.

"We should get ready," he said and rubbed the sleep from his eyes. There was no enthusiasm in his voice. "Duke will be waiting."

Lauren nodded and slumped into the bed when Julian left it. It was cold without him but she didn't want to move. She wanted to stay there all night, just kissing him and talking, and perhaps other things. She smiled at the sight of him walking naked around the room. He came back to her and raised an eyebrow. She groaned and pouted when he took hold of her hand and pulled her up, forcing her to leave the bed, but any annoyance she'd felt disappeared when she realised that they were heading for the bathroom.

A shower?

Showering with Julian was worth leaving the bed.

She followed him into the white and black bathroom, her gaze lingering on his bare backside. His firm cheeks dimpled as he walked. Her eyes roamed up his strong back, taking him all in. She'd explored every delicious curve of him with her lips but she wanted to do it all over again.

Julian turned the shower on. It was a cubicle separate to the bath and didn't look big enough to accommodate both of them. She didn't care if she spent the whole time squashed against him, they were going to shower together. She took the lead, luring him into the shower. The water was hot and soothing. Julian stepped in and pulled her close, so their fronts were flush together, and kissed her. His hands skimmed down her sides, making her wriggle as they tickled, but her lips didn't leave his. She kissed him back, slow and gentle, and warmed from head to toe. Julian tugged her closer, slanted his head, and brushed her lips with his tongue. She opened to him, her tongue meeting his and sliding sensually along the length of it. The water sprayed down on their heads, trickling over her lips and her cheeks. She didn't care. She didn't care about anything when Julian was kissing her, his lips firm and passionate against hers.

Lauren broke away before it became too much. Duke really would be waiting and if they didn't go to him, he was going to come to them. If she kept kissing Julian, they were going to end up back in bed. The thought of Duke disturbing them then made her blush from head to toe.

She turned in Julian's embrace and furrowed her brow when he stepped close behind her, pressing his front into her back. It felt too good to have his body on hers, his hands skimming up and down her arms, his lips pressing lightly against her shoulder.

He kissed along it to her neck and then brought his mouth to her ear.

"This is heaven," he whispered into it and she murmured in agreement. He kissed her earlobe. "I could stay here with you forever."

But.

She could sense it, knew him well enough to feel it coming. They couldn't stay here. They had a duty to do and he wasn't the kind of man to turn his back on his duty.

"We have to go and finish this," she said and turned to face him. His pale blue eyes held hers and the fire in them made her cheeks blaze. She didn't think she would ever get used to the hungry way he looked at her. Her gaze darted away. There were various bottles on the rack in the corner of the cubicle. Lauren picked up the shower gel and flicked the cap open, trying to distract herself. "We have to see it through to the end… so we can…"

She bit her lip, not quite brave enough to say what she wanted to. She glanced at Julian. He gave her a slight smile and dipped his mouth to her ear.

"So we can be together," he whispered with his jaw brushing against hers and then kissed her cheek.

Lauren nodded and dropped her gaze to his body when he drew back. Taking a deep breath, she squeezed some shower gel onto her hand and then rubbed them together to form lather. She nodded again, telling herself that she could do this, and smoothed the lather over Julian's chest. His body felt better than ever under her soapy fingertips, slick and slippery, the smooth contours a joy to explore. He leaned his head back when she worked her way down his stomach, paying close attention to each muscle, and kissing any cut that she came across.

"I told you I met an old friend," he said in a tight voice. His jaw tensed, the cords of his neck tightening with it, when she ran her fingers through his short curly hair. He closed his eyes and took a long deep breath, as though trying to find control. She skimmed upwards again, aware that she couldn't wash every inch of him without things getting beyond his control.

"And you didn't want to tell me in front of the others." Lauren squeezed behind him and washed his back, enjoying herself. "It's that important that you can't trust them with it?"

"After what happened with Leo—"

"You don't have to explain. If it's something important, it's probably best we don't risk it." She quirked an eyebrow and smoothed her hands over the twin peachy globes of his backside. They tensed. Little dimples appeared in their sides. "Who did you meet?"

"Zeus."

"Holy shit, really?"

Julian turned and frowned at her. She covered her mouth and smiled. She hadn't meant to swear but a real ancient Greek god had appeared to Julian. No wonder he didn't want to tell the others.

"Really." He took the shower gel from her and a wicked glint entered his eyes. Revenge. Her slow exploration of him had taken its toll judging by his erection. He was going to make her pay.

Lauren swallowed and then submitted to him when he swept soapy hands over her breasts. He relayed what had happened and what he'd discovered. She tried to listen but it was difficult with his hands gliding over her body. The attention he gave to the apex of her thighs was thorough, so much so that she was a quivering wreck and had climaxed by the time he'd finished.

He moved her to stand under the jet of water, his hands on her waist. Lauren leaned her head back and thought about the implications of what he'd told her as the haze lifted from her mind.

Lycaon had a weakness now. A weakness that only they knew. This time they would win. She was sure of it. She would defeat Lycaon so she could be with Julian.

He turned the shower off and stepped out of the cubicle. Lauren followed him.

She smiled when he wrapped her in a large cream towel and rubbed her down. She could get used to having such a handsome man pamper her. He stepped back and looked at her, slowly appraising the entire length of her body, his eyes full of fire. When he looked at her like that, she felt so beautiful. His love and attention made her feel as though there was no one else in the world for him, that she was a goddess. He made her beautiful.

He wrapped the towel around his waist and they walked into the bedroom. When he picked up his black shirt, she gave him an apologetic smile. Her claws had shredded it. He went through into the other room and to the door, unlocked and opened it. She wondered where he was going but he didn't leave the room. He bent over, out into the corridor, and then straightened, their bags in his hands.

"It appears Duke realised where we were," Julian said.

Lauren's cheeks burned. She really hoped that Duke hadn't dropped them off during any of their lovemaking marathons. She hadn't exactly been quiet.

Julian walked back to her and handed over her backpack with a wicked smile. Lauren dumped her backpack down on the crumpled blue bedcovers and busied herself with finding something to wear, another blush threatening to scald her face.

She pulled some fresh clothes out, making sure that her underwear matched this time. Her dark red roll neck jumper would keep her warm and hide the marks on her throat. She coupled it with the deep blue jeans she'd been wearing the day before and dressed quickly.

Julian was sitting on the blue couch in the other room and tying the laces on his boots by the time she'd finished fastening her jeans. He stood and flashed a brief smile at her as he walked into the bathroom dressed in his usual attire of black shirt and trousers.

She tugged her socks and trainers on and then ran her fingers through her hair. It was messy and damp.

Julian walked back out of the bathroom, his wet black hair a mass of haphazard spikes across his forehead. He clawed it back, stalked across the room, grabbed her around the waist and pulled her to him. Her hands pressed against his chest and her eyes widened when he dipped his head and kissed her. There was nothing gentle about it this time. It was fierce and dominant, a hungry clashing of lips and tongues that melted her inside. She closed her eyes and leaned into the kiss, absorbing all of the need in it and the sheer act of possession behind it. It left her in no doubt of what he was thinking and why he was kissing her like this again. He wanted her to know that she was his and his alone. She didn't have a problem with that. She didn't want to be anyone else's. They belong with each other and to each other, and nothing or no one would change that.

He pulled back and pressed a kiss to her forehead, holding her close. She leaned her head against his chest and listened to his heart beating steady and hard against her ear. His hands tightened against her shoulders and she could sense that he needed more than a kiss to reassure him that she was his. Drawing away from him, she looked up into his eyes and made sure that she had his attention. His eyes immediately locked with hers and her heart fluttered in her chest. He had bore his heart and soul to her, and he deserved something in return for that.

"Julian," she whispered and he blinked, slow and languid, making her heart jump again. She could do this. She held his gaze, letting him see and feel every emotion in her. "I can't… I'm not sure how to put this… but what you said before… you are my strength. You give me strength to do this, to go through with my destiny. From the moment I met you… you gave me the strength to do what was right and I… I wanted to be with you."

He opened his mouth to speak but she shook her head.

"You're my everything, Julian… without you I couldn't do this. You give me strength, and you make me feel so loved and you take away my fear. I don't deserve someone like you, but I'm glad that I have you, that you're mine… because I'm yours. You're all I want. You're everything I need… and I love you. I love you with all of my heart."

He smiled, pulled her back into his arms and kissed her. Not fierce this time but slow again, barely brushing his lips against hers. The light touch warmed her more than the hard one had, making her feel giddy. She closed her eyes and smiled against his lips, happy that she had put him at ease and that she had opened her heart to him, showing him that she really did love him and that she would never leave him.

When the kiss threatened to lead to other things, she pushed back and smiled into his eyes.

"Duke really will come and get us," she said with a shy smile. Julian's eyes narrowed on hers and he nodded slowly. She could see that he really didn't want to leave the room, just as she didn't. "We'll continue this later."

He smiled wide, flashing perfect white teeth, and pressed a brief kiss to her lips before breaking away from her. The hunger in his blue eyes when he crossed the room to his coat and looked back at her said that they would continue this later, there was no doubt about that.

He grabbed his coat and slipped it on. She didn't stop him when he fastened the collar so it hid the lower half of his face. She liked to see him but preferred that he hid the myriad of marks and bruises on his throat during the meeting.

She picked up one of her short katana and waited for Julian to fasten his long katana to his belt before heading for the door. He reached it before her, holding it open so she could pass, and she thanked him with a smile. They walked in silence, hand in hand, along the dim corridor and down the stairs to the ground floor. She followed her senses to find the others but they led her to the wrong room. The way Julian's eyes narrowed told her that he was smiling. She frowned.

"You will get there in time." He placed his hand against her back, guiding her to the right room.

Rome wasn't built in a day. Given time, she would master her new abilities just as Julian was master of his.

Duke and Astra were already in the room when they arrived. Duke gave her a knowing smile and Lauren looked away, busying herself with taking in her surroundings. It was a large drawing room with dark green walls and little furniture. There was a fireplace behind Duke and Astra. Two green velvet-covered armchairs stood either side of it, forming a wide disjointed semi-circle with a green couch. It looked as though someone had pushed the couch back towards the wall to make more room. Lauren stood beside the fire, warming herself and leaning on the tall back of one of the armchairs. Julian remained standing a short distance away.

The door opened and Kuga walked in, rubbing the back of his head. He looked tired, his usually warm brown eyes dull. She went over to him and touched his arm, knowing without asking that he hadn't slept today. She missed Piper too, but her feelings of loss couldn't match Kuga's, not while she had Julian with her and not even if she lost Julian. Leo had betrayed Kuga. She didn't have family that could do that to her. The only thing that compared to it was Lycaon, her supposed father, killing her real parents. He was going to pay for it. She would avenge her parents, just as she would avenge Piper. If Kuga couldn't bring himself to kill Leo, she would do it for him. Leo had to pay. Piper hadn't deserved to die, not like that, not when she'd finally found herself.

Morgan strode into the room. Julian sidestepped towards her, closing the gap between them, his gaze fixed on the vampire. Astra scowled at Morgan and folded her arms across her chest, this time covering her breasts rather than pushing them up. Lauren noted her change in clothes. Tight black trousers and a t-shirt had replaced her usual slinky black dress. Either she had changed because she was gearing up for the fight or because of Morgan.

Lauren suspected that it was the latter.

Morgan smiled briefly at Astra and then his gaze slid to Lauren. His stormy eyes took in every inch of her, all of his hunger evident in them. She stared right back at him, unfazed by his appraisal and more interested in something else.

He was alone.

It surprised Lauren.

"Where are the hounds tonight?" Julian stared at Morgan, nothing but darkness in his eyes. Lauren hated that look in them. She grazed his fingers with the tips of hers, wanting to reassure him and tell him that he didn't have to fight with Morgan anymore because she was his without a doubt—she would never betray him.

"Feeding on the tripe the lord of darkness keeps in his refrigerator." Morgan slumped into the armchair Lauren had been leaning against and stretched his legs out in front of him. Did he ever bother to button his shirts all the way to the collar? The blood red one that he was wearing had at least the top four buttons undone.

"If we are going to work together, I would suggest that you watch your mouth or I may just change my mind about not toying with the dead." Duke's black tone told Lauren that it was no idle threat. Morgan's eyes narrowed on him, turning inky and fathomless. That was a threat too.

"Can we all play nice for a moment?" It came out a little harsher than Lauren had aimed for but everyone fell quiet and looked at her. "Erm, thanks."

They all continued to stare. She squirmed inside, trying to think of what to say now. She should have thought it through and then told them to shut up. Morgan made an annoyed sound and looked away from her, playing with his undone shirt cuffs. He couldn't have looked more disinterested if he'd tried. He was up to something and instinct said it was trying to get her to pay attention to him. She turned away to face Julian, unwilling to play games with Morgan that might upset him.

Julian's ice blue eyes shone with murder, fixed on Morgan. Lauren touched his hand and his gaze slowly shifted to her, warming as it did. His fingers tangled with hers and then he suddenly moved their hands and clamped hers tight in his, their fingers interlocked and palms pressed together. Staking his territory? Having men fight over her was a new experience and one she might have found intensely satisfying under different circumstances.

"So... we need a plan," she said and led Julian over to the others.

Astra had moved away from the fire when Morgan had sat down and Duke had gone with her. Kuga sat on the arm of the green couch.

Lauren tried to ignore the thunderous glare that she could feel directed at her back by Morgan. She could sense his intent. Murder. He wanted to kill Julian. She wanted to turn and call him over, order him to come and join the others, but didn't dare make him lose face. He could easily take away his offer of help.

Kuga toyed with a slim black mobile phone and then offered it to her with uncertainty in his eyes. "I got it this morning."

Lauren took the phone. A message.

A message from Leo.

"Greece?" she said and looked around at everyone. "Some place called Mount Lyceum."

Julian tensed. His fingers pressed hard into the back of her hand. She looked up at him to see him staring blankly at the far wall.

"There?" he whispered in a pained voice.

"It makes sense," Duke said. "It is close to where we found you."

Realising that was why Julian had tensed, Lauren placed her other hand over his, stroking the back of it in an effort to calm him. He wasn't there anymore. She would never let anything like that happen to him again.

"What a weak little guard dog," Morgan muttered. "My queen deserves a stronger knight."

"Shut up!" Lauren turned on him, her eyes narrowed into a glare. "You don't know a thing about Julian and what he's done for me. If he is my knight, then he is the only one that I need. What have you ever done to protect me?"

Morgan leaned into the tall back of the armchair and then casually waved a hand in the air. "I am here, am I not?"

Lauren laughed. "I practically had to drag you here by that leash you proclaim I hold. If you think you're a worthy protector of your queen, then prove it to me."

His expression turned thoughtful and then he smiled, as seductive as ever. He bowed his head. "What my queen wants... my queen receives."

Lauren trembled inside, the burst of adrenaline from confronting Morgan making her feel sick and weak. Julian squeezed her hand. Her gaze met his concerned one and she smiled to reassure him. She felt better now that it was out in the open. The challenge of proving himself could only make Morgan work harder. If he wanted that drop of blood, he was going to have to earn it. Snide remarks about Julian were a black mark against him and one he would have to fight to erase.

"It is a trap," Astra said, bringing Lauren back to what they had been discussing.

"But it does make sense that Lycaon would return there, to where it all began." Julian looked pensive. "Lycaon wants us to go to him and we should not disappoint him."

"No." Lauren thought about what Julian had told her in the shower. "We shouldn't. When does the full moon rise?"

"In only a few days," Morgan said before Julian could answer her. Lauren looked at him. "It calls me as it calls you. When the full moon rises, our desire to fight werewolves is strongest... your blood does not let us rest that night."

It was eerie to think that her blood was still inside him, compelling him to fight werewolves. Or at least Sonja's blood.

"I will make arrangements then," Duke said with a glance at everyone. "It will take time to get there with the vampires in tow. Unless they don't mind travelling in the day?"

Morgan scowled at Duke, black eyes reflecting the fire. Julian had explained to her that real vampires did go poof in the sun. When the sun rose, vampires were dead to the world. Lauren couldn't imagine them being able to find a way of travelling to Greece that would allow for most of their forces to be asleep during the day and still get them there in time to face Lycaon this full moon.

"The Fates have spoken. We will meet Lycaon under the next full moon," Julian said and Lauren knew without a doubt that he was telling the truth. It didn't matter what method of transport Duke chose, someone was watching over them and would ensure they reached their destination in time to face Lycaon that night.

Morgan finally joined the group. He stood halfway along the couch, between her and Kuga, an air of unease about him. If he had wanted to conceal the fact that he was keeping his distance from Astra and Duke, he should have tried harder. Still, he wasn't the only one feeling unsettled by the past few days' events. Everything was moving so fast now since Piper had died. Lauren felt as though the turbulent current was sweeping her along and she couldn't fight it, couldn't find her footing when she needed to most. She knew nothing of battles and was still learning to use all of her abilities. At this rate, she was going to drown.

Julian's arm settled around her shoulders. She looked at his fingers where they curved around her upper arm, pressing in and holding her tight. He was her anchor in all of this, her haven, and the one she could show her weakness to without fear of him seeing her as unworthy of leading them. He understood her better than anyone and could see through her fears. He believed that she was strong and, for him, she could be. She curled her fingers tighter around the case of her sword and stood taller.

"Kuga?" Duke said in a cautious tone. The question was there in his eyes for everyone to read.

"I'm going through with this." Kuga stood and straightened to his full height, his expression one of sheer resolve. She'd seen that look several times since Piper's death. Even though Leo was his brother, he was going to face him. He was going to avenge Piper just as he'd promised. She understood his need for closure. She wanted to face Lycaon for the same reason.

"Then we must devise a plan," Julian said.

Duke and Morgan nodded in agreement. Lauren looked up at Julian, unsure of how she could help. He was her commander. Millennia of experience and a human lifetime as a soldier made him more than qualified to come up with something that would end in Lycaon's downfall. She knew nothing of this kind of thing.

"This sounds boring." Kuga smiled at her. "You wanna leave the boring stuff to the old fuddy-duddies and go practice?"

Julian's hand dropped to her back. She glanced up at him.

"As your commander, it is my duty to do these so called boring things. I will see to it that we are ready for battle. It is better that you see to it that you are ready to fight..." His eyes narrowed as though he was smiling and then he looked at Kuga. "Both of you. This will not be easy, Kuga. You will face Leo."

Kuga nodded, his look grim.

"And I'll be ready for him."

Lauren went to the door with him and paused when she reached it, looking back at Julian. He was watching her still, his eyes holding a strange mix of hope and fear. Her grip on her sword tightened and she stared deep into his eyes, letting him see her resolve. There was nothing to fear, not for either of them. Lycaon would fall this time. She'd been training hard since his attack on the Paris office. She was stronger now, not just because her skill had improved but because she had something that she wanted to protect.

She wouldn't let anything happen to Julian.

She would train until the last moment so she could protect him, as he protected her.

He would never be alone again.

This time they would defeat Lycaon.

She would be ready for him.

CHAPTER 47

Lauren sat on the worn wooden bench with her back against the large whitewashed villa. She stared out over the scenery, enjoying the lingering warmth as it rose up from the terracotta tiles beneath her feet. The world smelt of earth and olives, and sunshine. An hour ago, she'd decided that she liked the scent of Greece. It relaxed her, which was exactly what she needed right now, on the eve of such an important battle.

She'd come a long way from home, and a long way from who she used to be. Now she was stronger, braver, and finally felt as though she knew who she was. Her destiny had been three thousand years in the making and she was going to grasp it with both hands and see it through. They would defeat Lycaon. She would get her happily forever after with Julian. Nothing was going to stop her.

Stretching her legs out, she tilted her head back. She'd never seen so many stars. The light from the two small oil lamps hanging from the veranda wasn't enough to obscure their brilliant orbs as they twinkled against their canvas of black silk. The moon was creeping higher, turning bright white as it rose. She'd watched it since it had first appeared on the horizon, blood red and large. Beautiful. She had never stopped to watch the moonrise before. Everyone talked about sunrise and sunset being magical, but nothing compared to the sight of the moon rising into a darkened sky.

Now it was pale and bathed the world in blue-white light, casting long inky shadows up towards her from the olive groves that surrounded the old villa. The peak of Mount Lyceum stood high in the distance behind her. She was always aware of it, of who was waiting up there and what tomorrow held. No matter how many times she tried to push it to the back of her mind, it kept coming back.

When they had been driving from the nearest city, she'd had trouble finding the mountain on the map. Julian had pointed it out for her. In modern times, it had a different name—Lykaion. She didn't like it. It sounded even more like Lycaon to her and had made her think about him the whole journey up to the villa. She had studied the mountain as they drove, the way it undulated and steadily grew to a peak. Julian had told her that the remains of the sacrificial altar and a large ash mound still stood there. When she had asked whether they had been in use when he had been born, he had laughed at her and told her that the temple had been used then and all the way back to Lycaon's time, and he was far older than Julian. That hadn't comforted her in the slightest. She had learnt that with age came strength for werewolves. If Lycaon was the first and older than Julian, what chance did she have of defeating him? That fear lingered within her, a quiet voice that wouldn't go away.

An insect chirruped, sending her nerves skittering and breaking her calm. The slightest noise made her jump tonight. She'd never stood on the brink of war before but Julian had told her that everyone experienced moments of unease and anxiety in the time before a battle. He'd admitted that even he was feeling unsettled. That hadn't reassured her at all. If Julian was nervous, then this battle had to be something to fear. She'd seen him fight and not once had he looked unsettled.

The trees led Lauren's gaze to the road that wound its way down into the valley below, twisting around the prominent bumps that gave Mount Lyceum a rolling look. She could see small farms and clusters of houses at the base of the mount, and some solitary buildings nearer to her. A car drove in the distance, its lights snaking around bends that were miles away. It was incredible how much she could see from only midway up the mountain.

It felt as though she could see to the edge of the Earth.

She looked over her shoulder at the wall of the villa, towards where the peak of the mountain stood. It was still a long way up and it would be a tiring walk tomorrow night to reach their destination. The three vans that Duke had hired had brought them this far, but the roads swerved away now and it would be too obvious to use them to go around the mountain and up the other side. They had to walk and she wasn't looking forward to it.

She turned away from the peak, tilted her head back and pushed tomorrow out of her mind. The stars twinkled and blinked above her, a beautiful arch across the sky that soothed and calmed her again.

Someone shouted, shattering the silence.

Lauren frowned and then relaxed again.

The journey to Greece had been long with Morgan and his men in tow. He'd brought over twenty of them. The villa wasn't large enough to accommodate so many and tensions were running high. When the vampires had awoken at nightfall, Lauren had come out onto the veranda with Julian and Kuga. They had gone off to scout the mountain. She hoped they would return soon. It had been hours since they had left her here promising they wouldn't be long.

The door creaked open and someone walked out. No heartbeat and the smell of sin. Morgan.

"You should not be out here alone." The reprimanding note in his tone made her frown.

"I'm not." She nodded towards the moon. "A goddess is with me."

Morgan laughed and came to stand beside her, towering over her. The oil lamp hanging high to her right lit his face but did nothing to warm his expression.

"The moon cannot protect you." The serious edge hadn't left his voice. He knelt before her on one knee. The usual darkness in his eyes wasn't there tonight. His look shifted, becoming relaxed at first and then changing to something else. Something that surprised her. He reached up, his hand stopping just short of her face and then he brought it down, as though stroking her cheek, before lowering it again. "I will protect you tomorrow... my queen."

He held her gaze for only a second before he cast it downwards, turning his head to one side.

It was strange to see him so concerned. All of his usual charisma and confidence was gone, stripped away. For once, she was seeing the real Morgan.

"Konstantin," she whispered and he looked at her out of the corner of his eye. She expected him to reproach her for calling him by his original name but he said nothing, just stared at her, waiting. She nodded.

He stood and dusted his knees off. She could feel the difference in him. For all his bravado and snide remarks, he really did care about what happened to her.

"I need a walk," he muttered and stalked off.

"Be careful."

Morgan stopped a short way down the hill and turned back to face her. He flashed her a smile and then he was gone, disappeared into the darkness. Lauren sighed.

A chill tripped down her spine and then a thin ribbon of smoke curled through the air from the corner of the villa nearest her. Lauren smiled. Duke had been there for hours. He had only made an exit when Morgan had come out, probably to avoid a confrontation. She wasn't alone.

"That vampire is a mystery," he said loud enough for her to hear and then stepped around the corner. He leaned against the wall and took another drag on his cigarette.

"He's the original." Lauren stared in the direction Morgan had gone. "I made him apparently."

"Nervous about tomorrow?"

Lauren shook her head.

"Julian and Kuga will return soon. There's no need to worry."

She hated how easily Duke could read her. She didn't mean to be so open with her feelings, especially her fears, but when it came to Julian, she had trouble hiding them.

Lauren glanced across at Duke and then over her shoulder at the wall behind her, towards the peak of the mountain. She could feel him.

"Lycaon is up there right now... waiting," she whispered and reached out with her senses in an attempt to pinpoint him.

The door burst open. Lauren jumped.

"I have had it with those filthy bloodsuckers!" Astra threw the last two words back into the villa. A tirade of comments was hurled back at her. She slammed the door and huffed. When she turned around, her eyes fell on

Lauren and widened. Lauren had never seen Astra look awkward before. Clearly, she hadn't realised that Duke wasn't alone out on the veranda. "Can you do something about them?"

Lauren shrugged. "I can speak with Morgan when he comes back."

"Even he cannot stand them." Astra shuddered and grimaced. "I hate the looks they give me."

Duke crossed the veranda to Astra and offered his arm. "It's a nice night for a walk."

Astra slipped her arm through his and Lauren smiled inside when she noticed the way they looked at each other. They were definitely in love. A soul-sucking demon and a necromancer. A month ago, she would have thought she was going crazy. Now it seemed almost normal. She'd grown strangely used to the existence of demons, people with phenomenal powers, and immortals.

In fact, she couldn't imagine the world as it had existed for her before, full of normal people with boring jobs doing everyday things. Here she was, on the eve of a fight to decide the fate of the world, with an army consisting of immortals, powerful humans, demons and vampires, and it all seemed so normal. She'd finally found herself—immortal demi-goddess and lover of the most handsome immortal the world had ever seen.

Lauren smiled when she saw said immortal walking up the hill towards her, Kuga in tow. Leaving the bench, she met Julian halfway and threw herself into his arms. He wrapped his arms around her waist and she looped hers around his neck.

"All is well," he whispered close by her ear. Lauren closed her eyes, enjoying the feel of his strong embrace. "The area is quiet. Not even a human nearby."

She set back on her heels, removed her arms from his neck and looked up at him. "Morgan will be disappointed. He went out for a 'walk'."

Kuga came to a stop beside Julian and gave him a dark look.

"You'd be surprised how far a man will go for blood. My feet are killing me." Kuga's shoulders sagged. "I'm going to sit down before I fall down."

Lauren smiled at him as he passed and then looked back at Julian. Now that Kuga had mentioned it, she could smell blood on him. The rich metallic scent of it made her stomach gurgle.

Julian offered his hand. She slid hers into it, not needing to ask what he had in mind. It was all there in his hungry eyes.

"A walk sounds divine," she said and let him lead the way.

They walked down the hill, through a quiet world bathed in crystal moonlight. The sense of peace it evoked suffused Lauren's body and, with Julian's hand in hers, she was finally able to find some calm amongst the storm of her emotions. Her shoulders fell, the tension in them melting away. When Julian was with her, she felt as though she had nothing to fear and that nothing could go wrong. Lycaon and tomorrow's battle drifted away to the far recesses of her mind, and she focused on her hand and Julian's hold on it. The connection between them wasn't enough. She needed more and knew how to get it. Blood wasn't the only reason to bite him. The connection she experienced then was intense and intimate, deep and fulfilling. It gave her a sense of calm and peace like nothing else could.

Her senses scanned the dark world around them. Kuga had been right. There wasn't a soul for miles.

They were alone.

A flush of heat coursed through her veins at that thought.

Alone with Julian, in a moon-bathed world, under a starlit sky. It couldn't be more romantic.

Her eyebrows rose when he stopped, removed his jacket, and laid it out on the dusty ground in an opening amongst the olive trees. He held his hand out, inviting her to sit on his coat. She smiled at his chivalry and removed her black trainers before sitting down. Julian took his boots off, removed his sword, and then sat close beside her. Lauren hugged her knees to her chest. Julian tilted his head back. Her gaze roamed to his face. She would rather watch him than the stars.

"What are you thinking?" he said in a low intimate voice.

"This is nice." Her eyes didn't leave his profile. "The clear night sky... the peace and quiet... the solitude."

"The company?" he said, glancing at her out of the corner of his eye. She nodded and looped her arm through his, curling up close to him. He leaned over and pressed a kiss to her shoulder. "It is nice... but it could be nicer. Come."

She almost fell over backwards when he suddenly lay down and placed his hands under his head as a pillow. Taking the hint, she lay beside him and rested her head on his arm. Her gaze still didn't leave his profile. She wanted to put it to memory. Every part of it. The gentle slope of his brow, the straight line of his nose, and the delicious curve of his lips. All of it.

Her friends would be so jealous.

God. She hadn't thought about them in so long. Perhaps when all this was over she could drop by and explain that she'd been so caught up in Julian that she hadn't thought to contact them. They would understand when they saw him. No girl on Earth wouldn't be caught up and distracted by a man like him.

"This is better." He sighed and his lips tilted into a slight smile but it soon faded. What was he thinking now? His expression had turned serious.

"Forget about it all," she whispered. "I don't want Lycaon wrecking such a beautiful night."

She wanted it to be perfect. A night to always remember.

"Lauren." Julian moved onto his side so fast that Lauren's head hit their makeshift blanket. She grimaced and frowned. He smiled but his eyes were still serious. "Nothing could ruin this night."

Lauren rubbed the back of her head and Julian replaced her hand with his own. He supported her head, cradling it in his hand, and narrowed his eyes on hers. The affection in them warmed her from head to toe. Not quick warmth, but a deep one that she felt right down in the marrow of her bones. Lasting warmth.

He brushed his fingers over her forehead and down her cheek. His eyes mesmerised her just as they had done when she'd first looked into them. Just as they always would.

"Nothing could spoil any moment I have with you like this. They are all perfect, each one, and they are all beautiful. They are elusive dreams made flesh and blood. You have breathed life into them just as you breathed it into me."

Lauren couldn't help smiling at him when everything he said was so romantic. She wanted to ask him if he'd practiced this speech when he was out with Kuga but remained silent, drinking in his tender look and his words of love.

"I think you breathed a little life into me too." She brushed the black strands of his hair from his eyes. The smile he gave her was affectionate but gained an edge of hunger when his gaze fell to her lips. They parted for him, an invitation she hoped he wouldn't refuse.

He leaned over and captured her mouth with his own, his kiss soft and slow, light brushes that made her giddy and hot. She could spend all night doing this. He stopped kissing her and she frowned when he pulled away, only for a shy smile to replace it when he pushed her hair behind her ears and cupped her cheek.

"You are so beautiful."

She shook her head, unable to take the compliment.

He nodded and smiled. "Beautiful."

His persistence paid off because a blush burned her cheeks. If she was beautiful, it was only because he made her feel that way.

"More beautiful than Illia ever was." That made her frown and Julian's smile turned reassuring. She knew that he loved her, that his feelings for her were different to the ones that he'd had for Illia, but she still didn't like hearing about her.

"We're the same," Lauren said.

"No, not the same." Julian swept his thumb across her lower lip. It tickled and she smiled. "You are so much more beautiful than she ever was because you are so caring and compassionate. So warm. You think of others and would think nothing of sacrificing yourself for their sake. You do all you can to protect those you know and care about. You are so different to her... and I love you so much because of it."

Lauren didn't quite know how to respond to that so she threw herself at him, tackling him to the ground. His head hit the dirt as her lips found his and she rewarded him with a kiss that was somewhere between desperate need and profound love.

He rolled her onto her back and took control of the kiss, turning it heated and heavy, a tangling of tongues and clashing of lips. She smiled against his mouth when their kiss began to slow, stirring different feelings in her. His lips barely grazed hers, teasing and tickling them, making her burn with a need for more, for stronger contact between them. Julian held back, clearly intent on torturing her until she reached bursting point and again took command of the kiss.

She didn't.

She laid beneath him, savouring every meeting and parting of their lips, every sweep of their tongues against each other, and the sound of Julian's heart beating strong and steady in her ears. She reached up and ran her fingers down his cheek, memorising the defined line of his jaw and the corded muscles of his neck. Her Julian.

His soft reverential kiss fanned the flames inside her, warming her through but not with hunger and need. The feeling went deeper than that. Beyond such base feelings and even happiness or love. It transcended them all, filling her with peace and a sense of forever. She didn't want this moment to end, and it felt as though it never would. Julian was hers now. He loved her as she loved him, and nothing would change that. Her heart belonged to him forever, and the one she could hear in her ears, beating hard now, was hers, and she would cherish it for all eternity.

Lauren sighed when his mouth left hers, trailing fire down her neck as he licked and nipped a path towards where he'd bitten her the day before, and stared up at the sky. The Milky Way twinkled at her, sparkling as she smiled. This didn't have to end. Tomorrow was just the beginning for them both.

Julian's hand skimmed down her side, coming to rest under her knee and raising it up. His leg nestled between hers and she moaned softly as his teeth sank into her throat. The connection ran as deep as ever, sedating her and making her smile widen.

She would never get enough of this. Intense warmth filled her and their emotions combined, entwining together and leaving her lost in them. She had never experienced something as profound as the feel of his fangs in her, something so incredibly deep and real that it touched her beyond words. Nothing could even come close. He drew slowly on her blood, reviving her hunger and her need for him, reigniting the passion that always burned within her heart for him.

A shooting star arced across the heavens.

She ran her fingers into Julian's hair and clung to him, holding him to her throat and wishing that they would have eternity together, like this.

The stars above blinked and glittered. The moonlight felt warm on her skin.

It was beautiful.

It was a night made for making love.

Love Immortal

A night made for them.
Tomorrow would be their night too.
Their victory.

CHAPTER 48

Julian broke away from Lauren as they neared the first checkpoint, leaving her with Duke, Kuga and Astra. He followed Morgan and his men, striding over the rocky terrain, his footing sure even though the only light in the world was the full moon.

"Morgan," he said and told himself that he could do this. For Lauren's sake, he could talk civilly to the vampire. Morgan turned and then stopped. His men continued.

"This is something I did not anticipate. I had thought my queen would be the one to bid me farewell with a kiss, not her knight." Morgan's sarcasm went ignored. Julian was here to say something important not get into a fight. His fight waited above them on the mountaintop.

Julian looked back at Lauren, sensing her more than seeing her. The distance between them was far enough that she wouldn't clearly hear him, not even on a night this still, but he would keep his voice low. He couldn't risk Lauren hearing him. It would only upset her and she was already frightened. He turned back to face Morgan.

"If I fall," Julian said.

"Then we all fall." There was none of Morgan's usual mockery in his voice. He was actually serious. Julian shook his head. Morgan nodded. "My queen will not fight without her knight."

"No. She will go on and finish this… she will have a knight still."

Morgan's left eyebrow rose.

"She created us both. It is our duty to protect her and you cannot turn your back on your blood. If I fall, you will protect her." Julian swallowed, his heart hurting at the thought of leaving this world and Lauren. He wasn't going to let it happen, but he had to be sure that Lauren wouldn't be alone on the battlefield if it should. He needed to know that she would be safe without him. "You protected her once, centuries ago, when you were only human. You must protect her again. You cannot let her fall."

Morgan placed a hand on Julian's shoulder. The gesture made Julian think of all the times he'd done something similar to his Arcadian soldiers. Reassurance. A gift of confidence and inspiration. It was something he'd never imagined that he would receive, especially from Morgan.

"We will not let her fall," Morgan said with a wide cocksure smile. "You have my word on that. I will see you both through this."

Julian wanted to ask why. This side of Morgan unsettled him and reminded him of when the vampire had been human. Last night, Lauren had mentioned that Morgan was acting differently. Was this what she'd meant?

"If you fall..." Morgan took a few steps backwards and then turned away. The moonlight glinted off the broadsword strapped to his back. "Who will clean my city for me?"

Julian smiled behind his collar. That was the Morgan he knew and preferred—the one with a price.

"Save some werewolves for me." Morgan held his hand up. "Tell our queen that I will likely need that drop of blood."

Morgan and himself both. This battle wasn't going to pass without bloodshed on both sides but he couldn't worry about that now. The others would take care of themselves. He had to take care of Lauren. He couldn't allow himself to be distracted, not this time, not when her fate hung in the balance.

He turned and started back down the slope towards Lauren. She was watching him, waiting with her hands clasped in front of her. Even at a distance, he could sense her worry. If he could take it all away, he would. He didn't want her to be out here on the battlefield, experiencing the horrors of it firsthand, but it was necessary. He could only protect her and stay close to her.

This was it—his final fight against Lycaon. By dawn, his duty would be over, regardless of the outcome.

If they defeated Lycaon or Lycaon defeated Lauren—either way it was the end.

If Lauren died, Julian would too.

He couldn't go on without her.

CHAPTER 49

Lauren tried to shake the tremble from her hands. It was only getting worse as she waited for Julian. Fear clutched her tightly, refusing to let go. It had whispered in her dreams, turning them into scenes of death that had seen her wake in a cold sweat. It whispered now in her heart, telling her that she would lose everyone in only a few short hours or less.

She looked up at the moon where it hung large and round in the clear inky sky, feeling the warmth of its light on her skin, but not even its presence soothed her tonight. Her gaze dropped to the peak of the mountain. It was still a long way above them, more than an hour's walk. She didn't like that they had split up so early into their journey. She had wanted to remain together for longer but the others were right, it was best to come at Lycaon from all angles at once. That way they had a better chance of surviving this battle.

A wolf howl made a thousand tiny needles prick her skin. Lauren tensed and stared at the mountain, knowing who had made that sound. Lycaon was waiting. She closed her fingers around the hilt of one of the two short katana strapped to her back. Instinct told her to run away, to grab Julian's hand the instant he returned and flee with him.

She looked at Kuga, seeing the determination in his eyes as he stared at the mountaintop. His strength radiated through her.

She couldn't run away.

The fate of the world depended on her now. It rested heavily upon her shoulders but she would bear it. She would defeat Lycaon because no other could. It was more than her duty.

It was her destiny.

A sense of calm washed over her, turning the air around her still and warming her skin.

Julian.

He strode towards her over the uneven dusty ground, purposeful and intent, full of the confidence and fearlessness that she'd admired since their first meeting. If her strength failed her, if she succumbed to her fear during the battle, she knew that Julian would be with her. He would protect her until she found her strength again and could go on. This wasn't just her fight. This was their fight.

All of them.

Not only her and Julian, but Astra and Duke too. It was Kuga's fight to avenge Piper and his brother's betrayal. It was even Morgan's fight to free himself. They all had a reason to be here and that reason would see them live through it.

She would defeat Lycaon. She wouldn't fail her friends as they fought beside her or the world as it waited, unaware that tonight could change everyone's fate.

Julian stroked her cheek. She took hold of both of his hands, clutching them a moment as she looked into his eyes. Most of all she couldn't fail Julian. She would defeat Lycaon for his sake. She would end his eternal suffering and his duty, and see to it that he was never alone again.

Lauren tiptoed, pulled down his collar and kissed him softly and slowly, letting all of her emotions bubble to the surface so he would be able to sense them. She didn't care that the others were only a few feet away. She had to let Julian know how much she loved him and that she was doing this for him.

When she pulled away, he was smiling. She smiled back at him, managing to hold it when it quivered with nerves, and straightened his tall funnel collar out so it hid the lower half of his face again. The moon cast silvery light on him, highlighting his dark hair and reflecting off the two silver bands across the collar of his long black coat.

Everyone was wearing black tonight. They all blended into the night. The only part of her visible under the strong moonlight was her bare hands and face where her long tight turtleneck ended. She adjusted the grips that held her hair back and then took a deep breath.

"Time to go," Duke said and started up the path towards the peak, Astra behind him. They would fight close together.

Her gaze strayed to Kuga. Who would fight with him? She didn't want him to be alone. She doubted that he could kill his own brother, but didn't doubt that Leo would kill him. Back at the villa, she'd left Julian talking to Duke and had gone to see Morgan. He'd promised that he would keep an eye on Kuga in exchange for another drop of blood. She would gladly pay that price for her friend's safety.

Lauren touched her neck. She'd given Julian so much more than that only an hour ago. Her blood made him stronger and she needed him strong tonight so they could have their eternity.

Kuga turned away and followed Duke.

They would meet up near the top when they had cleared the checkpoints that Julian, Duke and Morgan had planned. Lauren scanned the darkness along her and Julian's path. She could sense something in the distance.

"It is rude to make them wait," Julian said and took hold of her hand, leading her up the mountain.

As they drew closer to the checkpoint, Lauren could clearly sense the werewolves. Four of them. No. Six. Three each, although she suspected that it would be more like one for her and five for Julian. She was determined to kill at least one though.

She drew one of her swords, released Julian's hand, and drew the other. His remained sheathed. She didn't have his skill or grace. With her nerves eating away at her, she was likely to fumble with her swords if she went for a dramatic entrance as he would. Julian would wait until the first werewolf attacked before drawing his sword and striking it down in an instant.

Another howl pierced the night.

Another answered it.

Julian turned.

The hairs on Lauren's neck stood on end.

Lycaon.

Her senses sparked and she shifted, her eyes switching to silver and her fangs extending. Three more werewolves appeared out of the darkness, their massive bodies silhouetted in the moonlight. Lauren moved on instinct, cutting the down the first werewolf and then turning to block when she sensed more behind her.

Ambush.

She growled in frustration and pushed forwards, unbalancing the werewolf that had attacked her and slicing through its gut.

"Lauren," Julian called out to her and she backed towards him, defending as she went.

Her blade was a swift silver arc in the moonlight, cutting down another werewolf. More were coming, surrounding them, and Lauren's calm edge broke and her heart began to pound.

Lycaon had tracked them. Their plan was shattered. With the group so fragmented this low down the mountain, they didn't stand a chance. Lauren ducked under Julian's sword as he brought it around, decapitating another werewolf. She attacked with both of her blades, slashing the werewolves whenever they were within reach, and kept close to Julian. This wasn't good. Her pulse raced and she struggled to settle it. Her actions became choppy and desperate, as poor as they had been the night Lycaon had almost defeated her.

Lauren set her jaw and clenched her teeth. No. She was stronger than that now. Julian was with her and the werewolves were weak compared to those they had fought then. They could battle through this and reach Lycaon. He was coming for her. She could sense his approach. They just had to get rid of these werewolves.

Julian shifted again, his movements faster than hers, cutting down his enemies in quick succession. For each one he cut down, another two appeared out of the darkness to take its place. Lauren kept fighting, hacking away at them. They were defenceless against her swords without armour and it was easy to kill them but something said it wasn't going to remain that way. These werewolves were weak but numerous, probably sent by Lycaon to tire her and Julian out.

The smell of blood overwhelmed the scent of the night, swamping her senses.

She turned when she felt the air move behind her and stared up into the enormous yellow eyes of a werewolf. It was as big as the ones in Paris had been, its tufted dark fur silhouetted against the moon as it towered over her, making her feel tiny. It launched a paw at her, sharp black claws cutting through the night. She brought her sword up but it was too slow. She couldn't move fast enough this time. Her senses screamed at her to get away. It was going to rip her apart. It wasn't a pup like the others.

Lycaon was close.

His commanders had come.

Lauren bent over backwards to avoid the paw but the werewolf was already attacking with its other. She couldn't dodge it as it came straight down, aimed for her stomach. Immortal as she was, she couldn't fight with such a wound. She started to twist away, hoping to take the hit on her hip instead.

A loud bang split the night. Her eyes widened as she continued to turn, staring up at the werewolf as a bright red flash exploded from its chest. It disintegrated and the charred remains rained to the ground as dust.

Someone grabbed her and then the world disappeared. Darkness enshrouded her for a split second, a cold breeze caressing her skin and a feeling of ice in heart, and then the world came back and she was standing in front of Julian.

"Close one," Duke whispered into her ear, a hint of amusement in his voice. "Take more care. I wouldn't want to lose you too."

Lauren breathed hard, disorientated and trying to figure out what had happened. Duke must have saved her. The red flash and bang had been his gun. The momentary darkness had been him moving her. It had been so black and cold. There had been pain there, not physical but something deeper. Despair.

She shook the feeling away and realised with some relief that she and Julian weren't alone anymore. Kuga, Astra and Duke surrounded her, forming a circle with Julian that no werewolf could penetrate. They cut down any that came too close, a startling cacophony of flashes, bangs and the sing of metal.

Her heart levelled and she quickly assessed the situation, trying to figure out what was happening and honing her senses so she could fight with the skill she had when practicing. Lycaon was drawing closer. These werewolves weren't the lower ranks. Those lay scattered across the mountain, staining the earth with their blood. These were faster, stronger, and wore black armour that made them difficult to kill. But they would fall. No one would stand between her and Lycaon.

With a deep breath, she readied her swords, turning slowly in a circle. Which way was he coming from? The quicker she found him, the quicker this battle would be over.

Her blood chilled and she stopped. He wasn't coming down the mountain. He was coming up.

"I feel him," she said and pointed when Julian glanced at her.

He nodded. She didn't want him to go with her. Lycaon couldn't hurt him but the young man that had been with Lycaon last time could. It was Julian's plan to fight the young man while she took on Lycaon. They had to defeat him before they could cut Lycaon. If she cut Lycaon before then, he would realise that Selene had lifted her blessing and the young man would come to his aid. They would escape again.

Lauren came up beside Kuga, helping him as he blasted the werewolves. He was holding back and she knew why. He was waiting for Leo, saving his power for his fight against his brother. She scanned the darkness as she fought, cutting through the horde of werewolves blocking her path to Lycaon. They all shifted whenever she killed one, moving to keep the wall between her and Lycaon steady. The path behind them, up the mountain, cleared.

Kuga stopped and turned. Lauren blocked the swipe a werewolf made at the back of his head, chopping its arm off with one sword, and then decapitated it with her other.

"What's wrong?" she shouted over the growls of the werewolves and the clash of battle.

"Leo." Kuga's eyes narrowed. Lauren looked up the mountain. He was right. Leo was standing at least one hundred metres up, toying with a ball of electricity. Before she could catch Kuga's arm to stop him and tell him to wait for someone to go with him, he was running towards his brother.

Lauren hastily slashed the thighs of the werewolf coming towards her to incapacitate it and then chased after Kuga. She wouldn't let him face such a terrible task alone. Lycaon would have to wait. She only hoped that Julian would wait for her too. She didn't want him to fight alone either.

"Son of a bitch!" Kuga. A white-blue light blazed through the night, blinding Lauren. It hit something and shot off to one side, crackling as it disappeared.

She skidded to a halt on the rocky screed of the mountain a short distance from Kuga. Both of his hands were glowing, swirling orbs of pale blue electricity suspended above his palms. They lit him with eerie coldness, making his face a mask of pure hatred. It wasn't the emotion she could sense in him. His feelings were in disarray, his heart thundering as he faced down his brother.

Leo stood a few metres up the mountain from him. He hurled a globe of electricity at Kuga. Lauren flinched away, afraid that it would hit her. Kuga held his hands up and the bolt shot upwards. He'd deflected it.

"Why?" Kuga's voice was tight and strained, full of the growing pain that she could sense in him. He frowned and hurled two twisting spikes of power at his brother. Leo dodged them both. When they struck the ground, it shook.

"Power," Leo said casually and Lauren gasped at the same time as Kuga. She couldn't believe that Leo would turn his back on his brother and kill Piper for that reason alone. She knew that he didn't like the fact that Kuga was stronger than him, and was chosen for missions over him, but that wasn't reason enough to do what he had done. Leo pointed at her. Kuga didn't turn away from him. "They have a pathetic track record. She dies every time, little bro! Only Julian lives to tell his whiny tale."

Lauren's grip on her two katana tightened. How dare he insult her and Julian? Kuga held his arm out, blocking her path. She backed down. Kuga was right. This wasn't her fight. She couldn't rush in and take over. Kuga had to do this, or at least try to.

Gunshots rang out below them. Lauren didn't take her eyes away from Leo. She could sense everyone and, so far, no one had more than a scratch. It was difficult to remain here with Kuga when her heart said to go to Julian, but she wouldn't leave him, not unless something happened to one of the others or Julian.

Werewolves were closing in behind them, approaching cautiously as though they could sense the power in Kuga and Leo and knew it was dangerous for them to come close. Lauren readied her swords. She couldn't get in the way of Kuga's fight unless he was going to fail, but she could buy him time by taking care of the werewolves for him.

One of them appeared out of the gloom, teeth flashing bright white and yellow eyes reflecting the moonlight. She cut it down and then attacked the next, trying to keep an eye on Kuga and Leo at the same time.

"I had a choice." Leo raised his hands and they glowed white, the electricity encircling his fingers and sparking. It began to twist around like lightning, moving more rapidly, and Lauren could sense the rise in his power. "I chose the winning side."

"You're wrong!" Kuga stepped forwards. Bright blue threads of electricity danced around his hands, violently twisting and distorting as it crept up his arms. Lauren stepped back and quickly decapitated the werewolf that seized the chance to lunge at her. Instinct told her to run. Kuga was verging on losing control and she didn't want to be around if that happened. She didn't think that she could survive a direct hit by the amount of voltage Kuga could command. His fingers closed into fists. "You're going to lose."

Lauren leapt backwards when he launched forwards, attacking his brother at close quarters. The light was too bright and the noise to loud. All of it hurt, shocking her senses and numbing them, making it difficult for her to detect the werewolves and the others on her side. She tried to remain close but Kuga and Leo's fight was too fierce.

She moved further down the mountain, still fighting the werewolves to keep them away from Kuga. Rogue bolts of electricity shot out in all directions and the smell of Kuga and Leo's blood filled the air. The sky above them clouded and lightning slammed into the ground, hitting the rocks and some of the werewolves that were coming after her. She tried to get closer, wanting to help Kuga, but she couldn't get past the lightning.

Wherever she went, it followed, chasing her back as though neither brother wanted her to interfere in the fight. She backed off, unwilling to go too far in case he needed her, but needing to keep away from the tempest they had created so she stood a better chance of survival and her senses cleared.

She frowned when she had to take her eyes off the fight to defend herself against two werewolves. The first launched a paw at her head and the other shifted to attack her from behind. She ducked and rolled to avoid the paw, and then turned as she stood to face the other werewolf. It snarled, exposing huge canines that made her heart miss a beat, and attacked. Lauren leapt backwards, narrowly avoiding being hit by a bolt of lightning, and then launched forwards when the werewolf's paw had swung past her. She brought both of her swords around and chopped its arm off and then turned, kicked it in the chest, and quickly brought her swords over her head in a cross to block the werewolf behind her.

It attacked again and she jumped high into the air, flipping over to land behind the werewolf. She lunged forwards and rammed her two swords through its back and straight out of its chest. The scraping of metal against bone when she pulled them free turned her stomach. She breathed hard, struggling to keep calm and keep her senses focused on so many things at once. The werewolf fell to the ground in front of her. When it did, her eyes widened. The other werewolf came out of nowhere, hidden by the body of its comrade. It clawed her arm and she cried out and then slashed at it with her other sword. It yelped as she caught it across the chest. Lauren didn't hesitate. She gritted her teeth against the pain and attacked with both swords, cutting it deeper across the chest and then across the gut. The werewolf fell on top of the other one, convulsing and whimpering.

A howl echoed up the mountain.

Lauren tensed and listened to it, feeling the call in her blood.

Lycaon was growing impatient. He was waiting for her. Something deep inside said to go to him but she refused.

She turned back to the brothers in time to see Leo shove Kuga. He stumbled but regained his footing and then threw himself at Leo, a look of sheer determination on his face. The fight was messy, all kicks and punches, a battle of brute strength. She could sense they were both tired, drained by their power, and it seemed neither of them had the energy left to attack with it. She moved closer, unafraid now.

The werewolves remained down the mountain. She glanced at the group, singling out Duke as he blasted werewolves into oblivion, Astra at his back, and then Julian. He was moving gracefully through the werewolves, so quick that she could only see a silver flash as his sword connected with them and they fell. They were keeping them back, away from her and Kuga. Satisfied that they were in control of the situation, she looked back at Kuga and Leo. Her heart pounded at the thought that Kuga might actually win. She wasn't sure how he would be able to live with himself if he killed his brother, but she knew he had to do this, and she couldn't stand in his way. He needed his vengeance as much as she needed hers.

The smell of their blood and the thundering of their hearts filled Lauren's senses as she moved closer. Her fangs itched.

Kuga landed a solid punch on his brother's jaw and then grabbed both sides of his head.

Lauren's breath hitched in her throat. This was it. He wouldn't get another opening like it. Kuga froze, his eyes locked with his brother's, and Lauren's heart fell. He couldn't do it. The pain in his eyes and the spike in his feelings told her that clearly. It hurt him too much to kill his own brother. Leo's hands came up and clamped around Kuga's wrists. He jerked and released Leo, falling backwards.

Damn Leo. If Kuga couldn't do it, then she would. She would make sure he paid for what he'd done to Piper. Lauren ran at him, her swords raised, determined to finish him for Kuga. A flash of light blinded her and she raised her arm to shield her eyes. When her vision came back, Astra stood between Kuga and Leo, her hand around Leo's throat, holding him off the ground. Kuga stared up at her, looking as shocked as Lauren felt.

"Allow me," Astra said and then turned to face Leo. "Goodnight, sweet prince."

With that, she kissed him.

"No!" Kuga shouted and reached for them, sheer agony flashing across his face.

Leo's eyes widened and then rolled back. He slumped to the floor. No heartbeat.

Kuga screamed, clutched his head and fell to his knees. He tilted his head back to face the heavens and his scream became a roar of pain.

Lauren narrowly avoided the massive bright shockwave of electricity he released in all directions. She leapt high into the air, her heart in her throat and her hands over her ears to protect them from the loud terrifying tearing sound. She choked on the dust thrown up by the wave. Astra disappeared before it hit her. Lauren landed and tried to see the others but it was difficult through the hazy cloud of dust.

She stared hard down the mountain, needing to see that Julian and Duke were safe. The dust began to settle where she was and she saw the white wave shoot through the group of werewolves below her, almost hitting Duke and Julian in the process. Duke had barely reached Julian and disappeared with him when it struck where they were. Some of the werewolves leapt to avoid it. The others exploded, showering the world in blood and flesh. The shockwave ripped through the olive groves beyond the battle and disappeared.

Lycaon howled.

Lauren tried to get Julian's attention but he was deep in battle again, fighting the masses of werewolves that had managed to survive the shockwave.

A mighty roar filled her ears and a group of werewolves to her right went flying. Julian dodged them as they landed, a scowl on his face. Morgan appeared through the fray, grinning as he butchered the werewolves in his path, hacking at them with his broadsword. His men followed him. They broke away as they reached the main group of werewolves and Lauren couldn't watch as they fought. They were as rough and brutal as the werewolves, using sheer strength combined with claw and fang to fight.

Julian paused.

Lauren knew what he'd felt.

Lycaon was here and so was his right hand man.

Julian moved his blade into an attack position and leapt. Lauren ran down the mountain towards the others. She had to follow, but she couldn't leave Kuga to fight alone, not now that he was so close to losing control.

"Morgan!"

He turned to face her, his hand still closed around the throat of a werewolf, throttling it.

Lauren flung one of her swords around and pointed up the mountain. Bright flashes punctuated the darkness and wolf cries filled the night. Kuga had found something to take his anger and pain out on and the noises the werewolves were making were horrifying. She didn't even want to imagine what Kuga was doing to them.

"Take some of your men and keep that promise!" She turned and blocked a werewolf as it struck at her from behind. The force of the blow sent her skidding backwards towards Morgan. He caught her, his hands strong against her hips.

"Yes, my queen," he whispered against her neck and was gone.

She fell backwards and thrust her swords forwards, piercing her enemy through the chest. It slumped towards her, heavy on her katana, and she rolled so it fell to the ground. It barely took a moment for it to disappear, leaving only a wisp of fur behind. Lauren realised that the older they were, the faster they turned to dust.

Gunshots echoed over the mountain and the sound of lightning tearing the earth asunder drowned out the rapid beat of her heart. She pushed her worry to the back of her mind. Morgan could handle Kuga. Duke and Astra could handle the werewolves. It was exactly as they had planned now. Except one thing.

She looked down the mountain and focused. The metallic ring of swords clashing gave her a direction. She ran, ducking and dodging through the battle between her and her destination.

Between her and her destiny.

Lauren pushed herself harder when she saw that Julian was fighting both Lycaon and the young man. He couldn't defend himself against two attackers. Lycaon would prove a distraction and would leave Julian vulnerable to the young man's attacks. Turning her swords around in her hands so her blades extended behind her, she readied herself for the fight.

This was it.

This was her moment.

CHAPTER 50

Lauren ran hard down the mountain, her breathing as steady as her hands and her focus on the fight in front of her. She could see Lycaon and the young blond man both attacking Julian together. They were in human form, just as they had been in Paris, and she could sense their power now that she was getting closer to them. The young man was almost as strong as Lycaon, and Lauren knew that it wouldn't be an easy fight for Julian. Her senses locked on him and she focused on his feelings. He was tired, hurt in places, but her blood was still lending him strength. It would be a while before it wore off and she hoped it would give him enough time to defeat the young man. She was relying on him, and she believed in him. Together they would end this.

Lycaon swung his sword towards Julian's side as he blocked the young man. Lauren sprinted between them and stopped his sword with her own, her back against Julian's. The feel of him there gave her the strength to fight, to face her fears and Lycaon. Julian's hand briefly touched her other one. It was his silent way of telling her that they could do this and they would have their happily forever after.

She growled with effort and pushed Lycaon backwards, forcing him away from Julian. Julian moved off, leading the younger werewolf down the mountain. Lycaon's dark eyes brightened to yellow, narrowing on her, and his lips compressed into a thin line of fury.

"Leave him out of this." Lauren sneered and lashed out at Lycaon, forcing him to move further away from Julian. They would need space to fight if they were to keep things one on one with their opponent. "It's me you want."

Lycaon stood tall and smiled at her, his sword held out in front of him. The moonlight caught his eyes and they flashed gold. The look of victory in them made her want to growl in frustration and chop his head off. He was so confident that he would win, and she was going to use that against him. He came at her, almost faster than she could see, but she was ready this time. She blocked his attacks, covering all angles and not giving him an opening. It was difficult to stop herself from attacking him with all her strength and skill when all she wanted was revenge for her parents and Piper. She couldn't let her blade strike him though, not yet, not until Julian had disposed of Lycaon's guard and she was ready to deal the final blow.

Strands of Lycaon's long wavy dark hair fell out of his ponytail, dancing around with each quick attack that he made as he moved from one side of her to the other, leading her in a tight circle. Her own hair began to fall out of the grips, getting in her eyes. She fought on, not daring to brush it away in case it gave Lycaon the chance he was searching for. He looked different tonight, more vicious and dark than he had in Paris, and there was only malice in his eyes. He wanted her dead. She could feel his intent in every inch of her. He wanted to make her suffer and then watch her die. This man was no father to her. He was her enemy, and this would be her victory.

The tail of his long coat flared out as he turned away from her and distanced himself again. He stood a few metres away, breathing so deep that the material of his black coat stretched tight across his torso, emphasising the breadth of his chest and the difference in their strength. She could feel it in each thrust of his sword. He was so much stronger than her, but she wasn't going to give up.

She reached out with her senses, quickly checking the others as she circled with Lycaon, her eyes never leaving his. Morgan and Kuga were fighting together and she was glad to feel Kuga was more in control now, his focus on disposing of the remaining werewolves. Morgan was bleeding, but it wasn't slowing him down. He was fast and furious, violence beating inside him like a heart.

She could feel Duke. The world felt cold where he was, drained of life, and he had forsaken his guns in favour of his true power. Astra was fighting hard beside him, using Duke's guns to pick off the werewolves.

The werewolf numbers were dwindling. Her side were winning but she couldn't get complacent. She had to keep a level head and keep fighting because it wasn't over until Lycaon and the young werewolf had fallen. If she became complacent, Lycaon could easily kill her or the young man could kill Julian. She had to give it her all to make sure that didn't happen.

Lycaon rushed her and she blocked him and then leapt high in the air, flipping over at her peak and bringing her sword down hard. He blocked her just as she'd anticipated and flung her backwards, sending her tumbling along the ground. She kept a tight grip on her swords so she didn't lose them, and breathed heavily when she came to a halt. Her side was sore from the dirt and stones, but she had to keep up the pretence that she couldn't defeat Lycaon. She couldn't end it yet.

Lauren pushed herself up onto her feet and ran at Lycaon. He swung his long sword at her and she ducked to avoid it and then attacked. She pressed on, blocking and attacking in turn, ducking and dodging whenever Lycaon got too close.

The fight was fierce and fast but this time she could keep up. Julian had given it his all in their last few training sessions and she was glad of it. Lycaon really had been going easy on her the night they had fought on the rooftop and in her heart she knew that it wasn't because Illia had been his daughter. Julian was right. It was because Lycaon enjoyed toying with Illia's reincarnations. He taunted them and then, when he was invulnerable, he killed them. Not this time. This time the blood staining the battlefield would be his. Illia's duty to Zeus ended tonight.

The sound of their swords clashing rang through the night, a symphony that she fought to, her heart and hands steady. She didn't take her eyes off him, instead using her senses to tell her where Julian was and whether she was still one on one with Lycaon. The werewolves were keeping their distance, staying with her side and fighting them. Had Lycaon ordered them to keep back? Julian had told her that Lycaon was only interested in fighting her. Perhaps he wanted her to himself. That made two of them. She wanted this battle to be only between them, between her and her so-called father.

Lycaon smiled at her, a hint of amusement shining in his eyes. "I see you have improved."

Did it satisfy him that she was more worthy to fight and kill now? Did it add to the pleasure he was so evidently getting from fighting her? She held his gaze, her eyes narrowed and silver. Perhaps she was doing too well. She didn't want him to suspect anything. If he did, he might leave or might fight harder. She didn't think she could defeat him if he fought with all of his skill. She could sense that he was still holding back a fraction, convinced that he didn't need to bother using all of his strength on her.

When he swung at her, his long sword gleaming in the moonlight, she dropped her guard a little on her left side, enough for him to nick her shoulder with the tip of his blade. It stung but didn't stop her from fighting. His smile became a grin.

Good. He had to think that he was winning and that he was still invulnerable.

A cry off to her right made her heart jump. Julian. She couldn't look, couldn't take her eyes off Lycaon even if she wanted to. He would kill her if she did. He laughed.

"Shall I have my man butcher your precious commander? He is in the way. I have enjoyed our games, but it is time to remove you both permanently." His grin unnerved her. There was so much malice in it and amusement, a combination of dark and evil things that made her fear for Julian's safety. He was up to something. He raised his hand and made a shape in the air. An order?

Lauren attacked him but he blocked and forced her backwards. She skidded to a halt and brought her swords around to defend herself. Lycaon didn't attack. She breathed hard and cursed him. If he didn't attack her, she couldn't attack him. She couldn't risk cutting him.

The moonlight bathed his face in white, highlighting the silvery scars that ran through the dark stubble coating his jaw and casting dark shadows around his eyes that made him look truly evil when his irises reflected.

She told herself that he didn't look like her. He wasn't her father. Her real father was dead because of this maniac in front of her. A grin widened Lycaon's lips and his yellow eyes narrowed as he lifted his head to look down at her, a spark of amusement twinkling in them. He was enjoying their fight. Lauren frowned and readied her swords, bringing them around in front of her. It didn't matter that he was bigger than her, or stronger, or even better with a sword. She was going to win.

"We have been waiting so long for this moment. You do not know how often he begged me to let him fight against you both again. I have heard nothing but it for millennia, but we had to be sure that things would go our way, that our plan was finally coming to fruition, and that he was strong enough. Our meeting in Paris determined that." Lycaon backed away and brought his sword out to point at her. "Watch, dear daughter, as the man who killed your precious Arcadian all those centuries ago takes his life again."

Lauren's eyes widened. The attack in Paris had been nothing but a test to see if the young man was strong enough. He was. He had cut Julian without him even noticing. She couldn't stop herself from turning to face Julian. He didn't know. He didn't realise that the man he was fighting was as old as himself, older in fact, and what danger he was in. The man must have been the first one that Lycaon had turned into a werewolf. He would be as powerful as Lycaon.

Her heart clenched and she reached out to Julian with it, hoping he would sense her.

He blocked the young man's attack and then looked at her. The man struck at him with his katana but Julian was gone, leaping high in the air and turning heels over head. He landed gracefully just metres from Lauren.

"He's Lycaon's first. He killed you!" she said and bit her tongue before she begged him to drop back, just as Illia had done the night he had died. She couldn't do that to Julian, not even when she was afraid that Lycaon's plan would succeed and the young man would kill him. She had to stand back and let Julian do this. He needed to have his vengeance too.

Julian's eyes flashed silver and narrowed into a murderous look as he turned to face the young man hurtling up the hill towards him.

The young man grinned at him, revealing sharp teeth, and his eyes shone gold in the moonlight. Blood streaked his face, dark in his cropped blond hair and down his long military coat. Looking at him now, Lauren could see why Julian would have underestimated him three thousand years ago. He was slighter than Julian and very young in the face, his build of a teenager rather than a man.

He moved his katana, holding it out at his side, and his speed increased. He sneered at them. Julian attacked first, his cry long and loud as he struck swift and sure with his katana, forcing the man backwards. Julian's attacks were fiercer than ever, his moves fluid and fast. He easily evaded the attacks of the young man, keeping him on the back foot. She had never seen Julian like this. He was overpowering the young man and Lauren knew in her heart that he would be the victor. Lycaon had underestimated Julian's strength. That night in Paris, she had distracted Julian. He had been worried about her. Now he was giving it his all, and he would win.

Lycaon growled and she sensed him move.

Lauren turned to face him but couldn't dodge his heavy blade. It punctured her left shoulder, sending a shockwave of searing white-hot pain burning

Love Immortal

through her. She cried out, tears falling as she squeezed her eyes shut. He rammed the point of the blade deeper and then twisted, forcing her to her knees. Wave after wave of nauseating pain crashed over her, threatening to steal her consciousness. She looked up at Lycaon and her vision blurred. The satisfied grin on his face gave her the strength to continue. She wanted to wipe it off. She wanted to see the fear in his eyes when he realised that she was going to kill him. She wanted revenge for what he had done.

It was now or never. If she didn't attack now, Lycaon would kill her. Julian was fighting so hard that it was only a matter of time before his blade struck true and the young man died. She would see to it that Lycaon shared his fate at the same time. She wasn't going to let him defeat her.

Excruciating pain blasted through every inch of her when she tried to move her left arm. Lycaon's blade must have severed the tendons and broken bones. The sword fell from her limp hand. Lycaon pulled his blade out of her shoulder and she slumped forwards. Weak. She was being weak again when she needed to be strong. Her arm would heal. If she won the battle, she could sleep for a week just as she wanted to. If she didn't do something now, she would be sleeping forever.

With a cry of anger, Lauren lashed out with the sword in her right hand. It cut across Lycaon's legs. He froze and stared wide-eyed at her and then the moon. The night breeze blew the long strands of his black hair from his face. The bright moonlight made his skin white and his eyes dark. He raised a hand towards the moon.

Not willing to lose this chance as Kuga had lost his, Lauren forced all the pain to the back of her mind and launched herself upwards. She still wasn't fast enough. Lycaon shifted backwards as she thrust her sword forwards. The point of it struck his left shoulder and she screamed as she drove forwards, plunging it deep. If she couldn't kill him, she could at least even the odds.

Lycaon roared and swung at her, his blade a brilliant flash of silver. She rolled away, hitting the ground hard and coming to her feet a short distance from him, her sword still tightly clutched in her right hand. The warm feel of blood sliding down her arm made her nauseas and she swallowed against the pain, trying to retain her focus. She couldn't give in now.

"You think you can defeat me?" Lycaon brought his sword down in a swift arc at his side, ridding it of blood, and stalked towards her.

Lauren moved backwards, clutching her shoulder and trying to force the fog from her mind. It was growing hard to concentrate and she was getting weaker by the second. She shifted her focus to Julian for a moment, long enough to sense that he was still winning, and then back to Lycaon.

"I never lose to you," Lycaon said and continued towards her.

She shuffled back again and brought her sword around. Her hand shook and she couldn't get it steady again. Cold crept outwards through her body from the hot point on her shoulder. She shuddered, took a deep breath and blinked, finding it hard to focus now. She had to keep going.

"I will shake Olympus for what it has done to me." A grin tugged at the corners of his lips and his yellow eyes narrowed on her. "I will butcher Zeus and will slaughter Selene for daring to curse me like this!"

Lauren brought her sword up the moment he attacked and blocked him. She pushed against his sword, forcing it away from her, and attacked. Lycaon moved around her, his coat swirling in the warm night air. She couldn't keep up now. She gritted her teeth and her fangs extended, the world brightening as her eyes changed once again. She would use all of her strength, give her life if it meant that Lycaon was defeated and the world was safe.

She blocked each of Lycaon's attacks, growing wearier, and then her eyes widened when she caught sight of Julian. The young man lay at his feet, decapitated. It was now or never.

She glared at Lycaon, mustering the last of her strength, and told herself that she could do this. She could defeat Lycaon and be with Julian. She could end this nightmare and live her dream.

Lycaon rushed her but she was ready. She ducked to one side and came around behind him, slashing her sword down his back. He cried out and then turned on her. She didn't give him a chance, she moved as fast as she could, reaching him before he could even swing at her, and thrust her blade deep into his side. He growled and elbowed her in the face, knocking her away and sending her mind spinning. She hit the dirt and her heart leapt when the world came back into focus and Lycaon's sword was coming straight at her. She rolled but he caught her left arm again, slicing through it. The pain burned up her arm, numbing her.

Lauren pushed herself to her feet and attacked again, unwilling to give in now that she was so close. The smell of Lycaon's blood drenched the air around her, the scent driving her on as something deep inside her called for her to surrender to her desire for violence and bloodshed. She harnessed that desire, using it to drive her on and give her strength. When she had stopped fighting her instincts back in Paris, she had been faster and better with her sword. She needed that now.

She thrust her sword at him again, forcing him back, and then blocked the swing he took at her. Bright sparks showered down from their swords as they clashed and she leapt backwards, giving herself some room to regroup. Lycaon didn't give her time. He came at her and she struggled to defend herself against his attack. He was fast and relentless. Lauren watched for an opening, just as Julian had taught her to, and she smiled when she saw it.

With a long cry, she brought her sword up from below just as Lycaon brought his down from above again. He was slower then. Her smile became a grin when Lycaon tried to change his attack but it was too late. Her blade cut into his ribs below his right arm and she threw all of her weight into it, using it to propel her sword upwards until it hit his heart.

The world fell silent.

Love Immortal

Lauren stared into Lycaon's eyes. Victory no longer shone in them. There was only defeat.

Her hand slipped from her sword, leaving it buried deep in his chest. He took one last look at the moon and then fell, disintegrating into ashes before he could touch the ground. They scattered on the breeze, catching in the moonlight.

Lauren felt strangely light inside.

She stared at the spot Lycaon had been, clinging to consciousness.

It was over.

She had won.

Her head spun. She looked around at the dimming world, searching for Julian. Her senses were in disarray and the fire pulsing through her made it impossible to focus them. She couldn't feel him, or hear anything other than the ringing in her ears. Her body felt numb but she could sense the moonlight on her skin, warm and comforting. Selene. She was so tired. It felt as though Selene was calling her home to where she could sleep.

Julian wavered into view like a mirage, bloodied and beaten, his collar obscuring his face. She reached out a hand to him. She didn't want to go home without him.

Her knees gave out but she didn't feel the impact with the ground.

Her head throbbed with deep black waves that pulled her under, so strong that she couldn't fight them.

She drowned in the darkness.

CHAPTER 51

The world was too bright.

Lauren moaned and rolled over, curling up into a ball and burying her head in her arms. Her left one throbbed and protested, the spark of pain pushing awareness through her mind. The battle came flooding back, every second replayed before her closed eyes, from the moment they had left the villa to when Lycaon had stabbed her and she'd defeated him.

Gentle hands took hold of her arm, pushing her onto her back.

"You will hurt yourself."

Those whispered words made her heart sing and the tender tone in which they were spoken sent calm washing through her. She focused on him, feeling the sense of safety that he always gave her.

"Julian," she croaked. Her throat was parched and sore. She frowned and tried to open her eyes but the light made them water. She covered them with her right hand.

There was a click.

"You can come out now," Julian said.

Lauren peeked through her fingers. It was darker but the world was fuzzy and she couldn't make sense of it. Had he turned off the sun? Was she still outside? Something was covering her and the ground was soft. Light fingers caressed her brow and slowly moved her hand aside. She blinked several times, trying to clear her vision, and stared up at Julian. He gradually came into focus. He was standing over her, his hair mussed and his coat nowhere to be seen.

"It is good to have you back." He smiled.

There was so much emotion in his voice but it held nowhere near the amount that showed in his ice blue eyes. They fixed on her, intent and focused, full of love and fear, happiness and relief. She placed her hand over his where it rested against her temple and closed her eyes as she leaned into it. It felt so good against her. Comforting. Warm.

"I've worried you again," she whispered against his hand.

"I am growing used to it," he said and sat down beside her.

She rolled slightly to her right towards him. A mattress. She looked around. She was in a large low-lit barely furnished white room and it wasn't the villa.

"Where are we?" She tried to sit up but Julian stopped her, his hand firm against her good shoulder. She looked at her other one. Someone had strapped it up and she hoped it had been Julian because she was naked. The bandages wound around her chest and down her left arm. "How long was I out?"

"We are at a Ghost office in Athens."

"Athens?" Her gaze darted back to Julian. The table lamp illuminated his face. "When did we move here?"

"Three days after we defeated Lycaon and his army." Julian's fingers grazed her cheek and he smiled again. "Which would be make it four days ago now."

"I slept for a week?" Her eyes widened. She'd wanted to sleep for a week after Lycaon had stabbed her but she hadn't actually thought that she would.

He nodded. "We moved you here when you were stable and were healing."

Lauren looked him over. The cuts she remembered seeing on him during the battle were gone. He must have healed without her help. She'd been unconscious for seven days. She couldn't imagine what had happened in all that time.

She shot up into a sitting position and pain bolted down her left side. She clutched her arm and gritted her teeth.

"The others," she said from between her clenched teeth.

Julian pushed her back onto the bed and gave her a reprimanding look. "All well. Only minor injuries."

"Duke... Astra?" Each name was met with a nod. It was a relief to hear that her friends had survived. Almost all of them anyway. Leo had been her friend once, as had Piper. "Is Kuga alright?"

"Physically, yes. Emotionally? I am not so sure. I believe he needs to speak to someone, a friend." Julian paused and held her gaze, his beautiful pale blue irises reflecting his concern for Kuga and for her. "He has been asking about you."

"Can I go to him soon?" She wanted to go to him now but something told her that Julian was going to be a strict nurse and not let her out of bed until she'd fully healed. Her arm still ached but she could move her fingers. She only hurt when she moved too fast. Perhaps she could ask him to bring Kuga to her. She was well enough to see her friends and she could wrap up in a bathrobe.

"They are all waiting to see you." A frown darkened his eyes. "Even Morgan."

While Lauren didn't relish the thought of seeing him when she was in such a state of undress, she was glad that he'd survived.

"Did we lose many?"

Julian shook his head.

"I want to see everyone... but not here, not like some weak invalid. I'm strong... you said it yourself... and with you around I'm sure I'll be fine. Can we go and see them?" She took his hand, toying with his fingers as she waited for his answer. He looked as though he was going to say no and then nodded.

Lauren didn't stop him when he helped her from the bed and fussed over her. She could stand by herself and her arm didn't really hurt much, but having Julian mollycoddle her was too good to pass up. He helped her into her jeans and a loose white shirt, fastening them for her, and smoothed her hair. When he was done, she reached up and caught him around the back of his neck, bringing him down for a long slow kiss as a reward for being so sweet.

It had been a long time since someone had worried so much about her and had taken care of her. The last man to do anything like it was her father, and it had been scraped knees that needed nothing more than a sticking plaster. Julian was dealing with an injury a hundred times worse and it showed in the way he treated her as though she was fragile.

Even when he kissed her.

His grip on her sides was light, as soft as his lips as they danced against hers in a barely-there caress that made her heart float and made her smile.

He broke the kiss and gathered her into his arms, holding her gently. His heart beat steadily against her ear but she could sense the turbulent emotions running through him.

"I really did worry you this time, didn't I?" It was wrong of her to like the idea that she had, that he'd been worried about her and had watched over her for the past seven days.

"More than you could ever know." Julian pressed a kiss to her hair and her smile broadened. "It felt as though my world was coming to an end."

God. The man knew how to melt a heart. Lauren pulled back and saw the truth in his eyes. He'd been more than worried. He'd been afraid that he was losing her. Any sense of satisfaction she'd gained slipped away, leaving her feeling terrible for making him worry so much.

"I'm here now. Whole again." She squeezed his waist. Her arm hurt and she grimaced. "Almost."

A smile tugged at the corners of his mouth and he tucked her hair behind her ear, his blue eyes holding hers. "Watch what you say or I will send you back to bed."

"Will you come too?"

He looked thoughtfully at the ceiling and then down at her. He nodded.

It was tempting. She was sure that he would come to bed with her regardless though, and that he wasn't going to let her out of her room for long. She had to see the others while she could and see that they really were all right.

Julian took hold of her hand and led her through the building at a slow pace. It reminded her of the villa only it was far larger. She couldn't imagine there being arguments about the sleeping allocations here. There seemed to be plenty of room for them and all of the vampires. They passed so many bedrooms that she lost count, spread over two floors. She took everything in as they walked through the white corridors. The warm Mediterranean air relaxed her, filling her with a strange sense of peace as she thought about the fact that it was over now. She had defeated Lycaon.

On the top floor, the terracotta tiles were still warm under her bare feet.

They found Duke and Astra on a wide rooftop terrace. Duke was laying on a recliner under a vine-covered veranda, his white shirt half open and his left arm in a sling. Astra sat beside him, fussing over Duke's leg for some reason. She stopped when Lauren stepped out onto the rooftop and turned to face them. Instead of the usual coldness that Lauren had expected, Astra smiled. Lauren frowned when she saw that Duke's right leg was in a cast. Duke patted Astra's hand.

"She won't quit fretting over me." Duke grinned. Astra glared at him and took her hand away.

"I thought you were immortal?" Lauren said. She'd expected him to be able to heal like her.

Astra's gaze dropped to the floor.

Duke sighed and leaned back into the recliner. "It seems my goddess didn't keep her promise."

He sat up again and reached over with his good hand, settling it against Astra's cheek. Astra didn't resist as he brought her head around to face him. He smiled at her but she didn't smile back. Her expression was pure guilt.

"Astra didn't want to risk me." Duke looked at Lauren. He didn't seem angry. In fact, he seemed happy. "Instead of permanently taking my soul, she took responsibility to protect me during the battle so I would believe that I was immortal. Unfortunately, things didn't go to plan and I was a little cockier than I should have been. Now I'm like this for another five to seven weeks."

He shrugged. He didn't seem bothered by the fact that he wasn't immortal. Lauren remembered that he was already several hundred years old and had survived the battle, his reason for giving his soul to Astra in the first place. Immortality probably didn't matter that much to him anymore.

"Astra was completely unscathed of course." Duke grinned at her when Astra looked down at her knees again. It was strange to see the demon so uncomfortable and shy. Lauren wondered just what had happened while she was sleeping.

"Only because you were a fool, as usual," Astra said almost under her breath.

The tension between Astra and Duke was palpable, warning Lauren that it was best not to probe any further. At least not in their direction. She looked at Julian.

"Duke has a tendency to protect Astra," he said in a matter of fact tone and looked at them both.

"But she's immortal." Lauren frowned at Duke.

"Well, in my defence, I thought I was immortal too." Duke lit a cigarette, leaned his head back and stared up at the heavens. It was approaching dawn. The sky was already a rich shade of dark blue and the stars were no longer visible. "Someone could have told me that I wasn't."

"But Astra took your soul... Morgan felt it." Lauren couldn't forget the altercation in the hall back in Paris.

"Temporary custody. I thought it would last longer than it did but there was more of a delay between the procedure and the battle than I had anticipated." Astra's look of guilt was only getting worse.

Lauren smiled. "Astra did keep her promise then. She took your soul and made you immortal. It just didn't stick. I have to say… if I were in her shoes and someone I loved asked me to do what you asked her to do, I would have done the same as she did."

Astra's eyes shot wide and her pale cheeks darkened. Duke laughed.

"You didn't honestly believe that no one would notice?" Duke chuckled and then grimaced when he reached over and took hold of Astra's hand. Astra touched Duke's injured arm and frowned. "Come, my love, there's no need to be shy about it. Julian has known since the day he first met us."

Astra glared at Julian.

"It is obvious," Julian said with a slight smile. It fell off his face when footsteps rang along the hall behind them.

"Duke, Morgan says that—" Kuga stopped dead and stared at Lauren. He looked rough, his face covered in a myriad of cuts and black bruises. His warm brown eyes lit up when he saw her and before she could mention her bad shoulder, he pulled her into his arms and squeezed her tight. She clenched her teeth and bore the pain, not wanting to upset him by mentioning it. He was only glad to see her. She placed her right hand against his back and held him. She was glad to see him too. "Someone could have told me you were up and about."

Lauren could almost see the scowl he would be giving Julian.

"I'm only just up… and not really ready to be about." She wriggled her way out of Kuga's tight embrace, feeling the need for air. "But I wanted to see everyone… especially you."

Kuga smiled but she could see the strain in it. They had all the time in the world now for a long talk and she was going to see to it that Duke kept his promise and tried to contact Piper so Kuga could say what he needed to.

"Especially me?" Morgan said as he appeared behind Kuga. Lauren frowned at him. In return, he put on his best seductive smile. "I missed you too. Your guard dog wouldn't let me near your room."

Did he honestly think that would upset her? The thought of Morgan seeing her naked was disturbing. He raked stormy eyes over her, the intimacy of his look reminding her that he knew her body well. Or at least one of her bodies. He was never going to know this one.

Kuga released her and she hid the pain as she straightened out her arm. Julian was by her side in an instant, his hand against her lower back. She smiled up at him, thankful for the silent show of support and wanting him to see that she was fine.

"It is good to see you well again," Morgan said with the same look he'd worn in Greece that night. He'd been worried about her. Lauren had finally figured him out. For all his swagger, he had a good heart locked deep inside.

Julian was wrong about him. It wasn't her blood that commanded him to do her bidding and help them. It was his feelings for Sonja. She honestly believed that he had loved her. "I kept my promises."

She nodded and looked down at her wrist. "Two drops of blood."

"Two?" Julian's hand tensed against her back.

"Save them. You still owe me and I am sure you are going to need my help in the future. When it is a little more than a few drops, I will claim my boon." His smile didn't falter, not even when Julian went to step past her, murder in his eyes. "So what will you do now?"

Lauren placed her hand in Julian's and he stopped, looking down at their joined hands and then at her. She smiled at him, her eyes narrowing affectionately on his, trying to show him that he didn't need to worry. She was all his and nothing was going to change that.

"I haven't forgotten," she said to Morgan. "We will help you free Paris of werewolves, but we might need help too."

Duke sat a little straighter when she looked at him.

"Ghosts work in groups of five, yes?" Lauren's gaze worked over Kuga, Astra and Duke. She couldn't replace Leo and Piper, but she had to do something. She owed Ghost and felt her duty wasn't done.

Duke nodded.

"You only have three. What will you do?" Her stomach churned. Julian squeezed her hand and she was thankful for his support in this decision. She knew in her heart that he would want to remain with Duke and the others, just as she did.

"Continue," Duke said and looked at Astra and Kuga. They both nodded. His dark eyes shifted back to her. "The werewolves are still a threat. Their numbers will increase. We must maintain the balance. That is our new mission. I have cleared it with headquarters… but they have told me we need five in our team. You could say that we're open for applications."

Lauren looked at Julian. He smiled at her, a soft tender one that made her heart skip a beat.

"I am yours to command. Always," he whispered.

Her heart warmed to hear those words. She ignored the gagging noise that Morgan made.

"Then it's settled. If you'll have us?" Lauren gave Duke a hopeful look.

An amused smile tilted his lips, as though he found it strange that she was asking him such a thing. She had never been one to be presumptuous. For all she knew, Duke might have had another two in mind. He might not have been assuming that she and Julian would join them since they had always worked alone.

Duke nodded. "We would be honoured."

Kuga grinned. It was so good to see him smile again that Lauren couldn't help smiling too. Although the journey had been painful and difficult, Lauren had finally found out where she belonged—here, protecting it with her friends and her lover.

"I need to get out of here," Morgan muttered. His black look shifted when her eyes met his. He smiled and shook his head. "My queen, I will expect you and your guard dogs in Paris."

Lauren nodded. He regally waved a hand and then walked away. She didn't bother with saying goodbye. They would see Morgan soon enough. Paris was first on her list when Duke had recovered. She always kept her promises.

With a great show of effort, Duke got to his feet. Lauren tried not to smile at the way Kuga and Astra fussed over him in case Duke noticed. She was sure he wouldn't like it. He straightened up and looked across the terrace at her.

It would be strange to take orders from someone but she was willing to give it a shot, although something told her that Julian would become a joint leader with Duke. The two of them had always worked together as equals and nothing was going to change that.

Julian had said that he was hers to command, but it was the other way around. He was her last Arcadian. Her Arcadian. Her commander even though he didn't know it. Without him she wouldn't have discovered who she really was and she wouldn't have survived this far.

She would never have known true love.

Lauren turned to face him and stepped into his waiting arms. He lowered his mouth to hers and brushed her lips lightly with his, a tender kiss that brought relief and happiness. She finally felt at peace and she finally knew her place in this world—here in Julian's embrace, for eternity. Julian held her close but gently, his arm only barely touching her left shoulder but stronger against her right. Lauren smiled at how delicate he was being with her. He really didn't want to hurt her and it told her better than words ever could just how much he loved her. She caressed his lips in a light kiss, her emotions getting the better of her, joy and love beyond anything she had ever felt before, so deep that it brought tears to her eyes. Her eyes closed and she savoured Julian's kiss and everything she could feel in him. He was happy too. They were no longer alone. They had each other now and nothing would change that.

Julian broke away when she sighed and he placed a hand against the back of her head and brought it to rest against his chest. She stared out over the low white wall surrounding the terrace. The night was fading fast. The city was coming alive and, over the haphazard rooftops of Athens, she could see the distant ruins of the Acropolis on the hill.

Julian's steady heartbeat matched hers, soothing music to her ear. He pressed a kiss to her hair and lovingly stroked her good arm. She latched onto his feelings and smiled at the warmth of them. They were both glad that it was all over and they could start a new life together.

Lauren stared at three quarters full disc of the moon. It was pale against the lightening sky, high above the Acropolis, but beautiful all the same. She thanked Selene for giving her Julian and keeping her safe.

"The sun will rise soon," Julian whispered.

She nuzzled his chest, unwilling to let him go now that she was back in his arms.

"I'd like to stay and watch it," she said and blinked slowly, fighting the call to find somewhere to rest. She was safe here in Julian's embrace. He would never let anything happen to her. "It feels like more than a new day is dawning."

"It is," Julian murmured in agreement and kissed the top of her head.

Lauren smiled at the tender touch and watched the sky lighten, feeling the beauty and warmth of it deep in her heart and soul.

"It's a new world, a new life, with a new purpose. I'm free." She drew back and looked up at Julian. "We're free."

He smiled, his eyes narrowing affectionately on hers. That look would always melt her and make her want to kiss him.

"This is our new world." Lauren believed every word, felt the truth in them. They were in this together and that would never change. She was going to spend eternity with Julian. "Our new purpose. Our new life."

Julian dipped his head. His lips grazed hers in a slow, soft kiss that made her feel as though she was floating. She closed her eyes, leaning into the kiss and wishing it would never end. This was a perfect moment. One of many to come.

"Our love," he whispered against her mouth and she couldn't help smiling again.

Lauren looked deep into his stunning pale blue eyes, lost in them in an instant.

Julian stroked her cheek. She could see all of his love in his eyes, none of his feelings hidden now, all on show for her just as hers were on show for him. She loved him more than anything, would thank Selene every night for the life she'd been given and for Julian. He made her feel alive, made her strong, and she would love him until the end of time.

Julian lowered his head and paused when his mouth was close to hers.

The sun rose, chasing the chill from the world and heralding the start of their new life.

Lauren closed her eyes and smiled when Julian whispered against her lips.

"Our forever after."

The End

ABOUT THE AUTHOR

Felicity Heaton is a romance author writing as both Felicity Heaton and F E Heaton. She is passionate about penning paranormal tales full of vampires, witches, werewolves, angels and shape-shifters, and has been interested in all things preternatural and fantastical since she was just a child. Her other passion is science-fiction and she likes nothing more than to immerse herself in a whole new universe and the amazing species therein. She used to while away days at school and college dreaming of vampires, werewolves and witches, or being lost in space, and used to while away evenings watching movies about them or reading gothic horror stories, science-fiction and romances.

Having tried her hand at various romance genres, it was only natural for her to turn her focus back to the paranormal, fantasy and science-fiction worlds she enjoys so much. She loves to write seductive, sexy and strong vampires, werewolves, witches, angels and alien species. The worlds she often dreams up for them are vicious, dark and dangerous, reflecting aspects of the heroines and heroes, but her characters also love deeply, laugh, cry and feel every emotion as keenly as anyone does. She makes no excuses for the darkness surrounding them, especially the paranormal creatures, and says that this is their world. She's just honoured to write down their adventures.

To see her other novels, visit: http://www.felicityheaton.co.uk

If you have enjoyed this story, please take a moment to contact the author at author@felicityheaton.co.uk or to post a review of the book online

Follow the author on:
Her blog – http://felicityheaton.blogspot.com
Twitter – http://twitter.com/felicityheaton
Facebook – http://www.facebook.com/feheaton

Printed in Great Britain
by Amazon